BROKEN ANGELS

One cold spring morning in County Cork, two fishermen find a bundle of rags floating in the Blackwater River: the mutilated corpse of a retired music teacher. His hands and feet are bound, and his neck bears the mark of garrotting wire. The Garda want to wrap this case up before the press get hold of it. But when a second man is found murdered, the body bears all the same marks as the first. And Detective Superintendent Kate Maguire fears this case carries the hallmark of a serial murderer...

BROKEN ANGELS

BROKEN ANGELS

by

Graham Masterton

Magna Large Print Books
Long Preston, North Yorkshire,
BD23 4ND, England.

British Library Cataloguing in Publication Data.

Masterton, Graham
    Broken angels.

A catalogue record of this book is
available from the British Library

ISBN   978-0-7505-4078-0

First published in Great Britain in 2013 by Head of Zeus Ltd.

Copyright © Graham Masterton, 2011

Cover illustration by arrangement with Head of Zeus Ltd.

The moral right of Graham Masterton to be identified as the author of this work has been asserted in accordance with the Copyright, Designs and Patents Act, 1988

Published in Large Print 2015 by arrangement with Head of Zeus Ltd.

Magna Large Print is an imprint of Library Magna Books Ltd.

Printed and bound in Great Britain by
T.J. (International) Ltd., Cornwall, PL28 8RW

For my darling Wiescka
17 April 1946 – 27 April 2011
Always adored, never forgotten

Is milis dá ól é ach is searbh dá íoc é
Irish saying: 'It is sweet to drink
but bitter to pay for'

One

At first he thought it was a black plastic garbage bag that some Traveller had tossed into the river, full of dirty nappies or strangled puppies. *'Shite,'* he said, under his breath.

He reeled in his line and then he started to wade through the shallows towards it, his rod tilted over his shoulder. As far as he was concerned, the Blackwater was sacred. His father had first brought him here to fish for spring salmon when he was eight years old, and he had been fishing here every year since. It was Ireland's finest river and you didn't throw your old rubbish into it.

'Denis!' called Kieran. 'Where are you off to, boy? You won't catch a cold over there, let alone a kelt!' His voice echoed across the glassy surface of the water, so that it sounded as if he were shouting in a huge concert hall. The wind blew through the trees on the opposite bank and softly applauded him.

Denis didn't answer. As he approached the black plastic garbage bag it was becoming increasingly apparent that it wasn't a black plastic garbage bag at all. When he reached it, he realized that it was a man's body, dressed head to foot in black. A priest's soutane, by the look of it.

'Jesus,' he breathed, and carefully rested his rod on the riverbank.

The man was lying on his side on a narrow spit

13

of shingle, with his legs half immersed in the water. His hands appeared to be fastened behind his back and his knees and his ankles were tied together. His face was turned away, but Denis could see by his thinning silver hair that he was probably in his late fifties or early sixties. He looked bulky, but Denis remembered that when his father had died, his body had sat in his basement flat in Togher for almost a week before anybody had found him, and how immensely bloated he had become, a pale green Michelin Man.

'Kieran!' he shouted. 'Come and take a sconce at this! There's a dead fella here!'

Kieran reeled in his line and came splashing through the shallows. He was red-faced, with fiery curls and freckles and close-together eyes so intensely blue that he looked almost mad. He was Denis's brother-in-law, eight years younger than Denis, and they had nothing at all in common except their devotion to salmon fishing, but as far as Denis was concerned that was perfect. Salmon fishing required intense concentration, and silence.

Salmon fishing brought a man closer to God than any prayer.

'Holy Mother of God,' said Kieran, joining Denis beside the body and crossing himself. 'He's a priest, I'd say.' He paused and then he said, 'He *is* dead, isn't he?'

'Oh no, he's just having forty winks in the river. Of course he's dead, you eejit.'

'We'd best call the guards,' said Kieran, taking out his mobile phone. He was about to punch out

14

112 when he hesitated, his finger poised over the keypad. 'Hey ... they won't think that *we* killed him, will they?'

'Just call them,' Denis told him. 'If *we*'d have done it, we wouldn't be hanging around here like a couple of tools, would we?'

'No, you're right. We'd have hopped off long since.'

While Kieran called the Garda, Denis circled cautiously around the body, his waders crunching on the shingle. The man's eyes were open, and he was staring at the water as if he couldn't understand what he was doing there, but there was absolutely no doubt that he was dead. Denis hunkered down beside him and stared at him intently. He looked familiar, although Denis couldn't immediately think why. It was those tangled white eyebrows and those broken maroon veins in his cheeks, and most of all that distinctive cleft in the tip of his bulbous nose. His lower lip was split open as if somebody had punched him, very hard.

'The cops are on their way,' said Kieran, holding up his mobile phone. 'They said not to mess with anything.'

'Oh, I will, yeah! You should come round this side. He's starting to hum already.'

'I just had my sandwiches, thanks. Tuna and tomato.'

The two of them stood beside the body, not really knowing what they ought to do next. It seemed disrespectful to go back to their fishing, even though now and again, out of the corner of his eye, Denis caught the quick flashing of silver in the water. He had hoped to catch his first springer today, and the conditions were perfect.

'Who killed him then, do you think?' said Kieran. 'Whoever it was, they gave him a good old lash in the kisser before they did.'

Denis tilted his head sideways so that he could take another look at the man's face. 'Do you know something? I'm sure I reck him. He's a lot older than when I last saw him, if it's him, but then he would be, because it was fifteen years ago, at least.'

'So who do you think it is?'

'I think it's Father Heaney. In fact, I'm almost sure of it. His eyebrows used to be black in those days. I always thought they looked like two of them big black hairy spiders. You know, them tarantulas. He's not wearing his glasses, but I'd know that gonker anywhere.'

'Where did you know him from?'

'School. He used to teach music. He was a right whacker, and no mistake. There wasn't a single lesson went by that he wouldn't give you a smack around the earhole for something and nothing at all. He said I sang like a creaky door.'

Kieran sniffed and wiped his nose with the back of his sleeve. 'Looks like somebody smacked *him,* for a change.'

Denis didn't answer, but standing in the river next to Father Heaney's dead body with the wind whispering in the trees all around him made him feel as if he had been taken back in time. He could almost hear the school choir singing the *'Kyrie eleison'* in their sweet, piercing voices, and the sound of stampeding feet along the corridor,

16

and Father Heaney's voice barking out, '*Walk*, O'Connor! You won't get to heaven any quicker by running!'

Two

Katie opened her eyes to see John standing by the bedroom window, one hand dividing the rose-patterned curtains, staring at the fields outside.

The early morning sunlight illuminated his naked body so that he looked like a painting of a medieval saint, especially since he had grown his dark curly hair longer after he and Katie had first met, and he had a dark crucifix of hair on his chest. He was thinner, too, and much more muscular, from a year and a half of working on the farm.

'You're looking very pensive there,' said Katie, propping herself up on one elbow.

John turned his head and gave her the faintest of smiles. The sunlight turned his brown eyes into shining agates. 'I was looking at the spring barley, that's all.'

'And thinking what, exactly?'

He let the curtain fall back and came towards the bed. He stood beside her as if he wanted to tell her something important, but when she looked up at him he said nothing at all, but kept on smiling down at her.

She reached her hand up and cupped him in her left hand, gently stroking his penis with the tip of

17

her right index finger. '*This* fruit's beginning to look ripe already,' she teased him. 'Why don't you let me have a taste of it?'

He grunted in amusement. But then he leaned forward and kissed the top of her head, and sat down next to her. She kept on stroking him for a while, but he gently took hold of her wrist and stopped her.

'There's something I have to tell you, Katie,' he said. 'I was going to tell you last night, but we were having such a great time.'

Katie frowned at him. 'What is it? Come on, John, you've got me worried now. It's not your mother, is it?'

'No, no. Mam's fine for now. The doctors even said that she might be able to come home in a week or two.'

'Then what?'

He was just about to answer her when her mobile phone played the first three bars of 'The Fields of Athenry'. 'Hold on a second,' she said, and reached across to the bedside table to pick it up. 'Superintendent Maguire here. Who is this?'

'Detective O'Sullivan, ma'am. Sorry to be disturbing you, like. But we were called out to Ballyhooly because these two fisher fellas found a body in the river.'

'What does it look like? Accident or suicide or homicide?'

'Homicide, not a doubt about it. He was all trussed up like a turkey and strangulated.'

'Who's in charge up there?'

'Sergeant O'Rourke for the moment, ma'am.

But he thinks you need to come and see this for yourself.'

'Oh, for God's sake, can't *he* handle it? This is my day off. In fact this is the first day off I've had in weeks.'

'Sergeant O'Rourke really thinks you need to see this, ma'am. And we need somebody to talk to the media about it, too. We've got RTÉ News up here already, and Dan Keane from the *Examiner*, and even some girl from the *Catholic Recorder.*'

Katie picked up her wristwatch and peered at it. 'All right, Paddy. Give me fifteen minutes.'

She snapped her mobile phone shut and swung her legs out of bed.

'What is it?' asked John.

'The call of duty, what do you think? Somebody's found a body in the Blackwater. For some reason, Jimmy O'Rourke wants me to come and take a look at it first-hand.'

She stepped into the white satin panties that she had left on the wheelback chair beside the bed, and then fastened her bra. John said, 'You want me to drive you?'

She pulled on her dark green polo-neck sweater so that her short coppery hair stuck out like a cockerel's comb. 'No, thanks. I could be there for hours. But I'll call you as soon as I can. By the way, what was it you were going to tell me?'

John shook his head. 'Don't worry. It can wait until later.'

She buttoned the flies of her tight black jeans and zipped up her high-heeled boots. Then she went through to the bathroom and stared at her reflection in the mirror over the washbasin. 'Jesus, look at these bags under my eyes! Anybody would think I spent all night at an orgy.'

'You did,' said John. He watched her as she put on her eye make-up and pale pink lip gloss. He always thought that she looked as if she were distantly related to the elves, with her green eyes and her high cheekbones and her slightly pouting mouth. She was only five feet five, but she had such personality. He didn't find it difficult to understand how she had managed to become Cork's first-ever female detective superintendent. He also knew why he had fallen so inextricably in love with her.

She came out of the bathroom and gave him a kiss. 'How about Luigi Malone's this evening, if I don't finish too late? I'm dying for some of their mussels.'

'I don't know. Maybe.' But then he thought: *Over dinner, that could be the right time to tell her.*

He wrapped himself in his dark blue towelling bathrobe and followed her barefooted to the front door. She turned and kissed him one more time. 'You take extra good care,' he told her, like he always did. Then he watched her walk across the steeply angled farmyard, with his tan and white collie Aoife trotting after her. She climbed into her Honda and blew him a quick final kiss before she drove off.

Three

On the way to Ballyhooly she played Guillaume de Machaut's *'Gloria'* by St Joseph's Orphanage Choir, from their *Elements* CD. The singing was so piercing and so clear and so intense that it always made her feel uplifted, and she sang along, just as high as the boys in the choir but badly off key. Despite the crime she had to deal with every day – the violence and the drug peddling and the prostitution and the drunkenness – *'Gloria'* reminded her that there really must be a heaven, after all.

She drove along Lower Main Street until she reached the turning for Carrignavar. The road was narrow and bordered on each side by grey stone walls covered in ivy, but it was deserted, and she saw no other sign of life until she reached a farmhouse about three miles down the road. Seven or eight cars and vans were lined up along the grass verge outside the farmhouse gates, and inside the farmyard three squad cars were parked, with flashing blue lights, as well as two police vans and an ambulance.

A garda directed her in through the gates and opened her car door for her. As she climbed out, Sergeant O'Rourke came across the farmyard to greet her, holding up a large pair of green rubber wellingtons. He was a short, sandy-haired man, with a rough-cut block of a head that looked much too big for his body.

21

'You'll be needing these, ma'am,' he told her. 'What size are they?'

'Tens. But you wouldn't want to be wading in the river in stiletto heels, would you?'

She sat down in the driver's seat, unzipped her black leather boots, and put on the wellingtons. They were enormous, and when she started to walk in them, they made a loud wobbling sound.

'So, what's the story, Jimmy?' she asked, as she followed him around the side of the farmhouse. The farmer and his wife and two teenage sons were standing together in their front porch, glowering at them. Katie waved at them and called out, 'All right, there? Sorry about all the disturbance!' but they didn't reply. They looked like a family of ill-assorted gargoyles.

'What a bunch of mogs,' said Sergeant O'Rourke.

'Now then, Jimmy. Respect for your ordinary citizen, please.'

They walked together across the pasture that led down to the edge of the Blackwater, and the breeze whispered softly in the long shiny grass. As they came nearer, the black-clad body came into view, lying on its side in the shallows. Two gardaí from the technical bureau were crouching in the water next to it in pale green Tyvek suits, taking photographs. Three more uniformed guards and two paramedics were talking to a TV crew and two reporters on the bank. A little further away stood two men with fishing rods, smoking, and three small boys.

Sergeant O'Rourke pointed to the anglers. 'Those two fellas over there – they were the ones who were after finding the body. One of them says that he knows who he is – or he's reasonably certain, anyhow.'

'Really?'

'He's pretty sure that he's a parish priest from Mayfield, Father Heaney. Apparently he taught music at St Anthony's Primary School back in the eighties.'

'Good memory your man's got.'

'Not surprising, if it *is* him. Father Heaney was one of the twelve priests in the Cork and Ross diocese who were investigated seven years ago for sexual abuse. Taught the boys music? Taught them to play the fiddle, I shouldn't wonder.'

'Was he ever charged with anything?'

'I had O'Sullivan check for me. There were eleven complaints against Father Heaney in all. Inappropriate behaviour in the showers, that kind of thing. In the end, though, the Director of Public Prosecutions wouldn't take the matter any further because it had all happened too long ago.'

'But that's why the press are here? Because of the sexual abuse angle?'

'Partly, like.'

'What aren't you telling me, Jimmy?'

'Like I said, ma'am, this is something you need to see for yourself.'

He stepped down into the river and held out his hand to help Katie follow him. The water felt icy cold, even through her rubber wellingtons. Sergeant O'Rourke waded ahead and Katie came behind him, trying to keep the wellingtons from falling off. As they approached, the two gardaí from the technical bureau stood up and took a

23

few paces back. One was grey-haired, in his mid-forties. The other could have just left school.

'Well, he *looks* like a priest,' said Katie, bending over the body. 'Any identification on him?'

'Nothing, ma'am,' said the younger technician. He had a wispy blonde moustache and such fiery red acne that he looked as if he had been hit in the face point-blank by a shotgun. 'All we found in his pockets was a rosary and a packet of extra-strong mints.'

'He took care of what mattered, anyhow,' remarked Sergeant O'Rourke. 'His soul, and his breath.'

'Any ideas about the cause of death?' asked Katie. 'Not to prejudge Dr Reidy's autopsy, of course.'

The older technician cleared his throat. 'One of two or three things, I'd say; or a combination of all of them. He was garrotted with very thin wire, which was twisted tight at the back of his neck with the handle of a soup spoon. The same type of wire was used to tie his wrists and his knees and ankles. But he could just as well have bled to death, or died of shock.'

With that, he bent over the priest's body and turned him on to his back. The priest's left arm flopped into the water with a splash. The technicians had cut the wires that had fastened his knees and his ankles together, and then they had unbuttoned his black soutane all the way up to his waist.

He was wearing no underpants. His flaccid penis lay sideways on his fat white thigh, but underneath it, where his testicles should have been, there was nothing but a dark gaping hole.

24

'My God,' said Katie. She leaned forward and peered at the wound more closely.

'Whoever did it, it looks like they used something like a pair of garden shears,' said the older technician. 'You can tell by the slight V-shaped nick in his perineum where the blades crossed over each other.'

'Christ on crutches,' said Sergeant O'Rourke. 'Makes my eyes water even to think about it.'

'This didn't happen to him here,' the technician continued. 'He's no longer in full rigor, so he's probably been dead for at least three days. My guess is that he was strangled and castrated somewhere else and dumped here sometime last night.'

'What do you think, ma'am?' Sergeant O'Rourke asked her. 'Revenge killing, by somebody he messed with when he was teaching his music? There's been wagons of publicity about child abuse lately, hasn't there? The pope saying sorry and all. Maybe somebody's been holding a grudge against him all these years, and decided it was time to do something about it.'

'Well ... you might be right,' said Katie, standing up straight. 'But let's not jump to any hasty conclusions. Maybe his killer simply didn't like him, for some obscure reason or another. You remember that case a couple of years ago in Holyhill? That young woman whose husband died of cancer, and she stabbed the parish priest with a pair of scissors because she said that his prayers hadn't worked?'

'There's a few priests *I* wouldn't mind having a good old stab at, I can tell you,' said Sergeant O'Rourke.

Katie turned to the older technician and said, 'You can send him off to the path lab when you're finished. I think I've seen everything that I need to see.'

'Before you go – there's one quite interesting detail,' he told her. He held up the two lengths of brass wire that had been used to bind the dead priest's legs. The ends of both of them had been twisted into neat double loops, like butterfly wings.

Katie said, 'That's very distinctive, isn't it? Is there any particular profession that finishes off its wiring like that?'

'Not that I know of. But I'll be making some inquiries.'

'Okay, good.'

Katie waded out of the river and Detective O'Sullivan gave her a hand to climb up the bank. Immediately, the TV crew from RTÉ came over – Fionnuala Sweeney, a pretty gingery girl in a bright green windcheater, accompanied by an unshaven cameraman – as well as Dan Keane from the *Examiner,* red-nosed, in his usual raglan-sleeved overcoat, and a pale, round-faced young woman with very black curls and a prominent beauty spot on her upper lip, whom Katie presumed was the reporter from the *Catholic Recorder.* She had very big breasts and she wore a grey tent-like poncho to cover them.

Fionnuala Sweeney held out her microphone and said, 'Superintendent Maguire! All right with you if we ask you some questions?'

'Let me ask *you* a question first,' said Katie, sharply. 'Who tipped you off about this body being found?'

Fionnuala Sweeny blinked rapidly, as if Katie had mortally offended her. 'I couldn't possibly tell you that, superintendent. You know that. I have to protect my professional sources.'

'Oh, stop being so sanctimonious, Nuala,' said Dan Keane, lighting a cigarette. 'I had the same tip-off myself but the caller didn't leave his name, and I certainly didn't recognize his voice. In fact, I couldn't even tell you for sure if it was a man or a woman. Sounded more like a fecking *frog*, to tell you the truth.'

'All right, then,' said Katie. 'Ask me whatever you like. But I can't tell you very much at all, not at this early stage.'

Fionnuala Sweeney said, 'Your witness here identified the deceased as Father Dermot Heaney, from Mayfield.'

'No comment on that. Whatever the witness said to you, we don't yet know for certain who he is.'

'In 2005, Father Heaney was one of the priests who were investigated on suspicion of child abuse.'

'So I'm told. But as far as I know, the DPP took no action against him, and this may not be him. What's your question?'

'I just want to know if you'll be considering the possibility that one of Father Heaney's victims was looking to punish him for what he did. Or what he was alleged to have done.'

Katie held up her hand. 'Listen, Fionnuala, how many times? We haven't yet established the deceased's identity, not for certain. He might not even be a priest, for all we know. And even if it *is*

Father Heaney, we have no evidence at all who might have wanted to kill him, or what their motives might have been. All I can say at this stage is that we'll be searching this area with a fine-tooth comb, and interviewing anybody who might have witnessed anything unusual. If any of your viewers think that they can help us to identify the victim, and whoever wished him harm, then as usual we'll be very grateful.'

'Do you know what the cause of death was?' asked Fionnuala Sweeney.

'Again, we're not sure yet. Either Dr Reidy, the state pathologist, or one of his two deputies will be carrying out an autopsy as soon as we can arrange it.'

The girl with the beauty spot spoke with a lisp. 'Ciara Clare, superintendent, from the *Catholic Recorder*. If your dead man does prove to be a priest, you *will* be consulting the diocese, won't you, about the most discreet way to handle it?'

Katie frowned at her. 'I'm not sure I understand your question.'

'Well, this has been a very difficult time for the church, hasn't it?' said Ciara Clare. 'The bishop has asked the public for forgiveness for past errors, as you know. I'm only suggesting that this is a time for healing, rather than more scandal.'

'Excuse me, Ciara? Are you saying what I think you're saying?'

'I'm only concerned about this murder being sensationalized. I mean, it does seem likely that your man was killed by a victim of child abuse, doesn't it, in revenge for molesting him, and that could very well incite other victims to take the

28

law into their own hands. We don't want more priests to be attacked, whatever they might have done in the past.'

'That's about three too many *ifs*,' Katie told her. 'Like I said, we need to take this one step at a time. Just because the deceased is wearing a cassock, that doesn't prove anything at all. He may have been on his way to a fancy-dress party.'

Dan Keane took his cigarette out of his mouth and let out a cough like a dog barking. 'He was castrated, though, wasn't he? That would indicate some kind of sexual motivation.'

'I'm sorry, Dan. We'll have to wait for the pathologist's report to find out exactly what injuries he suffered.'

'You don't need a pathologist to tell you when a man's had his mebs cut off. Your anglers saw it with their own eyes. Gelded, that's what they said.'

'Well, I'd rather you kept that to yourself for the time being. You too, please, Fionnuala. And you, Ms–'

'I'm not sure I can do that, superintendent,' said Dan Keane. 'It's the best part of the whole story, don't you think? "Father loses fatherhood."'

'Dan!' Katie retorted. 'Do you want me to give you any further co-operation on this case, or not?'

Dan blew smoke and coughed again and said, 'Very well, superintendent. I'll hold off for now, until you get the pathologist's report at least. But if it comes out from any other source, I'm going to have to run with it.'

Katie walked back to her car and kicked off the huge green wellingtons so that they spun away across the grass. As she was tugging on her black leather boots again, Sergeant O'Rourke came up to her and leaned against the car door. 'I'm having the whole area searched for tyre tracks and footprints and any other evidence. The fields, the pathways, the river bed. Everywhere. We've already started a door to door in Ballyhooly and all the surrounding communities. Somebody must have seen something.'

'Thanks, Jimmy. Keep me in touch. For some reason, I have a very uneasy feeling about this one. I always do when the church is involved. You never get an outright lie, do you? But then you never get an outright truth, either. It's all incense smoke and mirrors.'

Four

Before she went home, Katie called in at the Garda headquarters in Anglesea Street. In the past two hours, a heavy blanket of grey cloud had rolled over Cork City from the south-west, and the sunshine had been swallowed up. As she parked her car, it began to rain, not heavily, but that fine soft rain that could soak through your woolly sweater in a few minutes.

She went up to her office and switched on her laptop. Then she picked up her phone and punched out the number for the state pathologist's office in Dublin. She got through to Dr Owen Reidy's secretary, Netta, and gave her a message for him to call her. Outside it grew darker and darker, and the rain began to sprinkle against the window.

Perched on top of the multi-storey car park opposite, she could see a row of twenty or thirty hooded crows. She stood up, went to the window and stared at them, and it was so dark outside that she could see her own reflection, with her hair sticking up. It seemed to Katie that the crows only gathered there when her life was about to take a turn for the worse. Maybe she was imagining it. Maybe she simply didn't notice them when everything was going well.

All the same, they made her feel strangely unsettled, and it wasn't only because of the man's body lying strangled and castrated in the Blackwater.

She sat down at her laptop again and checked the child abuse report for the Cork and Ross diocese, published in 2005. Father Dermot Heaney had been the subject of eleven different complaints, mostly of touching boys in the showers after sports, or helping them to dry themselves after swimming and fondling them while he did so. He had also taken boys out for spins in his car, parked in secluded places and encouraged them to engage in mutual stimulation.

In spite of everything, he had been very popular with some of the boys at St Anthony's – 'like St Francis of Assisi' – especially the boys who excelled at music, and those who came from poor or broken families. The report said: 'Father Heaney gave them his attention, his affection and many small treats, which they were rarely given at home. The principal reasons why they were so reluctant for so many years to lodge any complaint against him was their gratitude for his apparent acts of kindness and generosity, and their abiding guilt about what they allowed him to do to them in return.'

Katie phoned John, to tell him that she would be coming home when she had finished at Anglesea Street. He didn't answer, so she could only presume that he was out in the fields somewhere, bringing in his cattle. She smiled to herself. She had never imagined when she had first met him that he would make such a natural farmer. He had emigrated to California after leaving college, after all, to escape from Ireland, and set up a very successful online business selling alternative medicines. He hadn't come back to Ireland, not once in eleven years, until his father had died.

He hadn't intended to stay in Ireland for more than a few weeks, but his mother had assumed that he would take over his late father's place as head of the Meagher family, and all of his uncles and aunts and cousins had assumed the same, and he had found it impossible to refuse them – especially his mother. He had reluctantly sold off his dot.com business and returned to take over the farm.

Katie shrugged on her raincoat and was just about to leave when her phone rang. It was Jimmy O'Rourke, calling from the University Hospital.

'It's Father Heaney all right.'

'You're sure?'

'One hundred per cent. We called round at his bedsit in Wellington Road and his landlady said that she hadn't seen hide nor hair of him since

Sunday morning. She said this was very unlike him because he comes back almost every night for his tea, and he always tells her if he's going away for a couple of days. She recognized him from the picture I took on my mobile phone, so we wheeled her around to the path lab and she identified him in the flesh. Sobbed like a babby, poor old girl.'

'Thanks a million, Jimmy. But keep it to yourself for now. See what else you can dig up on him and give me a call if you make any progress.'

'What about the media, like?'

'I'll probably call a press conference tomorrow morning, but I want to be very careful about what we give out. I have a strong suspicion that there's a whole lot more to this than meets the eye. You heard what that girl from the *Catholic Recorder* was asking us to do – or what she asking us *not* to do, rather. I don't want to give the church the chance to put a lid on this before we've even started.'

'Okay, boss. We'll be searching Father Heaney's bedsit next, so if we come across anything interesting I'll let you know. *Lives of the Saints* and porn mags, that's what we usually find when we search a priest's room. And half-empty packets of fruit-flavoured jub-jubs. Don't ask me why.'

Five

It was raining hard by the time she turned into the driveway of her bungalow in Cobh, close to Cork harbour, and almost dark. Her sister Siobhán had switched on the lights in the living room but she hadn't yet drawn the curtains, so Katie could see her sitting on the couch watching the widescreen television. Barney, her Irish red setter, was lying at her feet, his ears spread wide like Falkor the flying dog in *The Never-Ending Story*.

Katie let herself in, took off her raincoat and shook it. Barney immediately came trotting out into the hallway to greet her, his tongue lolling out. She tugged at his ears and patted him and then she went through to the living room.

'Hi, Siobhán,' she greeted her.

'Oh, hi, Katie. What's the story? I thought you were spending the day with John.'

Katie sat down in one of the mock-Regency armchairs and unzipped her boots. Barney stood close to her, panting, his tail whacking against the side table. Katie had intended to redecorate the living room after her husband Paul had died, eighteen months ago, but she had never been able to find the time. Either that, or she had wanted to keep it the way it was, for a little while longer, anyhow. Paul had chosen the Regency-style chandelier and the Regency-striped wallpaper because he thought it was classy, as well as the gilt-framed reproduction paintings, most of them seascapes, yachts leaning against the wind.

The only picture that he hadn't chosen was the framed photograph of himself, sitting at a cafe table in Lanzarote during their last vacation, grinning, lifting his glass of sangria, with one eye closed against the sunshine.

'I was called out,' Katie explained. 'Two anglers found a dead body in the Blackwater, up at Bally-hooly.'

'I thought this was your day off. And they're *always* finding dead bodies in the Blackwater. There's probably more dead bodies in the Black-water than fish.'

'Well, *this* dead body was exceptional,' said Katie, taking her boots through to the hall, and putting them away in the shoe cupboard. 'He was a priest, for one thing.'

'I hope he gave himself the last rites before he jumped in.'

'You're too cynical for your own good, you. Anyhow, he didn't jump in, he was murdered and dumped there. Throttled – and I'll tell you what else, castrated, but don't you go telling anybody.'

'Castrated? You mean he had his whatsits cut off? Serious?'

Katie nodded.

'Ouch!' said Siobhán. 'Didn't do it himself, did he? I've read about priests doing that, because they can't take the temptation any longer.'

'Not likely, in this particular case. Not unless he was some kind of contortionist.'

'Urgh. I don't want to know all the grisly ins and outs of it, thank you.'

'Drink?' Katie asked her.

'No, you're all right.'

Katie went across to the side table and poured a stiff measure of Smirnoff Black Label into a cut-crystal glass. She took a large swallow, which made her give an involuntary shiver.

'So what are you doing this evening?' asked Siobhán. 'Will you be seeing John again, or do you want me to cook something? I still have some chicken stew left from last night, if you want me to heat it up for you. Or we could order a pizza.'

Katie sat down on the couch beside her. 'I don't know yet. I called John, but he's probably out chasing his cows.'

Siobhán was Katie's younger sister, the third of a family of seven children, all girls. She looked more like their father than their mother. She was taller than Katie, and plumper, with a rounder face and masses of coppery curls and sea-green, wide-apart eyes. Soon after Paul had died, Siobhán had broken up with her boyfriend, Sean, an estate agent with snaggly teeth and a Jedward hairstyle and a very high opinion of himself, and so she had moved in with Katie. It suited Katie, because Siobhán could take care of Barney while she was at work, keep the bungalow tidy and do the messages.

It also meant that Katie could keep an older-sisterly eye on her, because Siobhán had been wild when she was younger, and was still given to bursts of outrageous behaviour, such as climbing out of her car if other drivers cut her up and banging on their windows, or drinking too much in Kelly's Bar on a Saturday night and falling over in the road with her legs in the air and her black lacy knickers showing.

'What did you do last night?' Katie asked her. 'Anything good?'

Siobhán was silent for a moment, and then she said, 'I called Michael, if you must know.'

'I thought you and Michael had been finished for donkey's. Quite apart from the fact that he's married.'

'I still miss him. And he still misses me. He should never have married that Nola. What a drisheen! She's more like his mother than his wife. Always fussing. She never lets him go out for a drink with his pals, and he has to take off his shoes every time he steps into the house, and put the toilet seat down. And now she wants to move to Kinsale, because she thinks it's classier than Carrigaline. Well, it is, but that's not the point.'

'Well, there's nothing you can do about it. You had your chance, and you blew it.'

Siobhán was winding her curly hair around her finger. 'I think he's forgiven me, to tell you the truth. I only cheated on him once. Well, twice. Anyhow, he said that he'd like to meet me again, just for one drink like.'

Katie took another swallow of vodka and raised her eyebrows. 'Up to you, girl. But you're asking for trouble, if you want my opinion. You know what one drink can lead to, especially with you. And if Nola ever found out, she's not the forgiving kind, I can tell you that.'

Her mobile phone rang, and she picked it up. 'Hi, John! I've been trying to call you for the past hour! Did you get my message?'

'I did, yes. Sorry. Somebody left a gate open and half a dozen of the goddamned Jerseys got out. They were halfway to Rathcormac before we rounded them all up.'

'I had a hunch you were chasing after cows – didn't I, Siobhán?'

'That's what makes you such a natural-born detective,' said John. 'Listen – can we meet this evening? How about those mussels you were craving after?'

'I don't know. I'm not so sure I'm that hungry any more. And I'm tired, too.'

'Oh, come on.'

'It's your fault, John,' said Katie, winking at Siobhán. 'You were the one who tired me out.'

John said, 'Please, Katie. There's something really important I want to tell you. I should have told you last night but one thing led to another. I'll come and pick you up at quarter to eight. How's that?'

'All right,' said Katie, pushing her fingers through her hair. 'I'll go and take a shower. That should wake me up.'

She hung up and looked at Siobhán with her lips pursed and her eyebrows lifted.

'What?' said Siobhán.

'He says he has something really important to tell me.'

Siobhán frowned for a moment and then let out a high-pitched scream. 'I know what it is! He's going to ask you to marry him! He's only going to propose!'

'Oh, get away with you! Of course he's not!'

'I'll bet you he is! Think about it! Paul's been in

the ground now for more than a year and a half, I'd say that's a decent interval, wouldn't you?'

'Siobhán, I'm sure he's not going to propose. And what would I say to him if he did?'

'Well, *yes,* I hope! You know you love him! And he's gorgeous! That wonderful American accent! He sounds just like that fella with the really deep voice at the beginning of *Law & Order,* who says *"These are their stories!"*'

'I don't know. I'm not so sure I *do* love him.'

'Of course you do. And what's the competition? Roddy Phelan, at the Water's Edge Hotel?'

'I *like* Roddy. He makes me laugh.'

'I'm not surprised, girl. That haircut of his. Makes him look like a squirrel.'

'Anyway,' said Katie, 'I'm going for a shower. If anybody rings, I'm not here, and I'm not expected back, either.'

Standing in the shower, with her eyes tight shut, she suddenly felt very alone and unexpectedly vulnerable. Paul had been a chancer, and a gambler, and he had cheated on her with some of the brassiest women in Cork. He had been prepared to do anything for money – as his drinking friends at the Ovens bar used to say, he would have minded mice at a crossroads for you, if you had paid him enough.

All the same, she had known him since school, and in the early years of their marriage she had found him funny and enchanting. No matter how much of a loser he had eventually turned out to be, she had never imagined that there would ever be a time when he simply wasn't there any more.

Six

Five minutes before John was due to arrive to pick her up, the phone rang and it was Sergeant O'Rourke.

'We finished searching Father Heaney's room but to be honest, ma'am, we didn't find a whole lot. A box of Polaroids of young boys in their baydnas, paddling in the sea at Youghal, it looks like, but they must be more than thirty years old. Three diaries, bound in leather with locks on so we had to bust them open, and even when we did the writing's so small that you practically need a microscope to read it. Not only that, it's all in Latin, like.'

'I know a classics professor at the university,' said Katie. 'He'll translate them for us, although I expect he'll be asking a hefty fee for doing it.'

'Oh, very public-spirited.'

'Well, I could ask the vicars general if they could recommend a priest who would translate them for us free and for nothing – to make some amends for the clergy's transgressions, as it were. But I wouldn't trust any priest to make a totally unbiased translation, would you? Especially if Father Heaney's written anything incriminating in them, and if he's implicated other priests, too. The church takes care of its own, Jimmy, and we've seen just how much.'

'Okay, then,' said Sergeant O'Rourke. 'I've

bagged the diaries up anyway and I'll bring them in. And the Polaroids, too. It's a hell of a long shot, like, but maybe we can identify some of he boys in the sea.'

'Anything else interesting?'

'A whole heap of sheet music. All religious, I'd say. There's one here called *"Vir perfecte haec dies"* and here's another one called *"Panis angelicus"* and another one called *"Pie Jesu".*'

'How are you spelling "Pie"?'

'P – I – E, like.'

'I think you're supposed to pronounce that *pee-ay*, like the Latin for "pious", not *pie* like in steak and kidney.'

'Don't ask me, boss. They never taught us Latin at Templemore.'

'All right, Jimmy. Bring that in, too. You never know.' John's car had just turned through the front gate and its headlights were shining through the curtains, so that Katie had to lift her hand to shield her eyes.

'Okay, ma'am – and, just for the record, we didn't find any jub-jubs. Only rhubarb and custards, and they were so old they were stuck together.'

John rang the front doorbell and Siobhán answered it. He came in carrying a large bouquet of pink roses, in shiny gold paper, and a box of dog treats for Barney.

'These are *gorgeous,*' said Katie, taking the flowers. As she did so, Siobhán gave her a meaningful look behind John's back.

'You still feel like going out tonight?' John

41

asked her. 'I mean, if you really don't want to–'

'I haven't washed my hair and put on my best designer jacket for nothing,' smiled Katie, and kissed him. His cheek was still wet from the rain and he smelled of some musky, leathery after-shave. 'Besides, I'm starting to feel seriously hungry.'

They left Siobhán standing at the front door with Barney and climbed into John's dark blue Mercedes. They turned west towards Cork City and the raindrops glittered as they slid across the bonnet.

'You rounded up all of your cows, then?' asked Katie.

'In the end, yes. Poor old Gabriel was supposed to be helping me but he was more trouble than he was worth, as usual.'

'I think it's very good of you to keep him on, considering how useless he is.'

'Sure ... but apart from my mam, he's the last living connection with my dad, isn't he? The last person who went out drinking with him and got up to all kinds of shenanigans with him. My mam always thought that my dad was really miserable and tight-lipped – not to mention tight-fisted. But Gabriel saw a side to him that my mam never did.'

'Oh, really?'

'You bet. He was quite the practical joker, ap-parently. One evening a Gaelic band came to play at the Roundy House, where my dad and Gabriel usually drank, and my dad opened up a can of sar-dines and poured the oil over the seats of all their chairs. The landlord had about five cats to keep

42

the mice down, and for the rest of the evening they followed these guys round the pub, sniffing at their arses and licking their lips and mewing.

He paused, and grinned, and then he said, 'Hey – it must have been pretty funny at the time.'

'Hilarious,' said Katie, pretending to be totally unamused. 'I'm just glad that you haven't inherited your father's sense of humour.'

They drove along Horgan's Quay into the city, with the cranes and lights of the docks on the opposite side of the river. The rain was easing off now, although the streets were still glistening. John turned across Patrick's Bridge and parked close to Emmet Place, the wide pedestrian precinct in front of the Crawford Art Gallery. He opened the door for Katie and they crossed the precinct to Luigi Malone's restaurant. Three boys were skateboarding up and down the precinct, their wheels making furrows in the puddles.

It was bustling and bright inside the restaurant, but John had booked them a table in a relatively quiet corner. He ordered dry white wine and the waitress came and filled their glasses for them. John lifted his glass and said, '*Sláinte!*'

'*Sláinte,*' Katie echoed, much more quietly, looking him in the eyes. She waited, and then she said, 'So – what is it that you want to say to me that's so important?'

John opened up his menu and said, 'Let's eat first. I'm starved.'

'No – first of all tell me what you want to say to me. I won't be able to swallow a single solitary mussel until you do.'

John stared at the menu and said nothing for a

43

long time, even though it was obvious to Katie that he wasn't choosing what he wanted to eat. He always chose the same thing, anyhow, chicken *fajitas*.

'I'm, ah...' he began, but then he stopped and looked up at her. 'I'm in trouble.'

'Trouble? What kind of trouble?'

'Money. What other kind of trouble is there? Like everybody else in Ireland, Katie, I got caught with my financial pants round my ankles.'

'What do you mean?'

'I mean that when I sold my dot.com business in California and came over here, the economy was booming. The Celtic Tiger was roaring fit to burst. Share prices were buoyant, new businesses were starting up all over the place.

'Now, of course, it's all gone down the crapper. Prices have shot up. Property values have dropped through the floor. It was tough enough when times were good, making any kind of a living out of that farm. Now, it's impossible.'

'But you inherited it,' said Katie. 'Its value may have dropped, but you haven't lost any of your own capital in it.'

'The trouble is, Katie, that's not even half of the story. I made a very healthy profit from selling my business, for sure. But I invested almost all of it here in Ireland – about a third of it in new Irish companies, and the rest in big internationals. It was only a couple of years ago that businesses like Pfizer and Hitachi were falling over themselves to open up new factories in Ireland. I had every expectation that I was going to be seriously rich.

'Instead of that, I'm only about five euros away

from being bankrupt.'

Katie took hold of his hands across the table. 'What are you going to do? Can't your bank see you through?'

'My bank is in a worse mess than I am, believe me.'

'Well, I could maybe help you a little, but I don't have much.'

John smiled and shook his head. 'Thanks for the offer, sweetheart, but you have no idea how much I'm talking about. I'm talking millions of euros. *Millions.*'

'So what are you going to do?'

'I don't have any choice, sweetheart. I'm going to have to sell the farm and go back to San Francisco and start over, from scratch.'

It took Katie a few seconds to understand what he was saying. The background music and laughter in the restaurant sounded oddly muffled, as if she were hearing it underwater.

'You're selling the farm? And then you're going back to America?'

John nodded, and then grimaced, and it was only then that Katie realized that his eyes were crowded with tears.

She squeezed his hands tighter and said, 'You *can't.* Surely there's some way out of it.'

'Like what?'

'I don't know – *something.*'

'Oh, sure. I guess I could go busking on the corner of Patrick Street. The trouble is, I have not played the banjo since I was at college, and then I was all thumbs. And you don't want to hear me singing "Hey, Mr Tambourine Man", you really don't.'

'Don't joke with me, John.'

'I'm not joking, sweetheart. I wish to God I were. I've been trying to keep my head above water for months, but it's no good. I talked to my accountant yesterday and he told me that I was well and truly screwed. The farm goes on the market tomorrow, but I'll be lucky to get more than a hundred and fifty thousand for it. That's if I can sell it at all.'

Katie let go of his hands. She felt breathless.

'What about *us?*' she asked him.

'I haven't been able to think about anything else. I've been trying to find out if I can set up a new business here in Ireland, so that I can stay here. But it's a question of contacts, and suppliers, and most of all it's a question of investment. The shape the Irish economy is in right now, it's hopeless, and it looks like it's going to be hopeless for a very long time to come. Another decade, easily.'

He paused, and she could tell what was coming. Apart from the details, she could almost have said it with him.

'Two old friends of mine have started up an online pharmacy business in Los Angeles. It's going so well that they need somebody else to come on board and help them out. So far, it's the only realistic offer I've had.'

'I see,' said Katie. Paul had hurt her with all of his stupid affairs, but she couldn't remember when she had last felt a pain as intense as this. At least Paul had stayed with her and pretended to love her, even if he hadn't.

She started to speak, but then she had to clear

her throat. 'You do understand that I can't possibly come with you.'

John was dabbing his eyes with his paper napkin. 'I know that, sweetheart. I know.'

'John, I'm a detective superintendent. I've fought tooth and nail to get where I am. I've fought so much sexual prejudice and so much ill will. I've had to prove myself every single inch of the way. What do you think it would look like, if all of a sudden I turned my back on it all, as if none of it mattered?

'I have so many things to take care of. People, as well as police duties. I owe so many people so much. Besides, what would I do, in California? I couldn't join the police, could I? I could lie by the pool, I suppose, and count myself lucky that I was out of the rain. But what else?'

The waitress came over, smiling, and asked them if they would like to order.

John said, 'How about it? You still want those mussels?'

'You know what?' she retorted. 'I may be over-emotional, but I find it really difficult to cry and eat at the same time.'

Seven

Father Quinlan locked the door of the sacristy and started to come down the steps, but stopped abruptly. He thought that he had caught sight of somebody standing deep in the shadows on the opposite side of the car park. The single fluorescent light was buzzing and flickering intermittently, so that it was difficult to tell for sure, but Father Quinlan stayed where he was, his face strained, like a man who fears that the demon that has been pursuing him all his life may at last have caught up with him.

The rain had stopped about twenty minutes ago, but the wind still felt damp, and it carried with it all the sounds of the city below him, the traffic and the throbbing of oil tankers along the dockside and the doleful clanking of cranes.

Mrs O'Malley slammed the church doors so loudly that he jumped. 'Goodnight, Father!' she called out. 'See you tomorrow evening!'

'Yes, yes – goodnight, Mary!' Father Quinlan called back, with an awkward wave of his left arm. 'Thanks for everything!'

Immediately, however, he turned his attention back to the opposite side of the car park. Was that a man standing there, close to the side of that white minibus, or was it nothing more than a complicated pattern of shadows and overhanging branches?

Mrs O'Malley stopped, hesitated, and then came walking back towards him. 'Just one thing, Father. I couldn't finish the lily arrangement in the Lady chapel because Moran's only sent the five bunches instead of the six, but I'll bring in some more tomorrow before the bereavement Mass and sort them all out so.'

Father Quinlan gave her a quick, distracted smile. 'Yes, Mary. Bless you.'

Mrs O'Malley frowned at him. 'Is everything all

right, Father?'

'Yes, Mary. Of course.'

But Mrs O'Malley looked around, trying to work out what he was staring at. 'It's not them kids again, is it? They need a good lashing, that's what they need.'

'No, no. It's nothing. I was trying to remember where I left my address book, that's all.'

'On top of your car, it wouldn't surprise me, like that box of eggs you left there the other day.'

Father Quinlan said, 'Yes, I expect you're right. I really must learn to concentrate, mustn't I?'

Mrs O'Malley said goodnight again and walked off. Father Quinlan remained where he was for ten long seconds, and then slowly descended the rest of the steps. He was a very thin man, with a bald dome surrounded by a puffball of white hair. His eyes were deep-set and glittery and close together and his nose was long and bony, so that he resembled one of the elders from the *Planet of the Apes*. He walked with the stiff, disjointed gait of a man plagued by rheumatism.

He crossed the car park and reached his car, a ten-year-old blue Volkswagen Passat estate, which was parked underneath a horse-chestnut tree. Before he unlocked the door, he looked around again, but there seemed to be nobody in the car park apart from him.

You're giving yourself the heebie-jeebies for no reason at all, he told himself. *What happened, that was thirty years ago. You've done your penance, so God has forgiven you. Time has forgiven you, too. Even if you had gone to prison, they would have let you out by now.*

He opened the door, and was halfway into the

49

driver's seat when somebody stalked up to the side of his car, seized the top of the door and slammed it against his leg.

'Ow-ah!' he cried out, and looked up in shock. A heavily built man in a large grey raincoat was leaning against the door, keeping Father Quinlan's shin pinned against the sill. His face was covered with a white cloth with two circular eyeholes cut into it, and on top of that he was wearing a tall conical hat, marked on the front with a black question mark. He looked to Father Quinlan like one of the Nazareno priests who parade in Spain in Holy Week, or a member of the Ku Klux Klan.

Underneath his face covering he was breathing hard, as if he were furious.

Father Quinlan was badly frightened. 'Who are you?' he demanded, much more shrilly than he had meant to. 'What do you think you're doing? You're hurting me! *You're hurting me!* Leave go of the door, will you?'

'Hurting you, am I?' the man replied. 'Hurting you, am I, you miserable gobshite?' He spoke in a soft, hoarse roar, like the voice that a Father puts on to scare his little children. *I'm a monster, grrrr, and I'm coming to get you!*

'What do you want?' Father Quinlan screeched back at him. 'Is it money? Do you want my mobile? Take whatever you want, for the love of God! You're breaking my leg!'

'I don't want your money and I don't want your mobile and I couldn't care less if I'm breaking your leg. Get out of the car, Father. You're coming with me.'

The man took a step back and opened the door

50

wide. Father Quinlan immediately shouted out, *'Help! Somebody help me! Help!'*

Without hesitation, the man punched him in the face, breaking his nose with an audible snap. Blood gushed out of Father Quinlan's nostrils, instantly giving him a bloody red moustache and beard, and turning his dog collar bright red. He lifted both hands to his face, honking and bubbling, while the man stood over him, leaning against his car in exaggerated impatience.

'Have you finished your whingeing?' the man growled at him. 'You're coming with me, Father, whether you like it or not.'

Father Quinlan rummaged in his trouser pocket and dragged out his handkerchief. He dabbed at his nose and his handkerchief was instantly soaked red. *'Please,'* he begged. 'Please don't hit me again.'

'That's a laugh, that is, Father. I can remember asking the same thing of you once. *Pleading* with you. And what did you do?'

Father Quinlan looked up. 'Do I *know* you?' he asked, his lips sticking together with congealing blood. 'Are you one of my orphanage boys? It's not Dooley, is it?'

'It doesn't matter if you know me or not, Father. The point is that *I* know you.'

'But if you're one of my orphanage boys, and you think that I ever mistreated you, you have to give me the chance to tell you how sorry I am.'

'Mistreated? *Mistreated?* Is that what you call it? I've heard it called a whole lot of things, but *mistreated* – that takes the all-time fecking biscuit.'

'I was misguided, I freely confess. But, believe

51

me, it was all for the greater glory of God.'

The man leaned forward so that Father Quinlan could see his eyes glittering inside his eyeholes. His tall conical hat made him seem even more frightening, like a character out of a nursery rhyme, the Man in the Moon who came down too soon. 'Come on, Father. Time to pay the price.' He grasped Father Quinlan's right arm and lifted him up, out of the driver's seat. Father Quinlan sagged to his knees, but the man heaved him upright.

'Please, I'll do anything you ask,' said Father Quinlan.

'You're dead right there, Father,' the man told him. He frogmarched him to the far end of the car park, where a black Renault van was hidden in the shadows, close to the church wall. He opened the rear doors and threw him in like a bag of old bones.

Father Quinlan tumbled on to a heap of folded sacks, jarring his shoulder, but immediately pulled himself up on his knees. *'Help me!'* he shouted out. *'Somebody please help me!'*

Without another word, the man banged the doors, and locked them. Father Quinlan felt the van sway as the man climbed into the driver's seat, and then he started the engine and pulled away.

'Dear God in heaven,' whispered Father Quinlan, clasping his hands together. 'Please, somebody help me.'

Eight

Katie was rinsing out her coffee mug when Siobhán came shuffling into the kitchen in her stripy nightshirt, her cheeks flushed and her curly red hair all messed up as if she had been out sailing in the harbour.

'*You* came back late last night,' said Siobhán.

'Oh – yes. After John went home I went back to Anglesea Street. I had a whole lot of paperwork to catch up with.'

'At two in the morning?'

'I didn't feel tired, that's all.'

'Too excited, were you? I mean, he *did* propose, didn't he, the gorgeous John?'

'No,' Katie admitted. 'No, he didn't.'

'Oh, there's a disappointment,' said Siobhán, opening up a cupboard door and taking down a box of Special K. 'So what was this really important thing he wanted to talk to you about?'

Katie turned away from her. 'Nothing very much. He's thinking of selling the farm, that's all.'

'Serious?'

'Yes. His mother's too ill to help him out now and the way things are going he can't make it pay.'

'So what's he going to do now?'

Katie shrugged and said, 'Who knows? Listen – I have to get to work. Dr Collins is coming down from Dublin this morning to perform an autopsy on Father Heaney. She won't thank me if I'm late.'

As she went toward the door, Siobhán caught the sleeve of her blouse. 'Look at you, girl. Your eyes are all puffed up. You've been howling, haven't you?'

'Of course not. Hay fever, that's all.'

'He's never dumped you?'

'No, he hasn't. No.'

'Then what is it?'

'I'll tell you later,' said Katie. 'Right now I've got too much on my mind.'

'He's selling up and he's going back to the States. That's it, isn't it?'

Katie said nothing, but went through to the room that she still called the nursery, but which these days she used as her home office. This had been little Seamus's room, but she and Paul had stripped off the blue wallpaper and the rocking-horse frieze, and now the only reminder of Seamus was a small framed photograph taken on his first and only birthday.

She unlocked the top drawer of her desk and took out her nickel-plated Smith & Wesson .38 revolver. She flipped it open to check that it was fully loaded, and then she clipped it into the flat TJS holster on her right hip.

Siobhán came to the door and repeated, 'I'm right, aren't I? He's selling the farm and going back to the States.'

Katie could see half of her face reflected in the window. She looked strangely emotionless, even though her brain was feeling like smashed china. She closed the drawer and said, 'Yes, he is.'

'Are you going to go to the States with him?'

'Of course not. How can I?'

'You love him, don't you?'

Katie pushed past her into the hallway and took her raincoat down from the peg. 'Yes. No. I *can't*,' she said. 'It's out of the question.'

Siobhán said, 'Katie – you only have one life, girl. I could have stayed with Sean. Maybe I *should* have stayed with Sean, but what a gowl. Your John, you shouldn't let him go away without you. I mean it.'

Katie opened the front door. The sun was shining and she could see the sea sparkling between the trees on the opposite side of the road.

'I'll see you after,' she told Siobhán. 'I'm going round to Dad's for tea, but I shouldn't be late.'

She drove up to Cork airport. Dr Collins's flight from Dublin had arrived early and she was waiting impatiently next to the statue of Christy Ring, the champion hurler. Dr Collins was a tall, axe-featured woman with bronze-coloured hair pinned back in a lopsided pleat. She reminded Katie of Katharine Hepburn, if Katharine Hepburn had worn narrow horn-rimmed spectacles and sported a large mole on her chin.

'Sorry if I kept you waiting, doctor,' said Katie.

'I could just as easily have taken a taxi,' sniffed Dr Collins, wiping her pointed nose on her handkerchief. 'It would have saved you a drive so, and it would have saved *me* a twenty-minute wait in the cold.'

Katie opened the boot of her car and helped Dr Collins lift her suitcase inside. 'I wanted to talk to you about this autopsy before you got stuck into it,' she said. They climbed into the car and Katie started the engine and drove out of the airport.

'I prefer not to have my assessments second-guessed, if you don't mind,' said Dr Collins.

'Oh, I wouldn't dream of doing that. It's just that this case has some odd ramifications, and I think you ought to be aware of them. The victim is a one-time parish priest from Mayfield, Father Dermot Heaney. He was tied up and garrotted with wire, and he was also castrated.'

'So, he's been sent to meet his maker incomplete, so to speak?'

'In 2005 he was accused of child molestation, although the bishop stood by him and he was never prosecuted. But now the church seems to be taking a different view altogether. You'd think they'd be wanting to distance themselves from this whole business as far as they possibly could, wouldn't you? But they seem all too ready to suggest that one of his childhood victims might have murdered him in revenge. That he *deserved* it, almost.'

'And what do you think?'

'I haven't come to any conclusions, not yet,' Katie told her. 'Not enough evidence.'

'But?'

'But it surprises me that the church should be in such a hurry to admit that he was a child abuser. All I can say is that it's given them a legitimate excuse to ask us to keep our investigation as low-key as possible – in case more former victims get the idea of attacking the priests who abused them. It's a complete turnaround, though. When Father Heaney was first accused of abuse, in 2005, the diocese defended him to the hilt. They went so far as to claim that all of his accusers were fantasists.'

'Well, times have changed, haven't they?' said Dr Collins. 'It's all abject apologies and breast-beating these days, isn't it? *Mea culpa, mea culpa* – the hypocrites.' She took out her handkerchief again and unfolded it. 'I don't really see how this concerns my autopsy.'

Katie drove around the Kinsale Road round-about and headed into the city. 'It might not have any bearing on it at all. I simply wanted you to be aware of it, in case you come across some piece of forensic evidence that doesn't look like much on the surface of it, but which might explain why the church is so keen to suggest that Father Heaney was a predatory paedophile who got what was coming to him.'

As Katie turned into the entrance to the University Hospital, Dr Collins finished wiping her nose and looked at her sharply. 'You suspect that he might have done something much worse, don't you?'

Nine

Sergeant O'Rourke and Detective O'Donovan were waiting for her when she arrived at Anglesea Street. She put down her plastic cup of cappuccino on her desk, hung up her raincoat, and asked, 'What's the form, then? Have we found any witnesses yet?'

'Two, so far,' said Sergeant O'Rourke. 'One of them's the Ballyhooly postie. The other's an auld

57

girl who was taking her dog for a walk.'

'Go on.'

'The postie had made his delivery to the Grindell farm about 7.20 in the morning when a black van overtook him and nearly forced him into the ditch. He reckons the van was doing at least forty and you saw for yourself how narrow that road is.'

'I don't suppose he made a note of its number.'

'No, but he says it was a Cork plate right enough. And he did notice one thing about it, there was a white question mark stuck on to one of the back windows.'

'Well ... that should make it relatively easy to find. You'll put out that description, won't you?'

'Have already, ma'am.'

'What about the other witness? The old woman with the dog?'

'She was crossing the bridge between Bloomfield and Ballyhooly just after seven o'clock, she thinks it was. She says it was misty then, so she couldn't see too clearly. But she saw a black van parked down by the riverbank, with its back doors wide open, and a fellow dragging something through the water.'

'Did she say what this something was?'

'No, the mist was too thick. But she said it must have been heavy, like, because of the way that he was dragging it. I asked her to guess what it might have been and she said a sack of coal.'

'Could she describe the man at all?'

'Big, she said. Fat, in fact, and round-shouldered. He was wearing a grey raincoat and wellingtons, but what really caught her attention was his hat. She said it was tall and pointed, like a dunce's cap.'

'That's odd. Who wears hats like that?'

'Search me. Dunces, I suppose. Most of the time he had his back to her, but when her dog kept on barking he turned around for a split second and she glimpsed his face.'

'So? What did he look like?'

'Like I say, she only caught a glimpse, and she didn't have the best powers of description. Fat, she said, but she did make a point of saying that he wasn't ugly. Fat like a cherub, that's what she said, rather than fat like a pig.'

'Fat like a cherub? Okay ... I think I'd like to talk to her myself, to see if she can describe him a little more precisely.'

'I could take you to see her this afternoon, ma'am,' said Detective O'Donovan. 'There are still four or five more houses I have to knock at where there was nobody in this morning, so I was going back up to Ballyhooly in any case.'

'Good,' said Katie. 'At least we have an idea now of *when* Father Heaney was dumped in the river. Let's check all the CCTV cameras in a fifteen-mile radius... Cork City, Mallow, Limerick, Fermoy. We might be able to pick up this van on its way to Ballyhooly, find out where it came from.'

'Right you are. I'll get on to it.'

Just then Chief Superintendent Dermot O'Driscoll knocked at her office door. 'Katie – spare me a moment, would you?'

'Of course.' She always had time for Chief Superintendent O'Driscoll. He was a big man, with a red face the colour of corned beef and a wild wave of white hair. He was a man's man, an

59

enthusiastic follower of rugby and hurling, and a prodigious drinker on his days off, but he had supported Katie's promotion from the very beginning and he continued to defend her whenever he thought she needed it. He had great respect for what he called her 'detectivating talents' and he believed that women have a much keener nose than men for liars and cheats and chancers. 'Women can smell a load of cat's malogian a mile off.'

Sergeant O'Rourke and Detective O'Donovan left the office and Chief Superintendent O'Driscoll came in and hoisted his huge left buttock on to the edge of Katie's desk. He was eating a pasty and every now and then he had to brush the crumbs from his belly.

'How's it going, then?' he asked her, with his mouth full.

'Too soon to say yet. I think the autopsy will tell us a lot more.'

'Would you believe that I've just this minute had a phone call from the diocese offices on Redemption Road? The Right Reverend Monsignor Kevin Kelly, vicar general.'

'Oh, yes? What did *he* want?'

'He says that he might have solved our murder for us.'

'Really? I know that some clergy are supposed to be able to work miracles, but how exactly has he managed to do that?'

'He preferred not to tell me over the phone, but respectfully asked if we could pay him a visit at the diocese office.'

'Oh, well, fair play to him. If he asked us *respect-*

fully. And if he really has solved it, that will save us quite a bit of trouble, won't it?'

Chief Superintendent O'Driscoll finished his pasty and smacked his hands together to get rid of the crumbs. 'You never know, Katie. Stranger things have happened. About six or seven years ago I was totally stumped by a stabbing I was looking into, in Sunday's Well. I had no witnesses, no weapon, and no forensics at all. But as soon as the victim's name was printed in the paper, a priest rang me up and said that by chance he had got a crossed line when he was calling his mother, and he had overheard the dead fellow arguing with another fellow, and this other fellow had threatened to come around and stick a knife in him. The priest only caught the other fellow's nickname, which was Tazzer, but since the dead fellow had only ever known one fellow whose nickname was Tazzer, I was able to collar him in about half an hour flat.'

'And the priest was given a reward, I hope?'

'No. The budget didn't run to it. But he'll get his reward in heaven, one day, you can be sure of that.'

Ten

As he regained consciousness, Father Quinlan became aware that he could faintly hear singing – the high, sweet, penetrating voices of St Joseph's Orphanage Choir, singing *'Ave Maria'*.

61

He opened his eyes to see a triangle of sunshine on the ceiling. His vision was blurry and he felt as if he had been beaten all over. His nose was throbbing and blocked up with dried blood, his shoulders ached, and his ribs were so tender that he had to breathe in quick, shallow gasps. Both of his knees were painfully swollen, and even his toes felt smashed, as if somebody had repeatedly stamped on his feet.

He grunted and tried to sit up but he had been lashed with nylon washing line to the single bed he was lying on, and he could manage only to lift his head two or three inches. Apart from that, his neck was so stiff that he could hold it up only for a few seconds.

He was lying in an upstairs bedroom with grubby whitewashed walls and a floor covered in worn-out dark green carpet. Apart from the bed, the only other furniture was a sagging brown leather armchair. The windows were old-fashioned sashes, and the plaster on the ceiling was flaking and covered in hairline cracks, so he could tell that he was in an old, nineteenth-century building. Straining his head up a second time, he saw the flat pastel-coloured facades of shop buildings on the opposite side of the street, and the painted letters 'Tom Murphy Outfitters'. He recognized at once that he was on the third storey of a shop or office on the north side of Patrick Street, Cork's main thoroughfare.

'Dear God,' he breathed, through split lips, and let his head drop back. Judging by the sunlight, it must be about eleven o'clock in the morning. He could remember yesterday evening, stepping out

62

of the sacristy and locking the door and saying goodnight to Mrs O'Malley. He could remember thinking that there was somebody standing in the shadows close to his car, but he couldn't think what had happened to him after that. He couldn't even remember being beaten, although he must have been, and viciously.

From one of the floors below, he heard somebody galumphing down bare uncarpeted stairs, two or three at a time, and he immediately called out, 'Hey! Hey there! Is anyone there? Will somebody please help me?'

He heard a door slam, but then he could hear nothing but the beeping of traffic in the road outside, and the clattering of feet on the pavement, and the tremulous strains of *Ave Maria*.

'Will somebody please help me?' he repeated, so softly that nobody could have heard him except God or one of his angels. Then he said a prayer.

Domine Iesu, dimitte nobis debita nostra, salva nos ab igne inferiori, perduc in caelum omnes animas, praesertim eas quae misericordiae tuae maxime indigent.

'O my Jesus, forgive us our sins, save us from the fires of hell, lead all souls to heaven, especially those who are most in need of your mercy.'

Nearly an hour passed. The singing from St Joseph's Orphanage Choir went on and on – the *Kyrie*, the *Credo*, the *Agnus Dei*, and then the *Ave Maria* again. Father Quinlan found it deeply disturbing, rather than uplifting, as if it were being played for the express purpose of frightening him. Of course *Elements* was massively popular,

63

especially here in Ireland, and it was being played everywhere, in shops, in restaurants, in pubs even, but what unsettled him was the way that it was being played over and over.

'*Help!*' he shouted out, again and again, even though he doubted that anybody could hear him – or, even if they could, that they would come to set him free.

But without warning, the door handle rattled and the bedroom door was opened up. From where he was lying, he was unable to see who had just stepped in, but he twisted his head around and said, 'Please! Please help me, whoever you are!'

There was a moment's silence, and then he heard the same hoarse voice that he had heard in the church car park the previous night. 'It's *help* you're asking for, is it?'

'What do you want?' asked Father Quinlan. 'Are you trying to punish me, is that it?'

'Oh, I think you know only too well what I want,' the man replied. 'If justice is a cake, of sorts, I want my slice of it.'

'I don't understand what you mean.'

The man hesitated for a few seconds longer, and then came around and stood close to the side of the bed so that Father Quinlan could see him. He was wearing the same face covering with the eye-holes and the same pointed hat that he had worn the night before. He was bulky and tall, about six foot two or three, with a bulging belly that hung over the belt of his baggy grey trousers. He was wearing a shapeless grey jacket with sloping shoulders, and a grey flannel shirt. He kept wiping his hands together, and Father Quinlan felt that he had a soft and creepy air about him, a *dampness,* as if the palms of his hands and the creases between his thighs were constantly sweaty.

His hat was well over eighteen inches tall, and it looked as if it had been made out of frayed grey silk glued on to cardboard, with two pointed earflaps. On the front it was marked with a black symbol that resembled a question mark, but which could equally have been a billhook, or a farmer's sickle.

'Who are you?' Father Quinlan asked him.

The man produced an odd, high-pitched snorting noise in one nostril. 'It doesn't matter who I am, Father. It's all going to end up in the same bucket, no matter what.'

'You sound so much like little Charlie Dooley. Are you Charlie Dooley?'

'That's not a name I recognize, Father. The Grey Mullet Man, that's what they call me these days. Need some justice done? Need a score settled? Still haunted by some shameful memory that never seems to leave you go, no matter what? Send for the Grey Mullet Man, that's what. The Grey Mullet Man will do the business for you for sure and for certain, guaranteed.'

'Was it you who mangled me like this?' asked Father Quinlan.

'Oh. You don't think you deserved it?'

'I have confessed and paid penance for every sin that I might have committed, venial or mortal. I am in a state of grace.'

'You seriously believe that, do you?'

'Yes, my son, I do. I made my peace with God

a long time ago, and I am quite content that I have been granted His forgiveness. Now, what do you want from me? You have hurt me severely, you know you have, and I am pleading with you now to untie me and let me go. I think that you have broken at least three of my ribs and I need to get to the hospital.'

All the time Father Quinlan was saying this, the Grey Mullet Man was slowly shaking his head, his pointed hat tilting from side to side with the regularity of a metronome. When he had finished, the Grey Mullet Man said, 'Not a chance, Father. There's something altogether different in store for you, I'm afraid.'

'Then may the Lord have mercy on your soul,' croaked Father Quinlan.

The Grey Mullet Man made the sign of the cross. 'And on yours, Father,' he replied.

With that, he took out a large clasp knife and opened it with a snap. Father Quinlan immediately closed his eyes tight and began to pray. Whatever was going to happen to him now, he begged forgiveness for any transgressions that he may have overlooked and for which he had not done penance, and any offence that he may have unwittingly caused to others, but most of all he begged not to suffer any more pain.

Strangely, into his mind came a memory of standing in his mother's kitchen on a summer's afternoon. He couldn't have been more than four or five. His mother was mixing a large bowl of barmbrack fruit loaf. She had stirred in the caster sugar and the candied fruit peel, and had covered the bowl with a teacloth to give it time to rise.

He lifted one corner of the teacloth, dipped his finger into the pale brown mixture, and licked it. Then he dipped it in again. He could still taste the sweetness of the uncooked bread flour and milk. He could still see the sun shining in through the pots of geraniums on the kitchen windowsill. He could hear his mother walk into the kitchen behind him, the sound of her shoes on the quarry-tiled floor. She snapped, 'Sacred heart of Jesus!' and then she slapped him so hard around the side of the head that he fell over and hit his head on the table leg. All he could hear was a loud singing noise, and the blurry voice of his mother shouting at him. All he could feel was pain.

He started to cry, and as he lay on this narrow bed with the Grey Mullet Man standing over him, he started to sob yet again, more for his childhood self than the bruised and miserable old man that he was this morning.

'Ah, why are you crying there, Father?' asked the Grey Mullet Man, hoarsely. He was leaning over him so closely that Father Quinlan could smell the onions on his breath. At the same time, he was cutting through the washing-line cord that was keeping Father Quinlan tied to the bed, and dragging it loose.

'There, you're free so,' he said, and Father Quinlan opened his eyes. The Grey Mullet Man was looping the cord around his elbow as he did so, the way that women wind wool.

'You're letting me go?' asked Father Quinlan, painfully easing himself into a sitting position and dabbing at his wet eyes with his fingertips.

'Oh, nothing quite as merciful as that, Father.

You'll see.'

He took hold of Father Quinlan's left elbow and helped him to stand up. Father Quinlan took one step forward, but the pain from his broken ribs was like being stabbed with a large kitchen knife, and he had to stop for a moment, gasping for breath.

'I can't – I'm not sure that I can – perhaps I had better lie down again.'

'Of course you can, Father. We're only going through to the next room, like. You can manage that. A man of dedication such as yourself.'

'I really can't – I'll have to–'

But the Grey Mullet Man pulled him roughly towards the door – so roughly that Father Quinlan howled out in pain and his knees buckled.

'I can't I can't I can't oh Jesus I can't–!'

The Grey Mullet Man yanked him up on to his feet again, and this time the pain was so excruciating that the room darkened and he felt that he was going to faint.

'You should never say *can't,* Father. That's what you always taught your boys, wasn't it? Never say *can't,* always say *can.* "Do you think Our Lord Jesus said *can't* when he was toting the cross up to Calvary?" That's what you used to say to your boys, wasn't it, Father? "Pain brings you closer to God."'

'Please,' wept Father Quinlan.

The Grey Mullet Man ignored him and dragged him through the door and into the next room, ducking his head as he did so. This was a damp-smelling bathroom, with a streaky green linoleum-covered floor and flaking green walls. On the left-hand side stood a huge old-fashioned bathtub with lion's-claw feet and taps that looked as if they had been taken from the engine room of the *Titanic*. The inside of the bath was streaked with grey and rust-coloured grime, and the taps were continually dripping.

Next to the bath stood a toilet with a broken mahogany seat and a washbasin with a mirror above it. The mirror was fogged over, but it reflected the blue sky outside and the clouds that moved across it, like a dim picture of freedom and happiness soon to be lost forever.

In the ceiling, in between the two sash windows, a pulley had been fastened, with a long rope through it that dangled on to the floor.

'You're not going to hang me?' said Father Quinlan, in horror.

'Not in the way that you're thinking of, Father. But in a manner of speaking. You've heard of the *strappado?*'

'No, no, no, you can't do that to me.'

'Oh, I think I can so. How else do you think I can get you to reflect on what you did, and to see it for the heresy that it really was?'

'It was never heresy! It never was! It was all done for the greater glory of God, you know that! It was all done to open up the doors of heaven, so that God's light could shine on us directly!'

The Grey Mullet Man pushed his face so close that Father Quinlan couldn't focus on him. The smell of raw onions on his breath was overwhelming, enough to make Father Quinlan start weeping again. 'It was not done for the greater glory of God, Father. It was all done for the

69

greater glory of we-all-fecking-know-who. What *you* have to do, Father, is admit it.'

'You expect me to admit to something that I never did?'

'I expect you to confess that you did it.'

'I can't, no matter what you do to me.'

The Grey Mullet Man stepped back. His expression was now very serious, almost considerate. 'This will hurt, Father. That's why the Inquisition used to do it.'

Father Quinlan's narrow nostrils flared. 'I cannot tell a lie. I cannot perjure myself in the court of God Almighty. You can do your very worst.'

'Very well.'

The Grey Mullet Man laid his hands on Father Quinlan's shoulders and pushed him down until he was kneeling. Neither of them spoke as he cut off a length of washing line and then pulled Father Quinlan's hands behind his back, lashing his wrists so tightly together that he almost cut off his circulation. Then he took the rope that was dangling from the ceiling, looped it between his wrists and knotted it.

Of course, Father Quinlan knew all about the Spanish Inquisition, and the *strappado,* and he couldn't stop himself from making a whinnying sound in the back of his throat. As the Grey Mullet Man gripped the other end of the rope and pulled it sharply downwards, so that he was hoisted to his feet, he managed to stifle a shout of pain. But when the Grey Mullet Man pulled on the rope again, and again, and he was lifted clear of the floor, with his arms angled sharply upwards behind his back, he let out a shriek of sheer agony.

The ligaments in his armpits tore apart with an audible crackling sound, and his left arm, which he had dislocated as a thirteen-year-old boy playing rugby, was pulled completely out of its socket.

The Grey Mullet Man pulled him up until his feet were kicking eighteen inches above the floor, and then he wound the end of the rope around the bath taps, and tied it fast.

'I have nothing to confess!' gasped Father Quinlan. 'I have nothing to confess!'

The Grey Mullet Man stood in front of him in his face covering and his tall conical hat, absurd but sinister, like an evil clown. 'How does it feel, Father? Is it more painful than anything you have ever experienced in your life? That's what they say, people who have suffered the *strappado*.'

'I have nothing to confess! God has forgiven me!'

Father Quinlan's face was ashy-grey with agony, and his eyes were bulging. The Grey Mullet Man was right: the *strappado* was not only more painful than anything he had ever experienced in his life, it was more painful than he could have imagined possible. His torso kept twisting, which increased the grating and jabbing from his broken ribs, and with every attempt to lift himself upwards, the nerves and tendons in his arms tore even more.

As the minutes passed, and every minute took him further and further into hellfire, he began to believe that his sins must be unforgivable, and that God was not going to save him.

'Kill me!' he shrieked. 'Anything, anything, dear Jesus, rather than this! *Kill me!*'

Eleven

The oak-lined driveway that led them up to the offices of the diocese of Cork and Ross was dappled with sunlight, and Chief Superintendent O'Driscoll hummed tunelessly, as if he were feeling contented, like Winnie the Pooh.

'You know, I should have been a priest myself,' he remarked, as Katie turned into the visitors' car park. 'My mam wanted me to be a priest, but my auld fellow was dead set against it.'

'Oh, yes?'

'Don't get me wrong. My auld fellow was very devout, as bus inspectors go, but there were two things he didn't believe in. One was margarine and the other was celibacy.'

'Get out of here,' said Katie.

'No, it's true. He always said that if God had not wanted men to eat butter he would not have created cows, and if he had not wanted men to fornicate he would not have created women.'

Katie pulled down the sun visor and primped her hair with her fingers. This morning she was wearing her olive-coloured suit with its small tight jacket and pencil skirt, and a cream blouse with the collar turned up. John always called it her 'army uniform'. She liked to wear it when she was meeting men that she wanted to impress with her directness and no-nonsense attitude to crime.

She and Chief Superintendent O'Driscoll

climbed out of the car and walked across to the nearest entrance. The diocesan offices were stone-built and spacious, halfway between a cathedral and a country house, and set in acres of trees and fields. Earnest-looking young men in dog collars were hurrying up and down the steps, while five nuns in fluttering white habits were gathered in a circle, chattering and shrieking like seagulls fighting over a dead herring.

They were led up to the vicar general's office by a young priest with thick spectacles and protuberant teeth, and his hair sticking up at the back, who scampered up the staircase so quickly that they could hardly keep up.

The Right Reverend Monsignor Kevin Kelly was sitting at his wide oak desk, his fingers steepled as if he had been waiting for them with growing impatience ever since he had first called. Behind him, through the leaded windows, Katie could see a wide view of the sloping parkland that surrounded the offices, and in the near distance the rooftops and spires of Cork City itself, sparkling in the sunshine.

Two walls of Monsignor Kelly's office were lined with leather-bound books, while the third wall, mahogany-panelled, was dominated by a large oil portrait of the previous bishop of Cork and Ross, Bishop Conor Kerrigan, in his robes and his purple sash, holding a Bible and obviously trying to look faintly saintly, but not arrogantly so.

'Ah, Dermot! Thank you so much for coming,' said Monsignor Kelly, rising from his chair and holding out his hand. When Katie had first entered his office, she had thought that he was quite tall, but as he came forward she realized that his desk had been nearer than she had imagined, and that he was only a little over five feet five.

He was handsome, in a Roman emperor way, with his grey hair brushed forward and a prominent nose with a bump in it, but he had those eyes that Katie was always suspicious of, in men. A little too glittery, and a little too self-satisfied. *You women, I know what you're thinking, you can't hide anything from me.*

There may have been times when she was wrong, but Katie liked to think that she could tell when priests had broken their vow of celibacy, especially when they had broken it often, and discovered how intense the passions of the flesh could be. They had a way of eyeing her, both sly and patronizing, as if they had a good idea of what she looked like naked, but weren't going to compromise themselves by admitting it.

'You've not met Detective Superintendent Kathleen Maguire, have you?' asked Chief Superintendent O'Driscoll.

Monsignor Kelly took Katie's hand and clasped it for a moment without shaking it. His own hand was warm and strangely rough. 'I've not yet had the pleasure, no. But it was your detectives who broke up that church-robbing gang of Romanians last year, wasn't it, detective superintendent, and for that the diocese owes you a great debt of gratitude.'

'Please, monsignor, call me Katie. The media always do.'

'Ah yes, the media. Don't we all love the media?'

'Only when it suits our purposes,' said Chief Superintendent O'Driscoll.

'Please, sit down,' said Monsignor Kelly. 'I suppose it's partly because of the media that I've asked you to come here this morning. The bishop is very distressed about all of the sensational publicity that Father Heaney's murder has been attracting. Of course, it was very newsworthy, but he doesn't want it to be blown out of all proportion. As far as all this child-abuse business went, we thought we had just about weathered the storm, but then this.'

He lifted from his desk a copy of last night's *Examiner*, with the headline PAEDO PRIEST'S 'REVENGE' KILLING. Police Quiz Abuse Victims.

Chief Superintendent O'Driscoll sniffed and said, 'Yes, we've seen it. But I'm afraid we have no control over what the papers want to come out with.'

'Well, I'm aware of that,' said Monsignor Kelly. 'But fortunately, I believe that the mystery of Father Heaney's murder has been solved. Or perhaps I should say *sadly*, because a tortured soul appears to have met his maker as a consequence.'

'Go on,' said Chief Superintendent O'Driscoll. Katie knew how sceptical he felt about amateur sleuths. As far as he was concerned, most of them couldn't solve a fecking two-piece jigsaw puzzle, let alone a drug-related triple stabbing in Grawn.

With a pursed-up smile that was very close to triumphant, Monsignor Kelly passed Chief Superintendent O'Driscoll a crumpled sheet of lined paper torn out of a cheap spiral-bound notebook. Chief Superintendent O'Driscoll quickly scanned it and then passed it across to Katie.

'Where did this come from?' he asked Monsignor Kelly.

'It was pushed through Father Lenihan's letter box at St Patrick's on the Lower Glanmire Road, some time late last night or very early this morning. Father Lenihan called me at six o'clock, as soon as he found it. I instructed him to tell nobody but to bring it up here.'

'You didn't tell him to call us directly?'

'Well, no,' said Monsignor Kelly. 'It might have been a hoax, after all, and I felt it more prudent to take a look at it myself first, in case we were wasting your valuable time.'

Oh what a smooth customer you are, monsignor, thought Katie, *with your D4 accent and your carefully guarded smiles.*

'Having our time wasted, that's part of our job,' put in Chief Superintendent O'Driscoll.

'I appreciate that,' said Monsignor Kelly. 'But what difference would it have made? By the time Father Lenihan had found the note, it would already have been too late, wouldn't it? And obviously I wanted to keep any hoo-ha to a minimum. I have the reputation of the diocese to think of, Dermot, as well as the sensitivities of Brendan's family.'

Katie finished reading the letter. It was written with a green ballpoint pen that looked as if it were just about to run out of ink, in a narrow, backwards-sloping script.

To All Of My Family And Friends, and for Father Lenihan most of all,

I have no shame for what I have done but I know that I have to pay the price for it in the eyes of God and the Law and I would rather pay the price in a way of my own choosing. Father Heaney intrefered with me many times at St Josephs and for all of these years I have thought every day about what I allowed him to do to me, and what in return I did to him.

As you know I have never had a girlfriend or wife and could not think of becoming intimate with a woman because I always believed that as soon as I was undress she would be able to see what had happened to me. I felt as if my body was tatoo all over with Father Heaney's blacky fingerprints and I would never be able to wash them off. I scrub myself every morning and night with bleech but I never feel clean.

All the talk of abuse in the past few weeks has brought back too many memories and too much torment. I cant sleep for the terrible shame of it. I decided that I could only find peace if I took Father Heaneys life the way he took mine. I am ending things myself now and I will be gone by the time you read this. I know that what I am going to do is supposed to be a mortal sin, but how can it be a sin to kill yourself when you have been killed already?

Goodbye and God bless you, Brendan Doody.

'So who is Brendan Doody?' asked Katie.

'He is – *was* – the odd-job man at St Patrick's,' said Monsignor Kelly. 'He did other bits and pieces all around St Luke's Cross, for anybody who would pay him. Gardening, window cleaning, bit of decorating, that kind of thing. I met him

77

only a couple of times but he was a queer fellow. Always talking to himself. Well, more like *arguing*.'

'Did he drive a van?' asked Katie.

Monsignor Kelly shrugged. 'I wouldn't know that, Katie. You'll have to ask Father Lenihan.'

'Did he seem to you like the kind of person who was capable of murder?'

'Who knows what *anybody* is capable of, when they're pushed to the limits of their mental endurance? He was physically strong, yes, and he certainly would have been able to overwhelm Father Heaney and tie him up, and perform the act of mutilation that Father Heaney then suffered, may God have mercy on his soul.'

Katie turned the letter over. 'No indication as to *how* he might have taken his own life, or where? Or, indeed, if he's really taken it at all?'

'Father Lenihan went to Brendan's flat after he had found the letter but Brendan wasn't there. The door was unlocked and there were five or six empty whiskey bottles on the table, as well as empty beer cans. Father Lenihan phoned his mother in Limerick and his brother in Midleton but neither of them had seen hide nor hair of him.'

'I see,' said Chief Superintendent O'Driscoll. 'But before we jump to any hasty conclusions, we need to go looking for your man. We can't assume that he's topped himself until we find his body, and we can't be sure that this letter means anything at all until we've had the chance to talk to him – that's if he hasn't topped himself, of course. If he's such a queer fellow, maybe it's all in his head.'

'Do you think so?' frowned Monsignor Kelly. 'I'd say myself that this letter is a very credible confession of guilt – and, believe me, I've heard a few confessions in my time.'

Katie said, 'What the public don't generally realize is that whenever a murder is committed, at least half a dozen people come forward to confess that they did it. Sometimes they're seeking attention, sometimes they simply have a screw loose and really believe that they're guilty. Sometimes they're looking for nothing more than a decent supper and a warm bed.'

Monsignor Kelly raised his eyebrows. 'Oh,' he said – and then, after a long pause, 'The bishop and I were very much hoping that this would close the book, as it were.'

'It may,' said Katie. 'But first of all we have to be sure that Brendan Doody actually wrote this note himself; and if he really has committed suicide, or simply absconded. Do you think that Father Lenihan will have a picture of him that we can circulate?'

'I'm not sure, but I expect so.' Monsignor Kelly gave Katie the impression that he was both disappointed and cross. 'Would you like me to call him and ask him?'

'Don't worry, I'll be going down to see him myself so,' Katie told him. 'Is there anything else you have to tell us? The sooner we get this investigation up and running, the better.'

'No, no. I only wanted to show you the note. But I did want to pass on the bishop's extreme concern, and ask you if you could handle your inquiries as discreetly as you possibly can.'

'We'll not be making any sensational state-
ments to the press, if that's what you're worried
about,' Chief Superintendent O'Driscoll assured
him. 'We deal with evidence, monsignor, and not
with wild specumulation.'

Monsignor Kelly stood up and they shook
hands again. As they did so, he gave Katie an
intense, unblinking look, which she couldn't
clearly interpret. He was a cleric, but it put her in
mind of the looks that Cork gangsters like Dave
McSweeney would give her, if they thought that
she was coming a shade too close to discovering
what rackets they had been running lately.

On the way down the wide curving staircase, as
two young priests flattened themselves against
the wall to let them by, Katie said, 'What did you
make of that, then, sir?'

'I'm damned if I know yet,' said Chief Superintendent O'Driscoll, taking out his handkerchief
and blowing his nose. 'But you sensed the anx-
iety, did you? Fair play, Katie, somebody's
pruned a priest, dirty old whacker or not, but
why should that worry the bishop so much?'

'I don't know, sir, but I agree with you. Our
Monsignor Kelly was definitely trying a little too
hard to point our noses in one particular
direction – away from something that makes him
feel very uncomfortable.'

Katie held up Brendan Doody's green-scrawled
note. 'I'll tell you another thing,' she said, 'this
confession doesn't ring true at all.'

'He admits he did it, like.'

'I know. But it reads like it was written by an
educated man pretending to be uneducated.

There's misspellings in it, for sure, but whoever wrote it has misspelled words like "intimate" that an uneducated man would never have used in the first place. Like *"torment"*. Did you ever meet an odd-job man who talked about "torment"?'

They crossed the car park and climbed back into their car. Katie said, 'I just don't understand why the church is so set on laying the blame on this Brendan Doody fellow. I mean, is he really dead, or have they spirited him away for some reason so that we can never find him?'

Chief Superintendent O'Driscoll pulled a face. 'Let's see if he shows up first. And if he shows up dead, let's hope and pray that he really did do himself in. If he *didn't,* this case is going to turn into a right pig's dinner, and no mistake.'

Twelve

Father Quinlan heard a clock strike five somewhere in the street outside. His whole being throbbed with pain – every nerve, every tendon, every muscle – but he had been hanging here for so long that, in some otherworldly way, he had begun to grow used to it. He wondered if Christ had felt the same, nailed to the cross.

The afternoon sun had moved around, so that only a thin triangular slice of it was shining in through the windows. He was alone in the bathroom, but he could still hear the thin, high voices of the St Joseph's Orphanage Choir. They were

81

singing *'Bring Flowers of the Rarest'*, which was traditionally sung in May – next month – to accompany the crowning of a statue of the Virgin Mary with a garland of flowers. It brought a sudden flood of tears to Father Quinlan's eyes, even more copious than the tears that he had been weeping all afternoon because of the agony that he was suffering.

He sobbed, and his sobbing made his broken ribs grind against each other, and he cried out even louder.

'Where are you?' he shouted, or tried to shout, because his throat was dry and he could hardly draw breath. *'Where are you, you devil? Why don't you kill me and have done with it?'*

The singing went on, and again Father Quinlan thought that he heard somebody galumphing down a flight of stairs, but still nobody appeared. It was worse in a way to suffer alone than to be taunted by the Grey Mullet Man. At least when the Grey Mullet Man had been here he had felt as if somebody cared about his pain, even if he relished it.

Suddenly, however, the bathroom door opened and for a moment, before it closed again, he heard the choir singing louder:

'O Mary! We crown you with blossoms today,
Queen of the flowers, Queen of the May!'

He lifted his head, even though he could feel the tendons in his neck crackling. The Grey Mullet Man was standing on the other side of the room beside the bathtub, with his arms folded. He had taken off his grey jacket, and was now wearing an ankle-length apron made of red rubber. His bare

82

forearms were decorated with tattoos, mostly of fish, as far as Father Quinlan could see.

'Did I hear you calling out for me, Father?' he asked. This time, he spoke softly and melodiously, like a mother who hears her child crying in the night.

'I thought I was alone,' wept Father Quinlan.

'How could you *think* such a thing, Father?' said the Grey Mullet Man – but now his voice was hoarser and harsher, the same as it had been before. 'Don't you know that God is always with us, and even when God has to take His eyes off us, for a moment or two, one of His angels is always watching? We are *never* alone.'

'Why don't you kill me and put me out of my pain?' Father Quinlan asked him.

'Because I need to hear you confess your sin, Father, and I need you to tell me the names of all of those who were complicit with you in committing that sin, and most of all I need to know who instigated that whole terrible madness.'

'I can't,' croaked Father Quinlan.

'Can't, Father, or *won't?*' the Grey Mullet Man demanded, coming closer, with his rubbery apron rustling. He smelled of stale sweat and onions. The fish on his forearms looked like the sea monsters on medieval mariners' maps, with bulging eyes and thick lips. One of them had been cut open so that torrents of smaller fish were pouring out its belly.

Father Quinlan said, 'I took an oath of silence. All of us did. None of us can speak of what we did or who we did it with, or why.'

Without warning, the Grey Mullet Man

violently shook the rope from which Father Quinlan was hanging, so that Father Quinlan let out a girlish squeal of pain.

'At the very least you could confess your own sin, couldn't you, Father? Then who knows? I might be minded to let you down, if you did.'

'But it wasn't a sin. We never once thought of it – *ever* – as a sin.' Father Quinlan had to pause between each sentence to catch his breath, and to cough, but the Grey Mullet Man waited as if he had all the time in the world, gently swinging the rope backward and forward to make Father Quinlan feel even more defenceless than he did already.

'Oh, so it *wasn't* a sin. But if it wasn't a sin, what was it?'

'Let me explain to you why it was done. It was done – it was all done–'

'Go on, Father. Don't stop now.'

Father Quinlan closed his eyes. The pain was too much for him. He could see nothing behind his eyelids but solid scarlet, the colour of hell, but he could still hear the choir singing *'O Sanctissima'*, and the honking of traffic on Patrick Street outside, and the pitter-pattering of shoppers' feet, like the eager crowds hurrying in their sandals up Calvary Hill, to see Christ and the robbers crucified.

'It was all done for the greater glory of God. And of the diocese.'

'Come here to me? What you and your fellow priests did – exactly how was that supposed to glorify God? Or the diocese for that matter? What you and your fellow priests did, that was the work

84

of the Devil, that was, and no mistake about it.'

'You don't understand.'

'No, you're absolutely right, Father, I *don't* understand, and unless you tell me I won't understand, either.'

'What difference does it make? You're going to torture me and kill me whether I tell you or not. I would rather keep my oath to my brother priests, and to God.'

The Grey Mullet Man shrugged. 'It's your decision, Father. But I don't think you realize that there's a difference between torture and torture. Hanging there, I'll bet you that feels like torture. Oh, yes! But at least when you're hanging there, you still have a hope of surviving, like, and living a normal life afterwards. Maybe your arms will never be the same again, but you'll still be able to walk and talk and eat fish and chips and wipe your own arse.'

The Grey Mullet Man leaned forward. The flap that covered his face rose and fell as he breathed. 'Supposing, though, you had your feet cut off? Or maybe your hands? Supposing you lost your ears, or your nose, or had your eyes poked out? All without the benefit of anaesthetic, of course. That wouldn't just hurt while it was being done to you, would it? You'd know while it was being done that you would never be the same man again, ever.'

He said nothing for twenty long seconds, his face flap rising and falling, his eyes glinting through the cut-out holes. Then he whispered, 'Then, Father, *then* you'd be begging me to kill you. I promise you.'

He pushed Father Quinlan hard, and Father

Quinlan swung around and around, his legs kicking, screeching in pain.

'I'll confess!' he cried out. 'I'll confess! Please! Holy Mary, Mother of God, I'll confess!'

'Well, now, that's a start,' said the Grey Mullet Man. 'Why don't you mull it over a little longer, an hour or so maybe, just to make absolutely sure, then I'll come back and let you down.'

'Please,' Father Quinlan begged him. 'Please let me down now. I'll confess.'

But the Grey Mullet Man ignored him, and walked out of the bathroom, closing the door very quietly behind him. Father Quinlan spun slowly on his rope, both of his arms now dislocated from their sockets, humming rather than moaning, with a string of bloody dribble dangling from his lips. The choir sang,

Ye watchers and ye holy ones,
bright seraphs, cherubim, and thrones,
raise the glad strain, Alleluia!
Cry out, dominions, princedoms, powers,
virtues, archangels, angels' choirs: Alleluia!
Alleluia! Alleluia! Alleluia! Alleluia!

Thirteen

It was dark before the Grey Mullet Man came back, and the only illumination in the bathroom was the orange sodium light from the street lamps outside.

Father Quinlan had been fading in and out of consciousness, and he had been hallucinating, too. He had thought that he was walking along the seashore, taking a break from a weekend retreat at Myross Wood, near Leap in West Cork. It was a warm August afternoon with only a few horse's-tail clouds, but a stiff breeze was blowing off the ocean and making his soutane billow as he clambered up the rocks.

He was thinking deeply about the discussion he had attended that morning: about 'shepherding' and 'discipleship', in which new converts to Christianity were supposed to submit themselves completely to more mature members of their church, and obey them as blindly as a dog chasing a stick. 'The dog doesn't know *why* he's chasing the stick. He doesn't realize that the exercise is doing him good. But then he doesn't have to. His obedience is all that's important.'

Panting, his black boots sliding in the shale, Father Quinlan struggled up the side of a rough granite outcrop so that he could get a better view of the bay. As he approached the top, however, he saw a girl's red hair, blowing in the wind; and when he climbed up two or three more steps, the girl herself came into view.

She was kneeling in the grass, pale-skinned and pretty and completely naked. She stared at him as he appeared, but she didn't seem to be at all abashed. She had small breasts with pink nipples that were stiffened by the wind, and vase-like hips, and a small flame of red hair between her thighs. She was grasping in her left hand the erect penis of a skinny young man, who was lying on his back with his head behind the rocks, obscured from Father Quinlan's view. His pubic hair was ginger, too, and the girl had just pulled his foreskin down, so that his lavender-coloured glans was exposed. Her lips were wide open in an 'O', as if Father Quinlan had caught her just as she was about to take it into her mouth.

For five long seconds, Father Quinlan and the girl remained frozen in a tableau. The wind blew Father Quinlan's soutane, so that it flapped and snapped, and it blew the girl's hair in long art-nouveau skeins. The ocean gnashed at the rocks below them, and the gulls circled around them, screaming, but for all of that time, neither of them moved.

Father Quinlan suddenly jerked up his right hand, as if to give the girl a blessing, or an apology, or to wave goodbye. Then he turned and stumbled down the side of the outcrop, half jumping and half falling, until he reached the pathway that would take him back to the road.

He felt hot, as he walked, but not from embarrassment. He felt as if he had inadvertently opened up a furnace door and been scorched by the red-hot fires of temptation. For the first time in his life, he had seen with absolute clarity what kind of man he was, and what it was that he really lusted after, but had never allowed himself to admit to it. He had seen his own sin as vividly as if it had been depicted in a painting by Brueghel, with beetle-headed demons trying to drag him down to hell, and trumpeting angels trying to give him the strength and the courage to resist them.

It was not the red-headed girl who had aroused

him. He had seen her as a siren, yes – a seductress, like Eve, or Lamia, the beautiful child-eating granddaughter of Poseidon. But what had aroused him was the anonymous young man who had been lying on his back while the girl stroked his penis. So thin, so narrow-hipped, so boy-like. Father Quinlan had pictured himself kneeling in the girl's place, ready to take him into his mouth.

The Grey Mullet Man waggled the rope violently from side to side. 'Don't tell me you're actually *sleeping?*' he demanded.

'*Ahhhh!* Please!' gasped Father Quinlan. 'Please – please don't, that hurts so much.'

'You're ready to confess, then?'

Father Quinlan tried to raise his head. The Grey Mullet Man was still wearing the cloth over his face, and his red rubber apron.

'Yes,' Father Quinlan whispered. 'If that's what you want.'

The Grey Mullet Man untied the knots that fastened the rope to the taps, and lowered Father Quinlan to the floor. Father Quinlan's knees buckled, so that he slowly collapsed on to his right side. As his dislocated shoulder touched the lino, he screamed so loudly that the Grey Mullet Man said, 'Name of Jesus, hush, will you! You sound like a fecking chicken.'

'*O Holy Mary, Mother of God, O Holy Mary, Mother of God.*'

The Grey Mullet Man freed Father Quinlan's wrists and one after the other levered his arms down by his sides. Father Quinlan bit his tongue to stop himself from screaming again, and a runnel of blood slid out of the side of his mouth.

'Now then,' said the Grey Mullet Man. He forced his hands under Father Quinlan's armpits, and pulled him into a sitting position. Then he dragged him across the bathroom floor and propped him up against the wall, next to the bathtub.

'Right now, Father, let's hear your confession. Loud and clear, please.'

Father Quinlan closed his eyes. He was suffering such pain that he had almost forgotten how to speak. The Grey Mullet Man waited for nearly half a minute, but when Father Quinlan still hadn't confessed, he said, 'How about a little lubrication for the voice box? I was going to give you some later, in any case.'

He went over to a small pine cupboard that stood in the corner and took out a large glass jar. He came back and held it up in front of Father Quinlan's face and said, 'Open your eyes, Father. See this? John Martin's best honey, from Dunmanway. You always swore by it, didn't you? It's the bee's knees, that's what you used to say.'

The sun shone through the honey jar so brightly that it looked like an orange lamp. The Grey Mullet Man unscrewed the lid, and then produced a large stainless-steel dessert spoon out of his apron pocket. He poured honey on to the spoon until it was dripping in long strings to the floor, and then he held the spoon close to Father Quinlan's lips.

'Here you are, Father. Golden honey to give you a golden voice.'

Father Quinlan kept his mouth tightly shut and tried to turn his head away.

'Come on, Father, you know it's good for you.'
The Grey Mullet Man pressed the spoon hard against Father Quinlan's lips. The strong, sweet smell of it made Father Quinlan retch.

'Don't you think that honey makes *me* sick, even now?' said the Grey Mullet Man. 'I can't even *see* a jar of honey sitting on the shelf in my local shop and I feel like bringing up my breakfast. But if this is what it takes to make you confess, then so be it, Father. You'll just have to mortify the palate.'

Still Father Quinlan kept his lips closed. It was his final act of defiance. *You may force me to confess, whoever you are, but in my own eyes I committed no sin, and neither did my brothers. Everything we did was to please and glorify God, and to bring the brilliance of heaven to the diocese.*

Without hesitation, however, the Grey Mullet Man plunged his left hand between Father Quinlan's thighs and grabbed hold of his testicles through his thin woollen underpants.

'Ah, no, please,' said Father Quinlan.

'So you *can* speak, then? Alleluia! Let's get this honey down you, shall we, and then we'll see just how sweet you can talk to me.'

Father Quinlan closed his lips again, but the Grey Mullet Man gave him a quick, sharp squeeze between his legs, and immediately he opened up wide. The Grey Mullet Man jammed the spoon into his mouth so hard that it rattled against his dentures, and then said, 'Suck! Go on, suck! I want a clean spoon, Father.'

Father Quinlan sucked all the honey off the spoon and swallowed it. Although it was fero-

91

ciously sweet, it had a bitter aftertaste – but that may have been blood from his bitten tongue.

'Oh, you're a good, obedient fellow when you want to be, aren't you, Father?' said the Grey Mullet Man, standing up and screwing the lid back on to the honey jar. 'Now, let's hear you sing to me.'

Father Quinlan was desperate to wipe the sticky honey from his lips, but both of his arms lay by his sides, dislocated and useless. 'In the name of the Father...' he began.

'Go on,' the Grey Mullet Man chivvied him, in his sandpapery voice. 'And of the Son, and of the Holy Ghost, amen.'

Father Quinlan said, as loud as he could manage, 'I confess.'

'Good. You confess. You confess to *what*, exactly?'

'I confess that in the summer of 1983 – I used my influence as their spiritual shepherd – to persuade several young boys who were entrusted to my care...'

'Go on! You may have escaped penance for nearly thirty years, Father, but now it's time to beg for forgiveness.'

'To convince several young boys who were entrusted to my care...'

'Spit it out, Father.'

Father Quinlan looked up at him and shouted, '*I promised them that they would see God!*'

Fourteen

Katie drove Chief Superintendent O'Driscoll back to Anglesea Street. As they climbed out of the car, she looked up and saw a dirty white shirt blowing in the wind above the rooftops, its arms waving at her. It soared and circled high above her, and then abruptly lurched out of sight, like a drunk man being pulled into a pub.

Detective O'Donovan was sitting at his desk, waiting for her.

'Sandwich?' he asked her, lifting up a lopsided doorstep of soda bread, filled with bright orange cheese.

'No, thanks, Patrick. Let's just get going, shall we?'

Detective O'Donovan nodded towards the transparent plastic evidence bag lying on his desk, next to his unwrapped sandwiches. 'Father Heaney's diaries, or whatever they are. I thought you'd like to take a look at them before I sent them across for fingerprinting.'

Katie picked them up. There were three books altogether, bound in mottled brown leather, about the size of pocket Bibles. She pulled a rolled-up pair of latex gloves out of her jacket pocket and snapped them on. Then she opened the evidence bag, took out one of the books, and turned it this way and that, and sniffed at it, too.

'Smells like churches,' she said.

93

'The whole of Father Heaney's diggings smelled like churches. I'd say he was smoking incense instead of ciggies.'

Katie opened the book's cover. On the flyleaf – in tiny, crabbed writing – it had been inscribed with the words *'Quam Condeco Deus'*, and underneath the name *'St Joseph's Orphanage, Cork, 1983.'*

'"Quam condeco Deus"?' asked Katie. 'Something to do with God?'

'It's the same in all three books, ma'am. I looked it up on the internet. As far as I can tell it means *How to meet God.'*

Katie flicked through the book from beginning to end. Jesus – it would take even the best translators weeks to decipher all of this diminutive handwriting. Each page was filled with numbered paragraphs, and even though she couldn't understand very many words, she got the general impression that it was a compendium of ways in which a true believer could feel closer to God. *'Statua angelus usequaque commodo Deus'* – God is pleased by statues of angels, whatever *'usequaque'* meant.

'Okay, Patrick,' she said, returning the book to its evidence bag and handing it back. 'But tell the lab to photocopy them all before they do their forensics. I want it translated as soon as you like. We need to know how Father Heaney thought he was going to be meeting his maker, whether he planned it or not.'

They drove over the grey reflective river to the Lower Glanmire Road and parked outside the lofty pillared portico of St Patrick's. Father

Lenihan was standing outside, talking to two of his parishioners, and the wind was waving his white comb-over like a handkerchief.

As Katie and Detective O'Donovan climbed the steps he swivelled around to greet them, clasping his hands together and tilting his head to one side as if he were being deliberately unctuous. He was a very thin man, with long arms and long legs, like the long-legged scissor-man in *Struwwelpeter*. His eyes were blue and his face was very pallid, but his cheeks were two scarlet spots, as if he had been drinking, or making himself up to appear as a pantomime dame.

'You must excuse me, ladies,' he said to his parishioners, two rotund women in hats like cow-pats and cardigans of different shades of brown. 'I have to have a word with these good people here. Guardians of the law. They've come about poor Brendan.'

The two women shuffled reluctantly away, try-ing their best to remain within earshot. But Katie said, 'Let's go inside, shall we, Father? I'd like to see Brendan's living quarters.'

'Well, of course. There's been no news of him yet, I imagine? It was a hideous business all around, you know, such a shock, but on reflection it didn't entirely surprise me. I always had the feeling that Brendan was simmering away inside of himself with some kind of pent-up anger against the world, although I had no idea that it was all directed against Father Heaney.'

Father Lenihan led them through the church, and one after the other they all genuflected in front of the altar. Then he took them out of the

95

back door and into the flagstoned yard, to the single-storey stone outbuilding in which Brendan Doody had nested – more like a giant hamster, thought Katie, than a human. The main room had a high ceiling, with rafters that trailed long dusty spiders' webs, and it was filled from one side to the other with unbelievable clutter. Underneath the window, there was a broken-down sofa covered with a multicoloured hand-crocheted blanket, which Brendan Doody had obviously used as his bed. Next to the sofa there was a dilapidated basketwork armchair, but the rest of the room was jam-packed with tables and workbenches, all of which were covered with wrenches and hammers and paintbrushes and tins of screws and squeezed-out tubes of glue. The air was pungent with the smell of varnish and white spirit.

At the far end of the outbuilding, a makeshift partition had been nailed together out of chipboard, with a crude doorway cut into it, and behind this partition was Brendan Doody's kitchen and his washbasin. On the windowsill stood two half-empty bottles of medicated shampoo, for dandruff. The kitchen was equipped with no more than a two-ring electric hotplate, a brown plastic kettle and a row of cheap cooking spoons and spatulas. Katie opened one of the cupboards and apart from a box of tea bags and a packet of chocolate biscuits it was stacked with nothing but cans of tuna, probably thirty or more.

The only personal touch that she could see was a curled-up photograph on the fridge of a grey-haired woman in a turquoise cardigan, who Katie guessed was Brendan Doody's mother.

They went back into the main room. Father Lenihan laid his hand on the back of the sofa and said, 'I'd find him lying here sometimes, young Brendan. Not asleep, but staring up at the ceiling and whispering to himself.'

'Did you ever hear what he was saying?' Katie asked him.

'I caught a word or two, but I don't really care to repeat it. He was a poor unfortunate soul with a tortured spirit and I don't think it's for any of us to judge him.'

'All the same, if you heard anything at all that might explain what he did...'

Father Lenihan shrugged. 'I suppose you can't say ill of the dead. He used to whisper, *"You demon, Skelly, you'll be sorry one day."*'

'Skelly?'

'I didn't know it until yesterday, when Father Tiernan from St Joseph's called me. "Skelly" is what the boys used to call Father Heaney, on account of him being so bony, I suppose.'

'So on several occasions you actually heard Brendan Doody whispering what sounded like threats against Father Heaney?'

Father Lenihan looked uncomfortable. 'In a manner of speaking, yes. I mean, that's always supposing that I heard him right.'

'You've just told me that you clearly heard him say, *"You demon, Skelly, you'll be sorry one day."*'

'In a manner of speaking, yes.'

'Come on, Father, did he or didn't he?'

Katie looked acutely at Father Lenihan and the way that Father Lenihan's blue eyes kept darting towards the broken-down sofa as if he were try-

97

ing his hardest to imagine something that might not have actually happened.

Father Lenihan twisted his hands together and said, 'Yes, that's it. That's what he said right enough.'

'Very good, then. When did you last see him?'

'I, ah – I think it was about five to six, just before Mass. He said he was on his way to meet some friends.'

'Did he seem upset, or different in any way?'

Father Lenihan shook his head. 'He might have been, but it was always very difficult to tell with Brendan. Sometimes he shouted as if he was very angry, but it was only his idea of a joke. People like Brendan ... they don't always have the same sense of humour as the rest of the world. He used to think that people in wheelchairs were funny. He used to point at them in the street and laugh his head off. It was only because people in Cork got to know him that he got away with it without somebody beating the dust off him.'

Katie circled around the outbuilding, picking up screwdrivers and pliers and odd lengths of wire. One pair of pliers and a coil of brass wire she gave to Detective O'Donovan to drop into his evidence bag.

Father Lenihan said, 'I suppose with all this recent publicity about abuse, it was only a matter of time before it occurred to Brendan that *he* was entitled to take his revenge, too.'

'Do you think that Father Heaney *deserved* what was done to him?' asked Katie.

'Of course not! Thou shalt not kill, under any provocation whatsoever. Besides, I know for a fact that whatever Father Heaney did, he was truly repentant.'

'But you believe that Brendan had a very strong motive to punish him?'

'That depends on how forgiving you are, superintendent.'

'Hmm,' said Katie. She ran her fingertip along a small tenon saw, but its blade was rusty rather than bloody, and she put it down again. 'Did Brendan own a van?'

'No, not himself. He used to borrow one from the nursery up at Ballyvolane whenever he needed a van for any of his odd jobs.'

'What did it look like, this van?'

Father Lenihan pulled a face. 'It wasn't always the same van. I saw a blue one once, and a black one, but I'm not really the man to ask about vans.'

'The black one – did you notice anything unusual about it? Any markings?'

'Only a name that somebody had painted over, but you couldn't read what it was.'

Detective O'Donovan held up a spiral-bound notebook, and a green ballpoint pen. 'I found these on the table here, ma'am. This must be the pad he used to write his suicide note in.'

Katie took the notebook and leafed over a few pages. They were all blank, but when she angled it against the light she could still make out the indentation of somebody's handwriting. She passed it back to Detective O'Donovan and said, 'Yes, let's bag this, too – and the pen, please.'

She took a last look around, lifting up the cushion on the basketwork chair, and then the crocheted blanket on the sofa. The leatherette fabric was worn through, so that the springs were showing, and Brendan Doody had pushed dozens of crumpled-up sweet wrappers down the back of it, mostly Snickers and Aero bars.

'Well, he never let himself go hungry,' she remarked. She let the blanket drop back and then she said, 'Did Monsignor Kelly tell you that we'd be needing a picture of him?'

Father Lenihan led them back into the church and through to his dark panelled presbytery office. On the wall above his desk hung a very miserable-looking Madonna, as if she were mourning what the world had become, in spite of having sacrificed her only son. In fact, Katie thought she was the most dejected Madonna she had ever seen.

Father Lenihan shook two photographs out of a manila envelope and handed them over. 'This one – this small one here – that's your most recent. That was taken at a family christening three weeks ago. The larger one – Brendan's not so clear in this one, but that's him standing in the background with the cap on.'

Katie examined the photographs closely. Brendan Doody looked about five feet six or seven, podgy, with scruffy caramel-coloured hair that he had probably cut himself, and protruding ears. He had an expression that was both eager to please and slightly bewildered, as if he were excited by the events in which he was participating, but didn't quite know how to join in.

'Thanks a million, Father,' said Katie. 'These two pictures will be grand. We'll probably be putting at least one of them out on the TV news tonight. Meanwhile, if you can think of anything else at all that might help us to find him.'

'I'll try,' said Father Lenihan. 'But you've read his letter, haven't you, and you can tell for yourself that he was always quite a queer fellow. With us in *body*, as it were, but not...' and he tapped his forehead with his fingertip. 'Not entirely, anyhow.'

They shook Father Lenihan's hand and walked back down the steps of St Patrick's. As they did so, Katie looked across the river and saw the white shirt that had earlier been flying over the rooftops lying spreadeagled in the filthy grey water, its arms rising and falling in a sinuous mockery of a dance.

They climbed back into the car and slammed the doors. 'What do you think to that then, ma'am?' asked Detective O'Donovan.

'What makes you think I think anything?'

'Because it's plain bloody obvious that you do. You've got that look in your eye. That famous look that O'Driscoll calls your "cat's malogian meter".'

They backed out of the parking space in front of St Patrick's. Father Lenihan was still watching from the top of the church steps with his hands clasped.

'He was lying through his teeth,' said Katie.

'Father Lenihan? Name of Jesus, he's a reverend!'

'So what? You don't seriously think that reverends ever lie? All that codswallop about Brendan Doody whispering about Father Heaney being a demon, and how he was going to be sorry one day.'

'You didn't believe that?'

Katie shook her head. 'Not for a second. And

you could tell how uncomfortable Father Lenihan felt, saying it. But – somebody further up the diocesan food chain told him he had to say it, or words to that effect. Otherwise – think about it – there would be no witnesses at all who heard Brendan threaten Father Heaney before his murder.'

'Brendan didn't call him "Father Heaney", though, did he? He called him "Skelly".'

'Nice touch, that, I thought. It made his threat sound all the more authentic, because if Father Heaney had abused him at school, that's what Brendan would have called him. Anybody who went to St Joseph's would have known who "Skelly" was. I'll bet you still remember *your* schoolteachers' nicknames, don't you, even today?'

Detective O'Donovan thought about that as they waited at the traffic lights to cross back over the river. 'You're right,' he said. 'Father Duckfart. I don't even remember his real name now, but I'll never forget the noise he used to make, walking along the corridor. Some of the bold boys use to throw breadcrumbs after him.'

Fifteen

Katie went up to the media office and handed over the two photographs of Brendan Doody so that they could be sent to the RTÉ TV studios for the evening's six o'clock news bulletin, and then to the newspapers: the *Examiner* and the *Corkman* and the *Southern Star* in Skibbereen. She was just about to go back out again when Sergeant O'Rourke tilted his head out of the squad-room door and called out, 'Phone for you, ma'am!'

'Whoever it is, tell them that I'm somewhere else altogether, because I very nearly am.'

'It's personal, apparently. Aoife's Father.'

Aoife's father. Aoife, of course, was John's collie bitch. Katie stopped with her hand against the door. She closed her eyes for a moment, and then she turned around and walked back. Sergeant O'Rourke was trying hard not to smile at her as he passed her the receiver.

'*John*,' she breathed.

'Caught you at last! I've been trying all morning. You haven't been answering your mobile.'

'Not to you, no. I've been up to my ears. We're right in the middle of this Father Heaney murder. I'm just about to go back up to Ballyhooly.'

'Katie ... do you think we could talk?'

'What about? There's nothing more to say, is there? Whatever we feel about each other, you're going and I'm staying, and that's all there is to it.'

'Please. I have some ideas. Maybe we can work something out.'

'What, like alternate weekends? California one week and Cork the next?'

'Katie – please, just hear me out. Is there any chance I can meet you this evening?'

Katie's instincts said, *no, this is going to mean nothing but more arguing and nothing but more pain*. But she checked her wristwatch and said, 'I'm having supper with my father at seven. Why don't you come round then?'

'I wouldn't want to impose on him.'

'You won't be. He loves company and Mrs Walsh always cooks far too much. I can't guarantee what she's going to be serving us up tonight, but if you're prepared to take pot luck...'

'Sure. I'll eat almost anything, you know me. Except please, please, *please* – not that tripe again, that stuff that she boils in milk.'

Katie hesitated. She knew that this was a terrible idea, but she was already missing John badly. Just to see him and to touch him would make her feel that she wasn't completely on her own again. And maybe there was an outside chance that they *could* work out some way of staying together. Maybe she could talk to some of her contacts and find him a job here in Cork, although she knew that most of the major companies were shedding more and more staff every day. Two entire factories had closed last week, for good, Z-Line Electronics and Pargeter's Foods. But then again, maybe John could run his business completely online.

Detective O'Donovan came out of the gents' toilet, shaking his hands. 'Bloody dryer's bust again. Are we ready?'

Katie nodded.

'This is getting up your nose, this case, isn't it?' Detective O'Donovan asked her, as they crossed the car park.

'It helps when your witnesses tell the truth, at least to the best of their ability.'

'My father used to say that he wouldn't trust a priest to peel a turnip.'

'I'm beginning to agree with him.'

They drove up to Ballyhooly under a blue sky filled with tumbling white clouds. On the way they passed the driveway that sloped up to the Meagher farm at Knocknadeenly and Katie saw that there was already a sign outside it: FOR SALE, Christy Buckley Auctioneers. Detective O'Donovan saw it, too, but he made no comment.

Patrick O'Donovan had a fair idea of what was happening in Katie's life, as did everybody else at Anglesea Street, but mostly they respected her privacy and kept it to themselves. At least John was an improvement on her late husband, Paul, who had been a notorious local chancer. The number of times they had turned a blind eye to Paul's dealings in building materials of doubtful provenance, and to all of those cases of Johnnie Walker that he had offered at half price in the back bar of the Flying Bottle in Hollyhill, no questions asked.

Margaret Rooney lived in a small, cream-painted house on Ballyhooly's Main Street, with its red front door right on the road. Detective O'Donovan knocked and inside a dog started yapping. He knocked again and at last the door was unlocked. A vexed-looking woman appeared, with close-together eyes and lips that looked as if they had been tightly sewn together, like a shrunken head.

'Yes, what do you want?' she snapped, holding up hands that were dusted in flour. 'Can't you see that I'm baking?'

Detective O'Donovan leaned across and smiled at her, holding up his badge. 'Remember me from yesterday, Margaret? Detective O'Donovan.

I brought my boss to talk to you about that fat fellow you saw in the river.'

Katie held up her badge, too, and said, 'Detective Superintendent Katie Maguire, Mrs Rooney.'

Mrs Rooney frowned at them irritably. 'I thought I'd told you people everything you wanted to know.'

'Well, yes, you did,' said Katie. 'But we have some pictures now, and I was hoping that you'd be kind enough to take a look at them for me.'

'Pictures, is it?'

Katie held them up. 'We think they could be the man you saw in the river, but we really need to know for sure.'

Without a word, Mrs Rooney opened the front door wider and flapped her floury hand to indicate that they should follow her into her living room. Her dog was a brindled Boston terrier with bulging eyes and it jumped up and barked at them furiously as they came in, scratching at Katie's shiny new boots with its claws. *About as hospitable as your mistress,* thought Katie, *you little bush pig.*

'Sit down,' said Mrs Rooney, going through to the kitchen to wash her hands. 'You won't be wanting any tea, will you?'

'No, thank you,' Katie told her. She and Detective O'Donovan wedged themselves side by side in a high-sided two-seater couch, while Mrs Rooney came back in and perched herself in her armchair, surrounded by balls of fawn-coloured wool and knitting patterns.

The living room was so small that their knees almost touched, and the claustrophobic effect was

106

intensified by all the decorative china plates and religious plaques that crowded the walls. Mrs Rooney's dog kept circling around and around, snuffling and bumping them and stepping on their feet. There was a strong smell of burned milk, which reminded Katie of her grandmother's house.

'About what time was it when you saw the man in the river?' asked Katie.

'I wouldn't know exactly, like, I don't have a watch. But I'd say about five past seven. When I was walking past Michael Sullivan's house on the corner I saw Michael pulling open his bedroom curtains, and I know that he always gets up at seven.'

'So you were crossing the bridge, and that's when you first caught sight of this man?'

'I would never have seen him at all if Micky hadn't stopped and barked at him. It was so misty like, you couldn't see further than the other side of Grindell's farm, where the lane comes down to the river. That's where the fellow's van was parked with its doors open. It was black, the van, or maybe dark blue. I told Micky to come away but then I saw the fellow himself and he was all hunched over with his back to me, like, and he was dragging what I thought was a sack of coal.'

'Did you call out to him?'

'Why would I? I didn't know then that he was dragging a dead priest after him, did I?' She made a shivery noise and crossed herself. 'If he hadn't been wearing that hat, I would have walked on and thought nothing at all about it, but that hat made me stop and stare at him, like.'

'Oh, yes – that pointed hat that you told Detective O'Donovan about.'

Mrs Rooney said, 'That's right. Just like the dunce's cap they used to make us wear in high babies, whenever we got our sums wrong.'

'Detective O'Donovan tells me you caught a glimpse of his face.'

Mrs Rooney pursed her sewn-together lips and nodded. 'Yes – but only for an instant, mind. Like I told your man here, he was a big fellow, and he was fat, but in a sweet-looking way, if you know what I mean. There's a painting of a whole bunch of angels and cherubs in St Patrick's in Fermoy, and that's what he reminded me of. A cherub.'

Katie took out the photograph of Brendan Doody at the christening, and passed it across to her. 'Do you recognize this man here – the one with the circle drawn around him?'

Mrs Rooney put on her rimless spectacles and peered at the photograph as intently as if she were trying to burn a hole in it. 'No. I don't know this fellow at all.'

'Are you sure?'

'Never saw him before. Never.'

'He's not the man with the pointed hat you saw in the river?'

'No. That fellow was much bigger.'

Katie passed her the second photograph. 'How about him?'

Mrs Rooney looked at her impatiently. '*This* fellow is the same fellow as *this* fellow. But neither *this* fellow nor *this* fellow is the same fellow as the fellow I saw in the river.'

'All right, then,' said Katie. 'I'll send a sketch

artist up to see you, and you can describe your cherub to her. Will you do that for me? I can't tell you how important your evidence is, Margaret. You're the only witness we have so far. You're the only person who actually knows that the murderer looks like.'

'But what about this fellow?' asked Mrs Rooney, handing back the photographs of Brendan Doody. 'What's he got to do with it?'

'Him?' said Katie. 'I wish to God I knew.'

Mrs Rooney picked up her dog and stood looking at Katie for a long time, as if she were going to come out and say something deeply profound. Eventually she reached out and touched Katie's hair. 'You're too pretty to be chasing after murderers, girl. You should be chasing after a husband instead.'

For the first time in a very long time, Katie felt her cheeks blush hot.

'Thank you,' she said. 'I will so, when I get the time.'

Sixteen

The Grey Mullet Man bent down and picked up Father Quinlan, with his arms and his legs dangling like Christ being lifted down from the cross, and lowered him naked into the deep, empty bathtub.

Father Quinlan was aware of the chilly enamel walls all around him, but no matter how furiously he blinked his eyes he could see nothing but a milky-white fog, and his ears felt as if they had been packed with creaking wads of cotton wool.

He couldn't think where he was, or what he was supposed to be doing here. He was juddering with cold, but when he tried to wrap his aching arms around himself to warm himself up, he could feel the chicken-like skin that hung around his stomach and he realized that he had no clothes on.

Was this real? Was he awake, or was he dreaming it all? He could hear a choir singing *'Credo in unum Deum'* from Mozart's mass in C minor, so perhaps he had inadvertently fallen asleep in church. But he wouldn't be naked in church, would he, not unless he was dreaming? Perhaps he was dead. That was it. Perhaps his body was lying in a chilly back room at Jerh O'Connor's funeral directors, ready for embalming, and the singing was nothing more than mood music from the showroom, to console his grieving relatives.

Perhaps he was both – dead *and* dreaming. Did the dead dream? Was that possible?

But – 'How are you feeling now, Father?' asked the Grey Mullet Man, in his softer, more conciliatory voice. 'Still woozy, I hope, for your own sake.'

'Where am I?' he whispered. 'Am I dead?'

'Not dead yet, Father, but you've arrived at the end of the line. The place where all sinners eventually end up. You've admitted your wrongdoings, and here you are, all ready to pay the price for them.'

'Price? What price?'

110

'Come now, Father, you always knew that you would have to *pay* for your sins, didn't you? You didn't think that all you had to do was confess to what you did, and say how heartily sorry you were, and forty-nine Hail Marys, and that would be the end of it, amen?'

Father Quinlan strained his eyes and through the fog he could dimly make out the shadows of the Grey Mullet Man, with his dark circular eyeholes and his pointed hat.

'Who are you?' he said. 'Whatever you're going to do to me, you could at least tell me your name.'

'I told you my name, Father. The Grey Mullet Man.'

'That's not what your parents christened you.'

'No, but it tells you much more exactly who I am than the name that I was given – whoever gave it to me.'

'I don't follow you at all.'

'Think about it, Father. What does your grey mullet feed on?'

'What? What are you talking about? Your grey mullet is a fish.'

'Of course it's a fish! And it feeds on *sewage*, Father – that's what your grey mullet feeds on!'

'What?'

'Have you never stood on Patrick's Bridge and seen all of those dozens of grey mullet crowding around the outpipe? Raw sewage, they gobble it up. Not to mention food scraps and waste diesel oil and detergents and all of the other toxic sludge that we discreetly pour into our rivers and oceans in the hope that nobody will notice. Me – I'm just like your grey mullet, only human. I feed on all

111

varieties of filth, all manner of detritus, except that I find *my* filth floating around churches and schools and seminaries – wherever sanctimonious abusers like you are contaminating the clear waters of childhood innocence.'

'So what are you telling me? That you really can't bring yourself to forgive me?' Father Quinlan's tone of resignation was so black and despairing that it sounded almost as if he were making a joke.

The Grey Mullet Man's hat waggled as he shook his head. 'No, Father, to be honest with you, I cannot. Look – I'm in no position at all to say that *God* hasn't forgiven you. Jesus may have forgiven you, too, for all I know, and Our Lady may have decided in Her heart that you are truly, truly sorry for what you did. But not me, not myself. Nor have any of the other boys you used for your own self-gratification and your own self-glorification – and which of those was the worse I couldn't say, the gratification or the glorification.'

The Grey Mullet Man paused for breath. When he spoke again, he loomed so close that Father Quinlan felt his cloth mask flapping against his cheek.

'Nobody has yet coined a word horrible enough to describe what you are, Father, and even if they had, I very much doubt that anybody could ever bring themselves to speak it, for fear that their tongue would be blackened and blistered forever, and they would have to have it cut out.'

Father Quinlan was beginning to grasp that he must have been drugged, or anaesthetized. He was certain now that he wasn't dreaming, and that he wasn't dead. But he decided in a strange detached

112

way that he was ready for death. It wasn't so much the pain he was suffering – his dislocated shoulders and his cracked ribs and his broken toes. It wasn't even the humiliation of lying naked in a bathtub while he was insulted and reviled and told that his sins were beyond forgiveness.

He was prepared for death because he was certain in his own mind that during his ministry he had tried his very best to delight the Lord his God, even if he had failed. He believed that God had understood what he had been trying to do, albeit vainly, and would take him into His arms when he died, the way a Father holds a son who has done everything possible to please him, regardless of whether he has succeeded or not.

'Very well,' he said. 'In that case, you had better do your worst.'

The Grey Mullet Man needed no more prompting. Without hesitation he reached into the bathtub and manhandled Father Quinlan on to his stomach. Father Quinlan couldn't stop himself from gasping out in pain. There was still a half-inch of rusty water in the bottom of the bath, and it splashed into his face, so that he could taste it. It tasted as bitter as blood.

The Grey Mullet Man pulled back each of Father Quinlan's wrists, one after the other, like a garda making an arrest, and bound them together with wire, so tight that it almost cut off his circulation. He snipped the wire with a pair of pliers, and then rolled Father Quinlan on to his back once more. The pain from his shoulders was so overwhelming that all Father Quinlan could manage to say was *'daah!'*.

He lay there for a few seconds, shivering and gasping, but then he heard the sound of somebody else walking across the bathroom, and another voice. It was a reedier voice than that of the Grey Mullet Man, as if its owner were suffering from catarrh, or had just reached puberty. Father Quinlan strained his eyes through the fog and he could dimly make out another figure standing beside the bathtub, looking down at him. This figure appeared to be wearing a mask, too, and a tall pointed hat, but a hat that had two points instead of one – more like a bishop's mitre than the *capirote* of the Grey Mullet Man.

'Look at him now, the gowl,' said this second voice. 'You couldn't have imagined it, could you? The way he used to strut up and down the corridors, like a bantam cock! Cluck, cluck, cluck! I never once dreamed that I'd see him like this.'

Father Quinlan felt sure that he knew who this was. There was something in his sing-song, clogged-up intonation that brought back the grainy image of a boy's white face, in a gloomy changing room somewhere, a boy with short brown hair and wing-nut ears. The boy was crying. There were dirty tear stains down his cheeks, but Father Quinlan couldn't remember what he was crying about.

Perhaps if he could remember what the boy's name was, and what had upset him so much, he and the Grey Mullet Man might forgive him, and stop torturing him, and let him live.

Before he could think about it any further, however, he heard the door slam and more footsteps cross the bathroom floor, heavier this time.

Yet another smudgy figure loomed over the bath-tub and a third voice said, '*Well,* now! Look who it feckin' isn't! Queer Balls Quinny!'

This figure spoke in a derisive, Hollyhill accent. All the same his voice was high and clear, and every 'l' from 'well' to 'look' to 'balls' was pro-nounced with liquid precision, as if he had taken elocution lessons.

Father Quinlan squinted up at him. He, too, was wearing a conical hat. He was wearing a mask too, but it looked more like a pierrot's mask than a white cloth with holes in it. More theatrical than religious, but just as scary.

'Hullo, Queer Balls, how's it going, boy? Long time no see. Looking a little thin on top these days. How about a transplant? You could borrow some bazz from your bollocks.'

In response, Father Quinlan could only pant, his chest heaving laboriously up and down like a fox hunted to exhaustion. Apart from that, he couldn't think of anything else to say, or anything else to ask. Whoever these men were, it was clear that they were determined to punish him for something terrible that he had done to them, and there seemed to be no point in trying to under-stand why they refused to forgive him for it.

'Want to say a last prayer, Father, before we get down to business?' asked the Grey Mullet Man.

Father Quinlan shook his head. 'I've already tried to make my peace with God, thank you.'

'Fair play to you, then,' said the Grey Mullet Man. Then, without any further hesitation, he reached down and grasped Father Quinlan's left leg, dragging it upwards and hooking it over the left-hand rim of the bathtub, and pinning it there with all of his weight. The man wearing the white pierrot mask did the same with Father Quinlan's right leg, so that the priest was lying on his back with his knees wide apart. In this position, his buttocks didn't quite reach the bottom of the bath, so all of his weight was resting on his bruised and dislocated shoulders.

'God in heaven, what are you doing to me?' he screamed. *'Haven't you punished me enough? Please – why don't you kill me here and now!'*

'Soon enough, Quinny!' retorted the man in the pierrot mask. 'And you can count yourself as lucky, boy, believe me! Not like all of us poor bastards who have had to live with what *you* did to them for twenty years and more!'

The man in the bishop's mitre came up close beside the Grey Mullet Man. Whatever Father Quinlan had been anaesthetized with, it was rapidly beginning to wear off, and he could see and hear much more distinctly, although his eyes were still unfocused, and the voices of his tormentors still sounded as if they were talking with their heads in metal buckets.

The man in the bishop's mitre made a show of lifting up both of his hands, in the same way that a priest raises a chalice to be blessed at the altar, during communion. But when Father Quinlan realized what the man was actually holding up, his spine quivered convulsively with dread. *God in heaven, no. Merciful God in heaven, save me from this. Let my heart stop first, before they do this to me.*

'I'll bet you reck *this* well enough, don't you, Father?' taunted the Grey Mullet Man. 'Not too

116

many of *these* in the world, are there? Very special-ist piece of equipment, I'd say.'

'Please,' said Father Quinlan. 'You will never get away with this. The guards will find you, sooner or later.'

'They never found *you*, did they, boy?' the man in the bishop's mitre taunted him, and made six or seven slicing noises with the instrument he was holding up in his hands.

Father Quinlan recognized it, all right. It was made up of two half-moon blades, each about seven inches long, with wooden handles. The blades were joined at the top with a hinge, more like a pair of nutcrackers than a pair of shears. It was old, crudely cast out of blackened steel, although the edges of the blades had recently been whetted, and were shining, and very sharp.

O God in heaven, please, not this. When we used it, we used it for a reason. Not out of cruelty, not for revenge. When we used it, it was only for the greater glorification of God, and of the diocese.

Now the choir was singing *'Gloria in excelsis Deo'*. Outside the windows, a dark bank of clouds was rolling over the city, like a stallholder drag-ging a tarpaulin over his stall at the end of the day, and the interior of the bathroom was plunged into gloom.

'*No*,' said Father Quinlan.

But the Grey Mullet Man reached down and took hold of Father Quinlan's shrivelled penis between finger and thumb, and stretched it up-wards as far as he could. It looked like a mussel, dragged out of its shell.

'No,' said Father Quinlan, and then he started to

117

gabble under his breath, as if he were trying to break the world prayer speed record. *'O Lord, Jesus Christ, Redeemer and Saviour, forgive my sins, just as You forgave Peter's denial and those who crucified You.'*

The man in the bishop's mitre tilted over the bathtub, with the metal instrument in his left hand, and positioned Father Quinlan's crinkled testicles so that they bulged between its two crescent-shaped blades. Then he grasped the right handle, too.

'Count not my transgressions but rather my tears of repentance,' Father Quinlan gabbled. *'Remember not my iniquities but more especially my sorrow for the offences I have committed against You.'*

'Ready?' asked the Grey Mullet Man.

The man in the bishop's mitre nodded.

'Have mercy on me and deliver me from these terrible torments, call me and admit me to Thy most sweet embrace in paradise.'

Father Quinlan heard the crunch, and knew what had happened, but for some reason he felt nothing at all. But then the man in the bishop's mitre held his bloody hand up in front of his face and said, 'There, Father. Welcome to the heavenly choir.'

Father Quinlan looked at what he was holding, and then looked up at the man's expressionless mask. It was only then that he understood the enormity of what he had done, and what had been done to him, and it was only then that the pain and shock hit him as if he had stepped out in front of a hurtling express train.

Seventeen

John's silver Toyota was already parked outside Katie's father's house by the time she arrived.

Katie's father lived in Monkstown, on the west side of Cork harbour, in a tall green Victorian house that overlooked the half-mile stretch of water that separated Monkstown from Cobh, where Katie lived. On a clear day she could glimpse her own front wall behind the dark row of elm trees that lined the opposite shore, but this evening it had started to rain again, hard, and she could barely see the ferry that plied its way from one side of the inlet to the other. Through the sheets of spray, she thought that it looked like a ghost of all the ships that had left Cobh on other rainy evenings, carrying emigrants who would never come back to Ireland, ever. She didn't know why she thought that. Maybe she was just feeling tired and sentimental and upset about John.

She made her way around John's Toyota and up the steps to the front door. She had her own key, of course, in case of emergencies, but her father always liked to answer the doorbell himself. She waited, while the rainwater clattered from the broken guttering over the porch. She rang again; and at last her father appeared, with John standing close behind him.

'Ah, Katie! John thought that he'd heard the doorbell.'

'Dad – did I not tell you last week to buy yourself a new hearing aid?'

'There's nothing at all wrong with this one that a new battery wouldn't fix.'

'Then buy yourself a new battery, for the love of God. They hardly cost anything.'

'Maybe so. But how often does anybody ring the doorbell? That's nine euros to hear just three rings a month.'

John was smiling. He said, 'Hullo, Katie,' and held out his hand to her.

'Hullo, John. How's the form?'

As Katie stepped into the hallway, John tried to put his arm around her shoulder, but she ducked to one side and embraced her father instead. Her father seemed so shrunken these days. She used to think that he was so stocky, and bull-like, but now he felt like a laundry bag filled with old coat hangers. His wild white hair was thinning and there were wriggling veins in his temples.

'John's been telling me about all of his plans,' said Katie's father, as he led her through the hall to the living room, with John following behind. As usual, the hallway smelled fusty and damp. There were two chaise-longues, one on either side, that nobody had sat on in decades, and a long-case clock that ticked so wearily that Katie used to wonder that it didn't stop from sheer exhaustion.

However, there was a sharp little log fire crackling in the living room, and a spray of orange roses on one of the side tables, and a savoury smell coming from the direction of the kitchen. Katie's father had been almost inconsolable after the loss of her mother, three years ago, and of course he still missed her grievously, but Katie had recently found him a housekeeper, Ailish Walsh, who washed and cleaned and cooked for him, and gave him much of the companionship that he missed so much, and at last he seemed to Katie to be enjoying his life more. He had even joined the Fota Golf Club, even though by his own admission he played like a gimp.

'You'll have a sherry?' he asked her.

'I think I'd rather have a Paddy's if you don't mind. It's been one of those days. Manic.'

'Oh, yes. I read about that homicide you've been looking into – that priest. I'm only surprised that nobody's had a crack at one of them before.' He poured her a tumbler of whiskey and brought it over. 'Those pious gowls deserve everything they get. I'd castrate them, myself, I tell you, and stick their balls on cocktail sticks.'

'Funny you should say that,' said Katie. 'We haven't told the media yet, but that's exactly what was done to him. Well, not the cocktail-stick bit.'

'What? Somebody–?' and Katie's father made a slicing gesture in the air.

'Jesus,' said John. 'You've just made my eyes water. Do you have any idea who did it?'

Katie shook her head. 'Still working on it. We've been given a possible lead by Monsignor Kelly, one of the vicars general, but I'm not one hundred per cent convinced.'

'Monsignor Kelly?' said Katie's father, pouring himself another sherry. 'You're talking about Monsignor *Kevin* Kelly?'

'That's your man. He gave us a handwritten con-

121

fession from a handyman who worked at St Patrick's on the Lower Glanmire Road, a fellow called Brendan Doody. It seemed to be a suicide note, too, but so far we haven't found a body, or any evidence that Brendan Doody might have actually killed himself. That's why I'm not too sure about it.'

Katie's father slowly nodded. 'I knew Monsignor Kelly years ago when he was the Reverend Kelly, priest-in-charge at St Joseph's in Mayfield. Good-looking fellow, admittedly, but a bit on the short side, and I've never trusted fellows under five foot four.'

'That's kind of height-ist, isn't it?' said John.

'Oh, you know what these short fellows are like. Always overcompensating for their lack of inches, in one way or another. Little Reverend Kelly was very ambitious, as I recall, but devious. Well, maybe "devious" isn't exactly the word. I never thought that he would ever tell you a lie, straight to your face, but on the other hand I never felt that he was telling you the truth, the whole truth and nothing but the truth.

'I'll give you an example. The first time I met him, it must have been twenty years ago, easy. Some of the boys in the parish swimming club had complained to their parents that one of the young priests had been playing snap-towel with them in the changing rooms in what you might call rather too friendly a fashion. But the Reverend Kelly managed to persuade everybody that it had all been good clean fun. Horseplay, he called it, that's all, and no need to make a fuss.'

'And what did *you* think?'

Katie's father pulled a face. 'I thought that he was telling everybody what they wanted to hear, rather than admitting the very real possibility that the boys might have been interfered with. But you have to remember that, in those days, people were much more intimidated by their parish priest than they are today. In the end we took no action. After all, we had only the boys' word for what had been done to them. But I thought to myself: I don't entirely trust that Reverend Kelly. He's got more sides to him than a Rubik's cube.'

'My feeling exactly,' said Katie. 'Dermot agrees with me, too. But I don't really know what we can do about it.'

'You should talk to him again, on your own,' her father suggested. 'Go back over everything that he told you, in detail, two or three times, as if you suspect that there's something that doesn't quite sit right. That should get him well riled up. He's that kind of arrogant little whippersnapper who always likes to feel that he's in charge, isn't he, and you might be surprised what he comes out with when loses his temper.'

The long-case clock in the hallway struck a dolorous half-hour, and at the same time Ailish Walsh appeared in the doorway, a round-faced woman in a red-striped apron, with her grey hair braided into a tight coronet. She looked hot, but pleased with herself.

'Supper's ready,' she announced. And then, 'Hallo, Katie, how's yourself?'

'Grand, thanks, Ailish. Something smells good.'

They followed Ailish into the huge, old-fashioned kitchen, tiled from floor to ceiling in shiny

123

cream ceramics, with decorative green borders. A large deal table stood in the middle, spread with a checked green and white cloth. A woven basket at one end of the table was filled with freshly baked slices of soda bread; and at the other end, a deep earthenware salad bowl was crowded with rocket and lamb's lettuce and fennel, which looked as if they had been harvested from a nearby hedgerow.

Katie and John sat down opposite each other, while Katie's father took four bottles of Murphy's stout out of the fridge and poured out a glass for each of them.

'Here's to us, and the blood and bandages, and the general confusion of the clergy,' said Katie's father, raising his glass. 'The blood and bandages' was the red and white strip of Cork's champion hurling team.

'Here's to the future,' said John, looking directly at Katie.

'Now you're tempting fate, boy!' said Katie's father. He glanced from Katie to John and back again. 'My old grandma always swore that she could tell the future. She told my sister that she was going to marry the steadiest man in County Cork, and what happened? She ended up wed to a high-wire walker from Tom Duffy's Circus. He was steady all right on his high wire, rock steady, but he chased after every bit of skirt that ever came within sniffing distance.'

Ailish let down the door of the oil-fired oven with a reverberating bang, and took out a baking tray with what looked like eight golden-brown chicken legs on it. She used tongs to lay two on each plate, and handed them around the table, and then she took off her apron and sat down herself.

'Crubeens, my favourite!' said Katie's father, rubbing his hands together.

John poked at one of them of his with his fork. 'Wow. It's a been coon's age since I had crubeens. But they don't look too much like the crubeens my mam used to make.'

'These are what my auntie used to call "polite company crubeens",' said Ailish. 'In other words, you can eat them with a knife and fork.'

'Me? Polite company?' grinned John, still trying to catch Katie's eye. 'I'm honoured. You must tell me how you make them.'

'Oh, it's fiddly, like, but it's easy enough. You take the hairs off the trotters, of course, and you wrap them up in cheesecloth, just the same as you usually would, and then you boil them for two or three hours with onions and carrots and bay leaves and peppercorns.'

'And parsley,' put in Katie's father. 'Don't forget the parsley.'

'Parsley, that's right. But after they're done, and you unwrap the cheesecloth, you skin them, and you use your fingers to take all the meat off the bones.'

'Like you would at table, if you'd cooked them as normal,' said Katie's father.

Ailish said, 'You lay a piece of trotter skin on the bottom of a bowl, and fill it up with a portion's worth of trotter meat. Then you wrap it in cling film, and put it in the fridge for a couple of hours to set.

'Afterwards, you dip them in beaten egg and

125

breadcrumbs and bake them in bacon fat for half an hour, and there you have them, pigs' trotters you can eat without making a holy mess of yourself.'

'I hope you're taking this all in, John,' said Katie's father. 'You could serve them up at a barbecue, couldn't you, when you get back to California? They'd go down a treat, I'll bet you.'

Katie had cut her first crubeen in half but hadn't yet taken a mouthful. 'Do you have a date yet?' she asked him.

'Not a firm date,' said John, looking at her steadily. 'But my friends want me over there as soon as possible, and I can leave Buckley's to sell the farm for me. I'll be leaving by the end of April, I guess, at the very latest.'

'As soon as that? What about your mother?'

'She's in a very good home now. I couldn't take care of her any better.'

'This online pill business sounds like a very exciting business proposition, I'd say,' put in Katie's father, wiping his mouth with his napkin. 'Better than anything you'd ever be able to set up here in Cork, especially now.'

'What are you suggesting?' said Katie.

'I'm not suggesting anything, my darling. But each of us only has one life, and sometimes it's worth taking a risk, and going for something completely new. Sean O'Riordan offered me a partnership once, in Globetrotters, his travel business, on Grand Parade. Well, you know how *that* prospered, and think of all the wonderful places your mam and I could have visited, all over the world, but we never did. The furthest we ever went was Dingle, and then it rained for four days solid.'

'Come on. You wouldn't really have quit the Garda, would you?'

'Oh, I thought about it, Katie. I thought about it long and serious, believe me. Mind you, I was only a detective sergeant, I wasn't a superintendent like you. Not nearly so exalted, and not nearly so well paid, which was more to the point, so I was very cautious about risking my pension. But think about it, Katie. There's a whole lot more to life than chasing after small-time drug dealers and pimps and prostitutes and priests who should have kept their soutanes buttoned up. There's a whole world out there, with sunshine and money and *fun,* for the love of God.'

'Well, well. John *has* been working on you, hasn't he?'

John said, 'Katie – I've only been telling it like it is. You and I, we could have a really great life out there.'

'I told you before, John. How can I just drop everything at a moment's notice, and walk away? I've had years of training, years of experience. If I leave the Garda now, they're going to lose all of that. I have so many contacts, so many informants. Who's going to talk to a piece of work like Eamonn Collins if I go? Or a header like Eugene Ó'Béara?'

Katie's father put down his knife and laid his hand on her wrist. 'They'll find somebody to replace you, darling, don't you doubt it. You've been keeping Cork City free of crime for long enough, don't you think? Maybe it's somebody else's turn.'

'I mentioned on the phone that I had some

ideas, didn't I?' said John. 'Well, one of my ideas is that you could take up a senior consultancy position with Pinkerton's.'

'Pinkerton's? Are you serious? You mean Pinkerton's the private detectives?'

'That's right. The oldest and most well-respected security agency in the world. Would you believe that Abraham Lincoln used to hire Pinkerton detectives during the civil war? They have an office on Howard Street in San Francisco and as it turns out my very good buddy Jed Walters is a very good buddy of their director of consulting. Plays squash with him, in fact.'

'You see?' said Katie's father. 'You could be doing just as much good in America as you're doing here. And enjoying it more.'

He didn't add *'and* you'd be living with the man you love' but the implication was there. John was giving Katie a look that was both pleading and cajoling. Even Ailish was smiling at her, her eyebrows raised, with that sort of romantic twinkle in her eyes, almost maniacal, that women have at weddings.

'But how would *you* cope?' Katie asked her father. 'You get your arthritis when it's damp and your eczema when it's dry. Not to mention your angina.'

'Get away with you, girl,' he told her. 'I'm not completely helpless, you know. I've got Ailish here to look after me, haven't I? And I can always call on Siobhán, in case of dire emergency.'

Katie thought to herself: *Siobhán? Siobhán is a one-woman dire emergency in herself.* But to keep the peace at her father's supper table, she nodded and said, 'All right, da. Give me some time to think about it, that's all.'

'But you *will* think about it?' John asked her. Sweet Jesus, she had already forgotten how handsome he was, how chocolaty-brown his eyes were, and how the side of his mouth tilted up like that, as if he were amused.

'Look now – your crubeens are getting cold,' Katie's father admonished her.

'Oh. Yes. Sorry,' said Katie, although she had completely lost her appetite, especially for pigs' trotters, which had made her gag ever since she was little. She had always imagined them standing in a mucky pigsty. Didn't her father remember her at the age of six, sitting at the kitchen table until four in the afternoon, with a plate of untouched crubeens in front of her, refusing to eat them, but forbidden to go out and play until she did?

Eighteen

Ailish cleared away the dishes and washed them up with a furious clatter, while Katie found a tea towel from Lourdes and dried them for her. The two of them chatted about traditional Cork recipes like crubeens and drisheen and porter cake, and then their conversation turned to the schoolyard games they used to play when they were children, which children never seemed to play these days, like Rats and Rabbits and

Shadows and Red Lights, Red Lights, 1-2-3!

Ailish said nothing more to Katie about moving to California with John, but after she had hung up her apron she gripped both of Katie's hands tight and smiled and shook her head as if to say, *I'd go, girl, if I was you. Myself, I'd jump at it.*

'Goodnight, sweet Ailish!' called out Katie's father as she went to the front door and opened up her umbrella. Outside it was still raining, although much more softly now, so that the raindrops sparkled in the street lights like thistledown.

'Why don't I give you a lift?' Katie offered.

'Don't go troubling yourself, Katie. It's only a five-minute walk up Fairy Hill.'

'Goodnight, then. And watch out for those fairies. Mischievous little rascals, some of them!'

Katie and John and Katie's father sat in front of the living-room fire for another hour, as the logs gradually collapsed and disintegrated into ashes, and between them they finished off most of a bottle of Paddy's. Katie's father told them lurid stories about Cork in the 1960s, and the rival gangs who used to run the city's crime.

'There was one fellow, Jimmy Dunne, what a header he was. He had a penchant for cutting off his rivals' noses with a straight razor. Jimmy the Gonker they called him. He got his desserts in the end, though. The three Murphy brothers broke into his house one night and abducted him and his wife Eileen right out of their bed, and their five children all asleep and not one of them woke up. The Murphys took them to a cellar off Oliver Plunkett Street and did things to them that would make your hair stand on end. When we found

130

them, the two of them had been reduced to such a smush we couldn't tell which of them was who.'

He finished his whiskey and shook his head. 'It was all different in those days, though. Nobody had any money, or mobile phones, or credit cards, so mugging was almost unknown. And it was all local boys, who weren't the sharpest tools in the box, so we usually knew which eejit was going to commit what crime about five minutes before he'd thought about committing it himself. Before I retired, though, all of these Romanians and all these Nigerians started taking over, and Katie can tell you how wily they are. And ruthless.'

'Well, let's put it this way,' said Katie, 'if somebody crosses them, they think nothing of chopping off their ears or their fingers or even whacking off their feet.'

'That's right,' said Katie's father, 'and the trouble was, I could never make heads nor tails of what they were talking about, even when they were supposed to be speaking English. How do you take a witness statement from somebody who says "e don red" when he means that "things were getting serious"? It was bad enough in my day, trying to understand some of those young tearaways from Crosser.'

'Here's a sign of the times for you, da,' said Katie. 'Last Thursday we had the annual crime statistics in. Can you guess which criminal activity made the most net profit last year – apart from drugs?'

'Well, people smuggling, I'd say, and pimping.'

'Wrong, believe it or not. Second-hand clothes. You know, the bags of clothes that people put out for charities?'

John said, 'You're kidding, aren't you?'

'Not at all. There's gangs of Eastern Europeans driving around the south of the city at three o'clock in the morning, picking up the charity bags from people's doorsteps. They drive them across to Lithuania or Estonia or wherever, and they clean them, and smarten them up like new, and they can make a hundred and fifty thousand euros out of the contents of one forty-foot trailer – a whole lot more if there's handbags and shoes in it.'

'Is that for real?' John asked her. 'I guess it's criminal, but you have to respect their initiative, don't you? I mean, you wouldn't catch me driving around the suburbs in the middle of the night, picking up hundreds of plastic bags of smelly old sweaters.'

'Believe me, John, they don't deserve your respect. The clothes are not legally theirs and it's theft, however you look at it. There's three rival gangs of them and they're even more violent than some of the drug dealers. We had to send fifteen gardaí to break up a pitched battle on the South Ring Road last month, thirty or forty clothes collectors with knives and broken bottles and hurley sticks, and they're forever fire-bombing each other's vans.'

Katie's father stood up. 'All I can say is – come back, Jimmy the Gonker, you're forgiven, boy.'

'Are you going to bed now?' Katie asked him.

He nodded, and leaned over and kissed her. 'You and John have a chat together. See if you can work something out.'

'I never would have taken you for a match-maker,' said Katie.

'Me, my darling? Never. But I'm looking at life from the opposite end of the telescope from you, and everything that once seemed so grand and impressive has all shrunk down to size. I can see now what could have been, but wasn't, and I don't want you to get to my age and feel the same way.'

'Goodnight, da. Sleep tight.'

John stood up and clasped Katie's father's hand in both of his. 'Goodnight, sir. And thank you for everything.'

Katie's father shrugged, as if to say 'we'll see'.

When he had creaked his way upstairs, John sat back down again, much closer this time.

'How about another drink?' he asked her. 'We might as well see this bottle off.'

He poured them each a last glass of whiskey. Katie said, 'I'm going to be langerated, so whatever I say to you tonight, I don't really mean it.'

'You mean like you'll change your mind and come to San Francisco with me?'

'No, John. You know it's not fair to ask me that.'

'But Pinkerton's, that would be a fantastic job. Prestige, or what? And think of your golden suntan.'

'Pinkerton's do accept Irish citizens?'

'Not in their government departments, no. But on the private side, they'll consider anybody, regardless of creed, colour, nationality, disability or sexual orientation. Mind you, I'm not so sure about pretty red-headed drunks. Or pretty drunk redheads.'

Katie swilled her whiskey around in her glass. 'I

133

don't know. It seems so disloyal, even to think about it. You have to swear an oath, when you join An Garda Síochána.'

She raised her glass and said, 'I hereby solemnly and sincerely declare before God that I will faithfully discharge the duties of a member of the Garda Síochána with fairness, integrity, regard for human rights, diligence and impartiality, upholding the Constitution and the laws and according equal respect to all people.'

John stared at her. 'Jesus. You know if off by heart.'

'It's in my blood, John, that's why. I inherited it from my father, and my grandfather, too.'

'I love you, Katie. I'm just trying to find a way.'

Katie looked at him for a moment, and then she said, 'The week before last we raided a brothel off Patrick Street, and we rescued a girl who had been smuggled over from Albania, along with five others. She was fifteen years old, this girl, and she was a virgin before she was brought over here, a schoolgirl. She was locked in a room twenty-four hours a day, wearing nothing but a bra, and she was forced to have sex with at least a dozen men every day, seven days a week, any way they wanted, or else she'd be beaten black and blue. She told me she felt like she was dead.'

'Okay,' said John, seriously. 'That's great. That's fantastic, in fact. You gave the girl her life back. But you can't save every girl who gets abducted.'

'I know. I know that. But you should have seen her, John! You should have talked to her. How can I possibly stop trying?'

John was silent for a moment. Then he said,

'You never told me about this when it happened. In fact, come to think of it, you hardly ever talked about your work, did you?'

'Well – I never thought you'd be interested.'

'Are you serious? Of course I'd have been interested! For Christ's sake, sweetheart, your work is what you're all about! It's everything that makes you Katie Maguire. But now I feel like you've always kept yourself shut away from me – like you never trusted me to find out who you really are.'

'John – it was never that, I promise you. It was just that when you and me got together, I didn't want to bring my day's work home with me, all of that stabbing and beating and drunkenness and foul language. Apart from anything else, crime is boring and criminals are boring. They have a vocabulary of two words and their answer to everything is to give you a good reefing, if you're lucky. If they could only see themselves for what useless gobshites they are. You think I want to talk about people like that all evening?'

John took hold of her hand. She was still wearing the emerald-set ring he had bought her to celebrate his decision to stay in Ireland forever.

'I get it, Katie,' he told her. 'I understand completely what you're trying to say to me, and I really admire what you do. But your Father's right. You've achieved so much, and you've done so much good. But do you honestly want to end up as a grey-haired old biddy, surrounded by cats, wishing that she'd done more with her life than chasing after pimps and drug dealers and second-hand clothes thieves in one of the wettest cities in the world? I know how important it seems to you

135

tonight – but in twenty years from now?'

The dolorous clock in the hallway struck eleven, as if to emphasize the passing of time. Katie had seen it happen to other gardaí as they grew older – how they had graduated from Templemore with a bustling sense of public duty but had eventually settled into a kind of routine righteousness. It was the scumbags who wore you down in the end. You got up, you went out on the streets, you confronted young men with tattoos who were shouting all kinds of filth at you, you feckin' swamp donkey; or perspiring accountants who had embezzled a builder's merchants out of fifteen thousand euros' worth of loft insulation; or unintelligible pimps from Sierra Leone with diamond earrings and three-hundred-euro Nikes and shiny tracksuits. After a while you didn't even hear what any of them were saying, it all became a kind of grey noise; and at the end of the day you went home, you watched TV, you went to bed and stared at the ceiling, and listened to your husband breathing next to you, if you still had one.

Maybe the same thing had happened to her, and she had become institutionalized. Perhaps martyrdom had become a habit.

136

Nineteen

John reached up and held her face in both hands, and looked directly into her eyes. 'Still as green as ever, your eyes, like the sea.'

'Oh, stop. I'm surprised they're not bright red, after all this whiskey.'

He kissed her, and they held that kiss for a very long time, while the last of the logs lurched softly in the hearth. The tip of his tongue penetrated her lips and ran across her teeth, and then slipped into her mouth. Their tongues wrestled with each other but Katie didn't try very hard to resist. She had missed him so much, she had missed *this* so much, the feel of him close to her, the smell of him, his breath against her face.

He took hold of the small oatmeal-coloured cardigan she was wearing, and peeled it off her shoulders. Then he tugged her sleeves off, one after the other, and dropped the cardigan on to the floor.

'What do you think you're doing, boy?' she breathed, in a real back-of-the-number-seven-bus North Side accent. She loved the rasp of his stubble, and she deliberately chafed her face backwards and forwards against his cheek.

'Thought you might be hot,' he told her.

He unfastened the top button of her green silk blouse, and then the second button, and then the third. He curved his hand inside and cupped her left breast, and gently squeezed it through her bra.

'And what do you think you're doing now, boy?' she challenged him, but no less breathily.

'I'm reminding myself of what I'm going to be leaving behind me.'

His voice was like a soft blustery wind blowing across her ear. He was already unbuttoning her cuffs, and drawing her blouse off completely. It slid to the floor on top of her cardigan.

He kissed her again, her lips and her eyelids and her throat. Then he reached behind her and thumbed open the catch of her bra. He gently lifted it away and cupped her bare breasts in his hands as if he had been given two miraculous fruit to hold. His thumbs softly rotated around her nipples, until they tightened and knurled. She had large breasts for a small woman, and John had always told her how much he liked it when she turned around, and he could see the crescent moons of her breasts on either side of her back.

'What is this?' she asked him, biting at his ear-lobe. 'What are you trying to do to me? You know I can't come with you. I just can't.'

'Ow!' he said. 'You're hurting me!'

'Wimp,' she retorted, biting him even harder.

'Stop it. This has nothing to do with my going back to the States.'

'Oh, no?'

'No. I'm not trying to change your mind. This is just us, here and now, this evening, in front of the fire. I hereby suspend time. There *is* no to-morrow.'

138

He loosened her belt buckle and unzipped her tight black jeans. She pretended to resist him, but she lifted up her hips a little to make it easier for him to pull her jeans down and over her ankles. They had been lovers for over a year, and had slept together two or three times every week, and yet she felt both shy and highly aroused, as if this was the first time they had ever done it.

They kissed furiously and deeply, almost like two excited dogs trying to take a bite out of each other. As they did so, John yanked open the buttons of his own blue denim shirt, and unbuckled his braided leather belt. He stood up, stripped off his shirt and his white T-shirt, and then stepped out of his jeans. He lost his balance as he did so, and nearly fell on top of her, and they both laughed.

'*How* much have you had to drink?' she teased him.

'Not *too* much, you'll be happy to know.' As if to prove it, his boxer shorts were rearing up at the front, and Katie reached out and gripped his penis through the thin blue-striped cotton.

'An Garda Síochána ought to issue these instead of batons,' she grinned, squeezing him hard, her green eyes sparkling with mischief. 'Well – it's a sight harder than the regulation timber ones.'

John pushed her slowly back on to the deep tapestry sofa cushions and kissed her, but she still didn't let him go.

'Do you know how much I love you, Katie Maguire?' he told her. 'I love you more than all of the crubeens in Cork.'

'That must be the least romantic compliment

that any man has ever paid me.'

'What could be more romantic than that?'

'Oh, come on. Can you imagine if Shakespeare had written, "Shall I compare thee to a plateful of pigs' trotters"?'

'You compared my cock with a cosh.'

'Sure I did. But that *was* a compliment. Just look at it.'

With that, she tugged down his shorts and bared his erection. His glans was swollen dark crimson, and a clear droplet of anticipation was already winking at her in the opening. She cupped his tightly wrinkled testicles in the palm of her left hand, and wound his dark pubic hair around her right index finger. She loved his pubic hair because it put her in mind of Michelangelo's David, or some other classical male nude, like dark heroic flames.

He leaned over her, and whispered, 'I dream about you every night, Katie, do you know that, and I think about you every day.'

'But you're angry with me, aren't you, because I didn't tell you all about my work, and how much it means to me. And you're angry with me because I won't give it up and come to San Francisco with you.'

'I'm *not* angry.'

'Yes you are. I can tell.'

'Katie, you think you can read people like a book, and maybe you can, those criminals you have to deal with. But I'm me, and I love you, and I think you should give me some credit for being more complicated than that.'

'What are you then, if you're not angry?'

He didn't answer, but kissed her again – her hair, her forehead, her eyelids, the tip of her nose, and then her lips, almost as if he were giving her the sign of the cross in kisses. Then he sat up, and took hold of the elastic waistband of her pink lace thong, and drew it down over her knees and over her feet and dropped it on to the floor.

'Now I'm going to read *you* like a book,' he said. He had an expression on his face that she couldn't quite make sense of – lustful, yes, but *artful*, too, as if he knew exactly what he was going to do to her and what the effect would be.

He parted her thighs with both hands. She didn't exactly resist him, but she made him use some strength to expose her. She was waxed and hairless, and her lips opened with the faintest juicy *plick!*

John lowered his head and licked her clitoris with the tip of his tongue – just once, and then paused, staring directly into her eyes, as if he were savouring the taste of it. Then he licked her clitoris again, and again, and again, very lightly, but enough to give her a prickling sensation all the way down her spine and between her legs.

He looked up and said, 'See ... this is how I open the pages,' and he used his thumbs to separate her lips even wider, so that she was completely exposed to him.

'The left-hand page of the book, that's what they call the *verso*,' he said.

'Oh stop,' Katie protested, reaching out to catch at his hair, but he ducked his head sideways to avoid her.

'I'm serious. This is where I can read all about

your past. You were always on the wild side, weren't you, when you were growing up? Don't try to deny it – your father told me all about you. You were wild and stubborn, and always trying to show the boys that you could beat them at their own game. Which you did, by becoming a detective, and then the *top* detective.'

Katie didn't know if she was amused or embarrassed or aroused, or all three. 'You're a header, John. You really are.'

He looked up at her again, and smiled, but then he carried on. 'The right-hand page, that's the *recto*. That's where I can read your future. I can see here – yes – I can clearly see here that you're going to be making a break with your past, a truly spectacular break. You're going to find happiness, and personal fulfilment, and somebody who loves you not in spite of your being so wild and stubborn, but because you are.'

'And who taught you how to read a woman's fortune by opening up her legs?'

John smiled even more widely. 'Every woman carries her fortune between her legs, you should know that.'

'Sexist.'

'That's not sexist, that's a compliment.'

He knelt between her thighs, and took his penis in his right hand, and placed it so that his plum-like glans nestled between her lips, between *verso* and *recto*, the past and the future. She found his body irresistible, the hardness of it, his shoulder muscles sculpted into curves by eighteen months of physical work, ploughing and digging and log-cutting; and his narrow waist. She loved the dark crucifix of hair across his chest. But what was most attractive about him was not his body but the quiet respect he gave her, and his open admiration for what she was, and the way that he still found her a mystery worth exploring, even after all their time together.

The question was: should she give in to him?

There was a long silence between them, a sense that time was going by. John stayed where he was, making no attempt to push forward and penetrate her. She knew exactly what he was doing. If she allowed him to enter her, she was tacitly agreeing to give up everything in Cork – her career in the Garda, her family, her friends – and come with him to the States.

The clock in the hallway started to chime. Katie took hold of John's hips and slowly pulled him into her. He slid in so deep that he touched the neck of her womb and made her jump.

Twenty

She arrived home shortly after 2 a.m. It had stopped raining now and a soft wind was blowing from the south-west. As she climbed out of her car she looked up and saw the full moon for a second or two, peeping at her from behind the clouds like a nosy neighbour. And where have *you* been this evening, Katie Maguire, and what shenanigans have you been up to?

She unlocked the front door, took off her coat

and her shoes and went through to the living room. It was ridiculous, she knew it, but in a way she still missed coming home to find Paul snoring on the couch, with half a dozen empty bottles of Satzenbrau on the coffee table in front of him, and the television still flickering with the volume switched off. She had never known what unholy mischief Paul had been up to during the day, and what tangles she would have to sort out for him in the morning.

She went across to the sideboard and poured herself a glass of Power's. She didn't really feel like a drink but she didn't want to go to bed straight away because she knew that she wouldn't be able to sleep, and she didn't want to watch *Teleshopping* or *Shortland Street*.

She sat down in her armchair, her head bowed, and tried to make sense of what had happened this evening. Had she actually made up her mind to quit the Garda and go with John to the States? Or had she simply given in to her sexual frustration and the need for John to hold her in his arms? Had she been self-indulgent and weak, giving up on all her responsibilities, and all the hundreds of people who depended on her, or had she been incredibly courageous? Most of all, did she really have the nerve to go?

She was still sitting there with her drink untouched when the kitchen light blinked on, and she heard the fridge door open. 'Siobhán?' she called out.

A bottle clinked, and then the fridge door closed again, but Siobhán didn't answer.

'Siobhán?'

Still no answer. Katie waited for a moment longer, and then she stood up and walked through into the kitchen.

'Mary, Mother of God,' she said. Siobhán's short, balding ex-boyfriend Michael was standing at the counter, wearing nothing but a droopy pair of grey underpants. He was holding up a plastic takeaway curry container, and his mouth was half open, ready to take in a large forkful of chicken tikka masala.

'Michael,' said Katie. 'What in the name of Jesus do you think you're doing?'

Michael looked around the kitchen, as if she might be talking to another Michael. Then he said, 'Oh! I was feeling snacky, that's all. Siobhán said she didn't mind if I had some more curry so long as I faced the other way when I came back to bed and didn't breathe it all over her, like.'

'I don't mean what are you doing eating curry. I mean what are you doing here at all?'

Michael put down the fork and the curry container. 'Siobhán said that you were away for the night, like, and any road you wouldn't mind.'

'Well, the funny part about it is, Michael, I *do* mind. This is my house and I don't expect to come into my own kitchen in the middle of the night and find a strange man in his undercrackers eating some Indian takeaway.'

'Me? You can't call *me* a strange man, Katie. Come on, you've known me since school.'

At that moment, Siobhán appeared in the kitchen doorway, her messy red hair even more Gorgon-like than usual, wearing nothing but a T-shirt with The Script printed on it in large red letters. Her eyes were puffy, as if she had been smoking skunk.

'Katie? What's going on? I thought you were staying with John tonight.'

'Oh, yes? And why would you have thought that?'

'Because I know how you feel about him, that's why. I'm not *blind,* girl. I've been seeing how much you've been pining for him.'

'That's still no excuse for you to invite Michael here.'

Siobhán put her arm around Michael and gave him a squeeze. Although he was short and beer-bellied, and he had a shiny bald head, he wasn't bad-looking in a broad-faced, snub-nosed, twinkly-eyed way, and he was unfailingly good-humoured and always ready with a joke. Katie had always thought Michael would have made a perfect husband for Siobhán, but no husband would ever be a perfect husband for Siobhán because she could never stay faithful. Even at school the boys had called her Tootles because of her willingness to get down on her knees for any boy she fancied. She had discovered at a very early age what the way to a man's heart was, and it was a little lower than his stomach.

Michael said, 'Come on, Katie. No cause to get upset. I'll be gone after breakfast.'

'So where does Nola think you are?'

'I'm attending a company bash in Limerick so. You know, one of them morale-boosting things. Paintballing and bonding and all that malarkey.'

'She'd kill you if she knew you were here, with Siobhán.'

'She probably would, like. But, you know, this is just for old times' sake.'

Siobhán said, 'You're always judging me! Always acting all righteous and superior because I like a bit of fun! What harm are we doing to anyone?'

'Oh, none at all, apart from cheating on Nola.'

'Nola's not going to find out, is she?'

'I hope for your sake that she doesn't.'

'Well, I hope for *your* sake that she doesn't find out from you!'

'Are you threatening me?'

'I wouldn't dare, girl! You might arrest me! Mary, Mother of God, what it is to have a moral guardian for a sister!'

'Oh, get back to bed,' said Katie.

Michael put his arm around Siobhán and said, 'Come on, darling. I think it's time we called it a night, don't you?'

'You haven't had your curry yet,' said Siobhán, looking defiantly at Katie.

'Forget it,' Michael told her. 'I couldn't eat it now if I tried. My throat's gone all constricted, like.'

There was a long moment when Siobhán stared at Katie and Katie saw something in her eyes that she had never seen before. It wasn't hatred, but it might have been resentment. Perhaps she had always wanted to be like Katie, but had never known how. Katie thought: *If only I knew how.*

She slept badly, and dreamed that she was walking through the grounds of Blarney Castle in the pouring rain. She was sure that she could hear

147

little Seamus crying, but every time she stopped to listen, so that she could tell where the crying was coming from, she could hear only the rain, pattering on the grass.

She didn't know if she ought to call out for him or not. If she called out for him, the witches who clustered in the caves around the castle might realize that there was a child there, and go out hunting for him, rustling and cackling in the darkness. There was nothing that witches liked better than roasting babies on an open fire. It was said that almost every morning the ground-keepers of Blarney Castle found dying embers in the cave they called the Witches' Kitchen.

When she reached the top of the hill that over-looked the castle gardens, she decided to risk it. She took a deep breath and cupped her hands around her mouth and shouted out, *'Seamus! Are you there, Seamus? Seamus, my little darling!'*

She listened, and listened, and she thought she could hear him crying, but maybe it was only a seagull, because seagulls cry like lost children. She didn't know what to do next. She couldn't simply walk away and leave Seamus behind, could she? Even if he was dead, and lying in the Old Church Cemetery, he would be so lonely if his mother was living thousands of miles away, and how could she lay flowers on his grave?

Her phone started to ring. She opened her eyes and realized that she had been dreaming, and that she wasn't standing out in the rain, after all. In fact, the sun was shining through her yellow floral curtains, and her bedroom was filled with golden light.

She sat up in bed and shook her head to wake herself up. Then she picked up the receiver and said, 'Yes?'

'It's Jimmy, ma'am, Sergeant O'Rourke. Sorry if I woke you.'

'What time is it?'

'Ten past seven.'

'Jesus, sorry. I must have forgotten to set my alarm. What's the story?'

'We've got ourselves another one, ma'am. Another priest, with his mebs cut off. Well, we're not sure about the mebs yet, but from all the blood it looks like it.'

'Oh my God. Where?'

'A blind man couldn't miss him, ma'am. He's hanging by his heels from the flagpole outside of St Joseph's, thirty feet up. He's all bound up with wire, just like Father Heaney. Hands tied behind his back, knees and ankles tied together, and the same loops in the wire, just like Father Heaney. Somebody's given him a terrible mangling, too, by the look of it.'

'When was this?'

'Only about an hour ago. First light. A young fellow was delivering papers and he looked up and there he was. Poor kid thought it was a vampire and practically shit his pants.'

'You haven't cut him down?'

'I sent a young garda up on a ladder to cover him over with a groundsheet and we've set up a diversion around the Middle Glanmire Road. We don't want the kids to see him hanging there, on their way to school.'

'Have you called for the fire brigade?'

149

'We did, yeah, but they're all tied up with a big warehouse blaze out at Ringaskiddy, and they can't send us their emergency tender with the Hiab for at least two hours. So we improvised, and O'Donovan's arranged for the council to send us up a scissor-lift.'

'Any idea who he is, this priest?'

'Not so far. His face is mashed up something terrible.'

'Okay,' said Katie. 'Give me fifteen minutes and I'll be with you. Don't touch anything, though. Nothing at all. I want to see him exactly as he is.'

'Whatever you say, ma'am. I'll see you in a tick.'

Katie climbed out of bed. She didn't have time to take a shower, which she would have loved to have done, but she splashed her face in the bathroom basin and soaped between her legs. She smelled John, as she did so, and closed her eyes for a moment. But another priest had been mutilated and murdered, and there was work to be done, and so she towelled herself and hurriedly dressed. She chose her light grey polo-neck sweater and charcoal grey trouser suit. She wanted to feel businesslike.

Michael was sitting in the kitchen, wearing a bright blue sweater with a hole in the elbow, eating toast.

'Look, Katie,' he said, 'I want to tell you that I'm sorry. Siobhán told me that you wouldn't object at all.'

'Forget it, Michael,' Katie told him. 'I have a murder to attend to, and somehow that makes a little adulterous hanky-panky seem extremely unimportant by comparison.'

150

Michael smiled at her and shook his head. 'You're a highly unusual woman, if you don't mind my saying so.'

'Oh, yes?' said Katie, as she strapped on her wristwatch. 'And you're a very bold fellow indeed.'

'I'm scared enough of my Nola, believe me. And your Siobhán's a handful, all right. But you. I don't know at all about you.'

Katie gave him a grin and patted him on the cheek. 'In that case, Michael, it's just as well that you and I aren't having a fling, isn't it?'

At the front door, she paused and called out, 'Siobhán! You won't forget to take Barney for his morning walk, will you?'

All she heard from Siobhán's bedroom was a long-drawn-out groan, like a soul that wakes up to realize that it *is* in hell, after all.

Twenty-one

By the time she arrived outside St Joseph's, two squad cars were parked outside, as well as a bright yellow ambulance, and at least fifteen other assorted cars and vans and SUVs, including a green and white outside broadcast van from RTÉ, with a large white satellite dish on its roof.

As she climbed out of her car, she looked up at the flagstaff in the far corner of the car park. A heavy khaki groundsheet had been draped over the top of it, like a witch's lair out of a frightening fairy story, high on top of a pole. Hanging below

151

the hem of the groundsheet she could just make out one bruised and blood-encrusted hand.

A makeshift canvas screen had been erected around the orphanage, but the flagstaff was nearly thirty feet high and the screen did nothing to hide it from the crowds of onlookers.

Detective O'Donovan came up to Katie and jerked his head upwards. 'Morning, boss. Looks like the exact same thing was done to him as Father Heaney. God alone knows how they got him up there. There must have been two of them at least, I'd say, even three.'

'You've called the council for a lifting platform, haven't you?'

'I gave them another bell only a couple of minutes ago and told them to get their skates on. They said that it shouldn't be more than a quarter of an hour, but they have to drive it all the way over from their depot on the South Side, and it isn't exactly a Ferrari.'

Katie glanced across the road, where six or seven reporters were talking and smoking together behind the police barrier tape. She recognized Dan Keane from the *Examiner*, John McCarthy from the *Southern Star*, and Fionnuala Sweeney from RTÉ.

'Where's that girl from the *Catholic Recorder*? What was her name? Ciara something.'

'Haven't seen her. Maybe her editor decided that it was a waste of time, trying to play down a story like this.'

'Wouldn't surprise me at all,' said Katie. 'One castrated priest, you could put that down as a single act of revenge, couldn't you? But *two* castrated priests – that's beginning to look like a vendetta.'

They crossed the car park to the foot of the flag-staff. Katie had always thought that St Joseph's had a grim look about it, and she could only imagine how the hearts of little orphans must have sunk when they first arrived there. *Abandon hope, all ye who enter here.* It was a large flint-grey building with an octagonal frontage, standing on the corner of Mayfield Gardens and the Old Youghal Road. It had been built in the 1890s as an industrial school for 'neglected, abandoned and orphaned children'. Although there was a life-size statue of St Joseph standing over the porch, with an oddly ingratiating smile on his face and his arms outspread in welcome, its miserly little leaded windows might have been deliberately designed to starve its inmates of sunlight, and its overhanging eaves always reminded Katie of Sister Coleen, one of the most vindictive nuns at her primary school, in her slate-grey wimple.

Sergeant O'Rourke had been talking to the janitor, but now he came across and joined them. He hadn't shaved and underneath his lime-green tracksuit he was still wearing his orange-striped pyjama jacket.

'Morning, Jimmy. State of you la! You look like a sackful of badgers.'

'Sorry, ma'am, but I thought I should get here quick before some do-gooder tried to cut him down, like, and fecked up all the evidence in the process. I don't even have my Y-fronts on. Now you're here, I'll dodge back home in a minute, if you don't mind, and get dressed proper.'

153

'Have a decent breakfast while you're at it. I think we're going to be here for most of the day.'

Sergeant O'Rourke shaded his eyes and squinted up at the single hand dangling below the groundsheet. 'I climbed up the ladder myself and took a quick sconce at him, poor bastard. Somebody's given him one devil of a reefing, I can tell you that for nothing at all. I don't know hundred per cent for sure if he's been castrated, but his habit's soaked through with blood.'

'We don't have any idea who he is yet?'

Sergeant O'Rourke shook his head. 'There's been no clergy reported missing. Not so far, anyhow. We're calling him Father X for now. But I'll bet you money he's a one-time kiddy-fiddler.'

'Now then,' Katie cautioned him. 'Don't go jumping to conclusions.'

'How about going up there yourself and taking a lamp at him, ma'am?' asked Detective O'Donovan. 'I'll hold the ladder for you, and I promise no shaking it – cross my heart and swear on the Bible.'

Katie looked up again. At the moment, Father X's body was completely hidden in the dark shadows underneath the groundsheet, but Detective O'Donovan was right: before they lowered him down she needed to climb up and examine him closely *in situ*. First of all, they needed to work out how his murderer had hoisted him to the top of the flagstaff. It didn't seem likely that one man could have done it single-handed – not unless he had used a block and tackle or some other ingenious way of lifting him up.

Not only that, it was important for her to see

how his murderer had bound him. She had learned from experience that the way in which people tied knots was almost as idiosyncratic as the way they signed their names. She had also learned how much a victim's injuries could tell her. Every bruise and burn and ligature mark and stab wound was like a brain scan of a murderer's state of mind. Seething, or vengeful, or jealous, or just plain sadistic.

She hesitated, and then she said, 'Okay, then, fetch the ladder. But I warn you, Patrick, I'm not happy with heights – and if I feel so much as a quiver, you're back on crossing duty.'

While Detective O'Donovan and a podgy young garda went off to find the ladder, Sergeant O'Rourke sniffed and said, 'Why do you think they hung your man from the top of the flagpole like that? I mean, that's a hell of a lot of trouble to go to, wouldn't you say, just to make a point? Especially if nobody can understand what your point actually is.'

'Maybe it's a warning to other priests.'

'It could be, like. Or maybe they're trying to show the world that he was no better than vermin – the same way those farmers in Kerry shoot crows and hang them on their fences.'

Detective O'Donovan and the young garda came across the parking lot carrying a long aluminium ladder. With a sharp rattle, they lifted it up against the flagstaff and shook it vigorously to demonstrate to Katie that it was secure. Detective O'Donovan said, 'I'll go up first and pull that groundsheet off of him. Then he's all yours.'

Katie waited while he clanked up to the top of

155

the ladder, took hold of the groundsheet and dragged it sideways. It got caught on one of Father X's heels, and he had to shake it two or three times as if he were making a bed. At last he managed to disentangle it, and drop it with an airy rumble to the ground.

When he came down, he said, 'Take a look at his neck, ma'am. They've strangled him with some kind of cord. Not wire, like they did with Father Heaney.'

He took her elbow and helped her to mount the first step of the ladder. 'Up you go, ma'am. But take it easy, okay? We don't want to lose you, do we?'

'Don't worry,' she told him, although she couldn't help thinking: *if you only knew.*

She climbed up steadily until she reached the penultimate rung. She looked down and she could see everybody looking up at her – gardaí and technicians and reporters and the crowds of onlookers who had gathered behind the police cordon three streets away. She caught a flash of reflected sunlight, and saw that the cameraman from RTÉ News was focused on her, too. She suddenly felt as if she were very high up.

Sergeant O'Rourke was right – Father X looked exactly like one of those rotting crows that farmers tied to their fences. He was bedraggled, like a crow, and his black soutane had flapped open like a pair of broken wings.

His ankles had been fastened tightly to the top of the flagstaff with twenty or thirty turns of bright brass wire. His knees were wired together, and his wrists were wired behind his back. As

Sergeant O'Rourke had told her, the end of each wire had been twisted into two tidy loops like a butterfly's wings, in exactly the same way as with Father Heaney.

She climbed up to reach the very last rung, as high as she could, trying to peer down between Father X's legs. His soutane had the traditional thirty-three buttons – each one representing a year that Christ had spent on earth. Enough buttons had been left unfastened to expose his badly bruised shins and knees, but his blood-smeared thighs were bound so closely together that she couldn't see for sure if he had been castrated or not.

His soutane, however, had a glossy sheen to it that showed her that it was soaking wet. She reached across and squeezed the edge of it, and her latex glove was blotched with red.

'Everything okay up there?' called Detective O'Donovan.

Katie twisted around and said, 'I'm grand, thanks!' but as she did so she felt a sickening wave of vertigo and she had to grip the ladder tightly and close her eyes.

Holy Mary, Mother of God, please don't let me fall off. It's such a long way down to the ground.

She kept completely still, though, and after a moment she recovered her sense of balance. She opened her eyes and took a deep breath to steady herself. *Right. Now let's take a closer look at this fellow.*

She leaned as far to the right as she dared. Father X's nose had been broken in a zig-zag and his eyes were swelled up like two over-ripe damsons. His jaw was dislocated, too, leaving his mouth wide open in a silent shout.

From his thinning plume of white hair and the papery skin on the backs of his hands, Katie guessed that he was at least seventy, and probably quite a few years older.

She could see the cord around his neck that Detective O'Donovan had mentioned. It was very thin, so thin that it had cut deep into his flesh, and most of it was invisible. But there were two trailing ends, each at least seven or eight inches long, which his murderer must have gripped in order to strangle him. The cord was made of purple and blue threads, intertwined. It appeared to be decorative, but Katie couldn't imagine what it could have been used to decorate.

'Coming down!' she called, and carefully descended the ladder, one rung at a time. When she reached the ground and looked back up at the top of the flagstaff, it didn't seem to be very high up at all, but it had certainly felt like it when she was up there.

'What do you think?' asked Detective O'Donovan.

Katie shrugged. 'I still can't think how they hauled him up there, but I'd say that you're probably right, and there were two or three of them. All the same, I'm pretty sure that at least one of them was the same perpetrator who killed Father Heaney. Those loops at the end of each wire – we never told the media about those, did we?'

'So much for Monsignor Kelly and his suicidal odd-job man,' said Sergeant O'Rourke, wiping his nose with a crumpled Kleenex and making no attempt to hide his satisfaction.

'That's right,' said Detective O'Donovan. 'Your suicidal odd-job man couldn't have committed *this* murder because he's dead.'

'That's if he genuinely did go ahead and top himself,' said Sergeant O'Rourke. 'He could easily have changed his mind. We don't have any evidence, do we, except for that suicide note? We haven't found his body yet.'

'Well, no, that's true. But we haven't found him living and breathing either.'

'Maybe he was so pleased with himself for killing Father Heaney that he decided to go for another priest – this unfortunate old whacker here, whoever he is. On the other hand, maybe he didn't kill Father Heaney at all and he didn't kill this fellow either, and the perpetrator was somebody else altogether, although Monsignor Kelly wants us to believe that it *was* him, for reasons known only to himself.'

Katie said, 'Jesus! I thought I was confused before, but you've got my head spinning now. But – yes, I agree with you.'

'You do? I'm not even sure that I agree with myself.'

'No, Jimmy – neither I nor Chief Superintendent O'Driscoll were convinced that Brendan Doody killed Father Heaney, and I don't think he killed Father X here either. Come on, Doody just doesn't fit the profile. Whoever killed Father Heaney was carrying out a ritual revenge – very complex and very specific – the same as this killing here. He was sophisticated and he was cruel and he really took his time.

'But Doody – you only had to look at Doody's lifestyle to realize that he could never do anything like that. Whoever committed these murders doesn't push sweetie wrappers down the back of their sofa cushions. Doody wasn't exactly a retard, but from what Father Lenihan said, he was somewhat on the slow side. I don't believe that he would have hurt anybody unless he was really goaded into losing his temper. He surely would never have gone to the trouble of trussing his victims up with wire and torturing them. In my opinion, he would have simply bashed their skulls in with a hammer, and probably regretted it the minute he did it.'

'But why was the Right Reverend Kelly so keen for us to think that Doody *was* the killer?' asked Detective O'Donovan.

'That's the million-euro question,' said Katie. 'And when I tell him there's been a second murder, I'd very much like to hear what the good monsignor has to say for himself. Like you say, if Brendan Doody really *has* committed suicide, we can't blame him for this killing, can we?'

She looked up at Father X's body again, slowly rotating at the top of the flagstaff.

'Don't worry – I'll be going across to the diocese later to talk to Monsignor Kelly about it. I think he knows a lot more about this than he's been telling us.'

It took the scissor-lift nearly an hour to arrive, and by that time a blanket of cloud had slowly moved across the sky and the sun had disappeared. Not only that, a fretful wind had risen, blowing dust and dead leaves across the car park. Katie was beginning to wish that she had brought her coat.

While they were waiting, she went across and spoke to the media. She told them only that the body was that of an elderly man, so far unidentified, dressed in a priest's soutane. It was highly likely that he *was* a priest, but they couldn't be one hundred per cent sure. His assailant had bound him hand and foot with wire, and beaten him severely, but it wasn't yet possible to tell the full extent of his injuries.

'Gelded, was he, the same as Father Heaney?' asked Dan Keane, his pen poised over his notebook.

'Like I said, Dan, we can't tell that for certain. We have to get him down off that flagstaff first.'

'But it wouldn't surprise you if he was?'

'Nothing surprises me, Dan. Not any more.'

As she was walking back across the road, a white flat-bed truck appeared, with a scissor-lift platform on the back, and turned into the car park. Two council workers in orange fluorescent jerkins jumped down from the cab, Fat and Fatter. They stared up at Father X suspended from the top of the flagpole and shook their heads in disbelief.

'Holy shite, how did he get himself up *there?*'

'We don't have a clue,' said Sergeant O'Rourke. 'But what we'd like *you* to do is get him down.'

Long pause from Fatter. Then, 'He's dead, right?'

'There's no fooling you, boy.'

'Yeah, but the thing is, we're not allowed to touch him, not manually, with our hands, not if he's dead. Health and safety, like. EU regulations.'

161

'It's all right. Our technicians will be handling the body. All you have to do is get them up there and bring them back down again.'

'He's not infectious, is he?'

'I don't think so. The last I heard, you can't catch bruises or a broken nose.'

Fatter stared at him with piggy eyes. 'Are you taking the piss, like?'

'What do you think?'

Grumbling and muttering under his breath, Fatter heaved himself into the driver's seat and made a noisy performance of backing the truck up close to the flagstaff. As soon as had done so, the other council worker helped the two garda technicians to climb up on to the scissor-lift platform. Fatter gunned the truck's engine, and the scissor-lift gradually opened up like a concertina and raised the platform up to the same level as Father X's body.

It took over forty minutes for the two technicians to photograph Father X from every conceivable angle, and to take samples of the paint on the flagstaff. At last, however, they cut the wire that was bound around Father X's ankles and lowered him carefully on to the platform. The council worker whistled to his colleague that they wanted to come down again, and they slowly descended.

A paramedic wheeled over a trolley covered with a shiny green vinyl sheet, and together she and the two technicians lifted Father X's body up on to it. Katie stood close by while the younger of the two unfastened the remaining buttons of the dead priest's soutane, and the older technician meticulously snipped the brass wire that

162

bound his wrists, his knees and his ankles.

'I have no idea at all who fastens their wires in loops like these,' said the older technician. 'They're not like the work of any electricians that I've ever come across, nor telephone engineers either.'

'Picture framers?' Sergeant O'Rourke suggested.

'Jimmy – I thought I told you to go home and change and get yourself some breakfast,' said Katie.

'You did, ma'am. But I really need to see if he's been – you know – discombobulated.'

Father X's soutane fell wide open, exposing his bony, greyish-white body. He was covered in bruises – some crimson, some purple, some turning yellow – and it was obvious from the way that his arms lay askew that they must have been wrenched from their sockets.

His penis was still intact, lying against his left thigh like a featherless fledgling that had fallen out of its nest. But immediately below it there was no scrotum – only a soggy, gaping cavity, dark with clotting blood.

The older technician leaned forward so that he could inspect the wound more closely. 'There – see that V-shaped nick just above his anus? He was castrated by the same instrument as Father Heaney, I'd swear to it. Two overlapping blades, similar to sheep shears.'

'I was fancying a couple of sausages for breakfast,' said Sergeant O'Rourke. 'But now – I don't know. I think I'll stick to Shredded Wheat.'

'Was he alive or dead when he was castrated?' asked Katie.

'Oh, he was alive,' said the older technician. 'You have only to feel his habit. It weighs a *ton,* because it's absolutely drenched. There's no doubt at all that his heart was still beating when they cut off his testes.'

'So he probably died from loss of blood?'

'That, and shock, I expect. We'll just have to wait and see what the illustrious Dr Collins has to say about it. You never know. She always seems to have some theory of her own.'

'Well, I'm seeing her this afternoon,' said Katie. 'She said that she'll be finished with Father Heaney by three.'

Just then, a lanky young garda came loping across the car park and said, 'Excuse me, ma'am, but there's a woman here who thinks she knows who this is.'

'Good, I'll come and talk to her. Frank – can you cover the body with a sheet or something, just up to his neck? Make him presentable anyway. I may ask this woman to come and take a look at him. The sooner we know who he is, the sooner we'll be able to find out who wanted to cut his mebs off.'

She followed the lanky young garda to the police barrier that had been set up across the Old Youghal Road. A plumpish woman in a black coat and a black bonnet like a rook's wing was standing behind the yellow tape, clutching a large black handbag. Her mouth was so grimly turned down that she looked as if she were taking part in a gurning competition.

'Madam?' Katie beckoned her. 'Why don't you come and join me over here?'

164

The woman bent down and struggled awkwardly under the tape. She presented herself to Katie, panting slightly, still clutching her handbag as if she were afraid that somebody was going to try and snatch it away from her.

'I'm Detective Superintendent Kathleen Maguire. And you are?'

'Mary O'Malley. Mrs Mary O'Malley, but I'm a widow. My husband was taken from me seven years ago this Pentecost. It was the throat cancer, although he never smoked.'

'I see. I'm sorry. This guard tells me you might know who our deceased is.'

'My friend Eileen told me that there was a dead priest hanging from the flagpole outside of the orphanage, and so I came up here directly.'

'So, who do you think it is?'

'There's only one priest missing that I know of, which is why I thought it must be him.'

'Okay. So what's his name?'

'I arrange the flowers at St Luke's, see, but on Tuesday morning Moran's didn't send up enough lilies, they only sent the five bunches instead of the usual six, so I had to go in early on Wednesday morning before the bereavement Mass to finish off my arrangement in the Lady chapel.'

'Yes?'

Mrs O'Malley stared at Katie as if she were educationally subnormal. 'If it hadn't been for that, I wouldn't have gone in at all, would I? And if I hadn't have gone in, I wouldn't have realized that he was missing.'

'No, I don't suppose you would.'

'Father Lynott knew that he hadn't turned up,

165

because Father Lynott had to take the bereavement Mass instead, but Father Lynott said not to worry because at his age he's always taking odd days off without any explanation and we just had to be tolerant.'

'What's his name, Mary?' Katie asked her.

'Who?'

'The priest who's missing. The one you think might be our deceased.'

'Father Quinlan, of course. I just told you.'

'Of course,' said Katie, glancing across at the lanky young garda, who was rolling up his eyes in mock despair. 'Do you think you could come and identify the body? It wouldn't upset you, would it?'

'Not at all. He always looked like he was half-dead, anyway.'

Twenty-two

She found Monsignor Kelly on the touchline of the football field at Sunday's Well Primary School for Boys, watching a second eleven game against Holy Cross. He was standing in a small group with the principal and the principal's wife and several of the school governors and three priests – all of whom were holding on to their hats because the wind had risen, and everything was flapping – flags, coats, dresses and soutanes.

Katie and Sergeant O'Rourke walked up behind Monsignor Kelly, so close that Katie could

166

have tapped him on the back. At first he didn't look round, but Katie could tell by the way that his shoulders shrank that he was aware of her presence.

'Come on, Sunday's Well!' he shouted, still without looking round. 'You're three goals behind and it's almost half-time!' Then he turned to face her and said, much louder than he needed to, *'Katie!* This is a surprise!'

'Good afternoon, monsignor.'

'You must have some news for me, yes?'

'I think we need to talk in private,' Katie told him. She smiled at the principal, the curly-haired Martin Shaughnessy, and said, 'You don't mind my stealing the monsignor a moment, do you, Mr Shaughnessy?'

'You'll bring him back directly, I hope? Right now, our team needs all the spiritual help it can get.'

They walked together to the back of the school building, and went inside. It was suddenly silent in there, and smelled of paint and glue and children who were given a bath only once a month, if that. Katie led the way into one of the classrooms, and sat down on the edge of a desk. There was a large mural on the wall that the children had painted themselves: a forest, with twisted trees in it, and wolves, and dark creatures with yellow eyes that looked like leprechauns, or goblins.

'Well, what's this about?' asked Monsignor Kelly, chafing his hands. 'Have you found Brendan Doody yet? Is that it?'

'No, we haven't found Brendan Doody.'

'Threw himself off Patrick's Bridge, it wouldn't

167

surprise me, and floated out to sea. He'll be half-way to France by now.'

'That hardly ever happens, monsignor. In fact, it never happens. The tide always brings them back in again.'

Monsignor Kelly gave her that sideways look that meant 'you're a woman, don't you contradict me, even if I'm wrong'.

'As a matter of fact, most of the floaters get themselves stuck by Horgan's Quay,' put in Sergeant O'Rourke, with a cheerful smile and a twirl of his finger. 'They swirl around and around until somebody spots them and then we come along to fish them out.'

Monsignor Kelly said nothing. Katie could sense that he was deeply reluctant to ask her why she had come to find him. If Brendan Doody hadn't turned up yet, dead or alive, she could only be here because she had some more awkward questions to put to him. From the way his lips were so tightly pursed, she could tell that he wasn't in the mood this afternoon for awkward questions. Not that he often was, she imagined, even from God.

'Do you happen to be acquainted with a Father Vincent Quinlan from St Luke's in Montenotte?' Katie asked him.

Monsignor Kelly's eyes darted from side to side like two minnows in a jam jar, as if he were trying to decide what the right answer was. 'I'm not sure. Is there any special reason why I should?'

'He's been serving at St Luke's for the past eighteen years, so I'd be surprised if you hadn't come across him once or twice, at least. And he was sent there after several boys at St Andrew's

168

Youth Club accused him of molestation. He was never formally charged, because there wasn't sufficient evidence, but I would have thought that the diocese would have kept him on their radar, at the very least.'

'That would imply that we didn't trust him, wouldn't it?'

'Not necessarily. But it's always better to be safe than sorry, isn't it?'

Monsignor Kelly's face reddened. 'We're not like the Spanish Inquisition, Katie. We believe in forgiveness, and forgiveness means forgetting, too. If a priest has shown himself to be truly penitent, we don't feel that we have to regard him with suspicion for the rest of his life.'

'Well, thankfully, monsignor, you won't have to do that with Father Quinlan.'

'Oh, yes? And what would be the reason for that, exactly?'

'Father Quinlan was found this morning hanging from the top of the flagpole outside St Joseph's, upside down. He was hog-tied with brass wire and throttled with string, and he had been beaten so viciously that almost every bone in his body was broken. He had been castrated, too.'

The flush on Monsignor Kelly's face drained away as swiftly as if Katie had pulled out a plug. He said, 'Name of Jesus,' and crossed himself, and then he promptly sat down on one of the child-sized chairs.

'Murdered? My God. And then castrated?'

'Not in that order, by the look of it.'

'Jesus.'

Katie stood over Monsignor Kelly for a few

moments, saying nothing. He kept shaking his head and crossing himself, and glancing up at Katie because he knew what she was going to say next. In fact, it was so obvious that she hardly had to say it at all.

'The way that he was tied up and mutilated, monsignor ... we don't have definitive evidence yet, but in my mind there's very little question that he was murdered by the same perpetrator as Father Heaney.'

'So what do you want me to say to that? "Dear God Almighty, I've been taken for a fool, and Brendan Doody is still alive after all!"?'

Katie leaned over him, in his little chair. 'I have no idea if Brendan Doody is still alive or not. He may have murdered Father Heaney, but if he did, he probably murdered Father Quinlan, too. Personally I don't believe that he murdered either one of them. I don't believe that he wrote that suicide note either.'

'And what are you implying by that? What are you accusing me of, Detective Superintendent Maguire? Stupidity, or forgery, or conspiracy, or maybe you're accusing me of all three?'

'I'm not accusing anybody of anything at all at this early stage. We haven't even finished our autopsy on Father Heaney yet. But I want you to be aware that I won't bend to any pressure from you or anybody else to close this case before I'm satisfied that we've thoroughly examined all of the evidence.'

Monsignor Kelly was plainly furious and Katie could tell that he was tempted to jump to his feet. But even if he jumped up, he would still be no taller than she was, so in spite of his fury he stayed where he was, crouched in his little child's chair, and he lowered his voice so that Katie had to lean even closer and Sergeant O'Rourke wouldn't be able to hear him.

'Let me tell you this,' he said. 'Only one other person in all of my years in the church has dared to suggest that I have conducted myself at any time with anything but the greatest of propriety. And that person bitterly regretted having uttered that calumny for the remainder of her life. And I mean *bitterly*.'

Katie narrowed her eyes at him.

'Are you threatening me, monsignor?'

'I'm giving a word to the wise, that's all, detective superintendent. *Cineri gloria sera est.* You may solve this case, and you may be given all the credit for solving it, but applause is of no use to those who can no longer hear it.'

'You *are* threatening me, aren't you?'

'I'm simply making it clear to you that the reputation of the diocese could depend on this, and that the diocese has some very powerful friends in all kinds of high places – people who it would be advisable for you for your own safety not to cross.'

'I could arrest you for saying that to me.'

'I never said a word, Katie. I was just trying to be helpful.'

'In that case, *be* helpful,' said Katie, standing up straight. 'Who do you suggest I ought to go looking for – apart from Brendan Doody? Who else can I arrest without ruffling any diocesan feathers?'

171

Sergeant O'Rourke caught the sarcasm in her voice, and realized that there was a confrontation going on here. He came and stood at her right-hand side, his arms folded, to give her support.

'I really don't know,' said Monsignor Kelly, looking away. 'I still think that Brendan Doody is your most likely suspect, but then I'm not a detective, am I? I'm one of the vicars general, that's all. What do I know, except of the ways of God?'

Katie said, 'I'll talk to you again later, monsignor, after I've been to see Dr Collins. Look – half-time's over. The Sunday's Well boys are going to need all the support you can give them. You'd better get back out there on touchline and get down on your knees and start praying.'

Monsignor Kelly stood up, and his little chair tilted back and clattered on to the floor. There was a look in his eyes that Katie recognized. She had seen it in the eyes of drug dealers and fraudsters and murderers and wife-beaters, but she had never seen it in a cleric's eyes before. It was a look that said *bitch*.

Twenty-three

'Fascinating, this case,' said Dr Collins, lifting up the green sheet that was covering Father Heaney's body. 'Well ... *both* of them, in fact. Fascinating.'

Her bronze-coloured hair was still tacked up in a chaotic French pleat, and her starched overall was buttoned up wrongly, but she seemed much calmer and much more approachable than when Katie had picked her up at the airport. It obviously put her at ease, being surrounded by the dead. The dead spoke to her unambiguously in the language of bruises and contusions and swollen blue tongues. The dead never argued, and they were never hypocritical.

Katie and Dr Collins and Sergeant O'Rourke were gathered around Father Heaney's autopsy table. It was right at the far end of the long, chilly pathology laboratory at the University Hospital. The opalescent light that shone in through the clerestory windows gave the laboratory an almost spiritual appearance, as if it really was the waiting room to heaven, and when the coroner had finished examining the dead, and sewing them up again, angels would come in through the double doors in a fluster of white feathery wings to carry them away.

Four other bodies lay in an orderly row on the opposite side of the laboratory. Sheets had been drawn up to their chests, and although their faces were waxy, they all looked serene, as if they were dreaming rather than dead. They were a family of four – father, mother and twin boys of nine – who had all been killed instantly in a head-on collision on the N25 at Carrigtwohill.

Next to the door, Father Quinlan's body was still completely shrouded. The paramedics had wheeled him in less than twenty minutes ago, and Dr Collins had only had time for a very cursory look at him.

Katie had seen for herself that Father Quinlan

was stone dead, hanging upside down from the flagstaff. All the same, she couldn't stop herself from glancing over at his trolley from time to time, just to make sure that she hadn't seen the sheet stirring. After her first visit to a mortuary, as a young garda trainee, she had suffered weeks of nightmares about bodies suddenly sitting bolt upright.

Dr Collins noticed her repeatedly turning her head. 'It's quite all right, detective superintendent. He's as dead as mutton, I promise you.'

'What? Oh, yes, I know he is. It's only my imagination, working overtime.'

'Don't worry,' Dr Collins told her. 'I used to get the heebie-jeebies, too, when I was a junior.'

Katie said, 'It was my husband's fault – my late husband, Paul. He used to love all of those zombie films. You know – *Night of the Living Dead,* that kind of thing. They were all total rubbish, those films, and those zombies – they were nothing compared to the drunks you get outside the Maltings on a Saturday night, believe me. But they still frightened the shite out of me.'

Dr Collins smiled. 'In the path lab, the middle of the night was the scariest, on the graveyard shift, when I was all alone with the recently departed. All of those people lying there, and no matter how hard you listened, you couldn't hear a single one of them breathing, because none of them were.'

'You're giving me the shivers,' said Sergeant O'Rourke.

Dr Collins drew the sheet away from Father Heaney's naked body, and folded it up. His face

174

had begun to collapse like a rubber Halloween mask, and his hands could have been mistaken for empty household gloves. She had cut open his torso in a dramatic Y shape and then sutured him up again. His skin had turned grey but he was blotched all over with florid crimson bruises. Katie was reminded of a pair of rose-patterned curtains that used to hang in her mother's sewing room.

Dr Collins prodded Father Heaney's distended stomach with her forefinger. 'You can tell by the colour of these contusions that they were inflicted only a short time before death,' she said. 'I found some extremely deep internal bruises, too, which have only just begun to appear on the skin surface, and it's likely that he has others that will never emerge at all.'

She lifted his left shoulder and turned him on his side so that they could take a look at his back.

'Most of this bruising, though, is quite superficial. It shows us clearly that the victim was punched and pushed around, so that he collided with doors and walls and various items of furniture. You see these parallel bruises? Tramlines, we call them. These tell us that he was beaten with a cane or a walking stick of some kind, in the same way that you would thrash a misbehaving donkey, say, or a very naughty schoolboy.'

Next she held up one of Father Heaney's hands. 'His wrists were tightly secured with wire – just before he was castrated, most likely, to prevent him from struggling. It's no ordinary wire either. You'll be intrigued to hear that it's seventh-octave harp wire.'

175

'It's what?' said Katie. '*Harp* wire?'

Dr Collins nodded. 'I confess that I wouldn't have known what it was myself, but one of your young lab technicians is a keen amateur harpist. Let me check my notes here, what he told me about it. Yes – apparently they use this particular wire for the clàrsach, the Irish low-headed harp. It's made of braided phosphor bronze wrapped in nylon, although your technician tells me that a real aficionado would only consider silver or gold monofilaments.'

'My Uncle Stephen used to play the clàrsach,' said Sergeant O'Rourke. He sniffed, took out his handkerchief and wiped his nose. 'He could reduce a whole parlourful of people to tears, believe me. He knew only the one tune, "Brian Boru's March", and that's about the most depressing piece of music you ever heard in all your born days.'

Dr Collins raised up Father Heaney's right knee. 'After he was castrated, Father Heaney's knees and ankles were bound together with the same type of wire, and then he was garrotted. Again with the same type of wire, with a soup spoon handle to tighten it like a tourniquet. The soup spoon is engraved with the initials HM, which tells us that it came from the Hayfield Manor Hotel. There were no fingerprints on it, I'm afraid.'

'What did they use to castrate him?' asked Katie. 'Our technician thought that it was shears. You know, like they shear sheep with.'

'The wonders of the internet,' said Dr Collins. She picked up her Apple laptop from the table where all of her instruments were arrayed, opened it up, and passed it over so that Katie could see what was on the screen.

She saw a picture of a bespectacled grey-haired man who looked like a professor. He was wearing latex gloves and holding up a pair of crudely fashioned metal shears. Unlike sheep shears, however, these had half-moon-shaped blades and they were hinged at the top.

'*Castratori,* these were called,' Dr Collins told her. 'They were specifically designed for the castration of young boys, so that their voices wouldn't grow deeper when they reached puberty.'

'You're talking about *castrati,*' said Katie.

'That's right. In the sixteenth century women weren't allowed to sing in church, or on the stage, so they used boys instead. *Castrati* became fantastically popular and they were still in huge demand right up until the nineteen hundreds.'

'But – Christ on a bicycle,' put in Sergeant O'Rourke. 'To cut a young lad's mebs off, just so he could sing like a girl. It doesn't bear thinking about.'

'It did if you were a dirt-poor family with half a dozen children and this was your only chance to make any real money. The very top *castrati* – the ones who became professional opera singers, or the ones who were chosen to sing in some of the great church choirs – they were like today's rock stars. World-famous, and idolized, and very wealthy. You can forget about Bono. Farinelli, in the eighteenth century, was openly compared to God.'

'How about that, then? I didn't know God had a squeaky voice.'

177

'*Castrati's* voices weren't at all squeaky,' said Dr Collins. 'They had extraordinary pitch, like a woman or a pre-pubertal boy, but much stronger and much more resonant. After they were castrated, their vocal cords grew only to the same length as a female high soprano, but their pharynx and oral cavity were fully developed, and they had the lung capacity of an adult male.

'Farinelli's voice spanned three octaves, and he could hold a note for whole minute without taking a breath.'

'Sounds exactly like my Maeve,' put in Sergeant O'Rourke.

Katie looked again at the bloody cavity where Father Heaney's scrotum had been sliced off, with its flaccid lips. 'The question I'm asking myself is, why?'

Dr Collins said, '*Why* is your area of expertise, detective superintendent, not mine. The only question I'm here to answer is *how*.'

'But if you castrate a grown man it doesn't affect his voice, does it, even if you allow him to live?'

'No, of course not. When a boy reaches puberty, testosterone lengthens his vocal cords by more than sixty per cent, while a girl's vocal cords lengthen by only half that, or even less. Testosterone also thickens up a boy's vocal cords, which helps to give him a deeper voice, and that thickening is permanent.

'In boys, the thyroid cartilage increases in length three times more than it does in girls, which gives men their Adam's apple. You can't reverse any of these physical changes by castration or hormone injections or any other means.'

Katie slowly shook her head. 'So these two priests were castrated only to cause them suffering, or to humiliate them as men, or to make some point that we don't yet know about? Or all three?'

'I think it was revenge,' said Sergeant O'Rourke. 'That's the most likely motive, the way I see it. This was done by somebody who was molested when he was younger. And of course, once he'd tortured them, and castrated them, he didn't have much of a choice. He had to kill them.'

'You're probably right, Jimmy,' Katie agreed. 'But think about it: if the perpetrator was trying to punish these priests for molesting him, why didn't he cut *everything* off?'

'What?'

'Why didn't he cut their penises off, as well as their testicles?'

'Now *that* is a very interesting question,' said Dr Collins. 'Especially if we're talking about a victim who was forced to give oral sex, or who was sodomized. It's the penetration that abuse victims find the most traumatic – the feeling that they've been physically violated. I've talked to dozens of rape victims, and they almost always have a vivid mental picture of their rapist's penis – even when they can barely recall what his face looked like.'

'*Don't*,' said Sergeant O'Rourke. 'I can remember like it was yesterday Father O'Grady standing by the lockers and calling out, "Look at this, O'Rourke!" and there it was sticking out of his soutane like one of McWhinney's Bigfoot

179

sausages. I ran off so fast my rubber dollies never touched the floor.'

'I hope you reported him,' said Katie.

'Get away with you, I was only seven and I was much too scared, and it would have only been my word against his, and in any case he's long dead now and St Peter will have decided how to punish him. If there's any justice in the world he'll be grilling his sausage in hell.'

Dr Collins said, 'I should finish examining Father Quinlan by midday tomorrow, detective superintendent, so that may tell us more. So far, however, I can formally tell you that the primary cause of Father *Heaney's* death was strangulation.'

'He didn't bleed out?'

'That wasn't the primary cause, no. He probably would have died from loss of blood if he hadn't been garrotted first. His inferior vesical artery was severed when he was castrated, and he also suffered a ruptured spleen, which caused more blood loss internally. He also had three broken ribs and massive internal bruising.'

She held up her latex-gloved hand and counted on her fingers. 'But these are all the things we *don't* have. *One* – we don't have any fingerprints or distinctively shaped bruises or marks on his body that could help us to identify his assailant. *Two* – we don't have any saliva or other bodily fluids either on his skin surface or in any of his body orifices that might yield incriminating DNA. *Three* – we don't have any epithelial cells under his fingernails that might have resulted from scratching or fighting with his assailant.

180

Four – we don't have any human or animal hairs or any foreign fibres.'

'So – *five*,' said Sergeant O'Rourke, sticking up his thumb, 'we seem to be well and truly clueless.'

'I admit that it's not going to be easy, especially if Father Quinlan's body is the same.'

'We have the harp wire,' said Katie. 'There can't be too many places in Cork where you can find wire like that. A music shop, maybe. Or a college that teaches music. Or an orchestra.'

Sergeant O'Rourke took out his Blackberry and prodded at it, frowning. After a minute or two, he said, 'There are six music shops in the city itself, like, and another five within a twenty-five mile radius – in Mallow and Bandon and Carrigaline.

He did some more prodding, and then he said, 'We have at least five music schools in the area, including the Cork School of Music on Union Quay and Cork City Music College, but some of them teach only keyboards or guitar.'

'Well, we're going to need to do some legwork,' said Katie. 'Call O'Donovan and Horgan and have them start to go round the shops. Tell them they're looking for – what was it? – seventh-octave harp wire, and the names of anybody who buys it from them.'

She turned back to Dr Collins and said, 'I'll come back tomorrow, when you've finished with Father Quinlan.'

As she did so, however, she was sure she saw movement under the green sheet that covered Father Quinlan's body. Only a slight stirring at first, followed by a moment's stillness, but then a quick, convulsive shake, as if Father Quinlan had

181

woken up and was struggling to pull the sheet away.

'*He's still alive!*' Katie whispered. She felt as if her scalp were shrinking.

'What?' said Dr Collins, staring at her.

Katie pointed toward the trolley. 'Father Quinlan – he's still alive! I just saw him move!'

Sergeant O'Rourke said, 'There's no way! Didn't we see him dead as a doornail? The paramedics checked his pulse and his pupils and nobody gets any deader than he was.'

Even as he was speaking, however, the sheet suddenly humped up and shifted rhythmically from side to side. It looked as if Father Quinlan had heard them talking and was waving his left hand in an effort to attract their attention.

'This is impossible,' snapped Dr Collins, as if it was a personal affront that anyone should come back to life after she had conclusively decided that they were dead.

She crossed over to the trolley and wrenched off the sheet. Sergeant O'Rourke crossed himself and said, 'Name of Jesus,' under his breath.

Father Quinlan was still lying on his back with his eyes closed, as bruised and broken as Father Heaney – worse, if anything, because his shoulders had been dislocated and his arms were lying at his sides at such an awkward angle.

Out of a glistening hole in the left side of his stomach, just below his ribcage, a wet, dark, narrow-nosed creature was rearing up. It was writhing around and around, frantically trying to get itself free, and it was this convulsive writhing that they had mistaken for Father Quinlan

182

attempting to tell them that he was still alive.

'A *rat*,' said Dr Collins, and her voice was soaked with genuine horror.

The rat continued to twist itself around, although for some reason it made no sound, no bruxing or chattering like a rat would normally do to show that it was stressed. Dr Collins reached across to the table where she kept all of her surgical equipment and found herself a thick pair of red industrial gloves. She pulled them on, and then she grasped the rat in both hands and started to tug it inch by inch out of Father Quinlan's body.

'Jesus,' said Sergeant O'Rourke.

The rat emerged with a thick, glutinous sound that reminded Katie of rabbit guts dropping into the kitchen sink when her mother was preparing a rabbit stew, and it made her feel just as queasy.

Dr Collins stalked over to the opposite side of the laboratory, holding the waggling rat at arm's length.

'Sergeant O'Rourke!' she cried out, 'the locker, will you?'

Sergeant O'Rourke flung open one of the wire cages that were usually used as a temporary store for odd items of evidence, such as hats and shoes and purses. Dr Collins tossed the rat inside, where it landed with a heavy wet thump. She slammed the door and fastened it with wire.

'Rats,' she said. 'Rats and maggots. Ugh! They disgust me. Sometimes I think I should have been a florist, or a confectioner.'

Katie looked down at the soft, boggy hole in Father Quinlan's stomach. 'Can you believe it?

They must have sewed it up inside him. Holy Mary, Mother of God. You don't think he was still alive when they did it, do you?'

Dr Collins took off her industrial gloves and snapped on a pair of latex gloves instead. She went back to Father Quinlan's body, lifted his penis out of the way and opened up the wound where he had been castrated, parting the flesh with her fingertips as wide as she could.

'There,' she said. 'See those stitches? You're absolutely right. They pushed the rat inside him and then they sewed him up so that it couldn't escape.'

Neither Katie nor Sergeant O'Rourke said anything, and Sergeant O'Rourke kept his hand pressed over his mouth, as if he were concentrating very hard on the evidence, or trying to prevent himself from retching.

Dr Collins went back and peered at the rat through the criss-cross wires of its makeshift cage. 'I can't say yet if Father Quinlan was still alive when they did it. But look – they tied the rat's front and rear paws together with thread, so that it couldn't burrow its way out of him, and they must have severed its vocal cords, so that it couldn't make any sound. Maybe they thought that nobody would ever discover it was there, and he'd be buried with the rat still inside him.'

The rat hopped round and round, its back paws still fastened together. It was obviously in a panic, and it repeatedly hurled itself up against the sides of its cage.

Dr Collins said, 'See? It managed to bite through the thread that was holding its front paws together, and then it used its claws and its teeth to tunnel through Father Quinlan's intestines.'

Katie said, 'I want photographs of this, please, doctor, lots and lots of photographs. And CT scans. And blood samples. Both human blood and rat blood.'

'Oh, you'll get all of those, I promise you,' Dr Collins assured her. 'And by the looks of things, I'll be able to give you a lot more besides. Nobody can commit a homicide like this and leave no trace of themselves at all. It simply isn't possible.'

Outside, it was bright but still blustery, and as they came out of the front door of the hospital they were caught up in a whirlwind that stung Katie's eyes with grit.

'What do you think, boss?' asked Sergeant O'Rourke. 'Are we dealing with a header, or are we dealing with a header?'

'I think I need a drink,' Katie told him. 'We can stop at the Hayfield Manor on the way back, if you like.'

'What, and ask them if they've counted their spoons lately?'

Twenty-four

It was past seven by the time she arrived back at her desk at Anglesea Street. The last of the sun was shining through the window, and her pot plant cast a shadow on the wall that reminded

185

her of a scowling witch.

On the roof of the multi-storey car park opposite, even more hooded crows had gathered, their feathers ruffled by the wind. Under her breath, Katie said, '*Shoo*,' but of course they stayed where they were, a living reminder of the very close presence of death.

Detectives O'Donovan and Horgan came barging in through her office only five minutes later, both of them looking exhausted and smelling strongly of cigarette smoke. Detective O'Donovan slumped into the chair on the opposite side of her desk and dry-washed his face with his hands. Detective Horgan went over to the window and peered out of it as if he had seen something of riveting interest, like a girl undressing in a nearby apartment, or his long-dead grandmother walking along the street with her long-dead spaniel.

'Well?' she asked them. 'Did you have any luck?'

'Oh we did, yeah,' said Detective O'Donovan, which was Corkinese for absolutely no expletive luck at all. 'I don't know what it is about these sausage jockeys who run these music shops. It's like they've all got these scraggy little beards and slitty little specs and they can't give you a straight answer to a straight question to save their lives.

'Like, "Excuse me, boy, in the past six months have you happened by any chance to have sold any seventh-octave phosphor-bronze harp wire?" I mean, you feel like enough of a gowl just asking it.

'So they say, "Seventh-octave? Ooh no. But plenty of light-gauge *fifth*-octave. We've sold more light-gauge fifth-octave than you could shake a stick at. By the way, have you heard Jean Kelly? She played harp on the soundtrack for *Lord of the Rings*, and she's a Cork girl. You should hear her play Handel."

'And what does Horgan here say straight-faced? "I never knew that harps had handles." I swear to God.'

Without looking around, Detective Horgan opened his notebook and said, 'Only one harpist in the past six months was after buying any seventh-octave phosphor-bronze wire. Mary ó Nualláin, twenty-two years old. She regularly plays the harp during Sunday lunchtimes at the Ambassador Hotel. I very much doubt that when sweet Mary ó Nualláin bought her seventh-octave phosphor-bronze wire she was after killing dirty old priests with it.'

'All right,' said Katie. 'But I want you both back on the case tomorrow.'

Detective Horgan flipped his notebook. 'Bright and early, ma'am, don't fret about it. Tomorrow we're calling on the Cork Youth Orchestra and the Cork Pops Orchestra, and every freelance musician who ever plucked a clàrsach. We'll catch the plucker, believe me.'

'Michael,' said Katie, sharply.

'Yes, ma'am?'

'Stop trying to be funny, Michael, because you're not. Just find me the psychopath who killed these two priests, and as soon as you like.'

Before she left the office, Katie tried calling Siobhán to see if she had made anything for supper, but Siobhán must have gone out because she

187

didn't reply. Katie wasn't too keen on Siobhán's cooking anyhow, especially that chilli con carne she insisted on making almost every week, which was always runny like cheap dog food and always nose-streamingly hot.

She was too tired to think of cooking anything herself, so she drove into the centre of Cobh on her way home and stopped at Mimmo's in Casement Square for takeaway cod and chips. While she was sitting under the bright fluorescent lights in the corner of the chip shop, waiting for her order, her mobile phone warbled and it was John.

'How's my sexy superintendent? Not that I'll be able to call you that for very much longer. Superintendent, I mean,' he corrected himself hastily, 'not sexy.'

'I'm grand, John, but a little knackered, to tell you the truth. It's been a very long day.'

'Am I going to see you tonight? Where are you?'

'I'm sitting in the chipper, waiting for my supper.'

'You have to be kidding me! I could have taken you out. Or maybe cooked you something. You've never tasted my fluffy three-cheese omelettes, have you? *Mmmf!* They're to die for.'

'I'm sorry, sweetheart, but I really need an early night.'

'Okay, but I definitely want to see you tomorrow. Have you told your boss yet?'

'Have I told him what?'

'That you're resigning, of course. That you're coming to the States to be my bride.'

'Is that a formal proposal of marriage?'

'I don't know. Is it? Yes, I guess it must be.'

188

'I'm sitting in a chipper, waiting for a takeaway, and you're proposing marriage to me over my mobile phone? How romantic can you get?'

'I'll get down on one knee. Listen, this creaking noise is the sound of me getting down on one knee. Is that romantic enough?'

'I haven't told him yet, no. I've been far too busy today. You must have seen it on the news. Another priest was found murdered, up in Mayfield.' She lowered her voice because there was a knock-kneed young boy sitting close to her, and he was obviously trying to overhear what she was saying. 'Castrated, too, just like the one who was found in Ballyhooly.'

'I saw that on the news, yes. Couldn't miss it, in fact. But you're quitting, right? I didn't think that you would be handling the case yourself.'

'It's my case, John. Of course I'm handling it. I may be quitting but I can't just walk out with half of my investigations unfinished. And I have to give notice.'

John was silent for a few seconds, but then he said, 'You haven't changed your mind?'

The young Italian behind the counter lifted up a plastic bag and called out, 'Small cod, small chips, mushy peas!'

Katie waved at him and called, 'Small cod, that's mine!' To John she said, 'Listen, sweetheart – my order's ready. I'll call you as soon as I get home.'

'I just want to be sure that you haven't changed your mind.'

'Give me some peace, will you? I'll call you. I'll be home in ten minutes.'

189

When she turned into her driveway she was surprised to see that the bungalow was in complete darkness. There was a light in the porch, which was supposed to switch on automatically, but even that wasn't working. As she climbed out of her car she saw that the living-room curtains were still open, and that none of the table lamps were lit, although two of them were on timers, set for eight o'clock. Even the television screen was glossy black.

That Siobhán, she thought. *Sometimes I could kick her out and throw her clothes after her, she's always so selfish and so inconsiderate.* But then she thought: *I'll be gone soon, myself, and that'll put an end to that problem.*

She stepped into the porch, and as she did so, small pieces of white glass crunched under her shoes. She looked upwards. In all the time she had lived here, she had only had to replace the photosensitive bulb twice, and on one of those occasions Paul had been drunk and angry about something stupid and whacked it with a hurley stick. She could see that it had been shattered again, instead of burning out. Maybe Paul's ghost had come around to see how she was, and when he found that she wasn't in, he had smashed the bulb to tell how annoyed he was – and to make sure that she knew who had called on her.

She unlocked the front door and called out, 'Barney? Where are you, boy?' She hoped that Siobhán had taken him out for his walk before she went out clubbing, or wherever she had gone. The last thing she felt like doing right now was

190

mopping the kitchen floor.

'Barney? Are you there, boy? Barney!'

Barney always barked when she came home and jumped up against the kitchen door, but tonight there was silence.

'Barney?' she said. She switched on the pink-shaded lamp on the hall table. If Barney had been waiting for her behind the kitchen door, she would have seen him through the hammered glass, but inside the kitchen there was only darkness.

She opened the kitchen door and switched on the overhead light. No Barney. But there was a chopping board on the counter, with sliced-up carrots on it, and there were two saucepans on top of the hob, one filled with peeled potatoes in cold water and the other with purple flowering broccoli. Siobhán may have gone out, but she had gone out when she had only just started to cook them some supper.

Katie went to the back door and tried the handle, but it was locked and bolted from the inside, so Siobhán couldn't have taken Barney out into the small back yard for a pee behind the geranium pots, while she herself smoked a cigarette. That was her usual definition of 'walkies'.

Maybe she had taken Barney out for a serious walk, after all. But lighting-up time had been over an hour ago now, and Katie couldn't see her leaving the house in darkness, without even closing the curtains. And where the hell had she taken him? All the way down to the harbour? If she had done that, Katie would almost certainly have passed them on her way back from the fish

191

and chip shop.

She approached the living-room door, which was wide open. The only light came from a single street lamp outside, and the shadows of tree branches crawled backwards and forwards across the carpet like the long skeletal fingers of blind men, endlessly groping for their lost eyes. Rolled under the couch, boy, never find them there.

Katie felt a sudden intuitive tingle, all down the nape of her neck and across her shoulders, and before she switched on the living-room light she eased her nickel-plated revolver out of its holster, cocked back the hammer, and held it up high. Something was very badly wrong here, in this bungalow, and it wasn't only the broken light in the porch, or the darkness, or the fact that there was no sign of Siobhán or Barney.

Something smelled wrong, too. It was a strong, musky perfume, Estée Lauder or something similar – the kind that Paul's shirts used to reek of, after he had spent the night with some local brasser (swearing blind, of course, that he had stayed over in Limerick for a business meeting).

Keeping her revolver raised, she reached over with her left hand and switched on the overhead chandeliers. The first thing she noticed was that the large mock-Regency armchair in which Paul used to sit was lying on its side, and that one of the occasional tables had tipped over. The china shepherdess that had been standing on it had fallen against the skirting board and her head had broken off, although she was still smiling inanely.

Katie took two cautious steps forward, and it was then that she saw a plump bare foot, protruding from behind the couch. She recognized the sparkly purple nail polish at once.

She circled around the couch, her eyes darting from side to side, in case an intruder was concealed behind the curtains or hiding behind the door, or in case somebody had been hiding in the bathroom or one of the bedrooms and came rushing in from the hallway to attack her. Never assume a perpetrator has left the crime scene.

'Siobhán,' she said. Then, 'Siobhán!'

Siobhán was lying face down on the carpet behind the couch, dressed in her green boat-neck sweater and her tight black skirt. The hair on the crown of her head was thick with glistening blood and there were spots and squiggles of blood up the wallpaper.

Katie knelt down beside her, laying her revolver on the carpet close by so that she could reach it quickly if she needed to. Siobhán's eyes were closed, but when Katie leaned forward she could hear that she was still breathing. Katie turned her over on to her back, and felt for the carotid pulse in her neck. It was slow, just under forty, and thready.

'Siobhán, darling,' she said, gently shaking her shoulder. 'Siobhán, can you hear me?'

Siobhán continued to breathe slowly and thickly. She muttered, as if she were having a disturbing dream, but she didn't open her eyes.

Katie scooped up her revolver and went across to the telephone. She dialled 112, identified herself and called for an ambulance. 'And will you tell them to hurry, please. My sister has severe head injuries and she's unconscious. I'm worried that she could have a cerebral haematoma.'

'It won't be long, ma'am, I can promise you that. No more than five minutes, tops. I've diverted an RRV on its way back from Glanmire.'

Next she called Sergeant O'Rourke. She caught him as he was starting his supper.

'Jimmy?'

'Good timing, ma'am. There's an onion dumpling halfway from my plate to my mouth, and if you'd called me five seconds later you wouldn't have been able to understand a word I was saying.'

'I'm truly sorry, Jimmy, but something terrible's happened and I need you to drop everything and do some organizing for me. Can you contact the technical squad urgently and call in four uniforms at least.'

'Not another fiddling priest, for Christ's sake.'

'No. It's my sister. There's been an intruder here, at my house, and she's been beaten on the head, by the looks of it. She's concussed, and there's a whole lot of blood.'

'Get away out of that,' said Sergeant O'Rourke, in horror. 'Your sister Siobhán?'

Katie puckered her mouth tight and her eyes filled up with tears. She took a deep breath and then she managed to say, 'Some of the furniture was knocked over, but it doesn't look as if she put up a fight. Barney's missing, too. I haven't had a chance to take a proper look yet, but as quick as you like, Jimmy. I'll be waiting here for you.'

'Your own sister, in your own house. Jesus.'

'Please, Jimmy. Just hurry.'

'You can count on me, ma'am.'

Katie hung up the phone. She went over and knelt back down next to Siobhán. *Think of it. There I was, my darling sister, calling you every name under the sun, and all ready to kick you out, and all the time you were lying here, beaten and bloody. Sometimes God can give you what you want, but sometimes He can show you how much you didn't really want it, after all.*

Siobhán was still breathing steadily, although her pulse rate was fluttering. Katie laid a hand on her forehead and her skin felt sweaty and chilled. She was going into shock and she urgently needed warming up.

Katie went through to the bedroom, kicking open the door and switching on the lights, and quickly checking behind the door and underneath the bed. She threw open the louvred doors of her fitted wardrobes, but there was nobody hiding there. Nobody hiding in the alcove behind the curtains either.

Katie checked Siobhán's bedroom, too, and the bathroom. Whoever had broken into the bungalow and attacked Siobhán was gone, and probably long gone, too.

She lifted a thick plaid blanket out of the bottom of Siobhán's wardrobe and carried it back into the living room. She covered her sister with it, right up to her neck.

'There, sweetheart, that should warm you up,' she said.

But Siobhán only murmured, '*Mmmfffff,*' in response.

While she waited for the rapid response vehicle to arrive, Katie gave the living room a quick once-over, searching for any evidence that might tell her

195

who had attacked Siobhán, and why. Apart from the tipped-over armchair and the decapitated shepherdess, there were no other obvious signs of damage. From the injuries on the back of Siobhán's head and the way that Katie had found her lying face down, it looked as if she had been struck from behind by surprise, and the blood spatters on the wallpaper appeared to back this up. They rose up the wall in a near-vertical line, and they were entirely consistent with a repeated series of blows, like a handyman knocking in a nail, or a priest shaking an aspergillum, a holy-water sprinkler.

The living-room door was still wide open, but Katie had no latex gloves with her so she didn't touch the Regency-style handle. Instead, she reached up and pushed the door shut with the heel of her hand. She just wanted to make sure that nothing had been dropped behind it.

And there – as the door swung back – was the message. It had been scrawled on the wallpaper in letters over six inches high, in dark green felt-tip marker.

GOD SAYS KEEP AWAY!

Twenty-five

It was beginning to grow light outside when the surgeon came into the relatives' room. Katie stood up and said, 'How is she?'

The surgeon was Indian, with a hooked nose

and protuberant eyes. If he hadn't been wearing pale green scrubs, Katie could easily have mistaken him for the owner of the Bombay Palace restaurant in Cook Street. He laid his hand on top of hers and said, 'Your sister is out of immediate danger, detective superintendent. She will survive.'

'Thank God,' said Katie. 'When can I see her?'

'You can see her as soon as she has been taken back to ITU and we have made her comfortable. But before you do, I must advise you that she has suffered some very serious injuries. As you know, she was struck on the back of the head with some kind of blunt instrument. Three times, with considerable force. I would say that it was probably a hammer, because it has left a circular impression.'

'How bad is it?'

The surgeon shrugged. 'All three blows gave her depressed fractures of the cranium, with intracranial bleeding and brain contusions. We have stemmed the bleeding and relieved the pressure, but it is too early at this stage to say if she has suffered any permanent impairment to her mental faculties. We will have to wait until she regains consciousness before we can make any kind of meaningful assessment.'

'Thank you, Doctor...'

'Hahq is my name, detective superintendent. Not doctor but mister.'

'I'm sorry.'

'Please, no problem. You need to give all of your attention now to your sister. I hope that she makes a speedy and full recovery.'

197

The surgeon left the relatives' room, and as he did so John appeared with two plastic cups of coffee and two packets of ginger biscuits. He was wearing a battered brown leather jacket and jeans and he was unshaven. He had arrived at the hospital only thirty-five minutes after Siobhán had been admitted, and he had stayed there with Katie all night. They had tried to sleep, but Katie had been too fretful to close her eyes.

'Siobhán's out of danger, apparently,' Katie told him. 'They're taking her back to intensive care and then we can see her.'

'That's good news,' said John. 'Well – cautiously good news, anyhow.'

'O God, I hope so. The trouble is, I'm beginning to wonder if she was attacked by somebody who mistook her for me.'

'You're serious?'

'It makes much more sense, doesn't it? Siobhán doesn't have an enemy in the world. She gets on people's nerves, I'll give you that. She gets on *my* nerves when she behaves like a Stella. But I can't see her upsetting anybody enough to hit her on the head with a hammer.'

John said, 'I don't think they were after *either* of you. It's much more likely that it was a burglary gone wrong. Like I've been telling you all night, Siobhán probably came back and interrupted some scumbag ransacking your stuff. Or maybe she was home already and they broke in without realizing that there was anybody in.'

'But, John, there was no sign of forced entry – only that broken light bulb in the porch. And think about it. If Siobhán had come home and

198

found a burglar in the house, she would have challenged him, wouldn't she?'

'Well, either that, or tried to run away.'

'But if she had tried to run away, she would have headed for the front door, wouldn't she? And if she had challenged him, he would have started to hit her with his hammer when she was facing him, so she would have had defensive bruises on her hands and her arms.

'No – it looks to me as if the perpetrator walked into the living room while Siobhán's back was turned and hit her before she even knew that he was there. She didn't struggle, she didn't turn around. She never even saw who hit her.'

'And that's why you think he mistook her for you?'

'Yes, I do. If her back was turned, he didn't see *her* face any more than she saw his. Siobhán and I are both around the same height. We both have red hair, even if they are different shades. She wasn't wearing those huge hoop earrings like she usually does. If the perpetrator was a hired hit man, he might never have seen me in person, and he could have been relying on somebody's description.'

John sat down. Katie sat down next to him and he took hold of her hands. 'So, go on. Who do you think could have ordered a hit on you?' he asked her.

'Mother of God, John – it could have been any number of people. There's this Lithuanian lowlife, Evaldas Rauba. He's threatened me two or three times. I put his brother behind bars last year for smuggling in air pistols that had been converted to shoot nine-millimetre rounds – complete with silencers. Rauba stopped me in the street and said he was going to cut off my head and piss down my neck.'

John grimaced. 'You know some real charmers, don't you?'

Katie said, 'The only thing that doesn't really fit is why Rauba should send anybody to kill me with a hammer. Those Lithuanians have more guns than we do.'

'And why would a hit man take the time to write on your wall? "GOD SAYS KEEP AWAY!" I mean, what's all that about? God says keep away from what? God says keep away from the Lithuanians? And where does God come into it, anyhow?'

Katie suddenly had a mental picture of Monsignor Kelly, and the hard-eyed way in which he had stared at her before he returned to the football match at Sunday's Well.

No, she thought. *He's an arrogant, sanctimonious, devious little bastard, but I can't believe that he would actually pay somebody to kill me. Not one of the vicars general.*

Even so, Monsignor Kelly had given her the strong impression that he had a secret that he was desperate to hide. Was it so devastating that it was worth him breaking the First Commandment to protect it? It was unthinkable, but all the same she had to think it.

A plump, freckly nurse came bustling into the visitors' room and said, 'Katie? Katie Maguire? You can come and see your sister now.'

They followed her along the corridor and into the lift.

'She's not awake yet?' asked Katie, as they rose up to the fourth floor.

'Not yet, no. But her vital signs are good. Pulse, respiration, blood pressure. She'll be going for another CT scan this afternoon.'

She led them into Siobhán's room, which had a view towards the airport and the countryside beyond. Thick clouds were resting on the hilltops as if a dirty grey quilt had been laid on top of them, and it was just beginning to rain. The only sounds in the room were the hissing of Siobhán's oxygen and the *meep-meep-meep* of her heart monitor, and the pattering of rain against the window.

Siobhán's head was bandaged. Both of her eyes were swollen and crimson, as if she had been punched in the face. Katie pulled up a chair and sat down next to her, taking hold of her hand.

'Oh, Siobhán, you poor baby. Who could have done this to you?'

John cleared his throat and said, 'With any luck she might be able to tell us herself, when she wakes up.'

'*When* she wakes up. But who knows when that's going to be? I want to find the gowl right now.'

John was silent for a moment, but then he said, 'Maybe this isn't the right moment to bring this up, darling, but I do have to make some travel plans, and I have to make them real soon.'

Katie wasn't really listening and she didn't answer. John waited, and then he added, 'I also have to give the letting agency a definite decision on the apartment we'll be renting. Later today, if possible. It's directly opposite Russian Hill Park,

201

but I've beaten them down to a very reasonable price, only two thousand three hundred a month.'

He paused again, but when Katie still didn't answer him he said, 'I guess you could always join me later, if you still have unfinished business here in Cork.'

Katie turned around. Unshaven, with his hair all messed up, he looked even more macho and attractive than ever, as if he had been in a fight, and conclusively won.

'When were you thinking of actually going?' she asked him.

'End of next month. Even that's pushing it. My friends want me to start working for them a.s.a.p. I was hoping you might be able to persuade An Garda Síochána to waive your period of notice.'

'The end of next month? But that's only, what, six weeks away! I can't leave Siobhán until she's better, can I? And I'm certainly not going until I catch whoever it was who hurt her.'

'Of course. I understand.'

Katie stood up and put her arms around his waist. 'John ... I love you. I want to be with you more than anything else in the world. You know that.'

He nodded and kissed her on the forehead, but there was something distracted in the way he did it, as if he was already beginning to accept that they could never be together.

'Listen,' he said, 'why don't I take you to Jury's and buy you a decent breakfast?'

'I couldn't eat it, John. I'm sorry. I'll stay here with Siobhán for now and maybe we can meet up for lunch.'

'Okay,' he said, and kissed her again, on the lips this time, but it was more like a goodbye kiss.

She was still sitting beside Siobhán's bed when her mobile phone rang. It was Detective O'Donovan, calling from Anglesea Street.

'Sorry to hear about your sister, ma'am. How is she?'

'Serious but stable, thanks, Patrick. She still hasn't regained consciousness, so it's early days yet.'

'Well, we'll be saying a prayer for her so. You think they were after attacking you, rather than her?'

'I think they could well have been, yes. There must be at least a dozen villains who would pay good money to see me laid out.'

Detective O'Donovan said, 'The reason I'm calling is I got back the first of Father Heaney's notebooks, translated. I should have the other two by the middle of next week.'

'That was quick. Who did it?'

'Stephen Keenan, he's one of the Latin teachers from the Presentation Brothers College. He owed me a favour, like, so he said that he'd do it for free.'

'A Latin teacher owed you a favour?'

'It's a long story, but it involved one of his sons and a small quantity of illegal vegetation. I said I'd turn a blind eye.'

'All right. So tell me about this notebook.'

'I haven't read it all, like. But you'd think that Father Heaney was on the illegal vegetation, too. He keeps on about talking to angels, and sending messages to heaven, and how to communicate with God.'

'But that's what priests do all the time, isn't it? They communicate with God by praying.'

'Well, that's right, but when you pray it's only hit or miss if you get an answer back, isn't it? You can pray and pray until you're black in the face, but you never know if God's listening to you or not, do you? I mean, He may be listening to you, but when He hears what it is you're asking Him for, He could be saying, "Fat chance of that, boy."'

Katie was beginning to get a headache, and she rubbed her forehead with her fingertips. 'I'm not sure I understand what you're saying, Patrick. What's so different about the way that Father Heaney communicated with God?'

'Like I said, I haven't read all of it yet, and there's still two more books to come. But he keeps on talking about meeting God in person. Actually *seeing* Him, face to face. He says that there's a link between earth and heaven, a physical link, and there's a way to open it up. *"We can hear His voice with our own ears, and touch His hand with ours. The truth is that God is real."'*

Katie said, 'I think you're right, Patrick – he must have been smoking something. I mean, why should a priest need physical evidence that God is real? I thought priests had faith. Otherwise they couldn't be priests, could they?'

'Makes you wonder, though, doesn't it, like? What if God *is* real, like really real, and not just imaginary real?'

'Don't start getting all metaphysical on me, Patrick. I haven't slept all night. If you can make me another copy of that translation, I'll come into the office later today and pick it up.'

'Right you are, ma'am. But I'll tell you something else that Father Heaney says. He says, *"To call on God, we have to use the language that they speak in heaven, and call on him with the voices of angels."*'

'And that means what, exactly?'

'Feck knows, to tell you the truth.'

Twenty-six

John called just after eleven. He sounded as if he was walking along a busy street. He told her that he would have to cancel lunch because he had to show a prospective buyer around the farm, but he could meet her early in the evening.

'Okay,' she said. 'I'm not hungry anyway.'

'How's Siobhán?' he asked her.

'No better, but no worse. I haven't upset you, have I?'

'No, honey, of course not. But we do need to talk.'

'Yes,' she said. They both knew what they had to discuss.

She sat beside Siobhán until the hospital porters came to take her away for another CT scan. By the time she left the hospital it had stopped raining, but the sky was still grey and oppressive and she felt like a character in some depressing black and white art movie. She drove back to the

205

office, feeling exhausted and jittery from too much coffee.

She took off her raincoat and sat down to check her emails. She had only just switched on her computer when Detective O'Donovan knocked at her office door, holding up a copy of Father Heaney's translated journal.

'Here's the book, ma'am,' he said. 'And we've made some progress with the van, too, the one that Mrs Rooney saw by Grindell's farm.'

'Have we found it?'

'No, not yet, but...' he took a memory stick out of his breast pocket and held it up '...it was caught on CCTV at six twenty-seven that morning driving northwards out of the city centre, up Summerhill. That's less than an hour before Mrs Rooney saw the fellow in the dunce's cap dumping Father Heaney's body in the river.

'After that, it was seen at eight forty-seven going around the Magic Roundabout and then heading away up towards the airport.'

'Is that the last time it was sighted?' Katie asked him. 'It could be anywhere at all by now.'

'It depends on the route it took,' said Detective O'Donovan. 'It could have been driven on back roads all the way to Galway and not passed another camera all the way. But if it belonged to the same perpetrator who killed Father Quinlan, I doubt he took it very far. He might have abandoned it, of course, but if he did we'll most likely find it sooner rather than later.'

Katie said, 'Ask the airport police to check their car parks, just in case he left it there. What about the number plate, or anything else that might help us to identify it? Father Lenihan mentioned that Brendan Doody's van had lettering on the side, painted over.'

Detective O'Donovan pushed the memory stick into Katie's computer, and a CCTV picture appeared on her screen. A grimy black Renault van, with a white question mark stuck or painted on to its offside rear window.

'For sure, that must be the same van that nearly ran the postie off the road up at Ballyhooly. I checked the number plate, but it belonged to a ninety-three Ford Fiesta that was scrapped two years ago. I don't know if the question mark means anything. Maybe it means nothing at all, but I'm checking any trademarks that might have a question mark at the end of them.'

'Okay,' said Katie. 'Any luck with the harp wire yet?'

'Not so far, ma'am. We've checked every music shop in the city, and talked to the leaders of both orchestras, but not a sausage. Detective Horgan's gone off this afternoon to call on every harpist that he's been able to find, professional or semi-professional, about five of them, and a couple of amateurs, too. To be frank with you, though, I'm not too optimistic that we're going to find out where it came from.'

At that moment, Katie's phone rang. She picked it up and a voice said, 'Is that Detective Superintendent Maguire I'm speaking to?'

'It is, yes.'

'This is Garda Ronan Kerr from Cobh Garda station. You called us earlier this morning, yes, about an Irish setter called Barney? Well, he's just this minute turned up. A member of the public found him wandering around by the Heritage Centre and has brought him in to us.'

'Thank God. He's not hurt at all?'

'Not at all. He's soaking wet, like, and he's muddy, and he's starving hungry, but apart from that he's one hundred per cent.'

'Bless you,' said Katie, and put down the receiver. Detective O'Donovan said, 'Everything all right, ma'am?'

'Yes,' she said, 'everything's grand.' She was glad in a way that he was there, and that she had to keep her composure, because otherwise she would have burst into tears. *It's only tiredness,* she told herself, but she knew in her heart that it was much more than that.

She was gathering up her keys and her mobile phone, ready to go home, when there was another knock at her office door. To her surprise it was Dr Collins, with her hair pinned up unusually tidily, and wearing a double-breasted suit of green herringbone tweed.

'Detective superintendent, I'm so glad I caught you! I wanted to show you this in person.'

'Have you finished your post mortem on Father Quinlan?'

'Ugh, yes. Father Quinlan *and* his rat. It was a common brown rat, *Rattus norvegicus,* about a year old, and it was carrying both Weil's disease and salmonella. I would guess that it was caught in a sewage outlet, or possibly a cemetery. Not many people appreciate how many rats there are in cemeteries.'

'What was Father Quinlan's cause of death?'

'Oh, strangulation, no question, the same as Father Heaney.' She opened her briefcase and took out a clear plastic envelope marked EVIDENCE. Coiled inside the envelope was the thin, silky cord that had been tied so tightly around Father Quinlan's neck, purple and blue braided together.

'Before he was strangled, however, he was tortured in a similar way to the heretics who were tortured by the Spanish Inquisition. *Strappado*, they called it. His hands were tied behind his back and then he was lifted up clear of the ground. By all accounts *strappado* is by far the most painful form of torture there is. The Nazis used it in their concentration camps and the North Vietnamese used it, too, in the Hanoi Hilton.

'Father Quinlan was also given a merciless beating. *Merciless*. Five of his ribs were broken, as well as his collarbone and almost all of the bones in his fingers and his toes. I don't know what he did to deserve such punishment, but somebody really wanted him to go through hell.

'Next, of course, he was castrated with the *castratori*. Finally, the rat was forced into his body cavity, and sewn up so that it couldn't escape except by gnawing its way out through his intestines. I still can't be sure if he was garrotted before or after this was done. I hope for his sake that it was before. I would have had to see the crime scene, and how much blood he lost.'

Katie held up the clear plastic envelope with the cord in it. 'Have you found out what this is?'

'Yes, I have, which is why I wanted you to see it

for yourself. Again, it was my musical lab assistant who identified it for me. It came from a bassoon, apparently.'

'A *bassoon?*'

'That's right. He said that when they make the reeds for a bassoon, they often tie a knot around them, for decoration. It's called a Turk's head knot, because it looks like a turban, and this is the string they use – nylon string coated in beeswax.'

'So Father Heaney and Father Quinlan were strangled with two types of string from two types of musical instrument?'

'That's correct. Almost identical MO, but distinctly different garrottes.'

Katie sat down. 'Jesus. What's he going to use next time? Catgut, from a violin?'

'Let's pray that there won't *be* a next time.'

'Don't be sure about that,' said Katie. 'I have a very bad feeling that this fellow is only just getting started.'

Dr Collins said, 'I'm afraid I can't help you very much when it comes to tracking him down. The bassoon cord is distinctive, yes. So is the harp wire. But there was nothing else on Father Quinlan's body to identify his assailant – or *assailants* plural, since you say that there was probably more than one of them. No saliva, no blood, no hairs, no epithelials. No idiosyncratic bruises, such as might have been caused by a ring or a bracelet or a wristwatch. Nothing.'

'This is what convinces me that he's going to kill another priest,' Katie told her. 'He's on a crusade, yes, but his crusade isn't completed, and that's why he's being so careful not to leave any trace of

210

himself. He might not care if we catch him eventually. He might even *want* to be captured, in the end. Most crusading killers have a need to tell the world why they did it. But he doesn't want us to stop him yet.'

'I'll be re-examining both bodies tomorrow,' said Dr Collins. 'I've called Dr Reidy and told him that I won't be returning to Dublin for a day or two at least.'

'Well, if you can come up with any physical evidence at all.'

Katie picked up her keys again. Dr Collins hesitated for a moment, biting her lip, and then she said, 'You're finished for the day, then?'

'Yes. I don't know whether you heard but my sister was attacked and they've got her in intensive care. I was up all night and I really could do with some sleep.'

'Oh, I'm so sorry. What happened?'

Briefly, Katie told her how Siobhán had been assaulted. Dr Collins shook her head and said, 'Terrible, that's terrible. That's a terrible thing to happen. Terrible.'

'I'll see you again tomorrow, then?' said Katie.

'Look, well, under the circumstances – what with your sister and all – this is probably inappropriate,' said Dr Collins. 'But I'm all on my own here in Cork, and you have nobody to go home to, and I was wondering if I could buy you dinner this evening.'

Katie didn't know what to say. She could sense at once that this wasn't a casual invitation. This wasn't going to be two law-enforcement professionals sitting down over bacon and cabbage and

211

a glass of wine to discuss the technical ins and outs of a complicated case. This was supposed to open the door to something much more intimate. Dr Collins's cheeks were flushed, and she was biting her lip again, and she was staring unblinkingly at Katie as if she was willing her to say yes, but sure that she was going to say no.

Katie remembered being given a similar stare by Sister Bridget, at school, after Sister Bridget had asked her if she would like to have extra tuition in algebra, one to one, in the privacy of Sister Bridget's room.

Katie dropped her keys and her mobile phone into her bag. 'Thanks for the invitation, doctor, but I have to go all the way to Cobh Garda station to collect my dog, and then I have to go home and make sure that my house is locked up securely, and then, believe me, I'll be fit for nothing but crawling into my pit and dropping off before I have time to say my prayers.'

For some reason, she didn't mention that she would probably be meeting her lover, too. That would have sounded as if she were aware that Dr Collins was making a pass at her, and perhaps, after all, she was wrong, and she wasn't. Perhaps she was simply lonely and wanted somebody to talk to, instead of eating her dinner on her own.

'That's all right,' Dr Collins flustered. 'Perhaps we can do it some other time. Tomorrow evening, or the evening after. I just wanted you to know that what you've achieved here – well, you've really impressed me. It shows that a woman *can* make it to the top, even in a man's world like the guards. And a very attractive woman, too.'

212

Katie switched off her desk lamp, so that Dr Collins was standing in silhouette against the window. 'Thank you, doctor. Goodnight.'

Twenty-seven

John called her shortly before 9 p.m.

'I'm sorry, Katie. I'm tied up on the internet with Bob and Carl in San Francisco, and it looks like I'm not going to be finished till way after midnight. There's so much we still have to do to get this business up and running.'

'Okay. Don't worry. I'm really tired anyway.'

'I'll see you tomorrow, though, for definite. Maybe for lunch, if you can spare the time. I love you.'

'I love you, too,' she told him. A framed photograph of him stood on the telephone table, and she reached out and touched his lips with her fingertips. He was smiling in this photograph, but she hadn't noticed before now that he seemed to be looking over her shoulder, not directly at her, his attention caught by something far behind her.

She put down the phone and returned to the kitchen. She had been making herself a Gubbeen cheese sandwich with the intention of taking it to bed and watching television for an hour or two, but all of a sudden she wasn't hungry any more and she didn't feel so tired. Barney was asleep in his basket in the utility room, wuffling to himself. When she had brought him home she had given

213

him a bath and fed him and made a fuss of him, but he had still followed her from room to room in case she was thinking of deserting him again.

She undressed and showered and put on her long white linen nightdress, the one that John said made her look like a ghost. 'If you came into my bedroom in the middle of the night wearing that nightdress and going *Wooooooo,* I think I'd crap myself.'

To relax herself, she played the *Elements* CD from St Joseph's Orphanage Choir, very softly. Those sweet, high voices reminded her that life wasn't all torture and stranglings and hammer attacks. Not only that, she thought it was both apt and uplifting that this sacred music had been recorded by children from the same orphanage where Father Quinlan had been found hanging. It was almost as if they were trying to offer him comfort, to sing him on his way to heaven.

She opened her laptop and quickly read through the two post mortem reports that Dr Collins had sent her. Both of them were lengthy and highly technical, a list of almost every fracture and contusion in the medical lexicon. Some of the injuries she hadn't been aware of until now. Before he was castrated, Father Heaney had apparently been sodomized with a tightly rolled-up newspaper – a fact that Dr Collins had been able to establish because the lining of his rectum had not only been torn but stained with soybean oil, which was used as a solvent for newspaper ink, as well as carbon black, cadmium yellow and other natural pigments that were used to print colour photographs.

Katie had intended to make herself a cup of tea, but instead she went over to her drinks table and poured herself a large vodka. *Mother of God,* she thought, *revenge is one thing, but this is out and out sadism.* Each trauma that Dr Collins had listed was even more cruel than the one before, and she could only think that the perpetrator was either a psychopath or a demon. Demons, however, existed only in legends, and in the Bible.

She took a large swallow of vodka, and shuddered, the way that demons are supposed to shudder when they hear the name of God.

One thing of which she was increasingly sure, although she still had no evidence to back it up: Brendan Doody wasn't the man they were looking for. For some reason, Monsignor Kelly had tried very hard to convince her that he was the murderer. But there had been nothing in Brendan Doody's way of life that suggested a character so inventively cruel. He had painted fences for people, mowed their lawns and weeded their gardens; and there had been nothing in his shabby lodgings to suggest that there lived a man who was obsessed with inflicting agony on others.

It was 10.30 p.m. now, and she called the hospital to see if there was any news of Siobhán. 'Still the same, I'm afraid,' the nurse in the ITU unit told her. 'Unconscious, but stable. Mr Hahq will be coming to see her again at nine tomorrow morning.'

She went back to her laptop. Now she searched the internet for all kinds of pointed hats, to see if they could give her any clue to the identity of the man who had dragged Father Heaney into the

Blackwater River. Some of the earliest pointed hats had been found on mummies from the Iron Age, around 800 BC – *'Terrifically tall, conical hats, just like those we depict on witches riding broomsticks at Halloween or on medieval wizards intent on their magical spells.'*

Apart from the traditional dunce's cap, there was the *hennin* worn by French noblewomen in the fifteenth century – the archetypal pointed hats seen in fairy-tale illustrations of maidens imprisoned in castles. Then there was the *capuchon* worn during the Mardi Gras celebrations in Louisiana, the *Spitzhut* found in Bavaria, and the black sugarloaf hat favoured by witches. But it was the *capirote* that interested Katie the most. This was a cardboard cone worn by religious flagellants in Spain, often with a mask attached to cover the face. During the Spanish Inquisition, accused heretics would be forced to wear one during their public humiliation, their torture, and their eventual execution.

Katie thought: *What could have been more like the Spanish Inquisition than the way in which Father Heaney and Father Quinlan were murdered?*

It seemed almost certain that the murderer was taking revenge on molesting priests, but Katie couldn't help feeling that there was very much more to it than that. She had never found it easy to persuade boys to admit that they had been sexually abused by a member of the clergy: many of them simply wanted to forget that it had ever happened. But nearly as often, some of them still regarded the priest who had abused them with respect and affection.

216

'Suppose you're an adolescent boy,' the psychology lecturer at the police college at Templemore had once told them. 'Suppose you've been deprived of love and affection for your entire life, beaten and abused and neglected by your drunken, ignorant parents. Then suppose that a smiling friendly priest feeds you Mars bars and shows you photographs of naked women, and lovingly masturbates you. Would that really be your idea of hell?'

Katie googled for news reports about protests against abusive priests and came up with hundreds of thousands of results, although most of the reports related to America, and the archdiocese of Philadelphia in particular. But when she checked a story from the *Cork Examiner*, dated 29 April 2003, she came across a story headlined BISHOP URGED TO NAME MOLESTING PRIESTS.

She remembered the protest, although it had been mostly peaceful and no arrests had been made. She had been plain Detective Garda Maguire at the time. About thirty victims of child molestation had paraded along Redemption Road, nearly all of them disguised to conceal their identities. They had demanded that Bishop Kerrigan should publicly release the names of eleven Cork priests who were suspected of having abused the children in their care, both boys and girls.

There was a photograph taken as the protestors gathered outside the diocese offices. On the front steps, accepting a petition from the leader of the protest, was Monsignor Kelly himself, with an oddly glazed look in his eyes. He was surrounded

217

by five or six other clergy, all much bigger than him. They looked more like his bodyguard than his companions in the cloth. It was raining, and one of them was holding an enormous umbrella over his head.

The leader of the protest was Paul McKeown, director of the Cork Survivors' Society, which had been established to give psychiatric counselling to young men and women who had been abused by priests when they were younger. Out of everybody on the march, he alone wore no mask. He was tall, with dark curly hair, but his face was turned away from the camera, so Katie couldn't see clearly what he looked like.

Behind him, the rest of the protestors wore scarves or balaclavas or pale, expressionless masks. At the very back, however, Katie saw five protestors wearing pointed white hats, with white cloth flaps covering their faces. Any one of them could have matched the description that Mrs Rooney had given them. *Just like the dunce's cap they used to make us wear in high babies, whenever we got our sums wrong.*

But now she noticed something much more in the photograph. Some way behind the protestors in the pointed hats, two vehicles were parked. One was an old maroon Honda Accord, and the other was a black van. On the rear doors of the van, two white question marks had been painted, one on each door.

The van was at least fifty feet away, and it was out of focus, so it was difficult for Katie to make out its number plate. It was also difficult to see whether the question marks really were question marks. Although they were clearer than the single question mark on the back of the van that had been picked up on CCTV, they appeared to have been smudged or decorated in some way.

She picked up the phone and called Detective O'Donovan. 'Patrick? You're not in bed yet?'

'I'm watching the League of Ireland live. Galway United versus Sligo Rovers.'

'Well, I'm sorry to interrupt you, but in just a minute I'm going to be emailing you a photograph. It's a picture of a protest that was held in April 2003 by the victims of sex abuse by priests. Some of the protestors are wearing pointy hats like the man that Mrs Rooney saw in the Blackwater river. But there's also a black van in the background and it looks very similar to the van we've been trying to locate. I want you to get on to the picture desk at the *Examiner* and see if they can't dig up an original copy of that picture, so that you can send it to the photography unit at Phoenix Park and have them enhance it for us.'

'I see,' said Detective O'Donovan. He sounded deeply dispirited. 'Okay, then.'

'What's the score?' asked Katie. She could hear the roaring of the football crowd in the background.

'Galway three, Sligo nil.'

'I'm sorry.'

'So am I, ma'am. I support the Bit o' Red.'

Twenty-eight

Gerry O'Dwyer set the alarm of his music shop, stepped out of the front door and locked it. Maylor Street was almost deserted except for a group of young people on the corner, shuffling and shouting and smoking cigarettes. Gerry checked his watch as he walked toward Patrick Street. It was 11.07 p.m. He hadn't meant to stay so late, but his accountant was expecting his annual returns first thing tomorrow morning. She was off on holiday to Lanzarote next week and if she didn't complete his tax return by Monday then she wouldn't be able to complete it for two weeks, and he would have to pay a penalty.

Gerry thought how ironic it was that he had to hurry to hand her his accounts when he couldn't afford even a weekend's bed and breakfast break in Kerry for himself and Maureen. But with the Irish economy the way it was now, people were buying food and paying off their credit-card bills rather than spending their money on musical instruments. Almost every day one of his customers came into the Mighty Minstrel trying to sell him back one of the guitars or fiddles that they had bought from him when times had been prosperous. There was a saying in the Irish music trade that when you're buying it, it's a fiddle, but when you're selling it, it's a violin.

Gerry was a big man. At the Presentation

Brothers College he had been a star rugby player, and after he had taken holy orders he had coached the rugby team at St Joseph's. These days, however, he felt and looked worn down, both by time and circumstance. His thick curly hair was grey now, and his broken nose made him look more like a down-and-out boxer than a powerful second-row forward. His shoulders were rounded inside his shabby green tweed coat, and he shambled rather than strode.

He would never have admitted it, even to Maureen, but he felt that God had turned His back on him, even after he had given God everything, and more.

As he reached the corner of Patrick Street, a man came out of the doorway of Brown Thomas, the department store, and walked towards him at a sharp diagonal.

'Got a light there?' the man asked him, holding up a cigarette. He was thin, with a large narrow nose. He wore a black leather jacket, and he had silvery, slicked-back hair that gleamed in the street lights.

'Sure.' Gerry stopped, and reached into his pocket for his lighter. He didn't smoke himself, but there were plenty of times when he needed a naked flame for melting sealing wax and glue and burning through catgut. He flicked it alight and the man leaned forward with his cigarette between his lips, cupping his hands around Gerry's in a way that Gerry found almost too intimate.

The man blew smoke out of the corner of his mouth and said, 'Thanks.' Then he cocked his head to one side like an inquisitive spaniel and

221

said, 'I reck you, don't I?'

'You might well do,' Gerry told him. 'Were you ever at Pres?'

'Pres? Me? Too slow for a school like that, boy. I used to think the Straits of Gibraltar was called the Straits of Gibraltar because they wasn't gay.'

'Maybe you've seen me in my shop. The Mighty Minstrel.'

'That's the musical instrument shop? No, I was never in there – not musical, me – so it wouldn't have been in there that I saw you.'

'In that case, I really don't know. Now, you'll forgive me, I have to be getting along. I'm late enough as it is.'

'Hold on,' the man told him, lifting his cigarette hand. 'I can see you wearing a dog collar. That's it! I can clearly remember you dressed up like a priest. Now, would that be right, like? Was you ever a Father Whatever-your-name-is?'

'A priest? No. Never.'

The man shook his head. He had a sly grin on his face that Gerry didn't like at all, and he was still breathing smoke out of his nostrils from the last drag that he had taken of his cigarette. He could have easily passed as a demon.

'That is very peculiar,' he said. 'I could have sworn blind that you was once a priest that I used to know. He looked the spit of you, so he did, only twenty years younger. Same wonky snoz. Same sideways look in his eye, like he was hiding something inside of him he didn't want you to catch sight of, know what I mean?'

'No, I don't. And I really have to go.'

'Come on, I got it right here on the tip of my

222

licker. Father O'Grady, was it? No, not Father O'Grady. Father O'Gallagher, that sounds more like it. Father O'Gallagher!' The man paused, frowning, and took another drag on his cigarette. 'No – wait, that wasn't it either. It was – hold on – it was Father O'Gara! That's it, Father O'Gara! That's who you're the spit of! Father O'Gara, from St Joseph's!'

Gerry said nothing, but stepped to one side and started to walk away.

'Father O'Gara!' the man whooped after him, and his voice echoed around the near-deserted shopping street. 'That's who you are! I dare you to deny it! In front of God, I dare you to deny it!'

Gerry had crossed the pedestrianized side of the street but now he stopped at the kerb and turned around. 'You listen to me, my friend! I don't know what you think you're playing at, but my name is O'Dwyer and I was never a priest. Now do us both a favour and hop off, would you?'

Unabashed, the man came stalking after him, stiff-legged, still grinning. 'And what will you do if I don't, Father O'Gara? Call for the schickalony? They could check your fingerprints, couldn't they, and prove who you are?'

Gerry said, 'Get the hell away from me, before I do something to you that I'd regret.'

But the man came even nearer, and leaned forward, and stared up at him with triumphantly widened eyes. 'You mean like all of them other things that you regret, Father O'Gara? Like all them poor sobbing boys at St Joseph's? Oh, the tears that stained those pillows, Father, not to mention everything else they got stained with.'

'I never did that!' Gerry barked at him. 'I never once did that!'

'So you admit who you are!' the man retorted. 'You admit that you're Father O'Gara!'

Gerry pushed him square in the chest with both hands, and although he no longer possessed the strength of a rugby forward, the man toppled backwards on to the pavement, his legs flying up in the air. His cigarette rolled into the gutter in a shower of sparks.

'Right!' the man spat. He rolled over on to his side and climbed back on to his feet, panting with anger and effort. 'Right! That is fecking it! I'm telling you, that is fecking *it!* I claim ya!'

He came towards Gerry with both fists raised in a puny imitation of an old-style bare-knuckle pugilist. Gerry said, 'Don't even think about it. I could eat you for breakfast. Now will you hop off like I told you to?'

But the man kept edging closer and closer, jabbing at the air and snorting and saying, 'Come on, boy, come on!' Gerry lifted his hands and backed away from him. 'I'm not going to fight you, you gowl. Go home and sober yourself up.'

'What are you frightened of, Father? Frightened that somebody knows who you really are? O'Dwyer, my skinny arse. You're Father O'Gara from St Joseph's and you have hell to pay.'

Gerry kept on backing slowly away, both hands defensively lifted. He was so preoccupied with this prancing, jabbing idiot that he didn't hear the van that started up its engine and pulled away from the kerb less than two hundred feet off to his right. It accelerated towards him without any headlights, and he became aware of it only at the moment when he stepped backwards into the road.

He tried to leap back on to the pavement, but the man in the black leather jacket took two brisk steps towards him and pushed him in the chest, in the same way that Gerry had pushed him. The man didn't have much weight behind him, but he caught Gerry off balance.

Gerry stumbled and swayed, both arms whirling, trying to stop himself from falling over. He was too late: the van hit him with a deafening bang. It was going no faster than twenty miles an hour, but that was enough to send him tumbling across the street, over and over and over, until he hit a litter bin and came to a stop, his face bloody, his arms and legs awkwardly bent in a swastika pattern.

He lay with his cheek against the concrete, staring at the leg of the litter bin. He was still conscious, but the world was dark around the edges, and growing darker. He wasn't at all sure what had happened to him. His body felt as it had once felt when a rugby scrum had collapsed on top of him and he had been trampled by the boots of half a dozen of his fellow players as they tried to disentangle themselves.

He could see his left hand lying on the pavement and he tried to move it, but it didn't seem to be connected to his brain. He wasn't at all sure that his legs were still attached to his body. He wondered if he would ever be able to walk again.

A girl's voice said, 'Can you hear me? You're not

225

dead, are you?'

He tried to look up. All he could see was a pair of red wedge sandals and two skinny legs in tight black jeans.

Another girl's voice said, 'He's not dead, Mar, look. His eyes are moving. I'll call for an ambulance.'

There was a moment's pause. He heard feet scuffling on the pavement and several people talking, but he couldn't make out clearly what they were saying. The only distinct voice was that of a woman who kept repeating, 'You shouldn't move him. They teach you that in the Guides. You shouldn't move him. He might have broken his neck, like. Or ruptured his spleen or something.'

But then a man's voice said, 'It's all right. We'll take him to the Mercy ourselves. It'll be much quicker than calling for an ambulance.'

Gerry thought the man's voice sounded very melodious and soothing, almost like a mother calming her children, or an angel consoling a widower at his wife's deathbed.

'You shouldn't move him,' the woman repeated. 'He could be paralysed for life if you move him. I mean his legs look all wrong, don't they? All bent the wrong way, like.'

'Don't you worry, love. I'm a trained first-aider. St John's Ambulance, every weekend at Páirc Uí Chaoimh. The sooner we get him into A and E the better, believe me.'

'I still think you shouldn't move him.'

The world was growing even darker, but Gerry was aware that three or four pairs of hands were taking hold of him, and that he was being lifted up. He felt as if his insides had been crushed and that all of his bones were grating together. Logically, he knew that he should be in terrible pain, but perhaps the pain was so unbearable that his brain refused to acknowledge it.

He looked up and saw the street lights jiggling as he was carried across the road. The men who were carrying him stopped for a few seconds, and he heard two metal doors creak open. Then he was lifted into the back of a van and dropped on to what felt and smelt like a pile of empty sacks.

He tried to speak – tried to say, *'Where are you taking me?'* but all that came out of his throat was a breathy squeak, like the sound of a blocked nostril. The van doors were slammed shut, and almost immediately the van was started up and driven away. The driver didn't show any consideration for his injured passenger either. He drove fast and jerkily, and whenever he took a corner, Gerry slid from one side of the vehicle to the other, colliding with the wheel wells. He tried to cling on to the sacks, but they slid across the floor, too.

After five minutes of bouncing and jouncing, he realized in a fragmentary way that he wasn't being driven to the Mercy, because the Mercy was only round the corner from Patrick Street, where the van had hit him. They must be driving uphill, because the sacks were gradually creeping toward the van's rear doors, and he could hear that the driver had changed down to third.

Uphill meant north, away from the city centre. Uphill meant that he wasn't being taken to hospital at all, because the nearest hospital anywhere in this direction was in Mallow, which was over twenty miles away.

The van drove into a pothole, and then another, and Gerry was jolted violently up and down, banging the back of his head against the floor. It was then that the pain first hit him, and it was a pain like nothing he had ever experienced in his life. It felt as if he had been pushed alive between the rollers of a crematorium's bone crusher, and that he was being dragged into it, feet first.

The pain rose inexorably up his legs, into his groin, and then it overwhelmed his chest so that he found it impossible to breathe, let alone cry out for help. He blacked out for a few seconds, but then he regained consciousness, and all he could feel was icy-cold agony. He could never have believed that such pain was possible. His legs hurt, his pelvis felt as if it had been cracked in two like a broken washbasin, and his ribs were digging into his lungs. Even his teeth hurt, right down to the roots.

He saw black and red flickering in front of his eyes, and he passed out again, but again he came to, and the pain was still there, only even more unbearable.

O dear God, I beg you to save me from this. O dear God, please turn around and see me. I was only trying to please you, my beloved Lord. Please don't keep your back turned against me.

But the van kept on whining its way relentlessly up the hill, and the pain grew worse with every beat of Gerry's heart and every bump in the road surface. It was so intense, the pain, that it was

228

almost audible, like a high, terrible scream that was just beyond the range of human hearing.

The van slewed round noisily on what sounded like shingle; and then it stopped. Gerry lay on the sacks with his eyes closed, praying to be lifted out of there, but terrified that he was going to be manhandled, and hurt even more.

The rear doors were opened with a double bang, and somebody climbed up inside the van and knelt down next to him.

'How're you feeling, Father?' said the same sweet conciliatory voice that he had heard when he was lying stunned on the pavement in Patrick Street.

He managed to open one eye. All he could see was a dark blurry figure bent over him, wearing a pointed hood that completely covered its face, except for two ghostly eyeholes.

'I apologize if you feel battered and bruised, Father,' the figure told him. 'Unfortunately we had to snatch you quick, and that was the best possible way. Otherwise you would have kicked up all kinds of a fuss, right there in the street, and you're a big strong fellow still.'

'Doctor,' Gerry whispered. He felt a warm tear sliding out of the side of his one open eye. 'Please, get me a doctor.'

'All in good time,' said the figure in the pointed hat. 'There's plenty of other things we have to do first.'

'It hurts ... so much. I can't bear it.'

'What did you say yourself, Father? "Christ bore unimaginable pain on the cross to save our souls. The least we can do is return the favour."'

'I'll do anything,' Gerry pleaded with him. 'Just get me to a doctor. Please.'

'Well, like, the straight answer to that is no. Come on, lads, he's ready for shifting here! Carry him into the house, if you will, but make sure you carry him gentle. We don't want to be accused of being unfeeling, do we?'

'No!' said Gerry. 'Please just call for an ambulance. I won't tell them anything. I swear to God that I won't tell them what you did.'

'You swore to God that you weren't Father O'Gara. How do you expect me to trust your word now?'

'I promise on my wife's life. I promise on my daughter's life.'

'Oh, you've made all kinds of promises, haven't you, Father? "I promise you that this will be the making of you, young fellow." That was the favourite, along with "I promise you that this won't hurt you a bit."'

'Don't touch me, please. Don't try to move me. Just let me lie here till the ambulance arrives. Please.'

'In that case, you're going to have a fierce long wait, Father, because I'll not be calling for an ambulance. Not now, not later. Not tomorrow morning. Not ever. Look at you. Even when you were wearing the cloth you always thought you were such a sham-feen, didn't you? Such a hard man. Now look at you, whimpering like a baby.'

Gerry said nothing. He had just been deafened and blinded by a tidal wave of pain, and he couldn't think of anything else.

The man in the pointed hat shuffled to the rear of the van and jumped down on to the shingle. 'I'll be seeing you later, Father. Maybe you won't be hurting so much by then. Okay, lads. Take him away.'

Twenty-nine

Katie slept badly. She dreamed that an intruder had broken into the house and was hiding in another room, but she didn't know which one. In her dream, she stood in the corridor, perfectly still, holding her breath, but the intruder must have been holding his breath, too, because she couldn't hear him.

'Who's there?' she said, trying to sound authoritative. 'Whoever you are, you'd best be showing yourself, with your hands on top of your head.'

No answer. Perhaps she was mistaken and there was no intruder after all. But she didn't dare to go back to bed, in case he came rushing into her bedroom when she was asleep and attacked her with his hammer.

Her alarm woke her just before 6 a.m. She climbed out of bed and shuffled into the bathroom, and stood under the shower for over five minutes with her eyes closed. Afterwards, she stared into the steamed-up mirror over the washbasin as if she didn't recognize the face that was staring back at her. Her wet hair was plastered over her shoulders and her breasts like a merrow,

231

a voluptuous Irish mermaid.

Mary, Mother of God, she thought, *why does my life have to be such a mess?* She was tempted to ring up Chief Superintendent Dermot O'Driscoll and tell him that she was resigning, as of now; and then calling John to say that she would definitely come with him to San Francisco, whether he found her a job with Pinkerton's or not. She felt so exhausted. She felt so weighed down. She may have looked like a merrow, but a merrow who had to drag the whole of Cork City behind her in a net, with all of its chancers and drug dealers and pimps and political wheeler-dealers, while the love of her life sailed blithely away to the other side of the ocean.

She dressed in an oatmeal-coloured sweater and dark brown trousers. Then she went into the kitchen and made herself a mug of black coffee. She stood by the kitchen sink to drink it, looking out over her small back garden. The sky was grey and it was raining. The stone statuette of the Virgin that stood in the middle of the rockery had a drip on the end of her nose.

Her phone rang. It was Detective O'Donovan.

'Morning, ma'am. I got hold of that photograph from the *Examiner.* Tim O'Leary, the night editor, dug it out of the files for me. I'll be taking it around to the technical boys as soon as I can.'

'Thanks, Patrick. I'm going to the hospital now to see my sister but I should be in around 9.30.'

'Well, we're all praying that she gets better real quick. We'll probably get the forensics back later today – not that your man left us much in the way of physical evidence. Only that felt-tip marker and a couple of partials on the living-room door, but in truth they could be anybody's.'

'I'll see you later, Patrick. Thanks for your prayers.'

'They work sometimes, ma'am. I've had first-hand evidence, like.'

'You must tell me about it some time. I'm beginning to think that God's on His holliers.'

When Katie reached the intensive care unit, she found that Siobhán was still unconscious. She looked waxy and pale underneath her oxygen mask, but the nurse reassured Katie that her vital signs were stable, and her blood pressure had risen during the course of the night.

'After Mr Hahq has been to see her, we'll be sending her downstairs for another CT scan, just to make sure that there's been no more bleeding, among other things.'

Katie took hold of Siobhán's hand, and squeezed it. 'Come on, Siobhán. Remember that Sleeping Beauty game we used to play, when one of us would pretend to be asleep and the other one had to find a way to wake her up? You only had to tickle me and that was enough, but *you* – I could pour a cup of cold water over your face and you wouldn't even twitch.'

She paused, and the rain pattered against the window.

'We're not playing Sleeping Beauty now, Siobhán. We're all grown-up now, and we can't pretend any more, not about anything. Please wake up, darling. Please open your eyes. I know you want to win the game, but playtime's over.'

233

She was still talking to Siobhán when Michael walked into the room. He was wearing a droopy khaki anorak and baggy jeans and he looked worn out.

'Michael,' she said.

Michael lifted one hand to show how helpless he felt. 'Look at the state of her la. She could have been killed.'

'When did you find out?'

'Yesterday evening. I was trying to call her all day and she didn't answer her moby so in the end I phoned her work.'

'You know how badly she's been injured?'

Michael nodded. 'The nurse said that she's going to pull through all right, but they don't know if she's going to turn out doolally. You know, on account of the brain injuries.'

Katie didn't know what to say. Michael approached Siobhán's bedside and gently laid his hand on her forehead.

'You know something, Katie?' he said. 'We should never of split up, Siobhán and me. You never know when you've got something truly precious, do you, until after you've lost it?'

'You have Nola now.'

Michael kept his hand on Siobhán's forehead. 'I know,' he said. 'You don't have to fecking remind me.'

On the way back to Anglesea Street, her mobile phone played *The Fields of Athenry*. It was Chief Superintendent O'Driscoll calling her. She flipped her phone open and said, 'Chief? I'll be there in ten minutes.'

234

'Make it quicker if you like. I think we might have another dead priest on our hands. Well, he's not dead yet, not that we know of, but he's missing, and we've half a dozen witnesses who saw him run over right in the middle of Pana by a black van with a question mark on the back of it, and then bundled inside and taken away.'

'When did this happen?'

'Yesterday evening, around eleven, but would you believe that nobody reported it until an hour ago? All of the witnesses thought that the van was taking him off to the Mercy, but when one of them went to the A and E this morning to check if he was still living and breathing, she was told that he had never arrived there.

'We called Mallow General and Bantry General and St Anthony's Hospital in Dunmanway, but he wasn't taken to any of those, either – not that it was very likely that he would have been.'

'All right,' said Katie. 'I've just reached the Magic Roundabout. I'll be with you as quick as I can.'

She found Chief Superintendent O'Driscoll in the interview room, talking to a pale woman with close-together eyes and a dreary wing of grey hair down one side of her face, like a pigeon run over in the road. Inspector Liam Fennessy was standing by the window, cleaning his circular spectacles with his necktie, looking more like a young James Joyce than ever, while Detective Sergeant Jimmy O'Rourke was sitting close beside the woman, with a sympathetic hand on the shoulder of her rusty-red hand-knitted jumper.

Detective Horgan was leaning against the far wall, one hand cupped against his face to mask the fact that he was picking his nose.

'Ah, Katie,' said Chief Superintendent O'Driscoll. 'This is Mrs Maureen O'Dwyer. It was her husband, Gerry O'Dwyer, who was knocked down on Patrick Street last night and apparently abducted by the fellows who knocked him down.'

Katie pulled out a chair and sat down opposite Mrs O'Dwyer. 'We know it was him for sure?' she asked.

Without turning around, Liam Fennessy said, 'Two of the witnesses identified him, ma'am. He runs the Mighty Minstrel music store on Maylor Street.'

'Yes, I know the Mighty Minstrel, of course. And I think I know *him*, by sight anyway. But why should anybody want to knock him down and then abduct him?'

Mrs O'Dwyer looked across at Katie with red-rimmed eyes. 'We were married seven and a half years. He's a good man, like, but he isn't easy. He always says that his conscience is following around after him like a dog with the rabies, just waiting for the chance to jump on him and take a bite out of his neck.'

'His conscience? Why, what has he done to feel guilty about?'

'I've just been telling your man here. He wasn't always Gerry O'Dwyer. Before that, and a few years before he met me, he was Father Gerry O'Gara.'

'He used to be a priest?'

Mrs O'Dwyer nodded. 'He was one of the

236

priests they investigated at St Joseph's Orphanage for messing with the children. They never proved anything against Gerry, and none of the children ever pointed the finger and said that he'd been molesting them. He swore blind to me that he never did anything of a sexual nature with those boys. But all the same he felt the shame of being accused of it terrible hard, so he said, and he gave up the priesthood and changed his name and tried to start a new life.'

Liam Fennessy replaced his glasses and said, 'There you have it. A third priest suspected of molestation, whether he actually did it or not. Let's just hope for his sake that he hasn't been taken by the same perpetrators as Father Heaney and Father Quinlan.'

'You'll find him, though, won't you?' asked Maureen O'Dwyer, twisting her wedding ring round and round. 'You won't let them hurt him? He's such a good man.'

Sergeant O'Rourke said, 'We have gardaí out looking for him everywhere, Maureen, and we've sent a description of the van they took him in to every Garda station in Kerry and Limerick and Tipperary and Waterford. It's quite distinctive, that van. Sooner or later somebody's going to spot it. All you can do now is go home and pray. The good Lord will help you to get through this, I can promise you.'

Katie called a young female garda to come into the interview room and help Mrs O'Dwyer out of the building. When Mrs O'Dwyer had gone, Katie turned around and said, 'This backs up something I was saying to Dr Collins. It's almost like this perpetrator *wants* to be caught. Not just yet, but eventually, when he's finished punishing all of those priests that he believes deserve punishment. He could have used a different van but he wanted us to know that it was him. Or *them,* however many perpetrators there are.'

'He could have just sent us a text,' said Detective Horgan. 'Hallo, this is the Serial Scrotum Snipper, at it again. And the code word is "Ouch".'

Katie gave him a sharp, tight-lipped look to show that she was distinctly unamused. But she recognized that he might be on to something. 'I get the feeling that he could be using this particular van because it has some special significance ... something that he couldn't suggest to us if he were only sending us text messages. Like, this question mark painted on the back ... what does that mean?'

Liam Fennessy shrugged and pulled a face. 'It could mean anything at all or nothing at all. It could simply mean, "Who the feck am I and why am I doing this?" Or it could mean, "I'm keeping you eejits guessing, aren't I?"'

Chief Superintendent O'Driscoll looked at his watch. 'Whatever it means, we're going to have to take some serious steps forward with this investigation, and make them real quick. Katie – I've arranged a media conference for 14.30 and I need some ideas on what we're going to say to them. We'll have to be very diplomatic, like. There's a lot of people out there who think that any priest who molested the children in his care actually *deserves* to be mangled and have his mebs cut off.'

238

'Well, me included,' said Detective Horgan. 'In fact, I think they should do it publicly in Emmet Place and charge admission. And sell popcorn, too.'

Thirty

Gerry awoke to excruciating pain and the ethereal sound of somebody singing. Of course he recognized the song. It was *'The Rose of Allendale'*, a wistful ballad about a traveller separated from the woman he loves. But the singing was extraordinary – high and resonant, as if it were being sung in an echo chamber, with grace notes that were held for what sounded like minutes on end.

> *My life has been a wilderness*
> *Unblessed by fortune's gale*
> *Had fate not linked my love to her*
> *The Rose of Allendale.*

He didn't hear any more – *couldn't*, because he was suddenly swamped with such black, intense pain that it blotted out everything – his hearing, his sight, even his ability to think. He was aware of nothing except the sensation that every bone in his body had been fractured or broken or crushed, and that all of his internal organs had been ripped away from their moorings – his liver, his spleen, his stomach and his kidneys – and that

239

they were chafing and bumping against each other like dinghies in a stormy harbour, all tangled up in the fraying netting of his nerves.

For over five minutes he was unable to cry out, unable to do anything but shudder and snort and gasp. Gradually, however, the pain ebbed away, even though every breath hurt so much that it ended with a little mewl.

Whoever was singing, they had now reached the final chorus, and they drew out the very last note as if they couldn't bear for the song to end. Then there was silence, except for a door slamming and the sound of a car engine starting up.

'*God, please, God, please save me,*' Gerry whispered. He opened his eyes and tried to focus on the room around him, although everything was blurry. He was lying on the bare diamond-shaped springs of a single bed that creaked and scrunged as he tried to turn himself over. The room around him looked like the bedroom of a derelict cottage. A single small window was hazy with dust and spiders' webs, and outside he could see only the green leaves of an overgrown hydrangea, nodding repeatedly in the breeze.

The walls were papered with pale green chrysanthemum patterns, but the damp had stained most of the opposite wall with dark brown blotches, and on every other wall the paper was bellying out or peeling off altogether. The floor was covered with cheap pale carpet, but it was so filthy and spotted with mould that it was impossible to tell what colour it had been when it was first laid.

'Please, God,' Gerry repeated, but he was so sure that God was ignoring him that he could almost picture His turned-away shoulder and the back of His flowing white hair. Gerry was convinced that God could hear him, but was refusing to answer. Instead, he appealed to Jesus.

'O Lord Jesus Christ, most merciful, Lord of Earth, I ask that you receive this child into your arms, as Thou hast told us with infinite compassion.'

He didn't know if it was possible to administer the last rites to himself. After all, he was no longer a priest, but there was no other priest there. He closed his eyes and tried to imagine making the sign of the cross on his forehead with holy oil. 'By this sign thou art anointed with the grace of the atonement of Jesus Christ and thou art absolved of all past error and freed to take your place in the world He has prepared for us.'

As he mumbled out the last words of his absolution he became aware that somebody had very quietly eased themselves into the room and was standing very close beside him – leaning over him, in fact, listening to him.

He opened his eyes and saw that it was the man in the pointed hat and the face mask, the same man who had spoken to him in the back of the van.

'Please,' Gerry begged him. 'Would you get me to a hospital?'

'Oh – you think that all of your heinous sins are forgiven and forgotten, do you, Father O'Gara? I'm deeply sorry about that, but they're not at all – not by me and the lads, anyhow.'

'Please call for an ambulance. I can't bear this pain even a minute longer.'

241

'No such luck,' the man retorted. Gerry thought that his voice was oddly gruff, almost like a child pretending to be a grown-up. 'We've brought you here for a reason, Father. We've brought you here to show you that everything you do in life has a consequence, sooner or later, and that there's no getting away with acts of evil.'

'Who are you? Do I *know* you? What have I ever done to you?'

'Oh, you *know* me right enough, just as well as I know you. But you don't need to know my given name. I call myself the Grey Mullet Man these days, after those greedy fish in the River Lee that have such an insatiable appetite for raw sewage, because that's what you are, you and your holy brothers. The raw sewage of life. The pieces of shit that passeth all understanding.'

The man leaned even closer, so that Gerry could hear that he was whistling slightly through one nostril.

'Do you know what my grandpa used to say to me about the grey mullet? The best way to cook them is to boil them in a pan with herbs and spices and an old running shoe. After half an hour, you empty the pan, throw away the mullet and eat the running shoe.'

He stood up straight, and walked around to the other side of the bed, where there was a 1960s-style kitchen chair, with cream tubular legs and a pale blue vinyl seat. Gerry could see a two-litre Diet Coke bottle standing on the chair, although it was filled up with some clear liquid, not Coke. There were some other objects, too, that he couldn't make out clearly without turning his head, and his neck hurt too much for that.

'Me, I'm exactly like the grey mullet because when I've finished feeding on all of that sewage I won't be worth saving because I'll be too fecking polluted, through and through. My very flesh will stink of you and your sins. But I was polluted a long, long time ago, wasn't I, Father? I was ruined body and soul before I had a chance to find out who I was or what it was I wanted out of life.

'Maybe, just *maybe*, I would have chosen to be what you and your brothers wanted me to be. However, I fecking doubt it. In fact, I fecking know I wouldn't. But you never gave me the choice, did you?'

'God makes our choices, not us,' Gerry whispered.

'What? What did you say? You're trying to blame *God* now, are you, Father O'Gara? That is very peculiar, if you don't mind my saying so, because I don't remember seeing Himself in the room when you were doing what you did to me, giving you the celestial thumbs up.'

'I did nothing wrong,' said Gerry. The pain was returning and his voice rustled like a ghost, or a sheet of paper tossed across the road by the wind. 'I promise you, I meant only the best for you.'

'No, you never did. You meant only the best for yourself and that fecking Bishop Kerrigan. You wanted glory, Father O'Gara, all of yez did. Glory glory fecking hallay-*loo*-yah!'

'For the love of Christ, get me to a hospital,' Gerry wept.

'Oh, no,' said the Grey Mullet Man. 'This is where you confess to your sins and beg forgive-

243

ness from *me,* not from God.'

'I'm not asking forgiveness from God,' said Gerry. He paused for two painful breaths, and then he added, 'God doesn't listen to me anyway.'

'Why am I not surprised?' said the Grey Mullet Man. He took two black nylon cable handcuffs out of his pocket and came over to the side of the bed.

'Okay,' he said, 'we're going to sit you up now.'

'No!' Gerry whined at him. 'Please – no! I'm all smashed up inside. You'll kill me.'

'Well, Father, that's a risk we'll just have to take, I'm afraid.'

'No! Please, God, no!'

But the Grey Mullet Man took hold of Gerry's thick brown sweater by the shoulders and heaved him up into a sitting position. Gerry screamed, a long shrill scream of absolute agony. He could feel his bones crunching inside his body and his broken ribs digging into his lungs.

'Come along, Father,' the Grey Mullet Man urged him. 'This is nothing at all. You just wait till you see what I have in store for you next!'

Gerry was in too much pain to scream again but as the Grey Mullet Man began to drag him up the bed, two or three inches at a time, each time he shifted him Gerry let out a thin, quavering howl.

'Forgotten what a grand singer you are, Father,' said the Grey Mullet Man. He tugged and shuffled Gerry into a sitting position with his back to the bars of the bed's iron headboard. Then he took hold of one hand at a time and fastened his wrists to the bars with the nylon cable handcuffs.

244

By now, Gerry had passed out. His eyes were closed and his chin was resting on his chest, and there was a thin dribble of bloody saliva sliding from his lower lip. The Grey Mullet Man shook his shoulder and said, 'Father O'Gara? Father O'Gara, can you hear me? Oh – Father O'*Gaaaaa*ra!'

Gerry's eyelids flickered but he didn't respond. The Grey Mullet Man stood back and looked at him without trying to rouse him any further. Then he reached up and slowly drew off his pointed hat and the face mask that was attached to it. At the same time, the sun shone brightly through the hazy little window on the other side of the room and illuminated his face, almost as if it had been arranged as a stage direction.

His hair was straw-coloured, curly and coarse. His face was rounded, and his cheeks were plump, with a faint red flush on them. His eyes were small, but intensely blue. He had a blob of a nose and pouting lips.

Mrs Rooney, who had seen him dragging Father Heaney through the shallows of the Blackwater, had been right. He did look like a cherub. In fact, Father Machin had always compared him with the left-hand cherub in Rosso Fiorentino's sixteenth-century painting of two cherubs reading a book at the feet of the Madonna.

If he hadn't been so tall and so heavily built, he could have looked sweet and harmless. But for a man of his height and bulk to have such a cherubic face was strangely threatening, especially since he was frowning at Gerry like a vexed two-year-old.

245

He picked up the Diet Coke bottle from the kitchen chair and unscrewed the cap. He sniffed it, and puckered up his nose. He had always hated the smell of vinegar. It reminded him of the orphanage, and the pickled eggs that they used to serve at teatime, especially on St Paddy's Day, when they dyed them green. He used to sit alone in the dining hall until it grew dark, refusing to eat his pickled egg, and forbidden to leave the table until he did.

Sometimes he could persuade himself that his abiding hatred of the priesthood came from those pickled eggs, even more than what had happened to him later.

It was over an hour before Gerry regained consciousness. By the time he did, the sun had been swallowed up by low grey cloud and the bedroom was so dark that he didn't realize at first that the Grey Mullet Man was standing in the corner in his pointed hat and his mask, quite motionless, watching him.

'Ah, you're awake,' said the Grey Mullet Man, in a curiously high-pitched voice, but then he cleared his throat and added, 'You wouldn't have wanted to miss what I'm going to be doing to you next. Well, fair play, perhaps you would, but I wouldn't have wanted you to.'

Gerry tried to moisten his lips, but his tongue was as dry as a slug on a garden path. 'I don't know why you don't just strangle me, whoever you are, and have done with it.'

The Grey Mullet Man stepped out of the corner and came up to the side of the bed. 'Because justice has to be served, Father O'Gara. People so often misunderstand the Bible, don't they, when it tells us eye for eye, tooth for tooth, hand for hand, foot for foot. It simply means that the punishment should equal the crime. Not revenge for its own sake, but fairness. No more than what's deserved – but on the other hand no less either, and that "no less" – that's critical.'

He paused for breath, because he had started to pant. 'You put me through the fires of hell, Father. You put me through the very flames of Hades. And that's what I'm going to do to you.'

'In that case, may God forgive you.'

'Oh, He probably won't. I don't expect Him to. But to tell you the truth, Father, I'm long past caring, because what you and your holy brothers did to me was far worse than anything that Our Lord could ever have done, or ever can.'

He picked up the Diet Coke bottle and unscrewed the cap. He held it close to Gerry's nose and said, 'Smell that? Home-made napalm. Five indigestion tablets dissolved in ten teaspoons of vinegar and topped up with rubbing alcohol.'

Gerry looked up at him with swollen eyes and a terrible feeling of dread.

'You're really going to do this, aren't you?' he said. His ribs and his pelvis were hurting so much that he tried to shift his position, but he could feel his fractured bones grate together and he had to stay absolutely still for a few seconds while his brain tried to cope with the pain. 'There's nothing at all I can say to change your mind?'

Just then the bedroom door opened and two more men came in – one of them wearing a tall

247

hat like a bishop's mitre and the other wearing a chalk-white mask like a pierrot. They approached the other side of the bed and stood beside it with their arms folded. They smelled of cigarette smoke.

'Sorry we took so long, like,' said the man in the pierrot mask, in a muffled, cardboardy voice. 'The traffic on the South Ring was shite.'

'Just pleased to see that you didn't start without us,' added the man in the mitre.

'Oh, there's no way I would have done that, boy,' the Grey Mullet Man assured him. 'This is your day just as much as mine.'

He tipped up the Diet Coke bottle and filled up the palm of his left hand with a large blob of glistening, pungent gel. This he slowly rubbed into Gerry's scalp, like a hairdresser applying conditioner. Gerry snorted and tried to twist his head away, but again the tendons in his neck gave him a stab of pain, and the Grey Mullet Man was too strong for him.

The gel smelled strongly of vinegar, and as the Grey Mullet Man massaged it into his scalp, it felt chilly, too.

'I'm pleading with you,' he whispered. 'I'm pleading with you not to do this. Whatever you want me to say – whatever you want me to confess to – I will admit to it, I swear on the Holy Bible.'

'How can you confess, Father, when you're so sure that you never did anything wrong?'

'Because we did *not* believe – we never *once* thought – that what we were doing – was wrong. Not in any way at all. We devoutly believed – that we were giving you boys – the greatest gift that

248

one man can possibly bestow – on another.'

The pain of saying so much made Gerry's eyes fill with tears, which poured down his cheeks until they were shining.

'Would you look at him, for feck's sake?' said the man in the pierrot mask, shaking his head. 'I never thought I'd ever get to see Father O'Gorilla cry like a fecking babby.'

The Grey Mullet man took out a box of extra-long matches. He shook it in front of Gerry's face and said, 'You hear them matches chuckling, Father? Ask not for whom them matches chuckle. They chuckle for thee.'

Gerry stared at him with wet, reddened eyes. '*No,*' he mouthed, soundlessly.

The Grey Mullet Man took out a match and struck it. When it flared into life, he held it up for a moment. Gerry stared at it, and then closed his eyes, as if his closing his eyes could extinguish it.

The Grey Mullet Man said, 'I light this candle in memory of all the lost boys at St Joseph's Orphanage – of all the happy futures that were never to be – of all the terrible pain and humiliation they suffered. Most of all, I light it in the sure and certain knowledge that what they went through will never happen to another boy, ever. Amen.'

'Amen,' echoed the man in the bishop's mitre and the man in the white pierrot mask, and the Grey Mullet Man touched the burning match to the top of Gerry's head.

Instantly, with a sharp crackling noise, Gerry's hair burst into flame. For the first few seconds, he couldn't feel anything at all, but the fire burned fast and fierce, with flames leaping up more than two feet above his head, and as soon as all his hair was shrivelled, and the blazing gel began to burn his bare scalp, he let out a screech that made the man in the pierrot mask clamp his hands to the sides of his head.

Wearing a crown of living flames, Gerry threw himself wildly from side to side, so that the bed frame screeched and groaned in protest and its feet danced a frantic rumba on the floor. But the thin black nylon straps that were holding Gerry up against the bedhead were unbreakable, and in the end there was nothing he could do but sit absolutely rigid, his teeth gritted, his face contorted with agony, his fists clenched, while the fire flared up higher and then eventually died down.

After three or four minutes, the last flames licked at his blackened, bloody scalp, and then slunk off into oblivion. Gerry's head slumped forward. He was unconscious again from shock, and his whole body was quaking as if he were freezing cold. Acrid smoke rose lazily up towards the ceiling and then got caught in a draft and shuddered away.

The man in the bishop's mitre crossed himself. 'Well,' he asked, 'do you think he saw hell?'

'Only a glimpse of it, I'd say,' said the Grey Mullet Man. He screwed the top back on to the Diet Coke bottle and placed it back on the chair. 'But don't worry, he'll soon find out what it's really like, the same way that all of us did.'

Thirty-one

Katie's cappuccino had gone cold but she drank it anyway, tugging a tissue out of the box on her desk to wipe her mouth. She had just picked up her phone to call the hospital when John knocked at her office door. He was wearing his brown leather bomber jacket and a green and white check shirt and he had just had a haircut, so he looked five years younger.

'*Katie,*' he said, giving her that quick, cautious smile.

'John! Hi, darling. You've caught me right in the middle, I'm afraid.'

'No time for lunch, then?'

'We have a media conference at 2.30 and I'm trying to make some progress in this priest-killing case, so that we have something newsworthy to tell them.'

John came into the room and stood beside her desk. 'Hey – why sweat it?'

'What do you mean?'

'All you have to do is tell the press that you're investigating some extremely promising new leads, and that you're only a few days away from making an arrest, and that you'll get back to them as soon as you've had a late lunch at the Clarion with the man you love and maybe a half-hour's hanky-panky in a room upstairs.'

Katie gave him a mock-exasperated look. 'I

251

can't do that, because I *don't* have any extremely promising new leads, and because I seriously *do* have to make some progress. Nobody's supposed to know this yet, but another priest has gone missing – well, *ex*-priest – and we're seriously concerned that the same thing is going to happen to him – that's if it hasn't happened already.'

'You mean...?' John lifted two fingers and snipped them in a scissors gesture.

Katie nodded. 'And likely even worse, if what they did to Father Quinlan is anything to go by.'

'Jesus.'

Katie stood up and came around her desk and put her arms around John's waist. 'Listen,' she said, much more quietly, 'you don't know how sorry I am that all of this has blown up now.'

He kissed her – once, twice, three times. 'Come on, sweetheart. You have your job to do, I know that. Most important, though, how's your sister?'

'Still the same, the last time I saw her. I was just about to call and find out.'

He held her close. 'I'm really sorry I was so pushy when I came to the hospital. I guess I'm afraid that I'm going to go out to San Francisco and that you're never going to follow me. It's like every day a new reason comes up why you won't be able to.'

He hesitated, and then he said, 'What I was going to tell you today was that I really have to go as soon as possible. I can't even wait until the end of next month. The guys are screaming for me to get out there and organize all the online sales distribution.'

'Then you should go.'

He looked down at her, looked intently into her eyes. 'I don't want to go unless I'm one hundred per cent sure that you're going to be following me, once your sister recovers and once you've wrapped this case up. I don't want to go out there and discover that I'm never going to see you again.'

Katie pressed her head close against his chest – so close that she could feel his heart beating through his soft cotton shirt. When she breathed in she could smell cinnamon and oak aftershave, and just *him*. She couldn't find any truthful words to say to him, because she knew that, right at this moment, she couldn't promise on the Holy Bible that she *would* follow him to San Francisco; but she also knew that he couldn't possibly afford to stay here in Ireland.

'You know the old saying,' she told him. 'The test of the heart is trouble.'

At that moment, Detective O'Donovan appeared in the open doorway. He cleared his throat to announce his arrival, and John and Katie separated.

He held up a USB stick. 'Sorry to interrupt you, ma'am, but the photography boys in Phoenix Park just sent me this and I think you need to see it urgent-like.'

'Of course,' said Katie. She tilted her head up to give John a kiss. 'I'll talk to you later this evening, okay? Maybe we can manage to get together for a drink and something to eat.'

John said nothing, but gripped her hand tightly for a moment, and then left.

'Sorry, ma'am,' Detective O'Donovan repeated.

'No, you're all right. Let's have a look at what you've got there.'

Detective O'Donovan went across to Katie's computer with its wide-screen monitor and plugged in the memory stick. Instantly the black and white newspaper photograph of the Cork Survivors' Society demonstration appeared on the screen. There was Monsignor Kelly standing on the steps of the diocese building under that monstrous black umbrella, surrounded by his heavyweight priests, and there was Paul McKeown from the CSS confronting him, and the motley crowd of masked and hooded protestors gathered behind him, like refugees from a travelling carnival.

'This is a print taken from the original negative,' said Detective O'Donovan. 'The background's out of focus, like, but they used that Kneson Imagener software and you won't believe what they were able to bring up. Amazing.'

He clicked the mouse and the photograph jumped into sharp focus. He clicked the mouse a second time and the screen was filled with a close-up of the black van with the two question marks on the back doors. There was lettering on the van's side panel, too, and Katie could read it quite clearly.

'Get everybody in here,' she said. 'I want the whole team to see this. And Chief Superintendent O'Driscoll, too, if he's back from lunch.'

Within five minutes, Inspector Fennessy and Sergeant O'Rourke and Detective Horgan and three other detective gardaí had crowded into Katie's office.

'This has to stay strictly under wraps until I say

so,' Katie cautioned them. 'Before we tell anyone at all, I need to go and talk to Monsignor Kelly again.'

Sergeant O'Rourke went up close to the monitor and peered at it with a concentrated frown. After a while he turned around and said, 'These question marks on the back doors of that van, they're not question marks at all, are they? They're like those shepherd's crook things that bishops tote around with them.'

'You're right,' said Inspector Fennessy. 'Croziers, that's what they are. Two bishop's croziers.'

'Exactly,' said Katie. 'And look what it says on the side of the van. *Diocese of Cork and Ross. Redemption Road, Cork*. And the telephone number.'

Sergeant O'Rourke was slowly shaking his head from side to side. 'So this fecking van that this priest killer's been driving around in, and using for carting bodies around, it belongs to the church?'

'It obviously did at one time, anyhow,' said Katie.

'I can't say that I ever saw it around the city.'

'Well, you wouldn't really notice it unless you were looking for it specially,' Detective O'Donovan put in. 'They've blacked out the lettering on the side, and they've changed the number plate, but for some reason they never got around to painting out more than one of the two croziers.'

'Maybe they ran out of paint,' suggested Detective Horgan.

Sergeant O'Rourke said, 'Maybe they did. Stupider things have happened. You remember that fellow who killed a horse and cut off its legs so that it would fit into the back seat of his car and drove along Grand Parade with its head sticking out of the window? "He's like a dog, see, he likes the wind in his face," that's what he said when we stopped him.'

'So, what's the plan of action now?' asked Inspector Fennessy.

'A visit to Redemption Road, I think, don't you?' said Katie. 'Let's get right back to the root of this. Liam – I'd like you to come with me. I think I'm going to need your calculating mind.'

Katie wanted to catch Monsignor Kelly by surprise, so she drove to Redemption Road without calling his secretary first to make an appointment. A hard rain was rattling down and she and Inspector Fennessy ran across the car park outside the diocesan buildings with their collars turned up. They bounded up the stairs to Monsignor Kelly's office, and Katie gave a single sharp knock on his secretary's door before they walked straight in.

Monsignor Kelly's secretary was a washed-out looking nun with a pointy, pink-tinged nose. She had a half-finished chicken sandwich on her desk but her mouth was so small that Katie wondered how she managed to get any words out, let alone eat anything.

Katie held up her badge. 'Detective Superintendent Maguire. I'd like to see the monsignor, please.'

'Oh, I see. Oh. I don't know,' flustered the nun, and her nose blushed even pinker. 'Is the monsignor expecting you?'

'No,' said Katie.

The nun looked across at the open diary on her desk and frowned very hard, as if frowning alone could magically fill up this afternoon's appointments.

'I'm afraid he's not available. Not just now, anyhow.'

Before she could protest, Katie came around her desk and peered over at the diary for herself. *Five p.m. Golf with Councillor Murphy at Fota, weather permitting.* That's all he's got written down here. And what's the time now? Only just half past twelve. He's got a full four and a half hours free to talk to us. And besides that, it's raining buckets, so weather is *not* permitting.'

'I'm sorry, superintendent. It's not written down here but just at the moment he's holding a media briefing.'

'A *media* briefing? A media briefing about what? He knows that he's not supposed to talk to the media about the case we're working on. Not without consulting me first.'

'I'm not sure at all what it's about,' said the nun. She was becoming increasingly agitated, and kept tapping her fingers softly on her desk, as if she were trying to convey a warning in Morse code to the man in the room behind her.

'Well, who does he have in there? The *Examiner?* RTÉ? I didn't see any TV vans parked outside.'

Katie made a move toward Monsignor Kelly's heavy oak door, but the nun sprang up from her desk and intercepted her before she could knock, grasping the door handle possessively.

'I'll see if he can spare you a few minutes,' she

257

said. She reminded Katie of those thin, bruised, browbeaten wives who panic whenever the gardaí ask them where their husbands are, and swear to God that they haven't seen them in weeks, even though they're hiding under the bed in the children's room, or crouching in the bottom of the airing cupboard with a fitted sheet over their heads.

'This is a murder inquiry,' Katie told her. 'The monsignor has to spare us as much time as we require.'

The nun said nothing, but rapped at the door. 'Monsignor Kelly,' she called, weakly. There was no reply, so she rapped a second time.

'Monsignor Kelly – Detective Superintendent Maguire is here. She says that she needs to see you!'

There was a long silence, but just before the nun could rap a third time, they heard the key turn very quietly in the door, and Monsignor Kelly say, *'Come!'*

The nun opened the door and they all stepped into Monsignor Kelly's office. It was deeply gloomy in there, because none of the lights had been switched on, not even the desk lamp, even though the sky outside the window was as dark as slate.

Monsignor Kelly was standing a little way behind his desk in what Katie thought was an oddly forced pose, partly defensive and partly aggressive, with his right hand on his hip, and his left hand brushing back his hair. He looked like a man who has stumbled while getting off a bus, and hasn't quite retained his balance and his dignity.

Besides Monsignor Kelly, however, there was

nobody else in the room – only the faintly saintly portrait of Bishop Kerrigan.

'Katie,' said Monsignor Kelly, trying to sound warm. He came forward and held out his hand. 'I would have appreciated it if you had made an appointment, you know. It would have helped me to give you all the attention you deserve.'

Katie thought, *I can read that teeth-clenching smile, monsignor. You think I deserve shite.* She looked around the office and said, 'So – where are the media?'

'Media?'

'The media. Your secretary here told us that you were holding a media briefing. By the way, this is Inspector Liam Fennessy. I don't think you've met him before.'

'Media briefing...' said Monsignor Kelly, his hand held over his mouth as if he didn't quite understand what the words meant.

But at that moment a side door next to the bookshelves opened up and Ciara Clare from the *Catholic Recorder* stepped out, with the sound of a toilet flushing behind her. When Katie had first met her up at Ballyhooly – on the morning they had found Father Heaney's body in the Black-water – Ciara Clare had been wearing a large grey poncho to conceal the size of her breasts. Today she was wearing a tight V-necked sweater, which dramatized her enormous bosom with broad red and purple stripes. She was also wearing a very short purple skirt and shiny purple stilettos. Her curly black hair was messily pinned up with barrettes and Katie noticed that her cranberry-coloured lipstick had been freshly applied. The

259

beauty spot on her upper lip was more noticeable than ever.

'Well, well,' said Katie. 'Nice to meet you again, Ciara. I'm guessing that Ms Clare here is the media that you've been briefing, monsignor?'

'A reporter from the *Catholic Recorder* comes once every week for a private press conference,' Monsignor Kelly snapped at her. 'After all, the *Recorder* is the only organ through which the diocese can speak directly to the public at large.'

Katie was tempted to make a sarcastic comment about organs, but held her tongue. Instead, she said, 'I need to ask you some questions about some new evidence that we've come up with, monsignor. If you don't mind, Ciara?'

Ciara Clare picked up a long purple cardigan from the back of a chair and said, in her distinctive lisp, 'I'll call you later, monsignor, if that's all right, so that you can finish giving me all the details about that church youth festival at Clonmacnoise.'

She said it in such a flat, tele-prompt way that Katie immediately knew that she was trying to give Monsignor Kelly an alibi. Katie would have bet money that he hadn't even *started* to tell her about the church youth festival at Clonmacnoise, or any other diocesan events, for that matter. She could *smell* it, and it was all cat's malogian.

'Please, take a seat,' said Monsignor Kelly, once Ciara Clare had left the room and closed the door behind her.

'This won't take long,' Katie told him. She opened her briefcase and took out a print of the CSS demonstration photograph.

Monsignor Kelly studied the photograph and then gave Katie another tight smile and shook his head. 'I remember that day, Katie. Not with any pleasure, I might tell you. The so-called survivors were extremely aggressive.'

'Well, maybe they had some justification, but that's beside the point. I'd like to know about this van parked in the car park.'

Monsignor Kelly studied the photograph again. 'Yes ... it's the van we used to use for all kinds of odd messages around the diocese. Shopping, or picking up clothing donations, for example. Or carrying sports equipment. Or taking furniture from one church to another. You know the kind of thing.'

'Do you know what happened to it?'

Monsignor Kelly narrowed his eyes. 'What *happened* to it? What are you suggesting? How should I know what happened to it?'

'It isn't still owned by the diocese, is it?'

'Well, no. As far as I know, we got rid of it about three or four years ago. We have a new van now, white. In fact, we have two of them. I presume this van was sold in part exchange.'

'Who would know for sure?'

'Well, Father Lowery would know. He's in charge of transport and logistics. But does it *matter* what happened to it?'

'Yes, it does, monsignor. It matters very much.'

'May I ask why?'

'I can't tell you just yet, I'm afraid. But I may come back to you about it. Is Father Lowery based here? The sooner we can talk to him the better.'

Monsignor Kelly clasped his hands together.

261

Katie was trying hard to read his expression, but all she could tell was that his mind was working at very high speed.

'Father Lowery *does* have an office here, yes, but I'm not at all sure that he's going to be here today. There's a charity car boot sale at St Michael's Church in Rathbarry and he's more than likely there. Besides ... I think that protocol demands that I inform the bishop first that you want to talk to him. The bishop is not at all happy about An Garda Síochána questioning his clergy at random.'

'There's nothing random about my questioning, monsignor,' said Katie. 'This is a major murder case and the only protocol that comes into it is the protocol of finding out who killed and castrated Father Heaney and Father Quinlan before he does it to anybody else.'

Monsignor Kelly gave her that teeth-clenching grin again. 'Very well. I'll talk to the bishop directly and then I'll call you if I may and tell you where you can find Father Lowery. I won't delay, I promise.'

Katie went for the door, with Inspector Fennessy following close behind her.

'By the way,' Monsignor Kelly called out, 'any news yet of Brendan Doody?'

'Nothing so far. If he *has* committed suicide, as he threatened in his letter, he's certainly done it somewhere that's very hard to find.'

'He'll be found one day, Katie,' said Monsignor Kelly. 'And on that day I'll be proved to have been right about him, you mark my words.'

Katie had opened the door and was looking at

the pink-nosed nun, who was sitting behind her desk with a look of extreme agitation on her face. *You poor girl,* she thought. *When we're gone you're really going to catch it because you didn't manage to turn us away.*

On the way back to Anglesea Street it stopped raining, although the streets were still wet enough to make their tyres sizzle.

'So, what do you think, Liam?' Katie asked Inspector Fennessy, as they crossed the river. The sun was shining so brightly from the surface of the water that she had to fold down her sun visor.

'I'm thinking that not everybody in the clergy appears to be taking much notice of Archbishop Diarmuid Martin,' said Inspector Fennessy, slyly. Katie knew what he was getting at. During a recent ordination ceremony in Dublin, Archbishop Diarmuid Martin had resoundingly reaffirmed the church's commitment to priestly celibacy.

'I suppose it depends on your definition of celibacy,' said Katie. 'I think we're probably talking Monica Lewinsky here rather than going the whole hog.'

'On the other hand, she may have been doing nothing more than using his facilities,' Inspector Fennessy put in, in a tone of voice that suggested that he didn't believe it for a moment.

Katie shook her head. 'Number one, his door was locked, which tells us that whatever the good monsignor was doing he didn't want to be interrupted. Why should he be worried about being interrupted if he was doing nothing more

263

than telling a reporter from the *Catholic Recorder* about a teenage festival in Clonmacnoise?

'Number two, Ciara Clare had freshened up her lipstick, which suggests that she might have been doing something to mess it up. There was no food or drink in the room, so she couldn't have smudged it on a cup or a sandwich.

'Number three, and I'll bet you didn't notice this, the buttons on the front of Monsignor Kelly's soutane were wrongly fastened, right in the middle. In his hurry to make himself decent, he had missed out one buttonhole.'

Inspector Fennessy let out a *'pfff!'* of amusement. 'So Monsignor Kelly is a dirty old vicar general. But where does that lead us to?'

'I'm not sure, but it tells us a lot about his character. And there's no doubt at all that there's something about this priest killing that he's very anxious for us not to know.'

'I think the van could be key to this,' said Inspector Fennessy. 'When you asked him what had happened to it, he was far too shifty. It's my guess that he knows exactly what happened to it and he was simply stonewalling us.'

'I'm with you there, Liam. I think I can go back to this media conference and tell them that we've found a critical new clue. Meanwhile, see if you can locate Father Lowery. He must have a mobile, or you could try phoning St Michael's. I don't want you involving the local gardaí. You know what will happen if you do, they'll get all over-excited and one of them will blab what we're up to. If you can't get hold of Father Lowery on the phone, you'll just have send some-

264

body down to Rathbarry. Jimmy O'Rourke maybe. It won't take him more than an hour.'

They reached headquarters and climbed out of Katie's car. As they walked across the car park, Inspector Fennessy said, 'How about giving details of the van's appearance to the press? It must be kept *somewhere* overnight, and somebody must have seen it.'

'Not yet,' Katie told him. 'Like I said before, I think the perpetrator has left that crozier where it is for a reason. I think he knows *we* know about it. But I don't want him panicking and painting it out, or dumping the van altogether. He's taunting us. But he still has unfinished business and he's going to make sure that we don't catch him until he's done.'

'So you're sure that he's going to kill more priests?'

'I'm convinced of it now. I can just *feel* it. And, let's face it, how many priests were investigated for child molestation in Cork alone? Eleven? Twelve? We could be talking about much more than serial killing here. We could be talking about a massacre.'

Thirty-two

Gerry was woken by the same ethereal singing that he had heard before, *'The Rose of Allendale'*. This time it sounded even higher than it had before, almost falsetto.

265

Though flowers decked the mountainside
And fragrance filled the vale
By far the sweetest flower there
Was the Rose of Allendale.

He was still lying on the bare diamond-patterned springs of that iron-framed single bed, and his wrists were still secured by nylon straps to the bedhead, but three or four heavy woollen blankets had been dumped on top of him. They smelled musty and damp, but he was shivering with shock and he was glad of them.

His scalp felt as if it was still on fire, though he knew that the flames had long since burned themselves out. What he didn't realize was that almost all of his hair had been frizzled off, except for a few scrubby clumps at the back, and that there were several patches on the left side of his head that had been seared right down to expose his skull. He had two small devil's horns made out of curled-up blackened skin, and the rest of his head was scarlet and glistening with fluid.

He couldn't believe that it was possible for a human being to suffer so much agony, let alone *him.* The pain went on, and on, and on, like some terrible relentless noise that keeps you awake for night after night, and he prayed for it to end as he had never prayed before. His lips moved, and he could hear his prayer in his head, but the only sound that actually came out of his mouth was a soft, monotonous growl.

'*O holy Father, please turn Your head around for once and see my pain and take pity on me. I know*

266

that I have transgressed and let You down. Please end this torture, and take me into Your arms. Please God, let it all be over. Please. Even if there is nothing beyond death but eternal silence and eternal darkness, please take pity on me and let me die.'

He was still praying when the Grey Mullet Man reappeared. *Oh Jesus,* he thought, *not more torture. Not more pain. Nothing could be worse than this.* He had never felt so frightened in his life. Underneath the blankets, he wet himself, copiously, and his warm urine pattered on to the floor.

The Grey Mullet Man loomed over him for a while, sucking his cotton mask in and out as he breathed, so that – tantalizingly – Gerry could almost make out his features.

'You were *praying,* Father,' he declared, at last. 'You were only fecking praying, weren't you?'

'I'm in hell,' Gerry whispered.

'Come back to me?' said the Grey Mullet Man, cupping one hand to his ear. 'You're, where are you?'

'I'm – in – *hell!'*

'You're in hell, are you? Well, well. Hell. No better than you deserve, Father O'Gara. The hell that you put others through, that was a never-*ending* hell – whereas yours at least will come to a swift conclusion. Not as swift as you might have been praying for, but a little too swift for me and my friends.'

Gerry gave two or three agonized gasps, and then he said, 'We genuinely believed ... we truly and honestly believed ... that we would see God.'

'I'm sure you did,' said the Grey Mullet Man, in a mock-pitying tone. 'But don't you get it? That's

267

what makes everything you did to us all the more contemptible. How does a man get to see God? How does *any* man get to see his maker? Through *redemption*, Father, that's how. Through selflessness, and through his own devotion. Not through the wilful sacrifice of others.'

'I'm sorry,' said Gerry.

'Oh! You're *sorry!* I'm sure you are now, like. But whenever I saw you in that music shop of yours – and, believe me, I looked in to see you more times than you will ever know, you never looked sorry then, not once. Smiling and laughing you were, not sorry.'

'What are you going to do to me now?' Gerry asked him. His voice was little more than a high-pitched wheeze.

'I tell you, boy, what we're going to do to you now, you're going to love it!'

'*What?*'

'Don't be an eejit. I only said that mockeyah. You won't enjoy it at all. But if you accept it as a justifiable penance, maybe that will help you to get through it.'

'Please don't hurt me any more.'

The Grey Mullet Man leaned even closer, and for one split second Gerry thought that he knew who he was. There was something very distinctive in the way he spoke, something in his accent and something in the way that he would mix Montenotte words like 'contemptible' and 'redemption' and 'justifiable penance' with Blackpool street slang like 'gutty boy' and 'mockeyah'.

He sounded to Gerry like somebody who had first been brought up in the roughest and poorest of homes, but had later been adopted by a family who were much more cultured and prosperous.

He had a name on the very edge of his consciousness. *I know who this is,* he thought. *I'm sure I know who this is.* He was about to say the name out loud when the Grey Mullet Man gripped the edge of the blankets that had been heaped on top of him and heaved them all on to the floor. Gerry was jolted on to his side, right on to his smashed-up ribcage, and he felt as if he was being simultaneously stabbed by a dozen mad assailants with kitchen knives. He forgot everything then. The name. The day of the week. His own name, even. He almost forgot that he was human.

The Grey Mullet Man said, 'What you took from us, Father, was far worse than taking our lives. You took *us* – you took who we were. I used to look in the mirror every morning and see a face, and the face looked like me, but it wasn't me. Not any more.'

Gerry was in too much pain to speak. He gritted his teeth and made a sound like *'gah-gah-gah-gah'!*

'Right – let's get on with it, shall we?' said the Grey Mullet Man. He whistled sharply between his teeth, and the other two men reappeared, the one with the bishop's mitre and the one with the pierrot mask.

'He's conscious at last,' the Grey Mullet Man informed them. 'Conscious enough, anyway. I wouldn't want to go to all of this trouble for him not to feel a thing.'

'Holy Mary, Mother of God, he looks like five and a half pounds of raw liver.'

269

'Don't you start feeling sorry for him. Just remember what he did.'

'I don't feel sorry for the bastard at all, believe me. If I could find a way to keep him suffering like this for the next thirty years, then I would.'

'Give us a hand here to take his trousers off. Jesus, look, he's pissed himself.'

The Grey Mullet Man unbuckled Gerry's brown leather belt and then pulled down the zip of his tan corduroy trousers, the crotch of which was dark and sodden with urine. The man in the pierrot mask tugged them down, over his thighs, over his knees, and wrestled them right off, over his feet. Meanwhile the man in the bishop's mitre pulled his dark brown sweater right up to his chest. He must have pressed on Gerry's broken ribs, because Gerry screamed out, *'Dear God almighty! Don't!'*

With a grimace, the man in the bishop's mitre took off Gerry's pale blue boxer shorts, which were heavily stained with dark brown. He held them up and swung them from side to side and said, 'Shit himself, too.'

'Well, there's revenge for you,' said the man in the pierrot mask. He leaned over Gerry and said, right in his face, 'You did the same to *me* once, didn't you, you bastard, when I was in catechism, and only seven years old? I was dropping and you wouldn't let me go to the jacks. I stunk so bad the whole class crowded over to the other side of the room and you had to send them out to the playground ten minutes early.'

'I know who you are,' Gerry croaked at him. *'I know who all of you are.'*

270

'You think so, Father O'Gara? Pity you'll never get the chance to tell anybody, isn't it?'

'I know who you are, but most of all the Lord God knows who you are, and you will join me in hell, believe me, all three of you.'

'Sez you.'

The Grey Mullet Man came back up to the side of the bed and he was holding up that two-litre Diet Coke bottle of clear shining jelly. He shook it and said, 'We gave your brain a bit of a frying the last time, didn't we, just so you'd know what we thought of you? But now it's time to get down to the real business. Eye for eye, tooth for tooth, and manhood for manhood. Yes, Father O'Gara. You were a priest yourself. You know all about manhood, and what it means when you're denied it, either by the will of God or the whim of a man.'

Gerry was beginning to fade out of consciousness again. The room appeared to grow darker and darker, and the Grey Mullet Man's voice began to echo. He felt as if he were inside a theatre, with the Grey Mullet Man playing the stage magician, his two masked cronies acting as his assistants, and himself as the volunteer from the audience who was going to be made to disappear, or sawn in half – or something unimaginably worse.

The Grey Mullet Man unscrewed the cap of the Diet Coke bottle and again filled up the palm of his left hand with quivering transparent gel. Gerry could smell the vinegar.

'No,' he said. 'Not again. Please.'

The Grey Mullet Man stood beside Gerry for what seemed like forever, although in reality it was probably less than thirty seconds. Nobody

271

spoke. All that Gerry could hear was the creaking of the bedsprings underneath him, and the tappity-tapping of the hydrangea against the window, and the dog-like panting of the Grey Mullet Man and his two companions behind their masks. He realized with dread why they were panting. They were excited.

'No,' said Gerry. But he was helpless, and when the Grey Mullet Man began to massage his flaccid penis with gel, he was incapable of anything but jerking his hips from side to side.

After the Grey Mullet Man had applied a thick, cold coating of gel on to Gerry's penis and pubic hair, he screwed the cap back on the Diet Coke bottle and wiped his hands on one of the blankets.

'There now,' he said. 'That is what I'd call a Roman candle. A *Holy* Roman candle.'

He took out his box of extra-long matches, opened it up, and struck one. It flared up, but it broke and dropped on to the carpet, and the Grey Mullet Man had to step on it to put it out, and take out another.

'No,' Gerry repeated, although he wasn't sure if he had managed to say it out loud. He closed his eyes tight, so that he wouldn't have to witness what was going to happen to him next. But he couldn't block out the scratching sound of the second match, or the spitting sound that followed. There was a few seconds' pause when he felt nothing at all, and he thought: *Thank God, maybe this isn't going to hurt at all.* But then a searing heat exploded between his legs, hotter than a roaring blowtorch. He opened his eyes and to his utter horror he saw his penis stiffen and rise up, even as

272

it was lasciviously licked by flames, even as its skin was shrivelling and crinkling, as if he were being aroused by Satan himself.

Thirty-three

When she returned to her desk, Katie saw that her phone was flashing. She picked it up and found that she had a phone message from Dr Collins.

'Katie? That rat that was sewn up inside Father Quinlan's abdomen – I've analysed its stomach contents. There was some raw chicken, half-digested, also cheese and crispbread. That strongly suggests that the rat was kept in captivity for several days before Father Quinlan was murdered, and fed by its captor. So I'd say that its sewing up into Father Quinlan's body was almost certainly premeditated.

'There's something else that you should know about. Shortly before they were garrotted, both Father Heaney and Father Quinlan had ingested at least twenty-one grams of honey, which is about one tablespoonful. Neither of them had time to digest it properly, because it hadn't passed through the stomach into the small intestine to be broken down by enzyme action into glucose.

'I have more results for you, but these are definitely the most interesting. Perhaps we can meet later and discuss them over a drink.'

Katie leaned back in her chair, tapping her pen against her teeth. This was yet more proof that

Father Heaney and Father Quinlan had been murdered by the same person or persons. But why on earth would they have been swallowing honey, just before they were killed? She doubted if they had been eating it voluntarily. So why would their murderer feed it to them?

Was it symbolic? If so, symbolic of what?

At that moment, Chief Superintendent O'Driscoll knocked at her open door and said, 'The jackals are all here. Do you want to do the business?'

Katie flicked the live microphone in front of her – more to catch the attention of the media who had assembled in the conference room than to check that it was working.

'Good afternoon and thank you for coming, all of you,' she announced. She recognized most of the faces in front of her – Fionnuala Sweeney from RTÉ, Dan Keane from the *Examiner*, Mary Fitzpatrick from Cork 96FM radio news – even Ciara Clare, although she was now wearing her long purple cardigan, covering up the tight stripy top that she had been flaunting this morning.

There was a fusillade of coughing, and the quickly suppressed warble of a mobile phone. Then Katie said, 'The latest news I have regarding the murders of Father Heaney and Father Quinlan is that we are now one hundred per cent certain that both murders were committed by the same perpetrator. Although you may think that this was glaringly obvious from the start – both men tied up with harp wire and both of them castrated – there was always a remote chance that

274

Father Quinlan's murder could have been the work of a copycat.

'However, new forensic evidence has shown us that there was another common factor in their killings, which a copycat could not possibly have known about.'

'Can you tell us what that common factor is, ma'am?' asked John McCarthy from the *Southern Star*.

'Not just yet, I'm afraid.'

'Is that because you're afraid that this priest killer is going to strike again?' asked Dan Keane, loudly, without looking up at her.

'We're obviously concerned that he might. And the last thing we want is for somebody else to be imitating him. I think we have enough on our plate.'

'Is this the only progress you've made?' asked Mary Fitzpatrick. 'Confirming something that seemed self-evident right from the very beginning?'

'No,' Katie retorted. 'We're convinced now that the perpetrator's identity is known or strongly suspected by a member or members of the clergy.'

'Really? Do you have any idea *which* members of the clergy?'

'I can't release any more information about that, not yet.'

'How senior are we talking about? What about Bishop Mahoney? Does *he* know?'

'I can't say any more at the moment, or name any names, because the perpetrator may well try to harm or threaten to harm any informant before he gets caught. Not only that, our informant might be forced to come out for the first time and admit that *he* was a child molester, too, and that's how he knows what he knows. It's always a possibility.

'I believe that we're *this* close to making an arrest,' she declared, holding up her finger and thumb with only an inch between them. 'I have a great team here in Cork and we're receiving some truly invaluable help from the technical bureau in Dublin. But at the same time I strongly believe that we could catch this killer very much sooner if we were given more co-operation by the church. I'm not criticizing the diocesan authorities, but I'm certain that some individual who wears the cloth can give us a name, and save many more lives.'

'Can you tell us what led you to believe that a clergyman knows who the killer is?' asked Dan Keane. He had raised his eyes now, to look at her directly, his pen poised over his open notebook, and Katie could see that he was relishing tomorrow's headline already. MYSTERY CLERIC IS SHIELDING TWO-TIME PRIEST KILLER, CLAIMS TOP 'TEC.

'Not in any detail, no,' said Katie. 'But let's say that people sometimes try too hard to cover things up, and then it becomes blatantly obvious that they're hiding something.'

'Come on, you have to give us more than that!'

'I will, I promise. Let's just wait and see if this clergyman does the right thing, and tells us who the killer is.'

'You're positive now that you're looking for a serial killer?' Fionnuala Sweeney asked her. 'I mean, if you are, it makes it all the more urgent that this clergyman gets in touch with you, doesn't it?'

'I'm sure he's going to kill more priests, given the chance.' Katie replied. 'And now is the time for the church not just to apologize for what happened in the past, for all the abuse that was suffered by so many children, but for the clergy to make real and practical amends, regardless of the personal consequences to themselves. Whoever in the priesthood knows or suspects who this killer may be, they need to call me today – now – so that we can make an arrest and put an end to this butchery. They can remain anonymous if they like.'

The media all seemed to be reasonably satisfied with this. After all, nothing sold better than a story with a cliffhanger ending. The newspaper and TV and radio reporters shuffled out of the conference room and Chief Superintendent O'Driscoll came up to give Katie a pat on the shoulder.

'That was excellent, Katie. Nothing like leaving them panting for more.'

One of the last reporters to leave the conference room was Ciara Clare. She looked across at Katie and narrowed her eyes and for a split second Katie thought she was going to come over and say something, but then she turned away and followed the rest of the media out of the door.

Katie watched her go, and as she did so Ciara looked round just once more. Her expression wasn't at all hostile, but neither did she look defensive. If anything, Katie thought that she looked *anxious*.

Katie returned to her office and found Detective O'Donovan waiting for her with a slanted grin on his face. 'I'll tell you this, ma'am,' he grinned, 'there's one gligneen who's going to be *very* unpleased about what you just said in there, and that's for sure.'

'You mean Monsignor Kelly? Yes, I know. That was the whole point. Forgive me one moment, I just want to call the hospital and ask after Siobhán.'

As she waited for the nurse to come to the phone, she said, 'Any progress with the harp strings?'

Detective O'Donovan shook his head. 'Nothing at all. Nor with that bassoon cord, neither. We still have a couple of music tutors to call on, but if you ask me he bought those strings abroad, or maybe ordered them through the internet.'

'Try contacting any company that sells them online. There can't be all that many.'

The nurse interrupted her by saying, 'Hello? Is that Katie?'

'Yes, it is. How's Siobhán this afternoon?'

'Still not awake yet, I'm afraid, Katie. But her vital signs are improving. We'll be sending her down for another brain scan tomorrow afternoon.'

Katie said, 'Thank you, nurse. Maybe I can call again later,' and put down the phone. Detective O'Donovan waited for a while, and then he asked, 'How is she?'

'A little better, thanks, Patrick. But still not conscious.'

'I'm genuinely sorry.' He waited a few more moments, and then he said, 'I have Stephen Keenan downstairs. You know, the Latin teacher

278

from Pres. He's finished translating Father Heaney's notebooks.'

'Really? Why don't you ask him to come up?'

While she waited for Detective O'Donovan to fetch Stephen Keenan from reception, she checked her emails. She had received three, all of them from John. *'Miss you, sweetheart … please try to get away tonight'* and then *'Think I might at last have a serious offer on the farm!!!'* and then *'Love you, Katie, believe me, more than my life.'*

Detective O'Donovan came back, accompanied by a balding, round-shouldered man in his early forties, with a large nose and hairy blonde eyebrows. He was wearing a green tweed jacket with brown leather patches on the elbows and a row of different-coloured ballpoint pens in the breast pocket, and baggy grey trousers. Katie couldn't help noticing his worn-down brown shoes.

'Stephen Keenan, ma'am,' said Detective O'Donovan.

Stephen Keenan held out his hand and gave Katie a soft, complicated handshake, as if he were trying to convey to her that he was a member of some secret order. His eyes were bulbous, with a slight cast, so that Katie wasn't sure if he was looking at her directly, or at the framed photograph behind her of Commissioner Michael Staines leading the first Irish police force through the gates of Dublin Castle in August 1922.

'So, Stephen – you've finished your translation,' said Katie, trying to sound businesslike but not too intimidating.

Stephen Keenan held up a dog-eared green

279

folder and said, 'I have, yes, superintendent, although it wasn't easy, I can tell you. Father Heaney uses dozens of abbreviations and what I can only assume to be pseudonyms. Perhaps he was trying to protect some people's identity. His Latin isn't very grammatical either. If he had been in my class I would have given him no more than three out of ten. Well, maybe four, at a pinch.'

'Please – sit down,' said Katie. 'How about a coffee? Patrick, ask Branna to bring us some coffee, would you? Mine's a cappuccino. I'm dying of thirst here.'

Stephen Keenan sat down and opened up his folder. 'An awful lot of these notebooks are filled up with Father Heaney's ramblings about the possibility of a second coming of Christ, and the reality or otherwise of angels. At first, I couldn't understand why he bothered to write it all in Latin, but the more I translated, the more I realized that he seriously believed in the physicality of heaven.'

'He thought that heaven actually exists? Like, somewhere up in the clouds or wherever?'

Stephen Keenan nodded enthusiastically. 'Precisely that. You've got it. To him, heaven was as real as Cork City itself. Heavenly bricks and heavenly mortar. Streets, people – except that the people have passed over, and they're policed by angels rather than the Garda Síochána. Sorry – that was meant to be a joke.'

'All right,' said Katie, twitching the side of her mouth to show him that she had got it. 'But why the Latin? Millions of people believe that heaven is real, don't they? I don't know. It may be a bit *medieval,* but it's nothing you'd need to hide, like.'

'Aha! But Father Heaney and his pseudonymous friends not only believed in the physical existence of heaven, they believed that under certain circumstances heaven can actually be seen from earth. I'm serious. They believed that there are ways in which God can be persuaded to show His face to us, and give us a preview of paradise, if you like.'

'I see. It all sounds cracked as the crows. But I still don't understand why he needed to be so secretive about it.'

Stephen Keenan licked his thumb and leafed through six or seven sheets of handwritten notes before he came to what he was looking for.

'It's not the belief itself that he was trying to keep secret. It's what specifically needed to be done in order to coax God into granting us poor mortals an audience.'

'And what was that?'

Stephen Keenan took a pair of tortoiseshell half-glasses out of his inside pocket and put them on the end of his nose. Then he picked out a sheet of paper and started to read out what he had written on it, using a sing-song voice that Katie thought was highly appropriate, considering his subject matter.

'He starts by saying, *"Illic est dulcis sono quod Deus diligo"*, which roughly means, "There is some singing so sweet that God adores it." Or He thinks quite a lot of it, anyhow.

'He goes on to say that in the latter part of the sixteenth century, the Church of Rome set out to

281

produce music that would delight God so much that He would show His appreciation by appearing to us in physical form. This sort of music was highly complex and polyphonic, with much elaborate ornamentation, and for this it required voices in the higher register.

'In order to reach the high notes required, the papal choir used boys and male adult falsettists, many of them imported from Spain, because there was a papal injunction against women singing in public. But the children's voices were lacking in resonance and their career was very short-lived before they reached puberty, and the adult falsettists were considered to be inferior in tone and power to...' and here Stephen Keenan lifted one finger and said, 'wait for it – *eunuchs.*'

'He's talking about *castrati,*' said Katie.

'*Castrati* – absolutely. And this is how Father Heaney goes on: the first pope to make a serious attempt to see the face of God was Pope Sixtus V. He believed that if he could persuade God to manifest Himself on earth, that would prove beyond doubt the supremacy of the Church of Rome and his own supremacy as its spiritual leader. He issued a bull in 1589 which called for four *castrati* to be included in the choir of St Peter's in Rome.

'*Castrati* remained in the papal chapel for over three centuries, as each successive pope tried to perfect the singing that would coax God into opening up the doors of heaven and showing Himself.

'Father Heaney adds, perhaps at last we Catholics could end the Lord's Prayer by saying, *For*

282

Thine is the kingdom, the power and the glory, which had always been denied to us, because now we could see them for ourselves in all their splendour.

'There was a temporary hiatus in the use of *castrati* when the Papal States came under the rule of Napoleon in 1808, but after Napoleon's removal in 1815 they were revived and not finally excluded from the Sistine Chapel until 1902. The last *castrato* in the Vatican was Alessandro Moreschi who died in 1922, at the age of sixty-four. He was said by those who heard his singing to have a voice like the purest crystal.'

Stephen Keenan took off his glasses and looked up. 'The rest of this particular notebook is filled with historical notes about famous operatic *castrati,* and also with Father Heaney's own domestic details. For some reason he's even written his laundry list in Latin. Do you know what the Latin for "five dog collars, no starch" is?'

'Is that all he has to say about *castrati?*' asked Katie. 'We're trying to find a motive for Father Heaney and Father Quinlan being castrated, but this notebook doesn't really tell us very much more than we've theorized already, does it? Father Heaney for some reason had a very strong interest in the subject of *castrati,* but it still looks like somebody is taking his revenge for having been molested by a priest or priests. That's what Dr Collins thinks, anyhow. For want of any other explanation, I tend to agree with her.'

'Oh, no,' said Stephan Keenan, raising his finger again to interrupt her. 'There's very much more. This *second* notebook is all about Father

Heaney's time teaching music at St Joseph's Orphanage in Mayfield. I think this might well answer your question about motive.'

Thirty-four

'Father Heaney says that in May 1982, when he was teaching music at St Anthony's Primary School in Douglas – among other subjects, such as geography – he was called to a secret meeting by somebody whom he identifies only as Reverend Bis.'

'Reverend *Bis?*' asked Katie. 'What kind of a name is that?'

'I have no idea. But *bis* means "twice" in Latin.'

'All right, then, what did this Reverend Twice want from him?'

'Apparently, the Reverend Bis was deeply impressed with Father Heaney's music-teaching ability. Among many other accolades, St Anthony's had been voted top primary school choir for three successive years at the Cork Choral Festival, and they had been given the honour of singing for Pope John Paul II when he visited Ireland in 1979.

'Anyhow, Father Heaney went along to this secret meeting, which took place in a large private house in Lovers' Walk in Montenotte. Apart from Father Heaney and the Reverend Bis, the only other people present were two young priests, neither of whom spoke a single word throughout

284

the entire meeting, and a middle-aged woman who didn't say anything either but took shorthand notes of what was being proposed.'

'Which was?'

'That Father Heaney should take an extended leave of absence from St Anthony's and create a new choir at St Joseph's Orphanage, from scratch.'

'Did the Reverend Bis say *why* they wanted to create a new choir?'

'No, not in so many words. But he made it very clear that it would have to be the finest choir that the diocese had ever known, even better than St Anthony's. His exact words were *"a choir to delight the ears of God".*'

'That sounds the same as like what your Pope Sixtus was after,' put in Detective O'Donovan. 'Don't tell me this Reverend Bis was trying to cajole God into making a guest appearance in Cork. You can imagine it, can't you, God turning up in Knocka? "Aight, God? How's it hangin', kid?"'

Stephen Keenan turned around and said, 'You can laugh all you want, Patrick, but it does seem as if that *was* his intention. I'll tell you this, though – I have the distinct feeling from what Father Heaney has written here that the Reverend Bis was not your principal instigator of this plan to form a choir. Father Heaney refers to him several times as *cursor*, which in Latin doesn't mean the little arrow on your PC screen; it means "messenger".'

'So it was somebody else who wanted to put this choir together, and the Reverend Bis was

285

simply a go-between?'

'I'd say it was.'

'So what was the outcome of this secret meeting?' Katie asked him. 'Presumably Father Heaney agreed to do it.'

'Oh, yes! In fact, he was so inspired that he went home and prayed all night without sleeping to thank God for choosing him to be His vessel. The next day he wrote a hymn called *"Vox Angelus* – The Voice of an Angel"*. Composed it on the harp, because that was his instrument of choice, although he played violin and cello and piano, too.'

'He played the *harp?'*

'Oh, yes. He mentions it several times. He thought the harp was the musical equivalent of the wind blowing through angels' wings.'

'There was no sign of a harp in his room, was there, when we searched it?' said Detective O'Donovan.

'He explains that himself,' Stephen Keenan told them. 'His harp was damaged by the removal men when he moved to his new lodgings, and he couldn't afford to have it repaired and restrung, so he left it in his sister's garage in Ballincollig.'

Katie glanced across at Detective O'Donovan, who nodded to show her that he knew what she expected him to do – drive out to Ballincollig and bring the harp back to headquarters for fingerprinting, as well as authenticating what Father Heaney had written in his notebooks.

'Three other priests were brought in to organize the St Joseph's Orphanage Choir,' Stephen Keenan went on, and he counted them off on his fingers. 'Father O'Gara, Father Quinlan and Father ó Súllabháin. Each one of them had outstanding musical expertise – each different, but each complementary. According to Father Heaney, Father ó Súllabháin is one of the best voice coaches in Ireland when it comes to sacred music. He trained the North Monastery Boys' Choir before they recorded their album *I Love All Beauteous Things*. Father Quinlan plays woodwind – flute and bassoon – and Father Heaney writes that he's also a highly gifted arranger, both of ancient and modern music.'

'*Was* a highly gifted arranger,' Katie corrected him. She couldn't help visualizing that enormous rat, struggling gorily out of Father Quinlan's stomach.

'Yes, of course, I'm sorry,' said Stephen Keenan, and he flustered and dropped some of his papers on the floor.

'What about Father O'Gara?'

'Father O'Gara is a brilliant organist, so Father Heaney says; and an organist is essential for a top-flight choir. However, he was not very easygoing. Prickly, or *thorny*, if I've translated his Latin correctly. *Iratus*. He didn't tolerate any misbehaviour and he was never slow to use the pandybat.'

'I see. So these four priests were brought together by this mysterious Reverend Bis to develop a special choir at St Joseph's Orphanage. An exceptional choir, *a choir to delight the ears of God*.'

'But why St Joseph's, for feck's sake?' asked Detective O'Donovan. 'Have you seen the kids there, even today – and God knows what they were like thirty years ago. Underweight, most of them, or obese from too many chips. Rotten teeth, if they had any left. Accents like fecking chainsaws. Mouthy, smelly, ill-disciplined, Jesus. Why would you choose *them* to put a choir together?'

Katie sat back in her chair and pressed her fingertips to her forehead like a fortune-teller. She had *seen* this, right from the very beginning, but she had been far too slow in fitting all of the pieces together.

'What's the story, ma'am?' said Detective O'Donovan, in bewilderment.

'They chose them, Patrick, *because* they were orphans, not in spite of it.'

'What do you mean?'

'They chose them because nobody else in the whole world cared about them. Their parents were either separated or abusive or constantly langered or simply couldn't look after them. The social services were overworked and underpaid and couldn't wait to get them off their hands. Those boys were totally dependent on the priests and nuns at St Joseph's for everything. Food, drink, shelter, warmth, and most of all *affection*. That's why they were much less resistant than any other boys might have been to what the four priests who organized that choir wanted to do to them.'

Detective O'Donovan blinked at her. 'You mean, molest them?'

Katie fiercely shook her head. 'They didn't molest them. Well, they might have done, but they did something much worse than that. They castrated them. Do you know, I've been listening to that *Elements* CD in my car for weeks, thinking how beautiful the singing was, and of course it's beautiful. It's the same singing they had in the papal choir in the sixteenth century.

'It's the *castrati*. The orphan boys at St Joseph's were chosen for the choir by Father Heaney and Father Quinlan and Father O'Gara and Father ó Súllabháin, and they all had their little balls cut off so that they could sing like angels.'

'It's shocking, isn't it?' said Stephen Keenan, closing his folder. 'But after reading these note-books I think that's only the possible conclusion you can come to. You have to read between the lines, but it's all in here. Father Heaney doesn't once use the word "castrate". Instead, he refers to *purificationis*, or "ritualized purification", but I'm sure that by that he means castration. He gives times and dates of when they did it – sixteen boys in all. He doesn't name them, and he gives no clue to their identities, but I imagine the orphanage will have records.'

'But this happened in 1982,' said Detective O'Donovan. 'These lads have had over thirty years to get their revenge. Why in the name of Jesus have they decided to do it *now?*'

Katie stood up and went to the window. The hooded crows were still clustered on top of the multi-storey car park, their black feathers flutter-ing in the wind. There must have been at least twenty of them. She always felt that they were waiting for her, tattered but patient, because they knew something that she didn't, or couldn't, even guess at.

'Perhaps it was hearing that *Elements* CD,' she suggested. 'Like, you can't go anywhere just at the moment without hearing it, can you? They were even playing it in Brown Thomas the other day. Maybe it brought it all back. Or maybe it was all this recent publicity about child abuse by priests – that might have triggered them off.'

Stephen Keenan nodded. 'You could be right. All those stories in the papers, they've really opened up some cans of worms, haven't they? One of my best friends told me only last week that when he was nine years old he was systematically molested by his parish priest for over a year. He burst into tears when he told me – *cried*, like he was still a small boy. I didn't know what to say to him. "It's all over, Bryan, forget about it"? For him – *no* – it never will be over. The shame lasts for the rest of your life. The thought that you should have said no.'

Katie said, 'Being abused – God – that's bad enough. But can you imagine how difficult it would be to come out in public and say that you'd been castrated? It's not something you'd want your friends to know, is it, even if they've always thought that you were different.'

'What happens now, investigation-wise?' asked Detective O'Donovan. 'I'm taking it that we don't rush out and arrest every man with a squeaky voice and no stubble.'

'We have to have a long and serious think about strategy, that's what we have to do now,' Katie told him. 'After all, we're not just dealing with two present-day murders, are we? We're also dealing with sixteen cases of serious bodily harm, even if they did happen thirty years ago. Stephen – I'll have to ask you leave us now. We have some confidential things we need to talk about, and although I *do* trust you...'

Stephen Keenan gave her a small, round-shouldered bow. 'That's all right, superintendent. I understand perfectly. And I promise you that my lips are sealed about all of this translation.'

'Of course they are,' said Katie. 'Otherwise I'll have to have you arrested. But that was grand work you did there and we'll pay you for it. Send me an invoice.'

She called an emergency meeting in the conference room, with Chief Superintendent O'Driscoll, Inspector Fennessy and seven detectives, including O'Donovan and Horgan, as well as fifteen uniformed gardaí. Only Sergeant O'Rourke was absent: he had been unable to contact Father Lowery by phone, so he had driven down to Rathbarry to see if he could find him.

Katie very quickly summed up what they had deduced from Stephen Keenan's translation. Then she said, 'So far as we know, our perpetrator is still holding Father O'Gara aka Gerry O'Dwyer. No body has been dumped anywhere yet, so we have to assume that he's still alive, even if he's being tortured.

'It's essential that we don't alert the perpetrator to the fact that we've identified his motive. As I said before, I still believe that he *wants* us to catch him, eventually, because he believes that his cause is just and he wants to be able to explain publicly why he took his revenge on these particular priests.

'If there's one thing we can be relieved about, it's that he probably intends to kill only those four priests who organized St Joseph's Orphanage Choir – not every single priest in Cork who was suspected of abuse. But we don't want him to kill even one more priest, whatever that priest might have done. We don't have any idea where he's keeping Father O'Gara. I'm just praying that he isn't hurting him too badly. But at the moment, Father ó Súllabháin is staying at St Dominic's Retreat Centre in Montenotte, meditating. I've detailed six guards to give him round-the-clock protection, so he should be safe enough – for now, anyhow.

'I'll be going up to Montenotte myself to interview Father ó Súllabháin directly after this briefing. He must have some idea who our perpetrator might be. As far as we can tell from Father Heaney's notebooks, he and his brother priests, they castrated those boys. The whole experience must have been traumatic for all of them, priests and boys alike. Don't tell me that Father ó Súllabháin can't remember any of their names – especially those who protested.'

'They *all* would have protested, wouldn't they?' asked Detective Horgan. 'I can tell you for sure that I'd lose the head if somebody tried to chop off *my* caideogs.'

Thirty-five

A cattle truck had turned over on the Croppy Road south of Clonakilty town centre, and the traffic on the N71 was backed up for more than three kilometres. Not only that, it had started to rain again, cold and hard.

Sergeant O'Rourke overtook the long line of traffic on the right-hand side, until he was flagged down by a garda in a waterproof cape. He could see the filthy old truck resting on its side across the road, completely blocking it from one grass verge to the other. It looked as two of its front tyres had burst, because they were hanging down in rubbery rags, as if the truck driver had run over some witches. Seven or eight bewildered-looking cows were standing around, twitching their heads sporadically to fend off the rain.

At least three more cattle were sprawled in ungainly positions on the tarmac, either dying or dead already, one with its legs in the air. A tall fellow in a putty-coloured raincoat and a brown trilby hat was crouching beside one of them. He looked like an IRA gunman from the 1920s, but he was the local vet, more than likely. Three gardaí stood beside him with their arms folded and watched him work, with rain dripping from the peaks of their caps.

The garda in the waterproof cape tapped on Sergeant O'Rourke's window and he wound it down.

293

'You'll have to turn around and go to the back of the line, sir. You can't jump the queue like that. There's other people been waiting here for nearly an hour.'

Sergeant O'Rourke showed him his badge. 'I'm on very urgent business. I have to get through.'

'Well, I'm sorry, sergeant, but there's no way. You can see for yourself. We can't even get our own cars through until the tow-truck arrives.'

'Oh, yes? And when is that likely to be?'

'He said twenty minutes, like, but you never know. He was out clearing an accident in Rosscarbery when we called him.'

Sergeant O'Rourke said, 'I'm working on a major case and we're fierce tight on time. I need to get through here now.'

'Can't be done, sir. Sorry.'

Sergeant O'Rourke opened his door and climbed out of his car. He jostled past the garda in the waterproof cape and headed directly towards a uniformed sergeant who was watching the vet as he manipulated one of the cow's upraised forelegs, feeling for fractures. The cow was rolling her eyes in pain and bewilderment.

He held out his badge and said, 'Detective Sergeant O'Rourke, Cork City.'

The sergeant gave his badge the most cursory of glances. 'Oh, yes, detective sergeant? And what brings you down here on a day like this? Come to take some detecting lessons from us culchies?'

'I'm working on a major case.'

'Oh, yeah? Major, is it?'

'Sorry, but it's confidential.'

'Confidential?'

'That's right. I have to locate a very important witness. As soon as humanly possible, like. Your man here says I can't get past.'

The uniformed sergeant had a big face as orange as gammon skin, with pale blue eyes and gingery eyebrows.

'Normally, I'd say you could go through town, back up to Wolfe Tone Street and then along the Western Road. But the Western Road is closed because of a burst water main, so it looks like you're stuck here like the rest of us. Sorry about that.'

'If that's the situation, I'm going to have to borrow one of your squad cars from the other side of that truck.'

'You're what? You're messing, aren't you?'

'Sorry, sergeant. Serious.'

The sergeant shook his head. 'I could have one of my lads drive you. How about that?'

'Sorry. This is totally confidential. I need to have the car to myself.'

The sergeant shook his head again and continued shaking it. 'Can't do that for you, no matter what.'

Sergeant O'Rourke took out his mobile phone and punched out Katie's number. After a few seconds Katie answered him and snapped, 'What is it, Jimmy? Haven't you found Father Lowery yet? We're running out of time, for God's sake.'

Sergeant O'Rourke explained about the overturned cattle truck and the burst water main and the fact that he wanted to borrow a squad car. Then he handed his mobile phone to the uniformed sergeant.

'Detective Superintendent Maguire. Tell her that I can't have a car.'

The uniformed sergeant began to plead that he couldn't allow Sergeant O'Rourke to take one of his cars because otherwise Clonakilty Garda station could be short of transport that evening, and once the Kilty Stone and Mick Finn's and Phair's closed their doors they needed all the transport they could get.

At that point it was obvious that Katie had interrupted him, because all he said after that was 'yeah but – yeah but – yeah but–' and then he nodded, and nodded again, and said, 'All right, then. All right, then, agreed.'

He handed back the mobile phone. His mouth was puckered as if he had just bitten into something extremely nasty-tasting. 'Name of Jesus,' he said. 'Wouldn't like to work for *her*. Go on, take one of the cars. But bring it back to the Garda station as soon as you can, all right? Once we've cleared up all this mess, we'll take your own car up there and have it waiting for you. We're halfway up McCurtain Hill – take a left before Harrington's pharmacy.'

Sergeant O'Rourke climbed around the front bumper of the overturned truck and made his way through the long wet grass and weeds at the side of the road. Three Garda vehicles were parked at an angle in the middle of the road, two Ford Focuses and a Renault people carrier. As he reached the nearest car, he heard the sharp crack of a captive bolt stunner as the vet killed one of the injured cows. Before he could climb into the driving seat he heard another crack, and then another.

He started the engine, slewed the car around and drove away, with his windscreen wipers going at full speed – *whump, whump, whump, whump!* It sounded like the heartbeat of a man who realizes that a terrible creature is hot on his heels, but he can never outrun it.

It took him only another fifteen minutes to reach Rathbarry, in spite of the rain. It was a small, hilly, pretty little village in the middle of nowhere – what the Cork City people called 'up back of leap'. It had won awards for being tidy and hospitable, although this afternoon it was almost deserted.

He drove past the Cáiteach, the signpost in the centre of the village made out of upturned scythes and sheaves of corn, and on to St Michael's church. An elderly woman was standing by the grey stone wall outside, with a wet grey shawl draped over her head, and a wet grey curly-haired dog sitting beside her.

Two cars were parked at the opposite end of the wall, one with its engine running and a plume of exhaust twisting in the wind. Sergeant O'Rourke climbed out of the Garda car and approached the woman, turning up his collar against the rain.

'What's the story, girl?' he asked her.

The woman had a face as wrinkled as an old potato. She may have owned a set of dentures, but if she did, she hadn't put them in today. 'You'll be watching for the divil, won't you?' she said.

'I'm looking for a priest, as a matter of fact.'

'A priest, is it? They're divils, too, every one of

them. Is it Father Fitzpatrick you're after?'

'Father Lowery. He was only visiting.'

The old woman shook her head. 'Never heard of him. But I'll bet you that *he's* a divil, too.' Her dog looked up at her from beneath its dripping grey fringe as if it had heard this many times before and just wanted to go home to a bowl of dog biscuits and a basket with a warm blanket in it.

Sergeant O'Rourke left the woman and her dog where they were and walked up the path toward the church's main door. As he did so, the door opened and a big fifty-ish man appeared, with a brick-red face and sandy-coloured hair and a shirt collar that was two sizes too tight for him.

'Can I be helping you there?' he asked, locking the door behind him.

'I hope so. I'm looking for Father Lowery. I was told that he was visiting the church here for a car boot sale.'

'Oh, yes, indeed he was. But that was all finished by lunchtime. Every time we hold a car boot sale here, the heavens open. I sometimes believe that the Lord is trying to discourage us.'

'So Father Lowery's gone back to Cork?'

'No, not yet. He'll be spending tonight at Ardfield, at St James's, with Father Fitzpatrick. In fact, I don't believe he's left yet. A taxi arrived for him only five minutes ago – and, look, yes, that's it.' He pointed toward the car with the smoking exhaust. 'There, if you make quick, you can catch him.'

Sergeant O'Rourke clapped the red-faced man on the shoulder and said, 'Thanks a million.' He

298

hurried back along the path, his raincoat flapping, but just as he reached the gates, the taxi pulled away and headed off towards the village. He glimpsed a white-haired man in a black biretta sitting in the back seat, but then the car turned the corner and disappeared downhill out of sight.

Sergeant O'Rourke immediately ran back to the squad car. As he passed her, the old woman with the shawl over her head called out, *'Divils! Every last one of them! Evil incarnate!'*

He started the engine, released the clutch, and shot forward ten metres with a rattling spray of shingle. Then he handbrake-turned and sped back the way he had come, past the Cáiteach and down the hill. He wanted to catch up with Father Lowery's taxi before the driver reached the main road. If he was going to Ardfield, he would take a left, and then the first right. It was only about a ten-minute journey, if that.

But as the taxi came to the junction with the R598, its offside indicator started to flash. Its driver waited for a farm tractor to come trundling past, towing a trailer loaded up high with straw. Then he turned right, towards the sea, speeding away with an audible squitter of tyres. Not only was he heading in the wrong direction, but he seemed to be driving inconsiderately fast for a taxi driver with a geriatric priest for a passenger.

Sergeant O'Rourke turned right, too, and went after him. He had been planning on switching on the squad car's blue lights and overtaking the taxi as soon as possible, but now he held back. He wanted to see where Father Lowery was being taken. He wondered if Monsignor Kelly had contacted Father Lowery and warned him to make himself scarce for a while. Why else had it been impossible to contact Father Lowery by phone? He hadn't answered any calls to his mobile and the small boy with the clogged-up nose who had picked up the phone at St Michael's had sworn blind that he had looked everywhere but couldn't find him.

From Rathbarry, this road would take them due south, towards the sea, but then turn westward and run parallel to the coast, through Long Strand. After that, though, it turned northward again until it rejoined the main N71, so Father Lowery could be heading anywhere at all – to Skibbereen, in the west, or eastward even, back to Cork City.

The taxi drove faster and faster, until it was speeding along at nearly seventy, with a bridal veil of spray trailing behind it. Sergeant O'Rourke was finding it hard to keep up, although he didn't want to come so close that the taxi driver realized he had a two-bulb on his tail. In his white Ford Focus with its yellow and blue Battenberg squares, he could hardly have been more conspicuous, and he cursed his luck for having been obliged to leave his own unmarked car behind on the Croppy Road.

After less than two kilometres, however, without indicating that he was turning, the taxi driver swerved down the narrow road on the left that led to Castlefreke Warren and Donoure. That was one thing settled, anyway – Father Lowery was definitely *not* making for the N71.

As he approached the corner to follow him, Sergeant O'Rourke slowed right down to give the taxi driver plenty of time to widen his lead. This was a very quiet rural road and it was highly unlikely that there would be any other traffic, especially in this weather.

He still couldn't work out where the taxi driver was going. It was possible to get to Ardfield this way, but he would definitely be taking the scenic route, through villages and caravan parks and farms, and it would take three times as long as driving there directly.

The road was only single-track here, with Castlefreke woods on the left and the sea on the right. The sea was the colour of gunmetal and very choppy. On the horizon, through the rain, Sergeant O'Rourke could just make out the pale grey outline of a giant oil tanker heading towards the Atlantic, like the ghost of the *Lusitania*.

When he looked back to the road ahead, however, the taxi had vanished.

'*Shite,*' he said, under his breath. He could see at least half a kilometre in front of him, and the road was reasonably straight, but there was no sign of the taxi at all. He took his foot off the accelerator and leaned forward over the steering wheel, narrowing his eyes to see if there were any side turnings up ahead. *Feck it,* he thought. *How could I have lost him? But one second he was right there in front of me, I swear to God, and the next second he wasn't – just like some fecking magic trick.*

He drove another seven hundred and fifty metres and then he pulled in to the side of the road. The rain was easing off now, and so he set his windscreen wipers to intermittent. He was tempted to call control at Clonakilty Garda station and ask for directions, but if he did that, the local cops would want to know where he was and what he was after doing, and Katie had insisted that he tell nobody that he wanted to talk to Father Lowery, or why.

He turned the car around and started to creep very slowly back the way he had come. He had covered less than two hundred metres when he noticed that some of the bushes by the side of the road had freshly broken branches, and that there were four deep tyre tracks in the muddy verge. The taxi driver must have turned off the road for some reason, plunging straight into the under-growth, and headed towards the trees.

Sergeant O'Rourke drove on a few metres further and then parked the Garda car in a small gravelly lay-by. The woods were only about thirty metres away and quite dense – spruce and syca-more and maritime pine – and so the taxi driver couldn't have gone very far. Sergeant O'Rourke crossed the road, climbed up over the verge, and began to make his way through the bushes, his right elbow lifted in front of his face to shield it from a barbed-wire fence of brambles. All the same, they snatched and tore at his coat.

There was a strong fresh smell of sea in the air, mingled with the smell of wet undergrowth.

As he went further into the woods, he saw the taxi half-concealed behind a beech tree, not covered with leaves or branches, but parked in such a way that it couldn't be seen from the road. He circled around it, keeping at least twenty metres distant, but the driver's door and the near-side passenger door were both wide open, and the taxi was empty.

So where the hell were they? Father Lowery and his taxi driver?

Sergeant O'Rourke reached into his coat and lifted his SIG Sauer automatic out of his shoulder holster. He cocked it, and held it up high in both hands, and then he approached the taxi's rear door, his knees slightly bent, all the time glancing from side to side in case he was being watched.

He heard a sharp crackle of leaves and twigs, and he swung around with his automatic held out stiff-armed in front of him. God almighty. But it was nothing more than two squirrels chasing each other, tearing around and around and up and down trees.

He looked inside the taxi. On the back seat there was a folded copy of the *Catholic Recorder* and an open spectacle case, with the spectacles still inside, but no Father Lowery.

When he checked the front seat, however, Sergeant O'Rourke began to suspect that this wasn't a taxi at all. There was no two-way radio, no clipboard, no business cards, and nothing to indicate that the driver spent hours driving around or waiting for passengers – no crisp packets, no newspapers, not even a roll of extra-strong mints.

So what were they doing together in the woods, Father Lowery and a taxi driver who didn't appear to be a taxi driver at all? *Holy Mary, Mother of God, I dread to think.*

He ventured a little further into the trees. They

303

had started to drip now, from high above, and Sergeant O'Rourke grew jumpier with every drip. He was seriously beginning to think that however strictly Katie had told him to keep this investigation to himself, he needed help from the local boys.

He made a detour around a fairy ring of toadstools. His mam's mam had always told him that fairy rings were the entrance to the underworld, so you'd better not step inside of one, young Jimmy, unless you want to disappear for a hundred years and come back to find that all your loved ones are long since dead and buried.

A few metres past the fairy ring Sergeant O'Rourke saw a black biretta with a pompom lying on the ground. He walked over to it and picked it up. No doubt about it – it was the same biretta that Father Lowery had been wearing in the back of the taxi. Sergeant O'Rourke looked around, hat in one hand and gun in the other. Raindrops continued to fall from the trees – sometimes singly, sometimes several all at once, with a sudden clatter.

Off to his right, he saw a wide depression in the ground, filled with leaves and broken twigs. He approached it slowly. Lying in the middle of it, with his arms and legs spread wide in an X shape, as if he had fallen from hundreds of feet in the air, was Father Lowery. At least, he assumed it was Father Lowery. As he came closer, he saw that the priest had virtually no face. It looked as if he had received the full blast of a shotgun at what must have been point-blank range. His jaw was missing so that his tongue hung straight downwards like a plump lilac-coloured cravat. He had no nose at all, only two narrow triangular holes, but both his eyeballs had been blown upwards out of their sockets, still attached to the optic nerves, and were perched on his forehead, staring up at Sergeant O'Rourke as if they were waiting for him to put them back in again.

'Jesus,' said Sergeant O'Rourke. He crossed himself twice, and he was so shaken that it took all of his strength not to drop to his knees. He tugged his mobile phone out of his pocket to call Katie, but there was no signal, not here in the woods around Castlefreke, on the edge of the Irish Sea. He would have to go back to the Garda car and make his call from there. Meanwhile, where the hell was the taxi driver – if he really was a taxi driver? Had *he* shot Father Lowery, or had he been shot, too, by somebody else?

Sergeant O'Rourke began to make his way hurriedly back towards the road, panting, his feet chuffing through the leaves. He gave the taxi a wide berth, even though it was still parked behind the beech tree and its doors were still open. He looked left and right, and then behind him, to see if there was any sign of the taxi driver, alive or dead, but he could see nothing. He listened, but all he could hear was the trees dripping and the squirrels scampering and very far away, the mournful hooting of the oil tanker.

As he came around the beech tree, however, he found the taxi driver was standing in his way, waiting for him. A stocky man, wearing a brown tweed cap and a black nylon zip-up jacket. The lower part of his face was covered with a black woollen scarf, so that Sergeant O'Rourke could see only his eyes. He was carrying a shotgun, its barrels lifted almost vertical, as if he were just about to let off a shot into the treetops.

'You could of minded your own business, you know,' said the taxi driver. His voice was muffled, but he definitely sounded like a southsider from Cork City.

Sergeant O'Rourke pointed his automatic at him. 'Break the shotgun, all right?'

'Oh, yeah? And who's going to make me?'

'Break it, boy, and then lay it down on the ground. Slow and careful, on the ground in front of you. Then back away with your hands on top of your head.'

'I just said, who's going to make me?'

'I am, me. Because I'm going to count to three, and if you haven't done it by then, I'm going to shoot you. I'm not going to aim at your shoulders or your legs or anything like that. I'm going to shoot you straight through the fecking heart and fecking kill you, because I think you'll find that we're allowed to do that if a suspect's armed.'

The taxi driver stared at him for a moment and then he slowly shook his head and turned away, so that he had his back to him. 'You're a joke, you cops. *I'm going to fecking kill you.* What a fecking sham-feen!'

'Turn back around!' Sergeant O'Rourke shouted at him. 'Do you hear me, boy? Turn back around!'

The taxi driver continued shaking his head. Sergeant O'Rourke said, 'One – two–'

'What comes after two?' the taxi driver challenged him. 'Two and a half? Two and three quarters? You haven't got the balls!'

With that, he dropped to his knees and twisted around at the same time, firing his shotgun at Sergeant O'Rourke's stomach. Sergeant O'Rourke was knocked backwards, falling flat on the ground with his arms spread wide, just like Father Lowery. He hadn't heard the shot that had hit him, but he heard it echo through the woods, and the sudden flurry of birds that it had disturbed.

He tried to get up, but he couldn't. He had dropped his automatic when he fell, and when he turned his head sideways he could see it lying amongst the leaves. He willed his hand to reach out and pick it up, but his hand wouldn't respond. In fact, he felt numb all over. He couldn't feel his arms and he couldn't feel his legs.

With an effort, he raised his head and looked down at his stomach. The front of his coat had been torn to riotous shreds, and he could see pale coils of glistening intestine bulging out.

The taxi driver came up to him, with his shotgun tilted over his shoulder. He had taken off the scarf that had covered his face and now he looked down at Sergeant O'Rourke with an exaggerated frown of deep concern.

'I didn't want to have to do that at all,' he said. 'Why did you make me do that?'

Sergeant O'Rourke attempted to speak, but his lungs refused to give him any air. He felt as if were being suffocated.

'*Hnneeeep*,' he said, trying to breathe in.

'What's that, copper?'

'*Hnneeep.*'

'I told you, you should of minded your own

307

business. You're interfering in things you don't know nothing about. Well, I don't know nothing about them, neither, but I do know that you're messing with people who won't be messed with under any circumstances.'

Sergeant O'Rourke couldn't manage to draw in another breath. He looked up at the complicated patterns of branches above his head and it occurred to him that he was dying. He had never imagined that it would be like this, lying on his back in a wood. He was sure he could see faces in the spaces between the branches – not so much faces as an absence of faces. One of them looked as if it was winking at him, but that was only the wind blowing a single leaf.

He wished that Maeve were here, in her apron, smelling of baking, kneeling beside him and holding his hand. He wished that he hadn't been so impatient with her all their married life, and told her that he loved her more often.

'Does it hurt?' asked the taxi driver.

Sergeant O' Rourke gave the slightest shake of his head.

'Well, I have to say I'm surprised about that. Your guts are pouring out all over the shop.'

He looked down at Sergeant O'Rourke for a few moments longer, biting his lower lip, as if he were trying to come to a decision. Then he said, 'I have to go now. I'm sorry, but I can't be hanging around here any longer. Somebody might have heard my gun go off.'

He lifted his shotgun off his shoulder and aimed it directly at Sergeant O'Rourke's nose. The ends of the barrels were so close that Sergeant

O'Rourke could smell the sour reek of burned gunpowder from the cartridge that had hit him in the stomach. He wished that he had the breath to plead with the taxi driver not to shoot him in the face. He had seen Father Lowery's face and if he ended up looking like that, the funeral directors would have to close his coffin and Maeve wouldn't be able to kiss him goodbye.

'I'm sorry, like, but I can't leave you here alive,' said the taxi driver.

No, I assumed not, thought Sergeant O'Rourke, and he was amazed at how practical he was being, considering what was going to happen to him.

He hadn't heard the first shot and he didn't hear this shot, either, but he did feel a red-hot blast in his face as if a furnace door had slammed open right in front of him. Then nothing.

The taxi driver stood still for a while, as if he couldn't decide if he had done the right thing or not. Sergeant O'Rourke's head had been almost completely blown apart, and the top of his skull was three metres away, among the toadstools that clustered around the beech tree, with clumps of his hair still attached.

It started to rain again, pattering down through the leaves. The taxi driver walked back to his car and climbed into it. He saw his eyes looking back at him in the rear-view mirror. They seemed emotionless, but he knew that wasn't true. He just hoped that he got his reward for what he had done today, both on earth and in heaven.

Thirty-six

'Wait a second,' said Katie, as Detective O'Donovan opened the car door for her. 'I just want to see if I can get in touch with Jimmy.'

Detective O'Donovan waited patiently while she dialled Sergeant O'Rourke's mobile number. She was surprised that she hadn't heard from him sooner. It was very unlike him not to keep in constant touch when he was out on a case. In fact, he often irritated her by calling in every half-hour to tell her that he had nothing to tell her.

Katie heard a ringing tone, but Sergeant O'Rourke didn't answer. She tried a second time and still he didn't answer. 'No,' she said, at last. 'I'll have to try him again later.'

'You get an awful patchy signal down past Clon,' said Detective O'Donovan.

'Either that, or he's talking to Father Lowery and doesn't want to be interrupted. Anyhow, let's go and see what this Father ó Súllabháin has to say for himself.'

They drove across the river and up Summerhill until they reached St Luke's Cross, by Henchy's pub, where they turned right towards Montenotte. This was one of the more desirable districts of Cork, with mature trees and flint walls and panoramic views to the south across the River Lee and out towards the airport, and the hills beyond. From there you could see the weather rolling in a

310

good half-hour before it arrived. St Dominic's Retreat Centre was built on top of a hill, surrounded by neatly manicured lawns and rose beds crowded with red roses. The main retreat was a plain, stone-faced building with a grey slate roof and white-framed windows. Two Garda cars were parked outside, and two armed gardaí were standing by the front door, talking to one of the Dominican friars.

Katie climbed out of the car and walked towards them, and as she did so one of them nudged the other and they both stood up straighter. The friar appeared to remember that he was wanted urgently elsewhere, and hurried away.

'Afternoon, superintendent, and how's yourself?' said one of them, a hefty young man with ruddy cheeks, who looked to Katie like the bolder of the two.

'I'm grand, thanks for asking,' she replied sharply. 'I just came up to have a few words with Father ó Súllabháin.'

'He's in retreat,' said the garda.

'I know he's in retreat, but I still need to talk to him.'

'Well, he's isolated, like. Saying his prayers. Nobody's supposed to interrupt him.'

'That's too bad. I'm afraid that this inquiry is infinitely more urgent than the saving of Father ó Súllabháin's soul.'

'He's in room 202,' the garda told her. 'But like I say, he's in retreat, and I don't know if he'll talk to you or not.'

'Have *you* talked to him? Is he aware why we're giving him protection?'

311

'Not exactly, ma'am. No.'

'What do you mean by "not exactly"? You *have* talked to him and explained what's going on?'

'Not exactly, ma'am. No. To be truthful, we haven't actually seen him yet.'

'You haven't *seen* him?' said Katie, in disbelief. 'Name of Jesus, you're standing here guarding him and you haven't even *seen* him? And don't tell me "not exactly".'

'No, ma'am. Sorry, ma'am. But we've checked everybody going in and out. Even the bread delivery.'

Katie said to Detective O'Donovan, 'Come on, Patrick,' and the two of them pushed their way through the main doors into the reception area. Inside, the retreat smelled faintly of stale gladioli water and leek and potato soup. There was nobody to greet them, only a desk and an empty chair, but a sign on the wall directed them to the lift.

The hallway was long and hushed, with a pale blue carpet and pastel-pink walls. It was lined with antique chairs and side tables, and the walls were hung with serene landscapes and scenes from the Bible, like Christ washing His disciples' feet, and the conversion of Saul.

They reached the lift, pressed the button and stepped inside. 'Name of Jesus,' Katie breathed, still fuming. 'They haven't even *seen* him.'

The lift made a thin, keening sound, like Barney when he was locked outside the kitchen door. She stared at herself in the mirror on the opposite side of the lift. Her eyes were puffy and she thought she looked much more haggard than usual – but maybe it was only the lighting, directly from above, like being at the hairdresser's.

They reached the second floor and Katie led the way along the corridor. She reached room 202 and knocked.

'Father ó Súllabháin?' Pause. 'Father ó Súllabháin? This is Detective Superintendent Maguire from the Garda Síochána.'

There was no reply, so Katie knocked again. 'Father ó Síllabháin – I know you're in retreat, and you're praying, but it's absolutely critical that I talk to you. It's about Father Heaney and Father Quinlan and Father O'Gara, and St Joseph's Choir.'

They waited, but there was still no reply. Katie looked at Detective O'Donovan, who shrugged and said, 'Either he's deaf or he's climbing out the window.'

Katie tried the door handle. The door was unlocked, so she immediately opened it up and called out, 'Father ó Súllabháin? Detective Superintendent Maguire! I need to talk to you!'

She stepped inside, and the first thing she saw was an olive-green armchair, which was lying on its side. She looked around quickly, with Detective O'Donovan close behind her. The room was cream-painted and carpeted in dark green, with only one picture on the wall, a print of Christ in the Garden of Gethsemane, being comforted by an angel. At the right-hand side of the room stood an unmade single bed, with a pine bedside table and a yellow-shaded lamp. To the left, a washbasin with a mirror. She walked up to the washbasin and examined the toiletries on the shelf. Palmolive shaving foam, Aquafresh toothpaste, Savlon

313

antiseptic cream and a Dove roll-on deodorant for men. A yellow plastic razor and a splayed-out toothbrush were leaning side by side in a green plastic mug, like two drunks in a Patrick Street doorway.

'Deodorant?' Detective O'Donovan remarked, looking over her shoulder. 'That's progress. All of the priests I ever knew reeked of BO. And they always had smelly breath. Father Beckett, we used to call him Paint Stripper.'

Katie went over to a plain pine chest and pulled out the drawers one after the other. In the two small drawers at the top she found clean white Y-fronts, an empty spectacle case, a hotel sewing kit, some tissues and a three AA batteries, as well as a half-eaten bar of plain chocolate and a small Bible covered in white plastic that was so worn out that it was stuck together with yellowing Sellotape.

The three drawers below contained the clothes that Father ó Súllabháin had brought to the retreat with him – a black sweater, an oatmeal sweater, at least eight neatly folded shirts, and socks that had been paired and rolled up into balls.

'Right,' she said, 'Father ó Súllabháin's belongings are all here. But where is Father ó Súllabháin?'

'Maybe he just went to check on the cabbages.'

'I can't believe those two eejits downstairs. I gave their sergeant a specific order that they were to contact Father ó Súllabháin as soon as they arrived here and apprise him that he was going to be protected from now on by at least two armed gardaí, twenty-four hours a day.'

'Well, like I say, he's either gone to check on the cabbages, or he left here of his own free will, or somebody's come in here and abducted him.'

'That tipped-over chair. That makes me think he could have been taken against his will. And the bed's still messed up, even though it's five in the afternoon. But if he has been taken, the real question is when was he taken? And who took him? And *why?*'

'Could be our friend,' said Detective O'Donovan.

'You could be right. Maybe he got wind of the fact that we were on to him and decided to bring his next abduction forward a few days.'

'Maybe he thinks we know more about him than we actually do,' said Detective O'Donovan solemnly. 'On the other hand, maybe we *do* know more about him, more than we realize, but he doesn't know that, and neither do we.'

Katie blinked at Detective O'Donovan, and thought, *There's no answer to that.* But he obviously knew what he meant, and she kind of knew what he meant, and that was enough. 'Have those two uniforms start searching the building,' she told him. 'Every room, no matter who's in there or what they're doing. And call for some back-up from Mayfield to search the grounds. I'll go and talk to the director.'

They went back down to the first floor, taking the staircase this time, which was illuminated in reds and blues by a tall stained-glass window depicting a mournful-looking St Dominic, with one hand raised. Detective O'Donovan pushed his way back outside to talk to the two uniformed gardaí, while Katie went looking for the director's office. There was still nobody around, and the entire building was eerily silent, as if it had been evacuated.

She came to a door marked *Director: Benedict Tiernan, OP.* She gave a rapid knock but walked straight in without waiting for an answer. Inside, she found the director sitting at his desk, giving dictation to his secretary – a tall balding man in a white Dominican habit. He had a single grey cow's lick of hair, which was all that remained of a widow's peak. His eyes were very deep-set, with coal-dark rings around them, and he had a large predatory nose. The sun was shining through the window and it lit up his nostrils scarlet.

His secretary was a small fat woman in a pale green cardigan and a plaid skirt. She lifted her pen and held it poised in mid-air as if she was waiting for the director to tell Katie that he was too busy to talk to her, and continue his dictation.

Benedict Tiernan looked up at Katie with un-disguised displeasure. 'Detective Superintendent Maguire,' he said, in a rusty, tremulous voice that changed pitch from one sentence to the next. 'I wasn't expecting to see you in person.'

'I came to talk to Father ó Súllabháin,' she said. 'I thought I made it clear over the phone that I needed to interview him as soon as possible.'

'You did, superintendent. You did indeed. But I thought I made it clear to you that Father ó Súllabháin is in spiritual retreat. He is meditating, and praying, and we cannot disturb him. When you said "as soon as possible" I took you to mean when his retreat comes to an end, which

316

will be Sunday, after lunch.'

'Friar Tiernan, it is absolutely essential that I talk to him right now. A man's life could be at stake.'

She explained briefly about Father O'Gara and how he had been run over in Patrick Street and apparently abducted.

'Well, I'm extremely sorry about this,' said Benedict Tiernan, steepling his fingers. 'I was, of course, quite happy to give you permission to position guards around the retreat, as much for the protection of myself and my staff as for Father ó Súllabháin. I also understand that you cannot divulge to me the exact details of why Father ó Súllabháin *needs* protection, although I wasn't born yesterday, superintendent. I am quite aware of what goes on in the world, beyond the walls of this retreat.'

He paused. He sat back, and as he did so withdrew the end of his nose from the beam of light, as if he had switched it off.

'However, Father ó Súllabháin is here at St Dominic's under our protection. We are safeguarding his spirit as well as his body. I cannot allow you to speak to him until his time in retreat is over. Can you imagine if Jesus had cut short his forty days and forty nights of fasting in the desert? We would never have had Lent. Or only a very short Lent.'

Jesus, thought Katie. *And I thought Patrick O'Donovan was illogical.*

'I've ordered a thorough search, house and grounds,' she told him. 'Let's hope for his own sake that Father ó Süllabháin has simply wan-

317

dered off around your gardens somewhere, for a spot of contemplation.'

Eleven uniformed gardaí searched the house and its grounds for over an hour and a half, but eventually one of them came trudging up the car park to Katie and Friar Tiernan and shook his head.

'There's no sign of him at all, ma'am. We even took a sconce at the garden shed.'

Katie looked around, biting her lip in frustration. 'I can't believe that not a single person saw him leave.'

Friar Tiernan shrugged. 'As you can see for yourself, superintendent, St Dominic's is a place for reflection. Most of our retreatants are absorbed in prayer and in dealing with their own internal struggles. Why, the pope himself could probably walk past them and they wouldn't notice.'

Detective O'Donovan glanced across at Katie and the expression on his face said *what a load of bollocks,* and Katie agreed with him, but neither of them said anything out loud.

When Friar Tiernan had gone back into the house, Katie said to Detective O'Donovan, 'Are you sure you questioned everybody here? All of the friars? All of the kitchen staff? All of the – what does he call them – "retreatants"?'

'Every one of them, ma'am. Nobody saw a dicky bird.'

Just then, about hundred metres away, Katie caught sight of a gardener in a long brown apron pushing a wheelbarrow up the sloping lawn.

'How about him? The gardener? He must have

been outside for most of the day.'

Detective O'Donovan tapped his forehead with his fingertip. 'He's a pure stones, apparently. I was going to talk to him myself, but one of friars told me I would be wasting my time.'

'All right,' said Katie. She watched the gardener as he reached the top of the lawn. He looked young, only in his early twenties, with a small head and a pointed, leprechaun-like face. He was wearing a green bandana knotted so that it looked as if he had leprechaun's ears.

Without saying a word to Detective O'Donovan, Katie walked across the lawn and came up to the gardener as he tipped up a tangled heap of weeds and branches on to a compost heap. If he was aware that she was there, he didn't show it. He used his fork and a few kicks from his wellington boots to tidy up the compost, and then he turned around and started to push his empty wheelbarrow back down the slope. Katie kept pace with him, not walking too close. She didn't want to intimidate him. He glanced across at her now and again, but he still didn't say anything.

'What's your name?' she asked him.

He glanced at her again, and blinked.

'You can tell me your name, can't you? My name's Katie.'

'Don't talk to no strangers,' he said, in a peculiar, duck-like voice, as if he were quoting something that he had been told by his mother.

'That's all right. I'm not a stranger. I'm a police detective.'

'You're a lady.'

319

'I know I'm a lady, but you can have lady detectives right enough. Didn't you ever see *CSI*, on the television? They have lots of lady detectives. Ladies are good at being detectives, because they don't know how to mind their own business.'

The gardener gave a single honk of amusement, which Katie thought was promising. At least he had understood what she meant. They walked down the slope a little further, with the empty wheelbarrow making a trundling noise, when the gardener suddenly stopped and said, 'Tómas?' as if it were a question.

'That's your name, then? Tómas? That's a very good name, Tómas. Do you know what it means? It actually means "twin".'

The gardener frowned at her. 'I *am* a twin, but my brother died before he was born. I was alive, inside of my mam, but Brian was dead.'

'I'm sorry.'

'It's all right, like. I still used to play with him. I could always see him, even if nobody else could. That was because we were twins. I can still see him, but we don't play any more. Well, we're grown up now.'

Katie said, 'You must see a lot of things that other people don't see.'

'Yes,' said Tómas. 'But they don't like me talking about it.'

'Who doesn't like you talking about it?'

He looked up towards the retreat. 'The friars. They say that my brother's in heaven so how can I see him here on earth? But I know he's dead. I'm not thick. I know he's dead but I can still see him. He stands over there by that summerhouse, especially when the sun's shining.'

He picked up his edging shears and began to trim the grass around the rose bed. 'I'm not thick,' he repeated. 'I know the difference between alive and dead. I know *everybody* here, all of the friars, I know every last one of them. And I know all of the cleaners and all of the cooks and all of the people who come here to pray. When they arrive, and when they go. I don't know their real names, all of them, but I give them names. Like Mister Sadbeard, or Mrs Twix, because she's always coming out into the garden when she thinks there's nobody looking to eat a Twix bar.'

Katie watched him working for a while and then she said, 'There was a priest who would have come here last Sunday. His real name was Father ó Súllabháin, and he was staying in room 202.'

The gardener stood up straight. He had a single blonde whisker, disconcertingly long, growing out of the right side of his chin. Katie wondered why he never cut it, or plucked it.

'I think I know the fellow you mean,' he said, blinking. 'Not too tall, not too short. Round head, like a football. That's what I christened him. Father Football.'

'Did you see Father Football today, Tómas? Maybe he was going out for a walk, something like that.'

The gardener said, 'No. I haven't seen him since Monday afternoon at a quarter past two. He came out into the garden and sat in the summerhouse for twenty-two minutes and then he went back in again. He looked like he was praying, because he had his eyes closed most of the time, and he was going through his rosary nineteen to the dozen.'

He held up his left hand, and pulled down his sleeve to display a red plastic Swatch. 'See? I have a watch.'

'So you definitely haven't seen him today? How about new people? Have you seen anybody you didn't recognize? Anybody unfamiliar?'

'The guards. There's two of them, isn't there? Garda Here and Garda There, that's what I call them, because one of them always seems to be looking for the other one.'

'Have you given *me* a name yet?' asked Katie.

The gardener looked embarrassed and turned his head away. 'I haven't, no. I thought you were only visiting for a very short while and I don't usually give names to people who visit for only a very short while. Like you, and that fellow with you, and those three fellows who came this morning and went away again almost as soon as they'd arrived.'

He suddenly clamped his dirty grey gardening glove over his mouth, and his eyes looked stricken, as if he had just sad something that he shouldn't.

'What three fellows?' asked Katie.

'I'm not supposed to say. Oh, God. I'm really not supposed to say.'

'What? Why? Who told you that you couldn't?'

'Friar Tiernan himself. Friar Tiernan, he's the director. After they'd gone away those three fellows, he turned around and saw me trimming the rose bushes and he came down here himself

322

and told me not to tell anybody what I'd just seen. Nobody at all. He said that even if I did, nobody would believe me, just like nobody believes that I see my twin brother. And now I've gone and told *you.*'

Katie laid a reassuring hand on his sleeve. 'It's all right, Tómas. I'm not just anybody, I'm a police detective. You're allowed to tell me. In fact, it's your civic duty and you may even get a reward for it.'

'But supposing Friar Tiernan finds out?' said the gardener. He was growing extremely agitated, tugging at the fingers of his gardening gloves as if he had already been dismissed and told to take them off.

'Friar Tiernan is not going to find out unless I tell him and I promise you that I won't. Do you understand me? Cross my heart and hope to die. Now, you're very good at describing people – what were they like, these three fellows?'

The gardener kept on tugging at his gloves and looked deeply miserable. 'I saw only the backs of them, like. One of them was a real big fellow with curly yellow hair and one them wasn't so big but he was still biggish, you know, and he had dark hair. The third one of them I could hardly see at all on account of the van door was open and he was mostly hidden behind it.'

'They had a van?'

The gardener nodded. 'They came in a van and they drove it backwards all the way up the driveway, right up to the entrance. They opened the doors and then they closed the doors and drove off again.'

'And what did the van look like, Tómas?'

'I shouldn't be telling you this. I'll be done.'

Katie reached inside her jacket and took out a manila envelope with a picture of the black van with the crozier painted on the back.

'Is this the van that you saw?'

The gardener said nothing, but looked at the picture, and then stared at Katie, and nodded so furiously that she was afraid that his head might fly off into the rose bushes.

She walked quickly back to the house, where Detective O'Donovan and three uniformed gardaí were waiting for her.

'Well?' asked Detective O'Donovan, with a sloping smile. 'Did you get any good tips about how to grow bananas?'

'You can laugh,' Katie told him. 'But if you want the truth about anything at all, always ask the simplest person you can find. They won't have any agenda and they won't try to embroider the facts to impress you and they'll always remember things just the way they were.'

She paused, and then she said, decisively, 'Benedict Tiernan, OP, was giving us a whole lot of BS, I'm sure of it. Our perpetrator came here in his van this morning and I'll bet you money that he took Father ó Súllabháin away with him, and that for some reason Friar Tiernan gave him his full co-operation.'

Detective O'Donovan opened and closed his mouth, and then he said, 'You're joking, aren't you?'

'Not at all.'

'And what? You're relying on what some mong of a gardener told you?'

'I'm relying on my own instincts, if you must know.'

'So what are we going to do? Arrest Friar Tiernan on suspicion of being an accessory to kidnap?'

'We're going to leave Friar Tiernan well alone for now. First of all, I want to find out who drives that van. Haven't you heard from Jimmy yet? Surely he must have found Father Lowery by now.'

'I've been calling his mobile, but he's not answering. Neither is Father Lowery. I called St Michael's church in Rathbarry and they're not answering either.'

Katie checked her watch. 'He should have reported back by now. Let's give him another half-hour anyway.' She looked back towards the retreat. 'We're being given the runaround here, Patrick, but I know who I need to talk to next.'

Thirty-seven

Gradually the window darkened, although the hydrangea kept on tapping against it, *tappity-tap*, *tappity-tap*, like a ghost who had long since given up hope of being let in, but who continued tapping all the same.

Is there anybody there? said the traveller, knocking at the moonlit door.

Gerry opened his eyes. He was suffering such pain that he found it hard to believe that he was still alive. Surely you could die from pain alone. Surely there was a way in which you could wish yourself dead. *Dear God in heaven, please stop my heart. Please stop it now, so that I no longer have to go through this unbearable agony.*

But of course God had turned His back on him, and no matter how desperately he pleaded, God would pretend that He hadn't heard.

The room grew gloomier and gloomier, until it was almost completely dark. Gerry rose in and out of consciousness, like a swimmer dipping up and down in the ocean, except that he felt that the surface was on fire, as if it was spread with blazing oil, and whenever he reached it he was blinded and seared and deafened by his own screaming.

Without warning, the room filled up with dazzling white light. He tried to raise his head to see what was happening, but he didn't have the strength, and the tendons in his neck were too tight. *Please, Mary, Mother of God, let it be an angel, come to carry me away.*

'*Help me,*' he said, inside his head; but not out loud.

It wasn't an angel. It was the Grey Mullet Man, holding up a hurricane lamp. He was still wearing his mask and his pointed hat, but now he was covered in a long red apron that smelled strongly of rubber, and his forearms were bare, and covered in tattoos. He stood at Gerry's bedside for a long time without saying anything, staring through his eyeholes at Gerry's black and scarlet scalp and then turning to look at the shrivelled remains of his penis, like a burned-out indoor firework.

'How was *that* for a penance?' he said. 'The burning bush, no less! Do you think that the good Lord has seen fit to forgive you yet?'

Gerry stared up at him, but it took all of his concentration to cope with his pain and he could hardly think, let alone decide if he had been redeemed.

The Grey Mullet Man held the hurricane lamp closer, so that Gerry could feel its heat against his cheek and hear its snake-like hissing. 'I'll tell you what I think. I think you're nearly there, but not quite, like Christ on his way to Calvary, carrying His cross. You still have some way to go, and you don't have Simon the Cyrenian to carry your cross the rest of the way for you, I'm afraid. Not that I believe that Christ dropped the cross at all. It doesn't say anywhere in the New Testament that Christ dropped the cross. In fact, it doesn't say anywhere that He even carried it a single inch. But let's pretend that He did, like; and now you're carrying *your* cross, just the same.'

'John nineteen, verse seventeen,' Gerry croaked at him.

'Ah, there you are!' said the Grey Mullet Man, in triumph. 'I knew the priest in you would come out at last! No good denying it any longer, Father O'Gara! But you could still be wrong, you know, about Christ dropping the cross. It depends on your translation of the Greek word *opisthen*, for "after". Did Simon carry the cross *after* Jesus had carried it, like *after* in time? Or did he carry it *after* him, meaning behind?'

The Grey Mullet Man waited, and then he said, 'You don't look like you fecking care, to tell you the God's-honest truth, do you? So let's be getting on with it, shall we? Let's get on and bring your penance to its glorious conclusion. Lads, are you there?'

The man in the bishop's mitre appeared; and, close behind him, the white expressionless face of the man in the pierrot mask was looking over his shoulder.

Oh, Jesus, thought Gerry. *What are they going to do to me now? I'm already dying, so why don't they just leave me alone? Shock or septicaemia or dehydration or hypothermia – one or all of them will get me in the end. I don't need to go through any more torture. Please.*

The Grey Mullet Man carefully set the hurricane lamp down on the plastic-topped kitchen chair.

'By the way,' he said, snapping his fingers, 'I thought you'd be pleased to know that we have the last of you now. Father Heaney, Father Quinlan – yourself, of course – and now we have Father ó Súllabháin.'

'He's *here?*' asked Gerry.

The Grey Mullet Man shook his head, his mask flapping from side to side. 'Oh, no. It wouldn't have been appropriate to bring him here. Not a fitting fate for him at all. To be honest with you, Father, I didn't want to go and bring him in just yet. We still haven't finished with you, have we? And here we are, having to go out and catch ourselves another one. The last one, I'm happy to say.

'The trouble is, the schickalony have been a little quicker off the mark than we thought they would. So we had to make sure that they didn't mess things up for us.'

He took a craft knife out of his pocket and then leaned over to cut the black nylon straps that were holding Gerry's wrists against the bedhead. Gerry felt an overwhelming urge to throttle him, but he couldn't even feel his arms, let alone lift them up and seize the Grey Mullet Man by the throat.

The Grey Mullet Man dropped his craft knife back in his pocket and picked up a coil of shiny steel wire. 'Recognize this? Fourteen-gauge piano wire. Thin enough to hurt, Father, but not too thin to cut through your skin. Very popular with some of your lot for self-flagellation, and why not? You fecking deserve all the flagellation you can give yourselves, you perverts.'

The man in the pierrot mask came forward, took hold of Gerry's left arm, and pulled him over until he was lying on his right side. He held him there, gripping his sleeve hard to prevent him from falling back. Behind him, the Grey Mullet Man unwound a long piece of piano wire and clipped it off with pliers. Then he pulled Gerry's wrists together and bound them tight, around and around, until Gerry thought that he was going to cut his hands off altogether. Fortunately, he was so numb that he felt scarcely any more pain than he was feeling already. His hands felt ice-cold, and nothing else.

Once his wrists were wired together, the man in the pierrot mask let him drop back on to the bedsprings. They made a jouncing, squeaky sound, like they would have done if a couple had been making love on them.

Now the man in the bishop's mitre lifted Gerry's legs as far apart as possible, and the Grey Mullet Man wired each of his ankles to the bed frame. His legs had been shapely and muscular when he played rugby, but now they were lean and white as chicken skin, and streaked with dark hair.

'There now,' said the Grey Mullet Man, tossing the coil of wire to one side. 'All lashed tight and ready for the gelding. First, though, let's hear you singing for mercy.'

He went back to the kitchen chair and picked up a jar of clear honey. He unscrewed the lid, dipped a tablespoon into it, and came up to Gerry and held it over his lips. Some of it dribbled on to his chin and ran stickily down the side of his neck.

'Here you are, Father O'Gara. You know it's good for the larynx. You'll be singing sweeter than Pavarotti before you know it. Oh, I forgot. Pavarotti's dead. Never mind, so will you be, soon enough.'

'*Mmmffff,*' said Gerry, and kept his lips tightly closed.

'Come on, swallow it,' insisted the Grey Mullet Man.

Gerry still kept his lips closed, so the Grey Mullet Man nodded to the man in the pierrot mask and he gripped Gerry's nose between finger and thumb so that Gerry couldn't breathe. When at last he opened his mouth, the Grey Mullet Man rammed the spoon into his mouth

330

so hard that he broke one of his front teeth in half, and he swallowed the fragment of tooth along with the honey. He choked, coughed, gagged, and nearly vomited, but the Grey Mullet Man dug another spoonful of honey out of the jar and forced it between his lips.

'Now then,' he said. 'That wasn't so difficult, Father, was it? So, let's hear you sing for forgiveness. In your time, one-two-three, *la-a-a-a-a!*'

Gerry could do nothing but cough, and cough, and in the end he coughed so much that he let out a loud, cackling retch. The Grey Mullet Man said, 'Jesus, I'll be chugging myself in a moment if you go on like that. That's not what I was looking for at all. I wanted sweet, holy music. I wanted a song of redemption, not the sound of someone talking to Hughie.'

He started to sing, in a high, eerie voice – the same voice that Gerry had heard singing *'The Rose of Allendale'*:

Hallelujah, God with us!
Hope restored and death undone!
Sinners saved and captives freed!
Beautiful redemption song!

Gerry retched again. There was nothing in his stomach but honey and saliva and phlegm, so he couldn't vomit.

'I give up,' said the Grey Mullet Man. 'I fecking give up. Let's forget the sinners saved and the stone rolled back and get down to business.'

There was very little left of Gerry's penis apart from a blackened rag that looked like a burned

331

wash leather, surrounded by a cluster of fluid-filled blisters of differing sizes. His scrotum had been scorched red-raw, but the man in the pierrot mask was still able to grasp it in his left hand and squeeze it until Gerry's testicles bulged. Gerry thought that he might have screamed again, but he wasn't certain. Everything seemed like one continuous scream. Even the bright white light from the hurricane lamp seemed like a scream, rather than a light.

The man in the pierrot mask handed the steel-bladed *castratori* to the man in the bishop's mitre. The man in the bishop's mitre held them up in front of Gerry's face, chopping them open and shut so that Gerry understood what was about to be done to him.

'I know you, you gowls,' he breathed. 'I know all of your names.'

'And what good do you think that will do you, Father O'Gara? What are you going to do, rat us out to the angels?'

Gerry stared at the ceiling. He felt the cold sharp blades of the *castratori* on either side of his scrotum. Then they slowly closed together, and he felt them cut through every nerve and every tubule and every inch of flesh. They made a surprisingly sharp *crunch,* too, which distressed him even more than the pain. It was the sound of his manhood being taken away from him, irrevocably.

The Grey Mullet Man collected his severed testicles in his open hand, before they could drop through the bedsprings. He held them up so that Gerry could see them, rolling them in a bloody mess between finger and thumb.

'Do you think that this will help you to see God, Father?' he said, and even though Gerry couldn't see his face behind his mask, he felt sure that he was leering.

He was still taunting Gerry when his mobile phone rang. He reached underneath his apron with his clean hand, took it out and flipped it open.

'What's the story?' he asked. He clearly knew who the caller was.

He listened, and then he said, 'Jesus. Feck. All right, then. Jesus. That's going to put the cat among the fecking pigeons and no mistake.'

He closed the phone and pushed it back into his trouser pocket. Then he looked down at Gerry and said, 'No more time to waste, Father. Although you couldn't be any kind of a father now, could you, state of you la.'

It seemed to Gerry as if the light from the hurricane lamp was dimming, even though it was hissing just as loudly as before. *Sink,* he thought. *Let yourself sink under that sea, into that welcome darkness, into that numbing cold. Sink and never come back to the surface.*

He didn't feel the man in the bishop's mitre lifting up his head, quite gently, so that the Grey Mullet Man could loop the piano wire around his neck.

Thirty-eight

Katie returned home to feed Barney and let him out into the back yard to do his business. She also wanted to phone the hospital to see if Siobhán was any better, and try to get in touch with John.

There was very little change in Siobhán's condition. Not much better, not much worse, although the nurse told her that they were slightly concerned about her low blood pressure.

John wasn't answering his phones, either his landline or his mobile, so she left him a message to call her and to tell him how much she loved him. She wouldn't have time to see him this evening, what with the former Father O'Gara and now Father ó Súllabháin both missing, believed abducted.

She was opening up a packet of soda bread to make herself a ham sandwich when her phone rang.

'Boss? It's Patrick. I've just had a call from Inspector Pearse in Clon. He says that he's fierce concerned about Jimmy O'Rourke.'

'What? Why? The local guards aren't even supposed to know that he's down there.'

Detective O'Donovan told her about the overturned cattle truck on the Croppy Road, and how Sergeant O'Rourke had borrowed a squad car from the Clonakilty Garda.

'They have his Toyota at the station but he

334

hasn't shown up to collect it and they don't have the first idea where he is.'

'All squad cars have trackers fitted, don't they? Why can't they find him?'

'The tracker must have been disabled, like. That's all they can think of.'

'Did you tell them that he was on his way to Rathbarry, and who he was supposed to be seeing?'

'I did not, no. I thought that I had better speak to you first.'

'Oh, well, good man yourself, Patrick. But get back to this Inspector Pearse, would you, and explain what Jimmy was doing down there. You don't have to tell him *why* exactly he wanted to interview Father Lowery, only that it was part of a major case that we're looking into right now. And if they can locate Father Lowery, that would help, too. Can you call the diocese office for me and see if he's turned up back in Cork?'

'Right you are, boss. But there's one more thing.'

'Don't tell me. Not more bad news.'

'I'd say "unhelpful" rather than anything else. We paid a visit to St Joseph's, to check on their records for the time when the choir was being formed, and there are none. In fact, they have no records at all between 1966 and 1997. The secretary said that when they were moved into temporary offices in 1998, during a renovation of the main building, they were all destroyed in a fire. That includes attendance records, examination results, copies of birth certificates, even photographs. The whole lot.'

'I don't believe it.'

'The secretary swore blind that it was true. We could get a warrant, I suppose, and search their archives, but I doubt if we'll find anything.'

'There must be some record somewhere. Try social welfare, or the HSE.'

'I'm not about to give up yet, ma'am. You can count on it.'

'Keep in touch with me, Patrick. This is getting critical. Our perpetrator has got hold of two victims now and there's no way of telling how long he's going to keep them alive.'

While Katie was eating her sandwich, she sat on one of the kitchen stools and opened up her laptop to look up the Cork Survivors' Society. There were two numbers, one on Oliver Plunkett Street right in the centre of the city, and another in Glanmire, which was a collection of villages about four miles to the east of Cork, up the estuary of the River Glashaboy. It was the second number she wanted: it gave the name of the society's director, Paul McKeown.

She swallowed a mouthful of sparkling mineral water to help her sandwich go down, and then she rang him. The phone rang and rang for a long time before anybody answered.

Then, a cautious man's voice. 'CSS. Who's calling?'

'Is that Paul McKeown?'

'Who wants to know?'

'Detective Superintendent Katie Maguire, from Anglesea Street Garda station. I'm investigating the murders of Father Heaney and Father Quinlan, and I was wondering if I could have a

336

word with you.'

'I see,' said Paul McKeown. She could hear his steady breathing. 'I don't see how I can be of any help to you, superintendent.'

'Well, I think you could be, more than you know. Can I call around and see you this evening? It shouldn't take too long.'

'Very well. My wife is out at her book club tonight, so that should be all right.'

Katie looked up at the kitchen clock. Nine minutes after seven. The day was disappearing fast and yet it was becoming more and more tangled by the minute. She felt as if she had plenty of answers but none of the right questions to make any sense of them.

She felt, too, that she was still relying almost entirely on guesswork to take this investigation forward. It seemed probable that Fathers Heaney, Quinlan, O'Gara and ó Súllabháin had deliberately castrated young orphan boys in order to make their choir the finest in Ireland. Their spiritual motive appeared to have been to please God so much that He would deign to make Himself visible in some way, although how this could happen was not clear. Maybe they had expected it to happen for real, so that everybody would witness His appearance, and see heaven. On the other hand, maybe they thought that it would happen only inside their own minds, a private revelation for them alone.

What she couldn't work out, though, was Monsignor Kelly's involvement. She strongly suspected that he knew what had happened to the van with the crozier on the back, and she even suspected that he had a strong idea who had murdered Father Heaney and Father Quinlan. Yet she couldn't understand why he had been so eager to blame Brendan Doody. And where *was* Brendan Doody – alive or dead?

Not only that, where in the name of Jesus was Jimmy O'Rourke? She was beginning to grow seriously worried about him.

She closed her laptop, finished her sandwich and went into the hall to take down her raincoat. Barney came bustling after her, his tail whacking from side to side.

'Sorry, boy. No walkies just yet. I'll try to take you out when I get home.'

Barney made that keening noise in the back of his throat. She loved him dearly, but she was beginning to think that it was very unfair of her to keep a dog as boisterous and needy as an Irish setter when she couldn't take him for regular exercise or give him the attention he deserved. What was more, John had given him to her, and supposing she decided to let John go off to America and not go with him? Barney would be a constant reminder of the chance that she had given up, and the love that she had sacrificed.

She hunkered down and stroked him and tugged at his ears, which made him snuffle and stick out his tongue and dance excitedly on the carpet.

'What would you do, Barney? Stay or go? Go or stay?'

Barney cocked his head to one side, and gave her a sympathetic *wuff*.

It was already growing dark as she drove up towards Sallybrook. On her left, the huge oak trees were as black as blotches of Indian ink. On her right, she could see the wide curve of the River Glashaboy, reflecting the sky. She had always thought that there was something very secretive about rivers at night. No wonder so many people committed suicide in Cork by throwing themselves in the river. They knew that it would carry away all of their despair, and tell no one.

Paul McKeown lived in a large house halfway up a winding hill called Glen Richmond. It was a newish house, very neat, with a steep asphalt drive and a recently planted rockery and a double garage with white-painted doors. Katie climbed out of her car, walked up to the front door and pushed the bell, which rang with a full Westminster chime. A light went on behind the stained-glass window over the porch, and she could see a figure coming down the stairs, changing colour as it did so, from red to green to yellow.

He opened the door and said, 'Superintendent Maguire?'

'Mr McKeown. Sorry I had to call on you so late.'

She recognized him from the newspaper photograph of the rally outside the diocesan offices on Redemption Road. Tall – very tall – at least six feet three – with dark brown hair that was wavy rather than curly as it appeared in the photograph, but then it had been raining that day. He must have been about forty-two years old, and his hair was a little too long for his age, but it immediately told Katie a lot about his personality:

339

non-conformist; quite artistic; somewhat vain.

He was extremely handsome, in a dark, slightly satanic way. He had a long face with a straight nose and sharply chiselled cheeks, and a strong, angular chin. His eyes were greyish-blue, the colour of a cloudy afternoon sky. He was wearing a very white shirt with the sleeves rolled halfway up and a pair of indigo jeans with a plaited brown leather belt.

'Come on in,' he told her. She stepped inside and he took her through to a large living room with a polished oak floor and burgundy leather sofas. The decor was very minimalist. Above the fireplace hung a 42-inch plasma television, but there were no pictures or photographs anywhere. In the far corner stood a green bronze statuette of an angel at prayer, her wings spread wide, but apart from half a dozen white roses in a clear glass vase in the middle of the coffee table, that was the only decoration.

'Sit down, please,' he told her. 'Like I said on the phone, I don't know what I can do to help you.'

Katie sat on one of the leather sofas. 'You could help me by telling me the truth,' she said, giving him one of her really disarming smiles, her eyes all twinkly.

'The truth?' said Paul McKeown. 'I haven't said anything to you yet, so could I be lying to you?'

'You told me on the phone that your wife had gone to her book club.'

'I did, yes. What of it? She goes every Thursday.'

'You're not married, Mr McKeown. I looked

you up in our records before I came up here. You're on Wikipedia, too. You used to be married to Caoimhe ó Faoláin, the poet, the one who wrote *The Flowers of Cashel Beg*, but you were divorced three years ago.'

Paul McKeown didn't seem to be at all abashed that Katie had caught him out. He gave her a nonchalant shrug and said, 'Okay. I always tell people that I'm still married, especially women. I suppose you could say that it's a defence mechanism. The trouble with being Paul McKeown is that women either have a prurient interest in what was done to me, or they think they can help me to forget it – often both.'

'All right, I'll forgive you this one time,' Katie told him, not very seriously. But then she said, 'I told you why I wanted to talk to you. We urgently need some help to identify who might have murdered Father Heaney and Father Quinlan. So far as we know, they're currently holding another priest who came under suspicion for molestation, Father Gerry O'Gara, and they may have abducted a fourth, Father Michael ó Súllabháin.

'I have to caution you that all of this is absolutely confidential at this stage of our inquiry, but we have notebooks kept by Father Heaney that describe how these four priests were brought in to form a choir at St Joseph's Orphanage.'

'Go on,' said Paul McKeown. From the tone of his voice, she had the feeling that he knew, or at least suspected, what she was going to say next.

'I'll be blunt about it. At some stage, it appears that these four decided that the choir could only reach the height of musical perfection if some or

all of the boys in it were castrated, like the choirboys in the Vatican in the sixteenth century. So
that's what they did. They castrated them. That's
according to Father Heaney's notebooks, anyhow, so we have to be a little wary about the
veracity of it. There's a lot of cat's malogian in
those notebooks, too – about seeing God face to
face, and heaven being a real place. So what he
wrote about could have been nothing more than
the sadomasochistic fantasies of a very frustrated
priest. But on balance we don't think so.'

Paul McKeown thought about this for a very
long time before he said anything, his hands
steepled in front of his face so that Katie couldn't
clearly see his expression. Then he suddenly
stood up and said, 'Let me get you a drink,
superintendent. You look like a vodka lady to me.'

'I'd love one, to tell you the truth, but I'm
working, and I expect to be working for the rest
of the night, and through tomorrow morning,
too.'

'You're sure? In that case, let me press you to a
cup of tea, maybe, or coffee. Or a soft drink.'

'All right, then. Anything will do. Fizzy orange
if you have it.'

He went through to the kitchen and came back
shortly afterwards with a glass of bitter lemon for
Katie, with ice and a slice of lemon in it, and a
Satzenbrau lager for himself, which he drank
straight out of the bottle.

'I've heard about boys at St Joseph's being
given the snip,' he said, when he had sat down
again. 'There have been all kinds of rumours and
stories about it for years, but nobody has once

342

come out and said it straight.'

'You think it's true, then?'

'I'm sure of it, superintendent. But I think that a combination of factors has kept it quiet. Let me tell you this: I decided to form the Cork Survivors' Society in the summer of 1998, when I was twenty-nine years old. I was serially abused by the priests at the school I went to, and by one priest in particular. During that summer, purely by chance, I met three or four young men who had suffered similar experiences at *their* schools.

'None of us liked to talk about it at first. You don't want to, because it brings it all back to you, and when you grow older you can never understand how you allowed it to happen. I still wonder, after all of these years, if I was partly to blame. The worst thing of all is that some of the abuse was actually enjoyable, and it takes a very strong and well-balanced personality to admit to that.

'By forming the CSS, we were admitting openly that we had been molested by the priests who were supposed to be taking care of us, and we were actively seeking help and support from each other, and the community around us. Legal help, financial help, but most of all psychological help. We were also naming names, and making specific accusations against specific priests. On top of that, we were demanding that such abuse should never happen again, *ever*, not to one more little boy or one more little girl.'

He leaned forward, looking at Katie with a seriousness that made her think that *he* would have made a good priest himself, especially one to whom you could confess all your doubts.

'I'll tell you something, superintendent, the resistance we came up against ... well, I expect you know yourself what was done to keep us quiet. They promised us full and open inquiries, but all we got was secret reviews by the diocesan officials themselves, and frantic cover-ups. They promised us punishments – defrockings, dismissals – but all that happened was that the offending priests were moved to other parishes, where, of course, they continued to molest the children in their charge. The Garda Síochána assured us that they would investigate every accusation thoroughly, and that criminal proceedings would follow if they were provable and justified, but not a single criminal case was ever brought.

'It was all too long ago, and there was no forensic evidence. No priestly pubic hairs or gym shorts with dried semen on them for DNA tests. No witnesses, either, for the most part. No witnesses who weren't too frightened or embarrassed to speak out, anyway.'

He paused again, and then he said, 'Yes ... we heard all kinds of stories about the boys in St Joseph's Orphanage Choir. But once they joined the choir they were kept apart from the rest of the children, except during lessons, and they were all given special treatment. They were fed better, and given their own dormitory, and they were excused games and gymnastics.

'There were so many rumours about why they were treated so well, and some of those rumours came very close to the truth, like the rumour that they had paschal candles pushed up their backsides to make them sing higher. But not one of the boys themselves ever admitted what had *really* been done to them – not one – and after the choir was disbanded, and the boys grew up, not one of them ever made a formal complaint.

'I made enquiries, believe me, and tried to find out the truth of the matter, but their lips were sealed tight, all of them.

'The church was still capable of striking the fear of God into them, and they weren't only threatened with damnation, believe me. They were physically threatened, too – both them and their families. You think the criminal gangs of Cork have their heavies ... you should see some of the muscle that the church employs. All very discreetly, of course, Hail Mary, full of grace, Our Lord is with thee, *thump!*'

Katie said, 'Well ... they may have been too scared before now, but we think it's likely that one or more of those boys from St Joseph's has at last found the bottle to take his revenge. What I need, Paul, is names.'

'I'm sorry. I can remember only about four of them, and at least three of them are dead now.'

'That's a surprise. *Castrati* are supposed to live longer than your average man.'

'Not if they kill themselves, they don't.'

'What about the fourth?'

'Don't know. Haven't heard from him in years.'

'You can still tell me his name.'

'Denis Sweeney. He called me in the last week of 1999 and said that two of his friends from St Joseph's Choir had gassed themselves in their car and did I want to know why? He said he would meet me in the Long Valley on Winthrop Street and tell me all about it.'

'And?'

'I went to meet him but he never showed. I never heard from him again.'

'Are you sure you can't remember any of the others?'

'There were twins, I remember that. Very shy and never spoke to anybody. I think their name might have been Phelan.'

'Well, that might help us,' said Katie.

'Do you think these two missing priests might be murdered like the other two?' Paul McKeown asked her.

'Tortured and murdered, yes. I think there's a very high probability. And half of what was done to Father Heaney and Father Quinlan we haven't released to the press.'

Paul McKeown said, 'What price can you put on a child's lost innocence? How much should you pay for deliberately taking away a boy's opportunity to become a man?'

They sat together in silence for a moment. Somewhere in the distance they heard the grumbling of thunder, or it may have been a plane landing at Cork airport, sixteen kilometres off to the south-west.

'I'm sorry I haven't been able to help you very much, superintendent,' said Paul McKeown. 'But I'll ask around. One or two members of CSS might have a better memory than I have.'

'Thank you,' she told him. 'And you can call me Katie if you like. "Superintendent" always makes me feel frumpy, and old.'

Paul McKeown stood up. 'Thank you, Katie. You're anything but that, if you don't mind my saying so. I was expecting a high-ranking lady detective to have iron-grey hair and steel-rimmed spectacles, but when I opened the door, I have to tell you that I was very pleasantly surprised.'

Katie was about to tell him to get away with himself when her mobile phone warbled. 'Excuse me,' she said, and flipped it open.

'Superintendent ma'am? It's me again, Patrick.'

'What is it this time? Don't tell me another priest has gone missing?'

'No, ma'am. The opposite. There's been a fire at a derelict farm cottage about two kilometres west of Killeens. The fire brigade have just called us to say that they've discovered a body inside, all trussed up with wire. From the way they described it, it sounds as if it could be Father O'Gara.'

'Oh, shite,' said Katie.

Paul McKeown looked at her quizzically, raising one eyebrow.

'I expect you'll see it on the news tomorrow,' Katie told him. 'Meanwhile, like I said before, I don't think I have much prospect of getting any sleep tonight.'

Thirty-nine

She smelled the burned-out cottage long before she reached it – a bitter, black smell that was blown into her car through the vents in the dashboard. Then she turned a corner of the narrow country road and saw the blue and orange flashing lights in a field about two thirds of a kilometre off to her right, and tungsten floodlights.

She drove down the bumpy track that led to the cottage. Both red fire engines from the substation at Ballyvolane were parked at an angle beside the still-smoking building, as well as a fire brigade jeep. A Garda squad car and Detective O'Donovan's car were parked nearby.

She parked her own car as close to Detective O'Donovan's as she could, to allow room for the technical unit's van when they eventually arrived. She climbed out and Detective O'Donovan was there to greet her, unshaven, wearing his old brown leather jacket and pale blue jeans. He looked as washed out and baggy-eyed as she felt.

'What's the story?' she asked him.

He wiped his nose with the back of his hand. 'The fire was called in by a passing truck driver about twenty past ten. He said the flames were jumping up fifty feet into the air.'

Close to the cottage, the drifting smoke made Katie's eyes water. Detective O'Donovan led her across to the far side of the building, where a fire officer was standing talking to three firefighters as they rolled up their hoses. The fire officer had slicked-back hair and a pointed nose and reminded Katie of Bono from U2, even down to the amber-lensed sunglasses that he was wearing.

'Ah, the famous Detective Superintendent Kathleen Maguire,' he greeted her, with a grin that bared his teeth. 'Wasn't I reading all about you just the other day in the *Echo?* All them Romanian pimps you collared. Good on you.'

Katie gave him a much tighter smile in response. 'We've got ourselves a body here, then?'

'Right inside, in the bedroom. He's been badly burned, your man, but he wasn't burned by *this* fire, and he didn't die of smoke inhalation.'

Katie looked around at the outside of the cottage. It must have been at least eighty or ninety years old, maybe more. The walls were made of rough stone which had been rendered with a thick mix of lime and cement and painted pink. Now the pink was disfigured with patterns of jet-black soot, which looked as if exultant demons had danced wildly all around the cottage to celebrate its burning, and left their shadows behind.

Part of the roof had collapsed, but the single chimney stack remained. All of the plants and weeds around the walls had shrivelled, and all of the windows had been stained brown by smoke and cracked, or had dropped out altogether.

'This looks as if it was started deliberately,' said Katie. 'Like somebody poured an accelerant all the way around the cottage walls and then set it alight.'

The fire officer said, 'I'd say so myself,' as if he

were loath to admit that she was right.

'So it probably wasn't done with the intention of burning the cottage right down,' she continued. 'If they'd wanted to do that, they would have started the fire *inside* rather than outside. It isn't easy to set fire to a damp exterior wall.'

'You'll be wanting to see the body, then?' asked the fire officer, sounding a little testy.

'That's what I've come for,' said Katie, and followed him into the cottage.

The kitchen ceiling had come down, and so the floor was covered in blackened plaster mush and broken slates. Water was dripping down everywhere, and the walls were all streaked with grey. The blue flashing lights of the fire engines parked outside gave the interior of the cottage a jerky appearance, as if they were walking through a 1920s movie.

The fire officer high-stepped over a diagonal beam that had fallen across the hallway, and then turned around to offer Katie his hand, to help her over. Katie didn't know if she ought to feel pleased or patronized, but she accepted his assistance anyhow. He then piloted her towards the bedroom by placing his hand in the small of her back, and she realized that he had been acting offhand because he fancied her.

The bedroom had suffered very little damage, although like everywhere else in the cottage the window had been broken by the heat and its walls had been darkened by smoke. In the centre of the room stood a metal-framed single bedstead, with no mattress, and lying on it was a dead man, with his wrists fastened behind his back and his knees and his ankles bound together so tightly that his flesh bulged.

'Like some illumination on the subject?' the fire officer asked her, holding up a black rubber-covered flashlight. Katie took it and switched it on, directing it first of all at the dead man's face.

The whites of his eyes were speckled with tiny red petechial haemorrhages and he was staring sightlessly upwards. Although his face was swollen from asphyxiation and his mouth was dragged downwards in a grotesque parody of absolute agony, Katie recognized him at once from the photographs that Maureen O'Dwyer had lent them, especially his broken nose.

She shone the flashlight on to his scalp, with its crispy curls of black and scarlet skin, and then she turned it towards his genitals. Not only had his penis been burned to shreds, but it appeared from the dried runnels of blood across his right thigh that he had been castrated as well, although his legs had been so tightly bound together that it was impossible to be sure.

'Gave me a fierce funny feeling in the goolies when I first caught sight of *that*, like,' said the fire officer.

'I'll bet,' said Katie, without looking up at him. She went around to the other side of the bed and examined Gerry's body more closely. He was tattooed all over with scores of bruises. Some of them were dark crimson, indicating deep soft-tissue damage. Others were little more than finger marks where he had been pulled or pushed or dragged across the bed.

She pulled a pair of latex gloves out of her

pocket and snapped them on, tugging at each finger in turn. Very cautiously, she laid the flat of her right hand on Gerry's stomach, just above the raw, blistered weals where his pubic hair had been. She thought that his abdomen felt a little lumpy, but he had been beaten up so badly that a little lumpiness was hardly surprising. At least, she couldn't feel anything moving, or squirming, or desperately trying to gnaw its way out of him.

The technicians arrived, climbing noisily over the debris in their Tyvek suits.

'Well, well, another one,' said the older technician. He set his case down on the floor, and peered at Gerry's mutilated body with the slightly detached frown of a Pizza Hut customer making a selection from the salad bar. The younger technician stayed well back. 'Fecksake,' he said, under his breath. 'Look at the fecking state of that.'

'I want this one handed over to Dr Collins just like he is now, please,' said Katie. 'You can photograph him all right, but please don't cut any of the wire, and don't take any skin or hair samples. I think we'll get a more complete story if we examine him intact at the lab. Anyway, you'll have the bed and the whole of the rest of the cottage to process. That should give you more than enough to be getting on with.'

'Body bag then, Eamonn,' said the older technician. The younger technician stepped back out of the room with obvious relief, while the older one went back to his close-squinting inspection of Gerry's head and neck.

'This wire they've used to garrotte him, it's not the same type of wire as they used on the other

352

two victims,' he remarked, after a while. 'It looks more like steel to me than bronze. Given the musical subtext of the other two killings, I'd hazard a guess that it's piano wire. And look at the soup spoon they've tightened it with, that's different too, different shape.'

He cocked his head on one side so that he could see it better without touching it. 'There... I'm right. It comes from Jury's. The other two came from the Hayfield Manor.'

Katie said, 'That doesn't tell us much, does it, except that that our perpetrator steals cutlery from more than one hotel?'

But then she thought: *Who would find it easiest to steal cutlery from a hotel? Somebody who worked there, especially somebody who worked in the kitchen or waited on table. It wasn't important that the spoons came from different hotels. Hotels routinely employed casual staff – waiters and cleaners and dishwashers.*

She made a mental note to ask Detective Horgan to check up on all of the local employment agencies. It was a very long shot, of course, but several times in the past she had got results from even more remote possibilities than this.

'There's something else interesting here,' said the older technician. 'It looks likely that the burns on his scalp and his genitalia were caused by some type of inflammable substance. I've seen a couple of victims who were tortured with a blowtorch or had petrol poured over them, but these burns are not at all similar. See how they're confined to only one area, with clearly defined limits. If they were caused by a blowtorch they'd be spotty and irregular, and if they were caused by a liquid, like petrol or white spirit or lighter fluid, the blazing liquid would have run down over his face and his ears and his shoulders, and all over his thighs and stomach. You can see how the blood has run across his thigh where we're presuming that he's been castrated. Burning petrol would have done the same.'

'So what *did* burn him, do you think?'

The technician looked at Gerry for a very long time before he answered. Katie had to acknowledge that he was right, though. Gerry's scalp might have been burned almost down to the bone, but his face hadn't even been scorched. There was a straight burn line across his forehead as if he were wearing a red and black beret.

'Hmm,' said the technician. 'I'd hazard a guess at some kind of inflammable jelly. Something moderately sticky.'

'Something like napalm?'

'No, I don't think so. Napalm-B is what you get these days, which is a mixture of polystyrene and benzene, and once it sticks to your skin there's no way of getting it off you and it will burn right down to your bones. I'm not sure what caused burns like this. Some home-made mixture probably, but you should be able to analyse it when you get him back to the morgue.'

'Okay, thanks,' said Katie. 'Let me see the photographs as soon as you can, and any forensics you come across.'

'Of course. I think we need to catch this perpetrator somewhat smartish, don't you? Whatever your man did, he didn't deserve to die like

354

this. He must have gone through sheer bloody hell.'

Katie stayed at the burned-out cottage until the body was taken away. The sky was beginning to grow lighter, and there was an early morning shower of rain, which rustled through the hedge-rows and damped down the last smouldering rafters.

Detective O'Donovan sat beside her in the pas-senger seat of her car, and tried again and again to contact Sergeant O'Rourke. Still no response; and no sensible answers from Clonakilty Garda station either.

'Fecking culchies,' he said. 'You couldn't make it up. Their only dog handler is off sick with the runs. The dog's all right, but it won't let anybody else go near it. They're waiting on another canine unit from Ballinspittle.'

After that he checked his text messages. He read them slowly, moving his lips as he did so, and then he slid his phone shut, shaking his head.

'Everything okay?' Katie asked him.

'It's nothing. A slight difference of opinion with the beloved missus, that's all.'

'Oh. Not serious, I hope.'

'She wants us to move to Tipperary, to be near her sister. Her sister has the MS but four kids under seven to take care of. I feel sorry for her sister but quite honestly I can't abide the woman. Her husband was away for slates about six months ago and I can't say I blame him.'

Katie laid a hand on his shoulder. She didn't

know what to say to him, but he had made her understand that she wasn't the only person in the world who had to make a decision to stay or go.

Forty

She drove back to Anglesea Street and went to the ladies' locker room and took a short, lukewarm shower. The hairdryer was broken so she simply brushed her damp hair straight back. She changed her clothes – clean white underwear and a soft grey dogstooth blouse, with a knee-length black skirt and black tights.

She applied some fresh make-up in the steamed-up mirror and then she felt almost human again, in spite of being so bone-weary.

Chief Superintendent O'Driscoll was waiting for her in her office. He had brought her a cappuccino and a bacon and egg sandwich. He was eating a sandwich himself, which he repeatedly opened up and frowned into, as if he couldn't decide what the filling was.

'Oh, thanks, chief,' said Katie, sitting down at her desk. An untidy heap of memos and messages was waiting for her, as well as all the files on the Codreanu case that she had asked for, the Romanian girl-smuggling ring that she had broken up.

'Still no news of Jimmy,' said Chief Superintendent O'Driscoll. 'Two witnesses saw him arrive at St Michael's at about four o'clock, just as Father

356

Lowery was leaving in a taxi. Apparently Father Lowery was supposed to be going to St James's church at Ardfield, and Jimmy went after him. But that was the last that anybody's seen of either of them. Father Lowery never arrived in Ardfield, and he hasn't returned to his house in Douglas and neither has he shown up at his office on Redemption Road.'

He opened up his sandwich again and peered into it suspiciously.

'I've sent a dozen of the lads down to Clon to join in the search. There's over a hundred out now, from all over. Kinsale, Skibbereen, Rosscarbery, even a busload down from Limerick. We may be calling in one of the helicopters, too, if we don't find Jimmy soon.'

An Garda Síochána had two helicopters, known as the Air Support Unit, based at Casement airfield in Dublin. Not that any gardaí were allowed to fly them.

'There's still no trace of Father ó Súllabháin either,' said Katie.

'What about Father O'Gara, or Gerry Dwyer, or whatever his name is?'

'They're taking his body directly to the path lab. I've called Dr Collins and she'll be starting her autopsy first thing this afternoon.'

'Shite,' said Chief Superintendent O'Driscoll, to nobody in particular. 'This whole thing gets more fecking complimacated by the minute.' Then, 'How did you get on with that survivor society fellow? McKeown, is it?'

'That's right, Paul McKeown. We got on well, I think. He gave me a couple of possible leads to follow up.' She gave him a brief résumé of what Paul McKeown had told her about St Joseph's Orphanage Choir, and the special treatment that some of the choirboys had received from Fathers Heaney, Quinlan, O'Gara and ó Súllabháin.

'We'll be holding another media conference later today, won't we?' she said. 'I think it might be worth us asking the public if any of them was a member of the choir when it was first formed, or if anybody can remember the names of any of the boys who sang in it.

'I'm really keen to trace this Denis Sweeney and the Phelan twins. *Somebody* must remember them.'

'Don't bet on it,' said Chief Superintendent O'Driscoll. 'When it comes to the misdemeanours of the clergy, everybody seems to suffer from a dose of the collective amnesias.'

They were still discussing what to say to the media when Inspector Fennessy appeared in the doorway. From the stricken expression on his face Katie could tell at once that he had bad news.

'Andy Pearse has just called me from Clon.'

'What's happened? Have they found Jimmy yet?'

'Both of them – Jimmy and Father Lowery, too. They were deep in some woods off the R598, near Castlefreke Warren.'

'Name of Jesus,' said Katie. 'Dead?'

'Both of them. Somebody blew their heads off with a shotgun.'

Katie crossed herself, and couldn't stop herself from shivering, as if the ghost of a goose had walked over her grave. From time to time, every garda faced a terrifying, life-threatening situation. Last month, when they had raided the Romanian brothel on Prince's Street, one of the pimps had screamed at her and pointed a gun point-blank at her forehead, although it had later turned out not to be loaded; and she had lost count of the number of times that criminals had brandished knives at her, or baseball bats, or tyre levers, or even (once) an electric hedge-trimmer. But when one of their number was injured or killed it was just as painful and unexpected as a shot or a stab.

Jimmy O'Rourke had been experienced, and wise, and funny, and older-brotherly towards her. Not only that, he had been one of the few detectives at Anglesea Street who hadn't resented her promotion – or if he had, he had kept it to himself.

'What in the name of God would anybody have wanted to kill Jimmy for?' asked Chief Superintendent O'Driscoll, wobbling his jowls in disbelief. 'I mean, he was only making a routine enquiry, wasn't he? It's not like he was trying to pull anybody in, was it?'

Katie said, soberly, 'I don't think we should be asking ourselves why anybody would have wanted to kill Jimmy.'

'What do you mean?'

'I think the real question is, why would have anybody have wanted to kill Father Lowery?'

'God knows. It seems to be open season on priests at the moment.'

'No – not just any priests. When the diocese

disposed of the van with the croziers painted on the back of it, Father Lowery was the only person at Redemption Road who knew what happened to it, because he was in charge of transport. According to Monsignor Kelly, anyway. But it wouldn't surprise me at all if Monsignor Kelly also has a good idea of what happened to it, although he swore that he didn't.

'Nobody else but Monsignor Kelly knew that we were interested in talking to Father Lowery, and *why*.'

Chief Superintendent O'Driscoll flapped his hand dismissively. 'Come on, Katie. You don't seriously think that Monsignor Kelly had anything to do with this? He's one of the vicars general. If he did – Christ almighty – he was being reckless beyond belief.'

'I don't know. He could be panicking. When this castration thing comes out, the sky is going to fall in for the diocese of Cork and Ross, believe me. The child abuse scandal is going to seem like nothing at all by comparison.'

'You'll have to be very, very careful with this, Katie. The last thing we want to be doing is getting on the wrong side of Bishop Mahoney.'

'Who cares about Bishop Mahoney?' Katie retorted. 'The *last* thing we want to be doing is letting somebody get away with killing one of our own, even if they do wear their collar back to front.'

'I still want you to handle this with two pairs of kid gloves on. If we start suggesting that a senior cleric took out a hit on a priest and a Garda detective – well, you can imagine yourself what

360

kind of an unholy furore *that* would stir up. It's bringing me out in a cold sweat just thinking about it.'

'But Monsignor Kelly is the only person I know of who had any kind of a motive,' Katie insisted. 'And if it was him who had Jimmy and Father Lowery murdered, that establishes something else, too. Monsignor Kelly knows that the van is still being driven by the same man that Father Lowery gave it or sold it to. In other words, Monsignor Kelly has known all along who the priest murderer is. He had Father Lowery shot so that he couldn't tell us, but maybe Father Lowery had already told Jimmy who it was, and so he had Jimmy shot, too.'

'Katie – you're talking far too fanciful,' said Chief Superintendent O'Driscoll. 'If Monsignor Kelly has known all along who the priest murderer is, why would he keep it to himself? He's a man of God, when all's said and done. After Father Heaney, he wouldn't have allowed the murderer to go on to kill Father Quinlan and Father O'Gara – or even if he couldn't stop him, he would have told us who he was, surely?'

'Not necessarily,' Katie replied. 'Not if he was trying to cover up something else. Something much more devastating than four abusive priests cutting the balls off sixteen young orphan boys.'

'I can't think of anything much more devastating than that, I'll tell you.'

'It has to be a cover-up,' said Katie. 'I can *smell* it.'

'And what actually does a cover-up smell like?' Katie looked at him hard. 'It smells like incense,

361

that's what it smells like. Because what about this Brendan Doody character? First of all, Monsignor Kelly tried to pin the blame for Father Heaney's murder on him and make us believe that he had then committed suicide. But after that, Father Quinlan was murdered, and now Father O'Gara. Who killed *them?* Maybe Brendan Doody didn't commit suicide at all, and it was him. Or was it somebody else altogether – in which case, what happened to Brendan Doody?'

'We're still officially looking for him,' Chief Superintendent O'Driscoll reminded her.

'He's probably deep in a bog in County Mayo by now. Either that or he's walking around Cork in some kind of disguise and laughing his head off at us.'

'So what's your plan now?' asked Chief Superintendent O'Driscoll uneasily. 'Are you going back to Redemption Road to have a word with the good monsignor?'

'Not just yet,' said Katie. 'The first thing I'm going to do is go round to Jimmy's house and tell Maeve what's happened.'

'Of course.'

'After that I want to tie up all the loose ends in this case. I'm not going to talk to Monsignor Kelly again until I've seen Dr Collins's autopsy report on Father O'Gara, and got all the details on how Jimmy and Father Lowery were killed. When I *do* go back to Redemption Road, I want to know more about what's going on than Monsignor Kelly does. We might think that he's reckless, and that he's panicking, and he may be, but he's a very cute hoor, that one, cute as a fox.

362

I can see him taking a chance, but only if he's pretty sure that he can talk his way out of it.'

She turned to Inspector Fennessy. 'Liam – would you and Pat McFadden drive down to Clon and liaise with Inspector Pearse for me? I'd very much like to see what the technical boys come up with, and as soon as you can. Where Jimmy was shot and what he was shot with, what time of day, what these woods are like where they found him. And if the last time that Father Lowery was seen was in a taxi, find out the name of the taxi company, and who the driver was. I expect Inspector Pearse knows all of this already, but just double-check for me, would you?'

Inspector Fennessy said, 'Right you are, boss,' and left. When he had gone, Katie sat down in her chair and she and Chief Superintendent O'Driscoll looked at each other in mutual sorrow.

After a while, Chief Superintendent O'Driscoll picked up her grey metal wastepaper basket from under her desk and dropped what was left of his sandwich in it.

She spent over an hour with Maeve O'Rourke, in her airless front parlour in Sidney Park. Maeve was a small doll of a woman with fiery cheeks and wildly fraying white hair. She sat in her armchair in her black Marks & Spencer cardigan and her green leafy-patterned dress, hugging her stomach as if she had acute indigestion and letting the tears roll over her bright red cheeks without any attempt to wipe them away.

There was a framed photograph of Detective Sergeant O'Rourke on the sideboard next to a bowl of wrinkled apples, and on the mantelpiece stood another photograph of Jimmy and Maeve on their wedding day. Jimmy had one eye closed in his wedding picture because of the sunshine, but it looked as if he was winking.

Maeve O'Rourke's youngest daughter, Aileen, went next door and came back with one of their neighbours, Mrs Shand, and then the priest arrived, Father Murphy, stoop-shouldered and so ponderously bellied that he almost filled up the whole of the parlour on his own, and then two more neighbours, Mrs Monaghan and Mrs Feeney. Mrs Monaghan drew the curtains as a mark of respect and the parlour became so gloomy and crowded and there was so much sobbing that Katie at last gave Maeve O'Rourke a kiss of sympathy and promised to call her when she had more news.

'You won't be staying for a cup of tea?' said Maeve O'Rourke, with tears still rolling down her cheeks.

'Another time,' Katie promised her.

Outside, on the front step, a brisk wind was blowing from the south-west, and it was a relief to breathe some fresh air. From there, Katie could see Cork spread out along the River Lee, with the shadows of the clouds leaping silently over the city's rooftops like the shadows of some long-forgotten steeplechase. She climbed into her car and pulled down the sun visor. In the vanity mirror she was surprised to see that her own eyelashes were sparkling with tears, too, but maybe it was the wind, as much as her grief.

She drove back to headquarters, parked, and took the *Elements* CD out of her car. The hooded crows on the rooftops watched her walk into the main entrance, their feathers black and tatty in the wind. One of them let out a loud, abrasive caw, but the rest of them remained silent, as if they preferred to watch and wait.

She bought a cappuccino from the coffee machine and carried it to her desk. Her bacon and egg sandwich was still there, but she didn't feel at all hungry and she dropped it into her waste bin, along with Chief Superintendent O'Driscoll's.

She took the *Elements* CD out of its box and slid it into the Bose music player that stood on top of her filing cabinet. She played it very quietly, but all the same the high, clear voices of St Joseph's Orphanage Choir seemed to make her whole office resonate to the same pitch as *Gloria*. Even the glass in the windows sang.

She sat down and lifted a large sketchpad out of the bottom drawer of her desk. She opened it up and took a purple felt-tip pen from the mug that had been presented to her when she had graduated from Templemore. In neat block capitals, she wrote down the names FATHER HEANEY, FATHER QUINLAN, FATHER O'GARA and FATHER Ó SÚLLABHÁIN.

Although Father ó Súllabháin was still officially 'missing', she was realistic enough to acknowledge that there was very little hope of them finding him alive. Even now, while she sat at her desk and wrote down his name, he was probably suffering pain beyond human understanding.

After that she wrote down MONSIGNOR

365

KELLY, and beside it she wrote down the names of all those people she believed were under his influence, in one way or another – FATHER LENIHAN at St Patrick's, BRENDAN DOODY (alive or dead??), CIARA CLARE from the *Catholic Recorder* (sexual liaison??), BENEDICT TIERNAN, OP, at St Dominic's Retreat.

Next she wrote down all the answers to which she still didn't really know the questions. The four priests had been selected to form a world-class choir at St Joseph's Orphanage. They had been recruited to do it by some mysterious go-between called the REVEREND BIS. But who was the Reverend Bis, and whose instructions had he been following?

The idea behind the choir seemed to be that, somehow, God would be encouraged to show Himself in some physical form or other on earth. But why would anybody want to do such a thing, even if it were possible? And *was* it possible? Historically, had anybody ever attempted it before? And had they ever succeeded?

The three priests whose bodies they had found so far had all been tortured with extreme cruelty and finally castrated and garrotted. If Father Heaney's notebooks were even partly fact and not all pornographic fantasy, Katie thought it was reasonable to assume that these killings had been done by castrated members of St Joseph's Orphanage Choir, in revenge for what had been done to them when they were young. But who were they, these *castrati,* and how many of them had got together to punish the priests who had taken away their manhood?

Monsignor Kelly appeared to be doing everything he could to hinder Katie's investigation. He might even have ordered the murders of Father Lowery and Sergeant O'Rourke, although she had no proof whatsoever that he was responsible – not yet, anyhow. But why? What secret was he trying to suppress, if any? Then again, Chief Superintendent O'Driscoll could be right, and the only thing about him that supported her suspicions of Monsignor Kelly was the simple fact that she disliked him so much.

Katie picked up the CD box and tugged out the little booklet inside. It explained that St Joseph's Orphanage Choir had been formed in 1981 and disbanded in 1985. During those four years it had gained a reputation for being 'the sweetest and most melodious of children's choirs ever heard in Ireland or anywhere'.

The choir's appearances, however, had been inexplicably limited, and only ever in churches, even though they had won accolades wherever they sang. Their four choirmasters had explained that their singing was 'for the adoration of the Lord, not for entertainment', and that 'too many performances would jeopardize the extreme purity of their voices'.

They had made just one recording, at the cathedral of St Mary and St Anne – this collection of sacred songs, which had been chosen to represent the four elements of the world that God had created: fire; water; air; and earth. The original tapes had been mislaid or shelved until 2010, when they had been 'miraculously rediscovered' and brought out as a 'devotional tribute'.

Katie noticed that there was no mention in the booklet that *Elements* had been released to take advantage of the recent upsurge in sales of sacred music. Ensembles such as the Priests and the Benedictine Nuns and the Cistercian Monks of Stift Heiligenkreuz were bringing in enormous profits.

She had such a strong feeling that the key to these killings was here, in this recording, although she didn't yet completely understand why. Perhaps the surviving members of the choir had seen what a commercial success *Elements* had become and had broken their self-imposed silence to demand a share of the royalties. Perhaps the diocese had refused to give them any, on the grounds that they were all for charity – or refused to give them as much as they felt they deserved.

Perhaps it was nothing to do with money at all. Perhaps the recording had simply brought back all of the unbearable suffering that they had endured as young boys, and they had decided it was time to punish their four choirmasters for what they had done to them.

However, this still didn't explain what part Monsignor Kelly was playing in this tragedy. Katie could fully understand why he should be so anxious to suppress it. But surely the most effective way to suppress it would have been for him to help her to identify the priest killers as quickly as possible after Father Heaney was found dead, before any more of them were tortured and murdered.

She was still frowning and doodling when Detective O'Donovan and Detective Horgan announced their arrival with a knock and a cough.

'A bit of progress, I think, ma'am!' said Detective O'Donovan, waggling his notebook triumphantly.

'Thank God. I could do with a bit of progress.'

'Well – you told us to check out the music supply stores on the interweb, and that's what we did. There's an online company in Galway that sells Gaelic harps and all kinds of accessories for harps and other musical instruments besides – John Bestwick's Music Stores. And would you believe that one of John Bestwick's most recent orders was for fifth-, sixth- and seventh-octave harp wire. It came from a small group called Fidelio, who you can hire to play music for you at weddings and christenings and funerals, and also at receptions.

'Not only that, but Fidelio recently bought piano wire, too, in several different gauges. And here's the clincher, they bought nylon string and beeswax for tying new reeds on to bassoons.'

Detective Horgan said, 'These Fidelio characters are based in Cork City, so they say. There's an email address, but no postal address, but it tells you all about them and how to contact them if you want to have them singing at your daughter's wedding – or garrotting your parish priest, whichever you prefer.'

Katie ignored that last remark and said, 'Come on, then, show me.'

Detective Horgan leaned across her desk and used two fingertips to type out the URL. Immediately, the Fidelio website appeared, displaying a shining gold background with a heading in purple letters: *Fidelio: Sacred Music for your Special Occasion.* It showed a photograph of the inside of a church, with sunlight streaming in through the stained-glass windows, and three men in dark three-piece suits standing in front of it, their hands clasped over their crotches. They were heavily built men, all three of them, and in spite of their pious smiles they looked more like night-club bouncers than choristers. A pretty young blonde girl was standing beside them, wearing a clinging pale turquoise dress and holding up a violin.

'Would you credit it?' said Katie, shaking her head. The man in the middle of the group was the biggest, with curly fair hair and a face that was unnervingly baby-like for a man his size. 'How did that Mrs Rooney describe your man, up in Ballyhooly? "Just like a cherub."'

The two men on either side of him were slightly shorter, and not so broad-shouldered, but it was interesting was how much they looked like each other. They both had protuberant brown eyes and pointed noses and bulging cheeks, as if they both had their mouths full of too many biscuits; and they both had recessive chins, with six-o'clock shadow.

'Twins, I'd say,' Detective O'Donovan remarked.

'And I'd agree with you,' said Katie. 'They're twins all right. Does this website tell you what their names are?'

Detective Horgan scrolled down to the bottom of the website until he found the credits. *Vocals,* Denis Todd, Charles Wolf, Sean Whelan and Sinéad O'Shea. *Gaelic harp,* Denis Todd. *Piano,*

370

Charles Wolf. *Flute and other wind accompaniment*, Sean Whelan. *Violin*, Sinéad O'Shea.

'Well, there's three glaring pseudonyms for you,' said Katie.

'Pseudonyms?' asked Detective O'Donovan. 'So, what – you don't think these are their real names, like?'

'I wouldn't have guessed if Paul McKeown hadn't told me about some of the boys he remembered from St Joseph's Orphanage Choir – Denis Sweeney and the Phelan twins, they were the only survivors he knew of. And look at these three fellows.'

'I still don't get it.'

'It's simple. Denis Todd, as in Sweeney Todd, the demon barber – Denis Sweeney. Then Charles Wolf. The Gaelic for wolf is ó Faoláin, and the anglicized version of ó Faoláin is Phelan. Then Whelan, and Whelan, as you know, is the same name as Phelan. One Sweeney and two twin Phelans, just like Paul McKeown told me.'

'That's very impressive, ma'am,' Detective Horgan had to admit. 'I'm not surprised they promoted you, like.'

'You're the ones who found the website. Well done to both of you.'

'So what's the story now?' asked Detective O'Donovan. 'We find these Fidelio fellows and feel their collars for them?'

'Yes – like right now. You can find their address through their web provider, can't you? With any luck they won't have started on Father ó Súllabháin yet – or at least they may not have castrated him and killed him.'

371

Forty-one

At five past three that afternoon, four squad cars sped into opposite ends of Marlborough Street in the centre of the city, a narrow, pedestrian-only street that runs between Patrick Street and Oliver Plunkett Street. No sirens, no flashing lights. Passers-by stood back against the walls and took shelter in the entrance to O'Donovan's pub as five detectives and eleven uniformed gardaí scrambled out of their vehicles and shouldered their way into a narrow doorway next to Hotlox the hairdresser's. No shouting, only the syncopated drumming of boots on the uncarpeted staircase.

It was gloomy inside the building, and smelled of damp and the dustbins that were crowded into the hallway. On the left side of the second-floor landing there was a small bar called Dorothy's, whose only occupants were three elderly men sitting silently in front of their half-empty glasses of Murphy's, and a woman with a shock of bright red hair whose head was resting on the table, fast asleep, her face as yellow as a painting by Toulouse-Lautrec.

On the opposite side of the landing was a brown-varnished door with a wooden painted sign beside it saying, *'Fidelio Sacred Choir. Please Ring and Enter.'*

Detective O'Donovan didn't bother to ring. He rattled the door handle and it was locked, so he

372

turned around and nodded to the beefy garda who was carrying the small, 10-kilo, red-painted battering ram they used for narrow doors and hallways.

It took three deafening blows before the locks broke and the frame splintered and the door shuddered open. The red-haired woman in Dorothy's lifted her head from the table and screamed out, 'What the feck? Can't anybody get any feckin' sleep around here?'

Detective O'Donovan went in first with his gun drawn, closely followed by Detective Horgan and then by Katie herself. The offices of the Fidelio Sacred Choir were dark and empty, and smelled empty, in the sour hopeless way that only a damp building can. There was a half-torn poster for Fidelio on the wall, with Denis Sweeney and the Phelan twins standing together in their black suits trying hard to look sacred. A green metal filing cabinet stood under the window with all of the drawers pulled open, and empty, and a sofa with a brown stretch-nylon cover was lying on its back with its legs in the air.

'Damn it,' said Katie, holstering her gun and prowling from one room to the other and back again. There was no evidence here at all. No harp wire, no piano wire, no nylon restraints, no clothing, no blood.

'Go next door, would you, and ask them when was the last time that anybody was seen leaving this office,' Katie told Detective Horgan. 'Mind you, they all look too langers to know what day of the week it is, let alone who's been coming and going.'

'It doesn't look to me like our Fidelio fellows have been here in quite a few days,' remarked Detective O'Donovan. 'I checked their website before we came out, though, and they're still taking bookings.'

'They might be taking bookings but that doesn't mean they're going to show up.'

'So what do we do now?' asked Detective O'Donovan. Katie was just about to answer him when her mobile phone played *'The Fields of Athenry'*.

'Superintendent Maguire? It's Ciara Clare from the *Catholic Recorder*.'

'I'm sorry, Ciara. I'm totally up to my eyes in it right now. Call me back later.'

'But it's the monsignor.'

'What do you mean, "it's the monsignor"?'

'We were supposed to meet at lunchtime at Greene's, but he never came. So I called his mobile but his mobile's switched off, and so I called his secretary and his secretary said that he left his office this morning with a man she didn't know and wouldn't tell her when he'd be back.'

'So he missed a lunch appointment. What are you so upset about?'

'It's these priests who keep turning up dead. He's been really worried about it. He keeps asking me to see what I can do to keep it quiet, but it's gone beyond that now. I can't keep a story quiet that's on RTÉ every night and Sky News and everything.'

Katie said, 'What has he told you about these dead priests? Anything?'

'He just says that they did something with the

374

priests that they shouldn't have done, and they stopped it, whatever it was, but it's all come back to haunt him.'

'Where are you now?' Katie asked her.

'I'm back at the office on Grand Parade.'

'Well, meet me at Monsignor Kelly's office as soon as you can. I might be twenty minutes or so by the time I've finished up here, but wait for me. Of course, if you hear from him before that, call me at once.'

'I will of course. And – I'm sorry.'

'Sorry for what?'

'Sorry for everything, I suppose. Sorry for myself most of all. I didn't understand at all what it was that I was getting myself into.'

Detective Horgan came back across the landing from Dorothy's, flapping his hand in front of his face.

'Holy Mary, Mother of God, it was reekin' in there, I'll tell you.'

'What's the story?' Katie asked him.

'Those Fidelio fellows haven't been there too often lately, and they know that in the bar there because they can hear them practising their singing sometimes, which the barman said was very uplifting. But they was there last night, about eleven, up and down the stairs every five minutes, up and down, up and down, and in a hurry by all appearances.'

'Sounds like that's when they cleared the place out,' said Detective O'Donovan.

'Maybe they have an idea that we're close to them,' Katie agreed. 'Or... I don't know. Maybe they have some other agenda. Now that they've abducted Father ó Súllibháin, that's the last of their choirmasters, isn't it? The last of the priests who mutilated them. God alone knows what they're thinking of doing now.'

'Right,' she said, 'you and me, Patrick, we're going to Redemption Road. Michael, do you want to finish up here? Talk to the barman in O'Donovan's on the corner, and any regulars you can find in there. And the girls from the hairdresser's. You never know. They might have seen something that can help us.'

By now, most of the gardaí who had backed up their raid were milling around in Marlborough Street, chatting to each other. Katie beckoned to one of them and said, 'You, what's your name?'

'O'Dowd, ma'am.'

'All right, O'Dowd, I want you and two more guards to follow us out to the diocese offices on Redemption Road, and anywhere else we go to after that. I think we might need some back-up.'

'If you don't mind me asking, ma'am, who exactly are we after nailing?'

'If I knew, O'Dowd, I'd tell you, believe me.'

When they reached Redemption Road, Ciara Clare was already waiting for them outside. She was wearing a bright red dress of tight-fitting needlecord, with a matching bolero top, which she had obviously chosen to go to lunch at Greene's with Monsignor Kelly. She looked deeply anxious, and her matching red lipstick was splodged.

As they climbed the steps of the offices, Katie looked up and saw that the sky, for four o'clock in the afternoon, was growing threateningly dark, and that the wind was blowing even more strongly – that fresh, chill wind that precedes a thunderstorm.

Katie spoke first to Monsignor Kelly's secretary, the pointy-nosed nun with the diminutive mouth. She was just as distraught as Ciara, and kept twisting her sleeves as if she were trying to wring water out of them.

'Here,' she said, showing Katie the monsignor's diary. She spoke in a hurried, panicky rush, as if she had memorized what she was going to say and was frightened of forgetting it. 'He was supposed to be having lunch at 12.30 at Greene's on McCurtain Street with Patrick Mulligan from the Church Overseas Missionary Fund. Then he was supposed to be back here at 3.45 for a discussion group with the bishop and lay volunteers about the changing of Mass times in rural areas to make up for the diminishing number of priests.'

'But he didn't arrive at Greene's, did he?' asked Katie.

The nun gave Ciara a sharp, resentful look and said, 'No. Not according to Ms Clare.'

'In fact, he left here in the company of a man you didn't know?'

'Yes, at about ten minutes to twelve.'

'Can you describe this man?'

'He was tall. Big. His hair was curly. He was wearing a black sweater and black trousers a bit too short for him so they were flappy round the ankles. He had a bit of a belly on him, to be truthful.'

'He didn't give you his name and Monsignor Kelly didn't tell you his name either?'

The nun shook her head. 'I had never seen him before but Monsignor Kelly must have known who he was because he came out of his office directly and went away with him.'

'Was any word spoken between them?'

Again the nun shook her head. 'I have had no word from him since and he has been uncontactable on his mobile. The meeting about masses in pastoral areas was postponed until tomorrow when, please God, the monsignor will have reappeared safe and well.'

She crossed herself, twice, and her mouth looked even more pinched than ever.

'What about the fellow he was supposed to be meeting at Greene's for lunch?' asked Katie.

'Patrick Mulligan? I don't know about that.' She paused, and then she said, 'Ms Clare knows more about that than I do.'

'Did Mr Mulligan not call you to ask why the monsignor hadn't turned up?'

Again, the nun's eyes darted toward Ciara. 'No, he did not. I can only presume that he thought he might have made a mistake about the date.'

'All right,' said Katie. 'Patrick – do you want to take a quick look at Monsignor Kelly's desk, see if he's left any notes?'

'I can't allow you to do that,' the nun protested. 'The monsignor's desk ... it's private. It's confidential. It's *personal*.'

'Don't you worry.' Detective O'Donovan grinned at her. 'If I find any porn mags I won't say a word.'

Forty-two

Katie took Ciara outside, and they sat in her car together. The sky was almost completely black now, with only a silvery streak of light over the hills to the north-east, where the sun must still be shining.

'I think you'd better tell me what the situation is between you and Monsignor Kelly, don't you?' said Katie.

Ciara looked away, out of the passenger window. The trees along the driveway were thrashing so wildly they looked as if they were trying to uproot themselves.

'I don't know how it started, to be honest with you. I was sent to interview the monsignor about his favourite subject, which is involving lay people in church affairs. He was always quoting Jesus about that. *Go into my vineyard, too.*'

'It sounds as if the monsignor went into *your* vineyard, too, Ciara, if you don't mind my saying so.'

Ciara blushed and started to twist at the large silver cross studded with red glass rubies that rested in her cleavage.

'It happened by accident, almost. We had to stay overnight at a church conference in Limerick and he came into my hotel room by mistake. Mixed up the numbers, that's what he said. But then he said that the Lord must have mixed them up deliberately to bring us together. I was the Lord's creation, he said, and I was so beautiful that the Lord must have intended him to celebrate my beauty.'

Katie nodded understandingly. At the same time, she thought: *What a line that was, and from one of the vicars general, too. What's worse, this poor cow actually believed him.*

'That was the first time a man I really respected had told me that I was beautiful and I knew that he wasn't lying to me because he was doing everything in his power to resist me. I could see for myself how much he was struggling.'

Of course he was struggling, thought Katie. *You need to undo thirty-three buttons to get out of a soutane.*

'Tell me about these murdered priests,' she said, as gently as she could. 'You said that Monsignor Kelly was worried about them.'

'I went to see him at his office one morning and he was very shocked and very pale. I mean, dead white, white as a sheet. I thought he was ill at first, but then he told me that somebody had phoned him – somebody he hadn't heard from in a very long time – and that some awful trouble was brewing. I asked him what it was but he said he couldn't tell me because I was too young and I wouldn't understand.'

'So he didn't give you any idea what this "awful trouble" actually was?'

Ciara kept on twisting her cross round and round. Katie felt like slapping her hand and telling her to stop it, but she knew that it would only break Ciara's confessional mood, and the last thing she wanted to do was antagonize her.

'All he said was that *somebody* was blackmailing him into doing something that was impossible. He said that he had tried to make a deal with them, tried to meet them halfway. He even said that he had offered them money – lots of money – but they hadn't shown any interest.'

'That was the actual word he used – "impossible"? He didn't say that he didn't *want* to do it, or wasn't *capable* of doing it for any particular reason? He said it was *impossible?*'

Ciara nodded. 'He kept on saying, "It's impossible. It can't be done. It's impossible," as if I knew what he was talking about, but I didn't know what he was talking about, and he wouldn't explain what he meant.

'There was something else he kept on saying, too. "I'm caught. I'm trapped. Whatever I do, it's going to turn out badly."'

'But you still had no idea of what he meant?'

'No, although I was pretty sure it was something to do with these murdered priests. When Father Heaney was found dead, he called me and told me to go up to Ballyhooly and do everything I could to play the story down, like. He was raging when it was the top story on RTÉ, and then the *Independent*. But he kept on having these mood swings. Later on that same day he was much more positive, as if he had managed to sort something out. But when they found Father Quinlan hanging from that flagpole his mood went all black again, and ever since then it's stayed black and it seems to be getting blacker.'

Katie waited for a long moment, and then she said, 'Has Monsignor Kelly given you any idea at all who the killers might be? Do you think he knows who they are? Or at least has an inkling of who they are?'

'No. But they're boys who were sexually abused by priests when they were at school, aren't they? Getting their revenge, like.'

Katie neither confirmed nor denied it. She waited for another long moment, while the car trembled in the rising wind and the first few drops of rain fell on to the roof. In her rear-view mirror she could see lightning crossing the distant horizon like stilt-walkers. *Don't worry, the circus will be here before you know it. The clowns will be coming to get you.*

'Do you mind if I ask you one or two personal questions?' she said. She was very aware of Ciara's perfume. A strong, seductive scent, heavy on hyacinth and musk, just right for lunch with an alpha-plus male, especially an alpha-plus male in a thirty-three-button soutane. Chamade, something like that.

'You want to ask me about me and Kevin?'

'Yes. Do you usually go to bed together properly? You know, like lovers?'

Very long pause, more cross-fiddling, then, 'Sometimes.'

'Sometimes, but not as often as you'd like to?'

'He's very busy. And of course it's difficult. You know – if we were to be seen together.'

'So what is it mostly – oral sex in the office, like you did the other day?'

Ciara blushed, but Katie had been interviewing women about their sexual adventures and misadventures for a very long time, ever since she was a young garda on the streets of Cork on a Saturday night, and she knew how desperately most of them wanted to talk about it, especially to another woman.

'You wouldn't ever expect him to give up the cloth and marry you, would you?'

'Of course not. I couldn't ask him to do that. Anyway, he's a man of God. He's completely devoted to his calling.'

'Doesn't that make you feel a little bit *excluded?* I mean, there you are, giving him your best attention, as it were, and he's standing there thinking about the Virgin Mary.'

'He says that when I'm kneeling in front of him it's the same as kneeling in prayer because I'm worshipping his body, which was made by God, the same as mine was.'

And what happens when you swallow? thought Katie, although she never would have said it out loud, and she felt blasphemous even thinking it. *Transubstantiation?*

But her intimate questioning and her religious cynicism had served their purpose. She now had a confession from Ciara that Monsignor Kelly had outrageously abused his position as one of the vicars general in order to coax her into giving him sexual favours. It was a confession that Ciara might later try to deny, but not under oath, in a court of law.

As they climbed out of the car they heard the first rumbling of thunder. Ciara turned to Katie, her hair whipped by the wind, and said, 'You *will* find him, won't you?'

'Of course, we'll find him all right.'

'And what I told you – you know – about our relationship?'

Oh, that's what you call it, licking the mickey of some vertically challenged cleric, a relationship.

'Of course,' Katie told her, although she didn't say precisely what 'of course' was supposed to imply.

Ciara began to walk back across the car park towards her own car, a pale green Nissan Micra. As she did so, Katie's mobile phone played *'The Fields of Athenry'*.

'Katie? This is Nurse Monahan from the hospital. I'm happy to tell you that your sister has just regained consciousness.'

'Oh, my God,' said Katie. She pressed her hand over her mouth and burst into tears.

'She's well in herself, but–' Nurse Monahan started to tell her, but then thunder crashed right over Katie's head and drowned out everything else she had to say.

Forty-three

She pushed her way in through the hospital doors, lowered her umbrella and shook it hard. As she crossed the reception area, a voice called out, 'Katie! Hold on a minute, would you?'

It was Michael, wearing a saggy grey gaberdine raincoat with a tightly twisted belt, and carrying a plastic shopping bag from Tesco's.

384

'Michael! What's the story? Have you been up to see her yet?'

'Not yet. As a matter of fact, I was waiting for you.'

'What were you waiting for me for? Listen, I have to go up and see her. You know that she's recovered consciousness?'

'They told me, yes. I'm ashamed to face her, if you must know.'

Katie had reached the lifts now, and pushed the button for ITU. A small boy was standing close by, looking up at Katie and Michael and listening attentively to what they were saying, as if they were characters in a play.

'Push on, kid,' Michael told him, but he stayed where he was.

The lift doors opened. Katie stepped inside and Michael followed her. He held up the Tesco bag. It was covered with raindrops and obviously contained something heavy.

'I was under the sink this morning, looking for the tap to turn off the water because we had a leak in one of the radiators. That's when I found this. It was behind all of the dishcloths and the Brillo pads and all of that. It's me hammer.'

'What was your hammer doing there, under the sink?'

'That's exactly what I asked myself. I took it out and had a good look at it and it's got hair on it, I think, and what looks like blood.'

He was about to reach into the bag to take the hammer out and show her, but she said, 'No – leave it there. It's been contaminated enough already.'

385

Michael had tears in his eyes. 'It was Nola. It must have been. Only Nola would be mad enough to attack Siobhán with a hammer, for God's sake, and only Nola would be stupid enough to hide it under the sink without even taking the trouble to wash it. Jesus, I wish I'd never set eyes on the bitch.'

When they reached the third floor, Katie took out her mobile phone and called headquarters. 'Send O'Donovan round to CUH, would you? I'll be here with my sister in intensive care.'

She took the Tesco bag out of Michael's hand and spoke to him gently. 'I want you to wait right here in the corridor, Michael. I'll call you in a minute and you can see Siobhán, too, if the nurses will allow it. Meanwhile, please stay here. What happened, it wasn't your fault and you shouldn't be after blaming yourself for it. You've done really well to bring me the hammer.'

She could hear how calm her voice was, as if a ventriloquist were talking out of her mouth. Inside, though, her brain was kaleidoscopic with splinters of anger, not only at Nola for nearly killing her sister but at Michael for messing both women around, and at Siobhán, too, for having a relationship with a gowl like him.

Michael sat down on the end of a row of plastic chairs, his head slumped. Katie stood beside him for a moment and then walked along the corridor to Siobhán's room.

She found Siobhán propped up with pillows, with her eyes open. Her head was still thickly bandaged and her vital signs were still being monitored, but when Katie came into the room she managed a weak, disorganized smile.

One nurse was taking her blood pressure while another was writing up her notes. Katie put the Tesco bag down on the chair and walked around the bed to embrace her.

'Oh, you don't know how glad I am to see you with your eyes open! How are you feeling, darling?'

Siobhán shook her head and made a barely audible bleating noise, like a lamb caught in barbed wire. The nurse who was taking her blood pressure said, 'She can't talk yet, I'm afraid.'

'But she *will* be able to? In time?'

'You'd have to talk to Mr Hahq about that. We've done two more scans and there's some improvement, but it's very early days yet.'

Katie turned back to Siobhán, took hold of her hands and smiled. She *looked* like Siobhán, although her face was puffier than usual, but there was nothing in her expression that reminded Katie of her quick, mischievous self. She smiled back at Katie sweetly, but so tiredly that she could have been eighty years old.

'Is there anything she needs? Anything I can get her?' Katie asked.

'Not at the moment, Katie. We're still feeding her through the drip, although we expect to take her off that in a day or two. And she can't read yet, because her eyes can't focus well enough. It's grand that she can recognize yourself.'

Katie stayed by Siobhán's bedside until Detective O'Donovan arrived with two uniformed gardaí. Michael was still waiting obediently in the corridor, his head still bowed. Katie gave Detective O'Donovan the Tesco bag.

'Take him in and have him make a full statement. I want him to explain the whole background in his own words – like his relationship with Siobhán and how they split up and how he married Nola but then started seeing Siobhán again. Also, get this hammer over to the technical unit pronto.'

Then, *'Michael?'* she said.

Michael lifted his head. She had rarely seen anyone look so wounded. 'What is it?'

'Where is Nola working now? Is she still at Penney's?'

'No. Debenham's, in the make-up department. Jesus, I wish I'd never seen that woman's face.'

Katie nodded to Detective O'Donovan. 'Go and pick her up, too. Nola Lyons. Arrest her for attempted murder.'

'Right you are, then.'

Before she returned to headquarters, she visited the path lab. Father O'Gara's body had arrived from Killeens and was lying on a stainless-steel autopsy table while Dr Collins was circling around it, ducking and weaving with her digital camera, taking photographs from every angle.

Katie walked the length of the laboratory, between the sheeted figures that lay on both sides, deliberately keeping her eyes straight ahead of her and not glancing at any of them for signs of movement.

Dr Collins stood up straight as she approached. 'Ah, Katie. I've just finished taking my first round of pictures.'

She stepped back and put down her camera. 'Now, I think it's time to cut the wires and find out exactly what this poor wretch has had done to him.'

'God, he must have suffered some terrible pain,' said Katie, shaking her head over Father O'Gara's burned and battered body.

'Being burned to death – that's the most painful death of all,' Dr Collins told her. 'Not just anecdotally, but neurologically.'

'Anecdotally? How can anybody tell you what it was like anecdotally?'

Dr Collins went across to her instrument table and picked up a pair of sharp-nosed pliers. 'It's the fact that people rarely scream while they're being immolated. You look at those newsreels of Buddhist monks burning themselves to death. The agony is too overwhelming to think about screaming.'

She cut the wires that bound Father O'Gara's wrists behind his back. She held up the wire and peered at it through her glasses. 'I think your technician was right. This does look like piano wire.'

Now she could manoeuvre Father O'Gara's arms until they were parallel to his sides. His shoulders and elbows made a crunching sound as she did so, like a chicken's joints. She rolled him on to his back, and then she cut the wire that kept his ankles tight together.

At that moment, Katie's mobile phone played. She checked the screen and saw that Inspector Fennessy was calling her.

'Liam? What's the form?'

'We've had a sighting of the black van with the crozier on it, only about five minutes ago, out on the Carrigrohane Road, about a half-mile west of Ballincollig.'

'Heading?'

'West. We could set up a roadblock on the N22 at Clodagh, say. It didn't appear to be travelling very fast.'

'No – no roadblock. But try to pick it up and tail it. I want to know where they're going, these Fidelios. I mean, they don't seem to care that their van is so easy to pick out, do they? You'd have thought they would have had sense enough to drive around in a vehicle that was totally non-descript.'

Dr Collins was having a difficult time cutting through the thick-gauge piano wire that fastened Father O'Gara's knees together. It looked as if it had been wound around at least twenty times, and plaited together, too. She was twisting her pliers from side to side, and each strand gave way only reluctantly, with a flat ping-*snap!* sound.

'Right you are, then, ma'am,' said Inspector Fennessy. 'We'll put a tail on it but we'll keep our distance.'

But Katie suddenly thought: *The Fidelios don't seem to care that their van is so easy to pick out, do they? But why don't they care? They've abducted and likely killed all four of the priests who castrated them, and abducted Monsignor Kelly, too; and they must realize that we're out looking for them the length and breadth of County Cork.*

Then she thought, *shite,* and shouted out, 'Stop it!'

'What?' asked Dr Collins, looking up from her autopsy table.

'No, not you, doctor,' Katie told her. 'Liam – stop that van, and arrest whoever's driving it.'

'I thought you wanted us to follow it – find out where it's going, like.'

'It's not going anywhere in particular. It's a decoy, I'm sure of it.'

'A what?'

'A decoy. They made no attempt at all to hide that van, did they, when they dumped Father Heaney's body in the Blackwater, and when they ran over Father O'Gara on Patrick Street, and when they collected Father ó Súllibháin from St Dominic's Retreat Centre? For all we know, they made no more effort to hide it when they strung up Father Heaney, because it must have taken them long enough to do it, and it was only chance that nobody saw them – or remembers seeing them, anyway.'

'Well, I don't know, superintendent. You might be giving them credit for being as clever as you are, whereas they could be as thick as shite, and just careless.'

'I don't think so, Liam. They have an agenda, these people. They feel they have to do everything to make their revenge complete, I'm sure of it. They may not mind being caught after that ... but they don't want to be caught just yet. Stop that van as soon as you can. I'll bet you twenty euros there's only one person in it, and that's the fellow who's driving it, and I'll bet you he doesn't know a *castrati* from a castanet.'

'You're the boss, boss.'

She closed her phone and said to Dr Collins, 'How's it going?'

Dr Collins had her teeth gritted and was using her pliers to flex the piano wires backwards and forwards until they snapped.

'Nearly done it. Whoever tied him up like this was certainly making sure that he kept his legs together.'

Katie's mobile phone played again. This time it was John. He sounded tired and more than a little irritable.

'Am I *ever* going to see you?' he complained. 'I'll be probably be leaving the day after tomorrow. I know you're catastrophically busy, sweetheart, but we really have to work something out.'

'I'll call you, darling,' she promised him. 'As soon as this crisis is over, I'll call you and we'll get together and I'll make all of your wildest dreams come true. I mean it.'

'I feel like I haven't seen you forever.'

'I know, because I feel just the same way.'

She was talking to him and watching Dr Collins at the same time. Dr Collins snapped the last strands of piano wire that were keeping Father O'Gara's knees fastened together. Then she took hold of each knee and started to force his thighs apart. She had to grit her teeth and use all of her strength to separate them because it was less than twenty-four hours since he had died and he was still in full rigor mortis.

John said, 'Any chance that we can we meet tonight? Just for a half-hour maybe?'

'I don't know, John. I'll try, I really will. Let me give you a call later. By the way, I shouldn't be telling you this, but it looks like we've caught the person who attacked Siobhán.'

'Wow. Good work. Who was it? He wasn't trying to kill *you*, was he?'

'I did think to begin with that somebody might have been after me, but it wasn't a he, it was a she. Michael's wife, Nola. You know which Michael – Siobhán's ex-boyfriend. Well, not so ex, which is why Nola tried to kill her.'

'Jesus. You Maguires lead such goddamn complicated lives. But do try to meet me later, won't you? Just for a cup of coffee or something? I need to put my arms around you and smell your smell.'

'I'll do my best, my darling. I promise.'

Dr Collins had managed to prise Father O'Gara's knees apart by about twenty centimetres. She gripped them even harder, like somebody trying to lever open the doors of a lift, but when she parted them a little more Katie noticed that two single piano wires were still looped around his thighs, just above the knee. Dr Collins hadn't bothered to cut them because they weren't connected to each other and didn't prevent her from opening up his legs. But now that his knees were gradually being forced wider and wider apart, Katie could see that each loop was connected to one of two taut wires that ran up the insides of his thighs and disappeared into the dark, boggy hole where his scrotum had been.

She had seen wires like this before. Not rigged like this, of course, inside a castrated man's body, but in a booby trap where two wires were attached to the doors of a van. When the doors

393

were opened, the wires pulled two switches to complete an electrical circuit, and an explosive charge was set off.

Katie didn't say a word. A shouted warning could have startled Dr Collins into pulling Father O'Gara's legs even wider apart. Instead, she walked quickly around the autopsy table, came right up behind Dr Collins and seized both of her wrists, then threw herself backwards with all of her body weight so that the two of them fell on to the floor, their legs in a tangle.

'What on *earth* do you think you're doing?' Dr Collins protested, in a voice that was almost a scream. But Katie caught hold of the sleeve of her lab coat and dragged her across the floor, panting with the effort of it, her boot heels kicking at the vinyl tiles to give herself purchase. When they were well clear of the autopsy table, she scrambled on to her feet, pulling Dr Collins up after her, and shouted, *'Run! I think he has a bomb inside him!'*

The two of them pelted to the far end of the pathology lab and cannoned out of the double swing doors. Dr Collins stopped and looked back through one of the windows, but Katie snatched at her sleeve again and said, 'Out! Come on! Right out of the building! As far away as we can!'

'But, my *God!*' said Dr Collins. 'You're not serious, are you? A *bomb?*'

'Just keep going,' Katie told her. They ran along the corridor that led to the hospital's main reception area, their heels clattering, and as they did so, Katie lifted her mobile phone out of her pocket, ready to call for the army bomb disposal squad.

394

They had only just reached the reception area, however, when they heard the deep, dull thump of a bomb going off, and felt the shock of it travelling through the floor, like an earth tremor. The double swing doors flew open for a moment, and a shower of fragments came clattering through – glass, metal, part of a chair back.

The receptionist jumped up from her desk and said, 'Holy Jesus – what was that?'

'Call your security people,' Katie told her. 'Tell them this whole wing has to be evacuated, as quick as humanly possible. Then get out of here yourself.'

Katie and Dr Collins stayed in the reception area while the receptionist called the hospital's security team. Fire alarms began to ring all the way through the building, and Katie could hear shouting and footsteps running backwards and forwards. She called Anglesea Street and told them to contact the fire brigade and the bomb squad, and she also called Chief Superintendent O'Driscoll. For a change, he wasn't still out at lunch.

'They booby-trapped Father O'Gara's body? I don't fecking believe it! What did they do that for?'

'The same reason they're driving around in that van so openly. They're trying to divert our attention away from what they're really up to.'

'You and your instincts, Katie. If you ask me they're just a bunch of headers. Anyhow, you make sure that you stay well clear until the bomb squad get there.'

'No more news about Jimmy O'Rourke, I suppose?'

'Nothing. They'll be bringing his body back later today.'

'Okay. All right. I'll wait to hear from you.' Katie closed her mobile phone and then said to Dr Collins, 'I'm going back to take a look at the body. Do you want to come with me? You don't have to. It could be risky.'

'No, I'll come with you,' said Dr Collins. 'It's highly unlikely that they would have planted *two* bombs in the same body, wouldn't you say? That's my experience, anyhow. And even if they had, both bombs would have exploded at the same time, wouldn't they? One would have set off the other.'

Katie grimaced, and said, 'Okay, then. Let's pray to God that you're right.'

They pushed open the double swing doors and cautiously re-entered the laboratory. The explosion had blown almost all of the sheeted bodies off their trolleys and on to the floor, so that they were lying on top of each other in a ghastly parody of a rugby scrum. The trolleys themselves had all been pushed into the opposite corner, although only three or four of them had been tipped over.

The laboratory was still hazy with smoke, but there was no chemical smell, only the stench of scorched human flesh. Katie guessed that Father O'Gara's body had been packed with some kind of plastic explosive such as Semtex, or more likely C-4, which was highly malleable and had no odour at all.

She walked across the debris-strewn floor, her

boots crunching on broken glass. Father O'Gara had been so spectacularly blown up that at first she couldn't work out what she was looking at. The middle part of his body had been blown wide open. His ribs were splayed apart, while one of his legs was standing in the washbasin on the opposite side of the laboratory. There was no sign of the other leg.

Most extraordinary, though, were the translucent beige curtains that hung over the autopsy table where Father O'Gara's remains were lying. They were all caught up in the fluorescent light fixtures in the ceiling, a vast and complicated spider's web of human viscera. Katie could almost imagine a large beige spider running across the ceiling, making the long strings of connective tissue tremble as it hurried to make sure of her prey.

The sun shone down through the clerestory windows and illuminated the membranes, so that Katie could see the blood vessels branching through them.

Dr Collins reached out with her latex-gloved hand and gently tugged at them. Part of the curtains slithered down, but most of them were inextricably entangled in the lights.

'Look at this,' she said, making it all sway. 'I've never seen anything like this in my life. Eight and a half metres of human intestines. One man's entire insides.'

Katie was too concerned with peering into the blackened barbecue pit that had once been Father O'Gara's abdomen. She could see the remains of what looked like a metal switching device, and the two wires that had obviously been the trigger mechanism, all twisted and tarnished. She recognized this bomb-making technique, and it wouldn't take her long to find out who had planted it. What she needed was a quiet chat with her old friend Eugene Ó Béara, who had never openly boasted of any relationship with the Provos because he didn't have to. Everybody knew who Eugene Ó Béara's closest friends were.

She turned to Dr Collins, about to say something to her. Quite unexpectedly, Dr Collins had pulled off her latex gloves, taken off her glasses and cupped one hand over her mouth and her nose. Her eyes were brimming with tears. Katie went over to her and laid a hand on her shoulder.

'It's the shock,' said Katie. 'I have to tell you I'm feeling a little off balance myself. Come on – I think you and I need to get out of here.'

Forty-four

They waited outside the hospital until Chief Superintendent O'Driscoll arrived, closely followed by the army bomb squad and two crime scene technicians, as well as nine uniformed gardaí and most of the local media. The car park was crowded with khaki trucks and Land Rovers and police vans and 4x4s.

Chief Superintendent O'Driscoll went inside the pathology lab to see the destruction for himself, and then came out again, his cheeks wobbling in disbelief.

'That would be have been a fecking massacre if they hadn't all been dead already.'

'I'll go back to headquarters now and write up a report,' Katie told him.

'No, you won't, girl. You'll go home and get yourself some rest and something to eat and I don't want to see you back until tomorrow morning. There's nothing more you can do here, and Liam Fennessy's taking care of things as far as the good Monsignor Kelly is concerned.'

'I'll be grand,' Katie insisted.

'No, you won't. You've had a bad shock and you look as deathly as that lot inside of there. You're taking on too much here. You're worse than Boyle Roche's bird, for God's sake. You can't be in three places at once.'

'All right,' Katie conceded. She turned to Dr Collins and said, 'How about coming home with me? I'll have to go out of the way to see my father, if you don't mind that. I need to tell him the news about my sister. But I could do with the company, to tell you the truth.'

'Yes,' said Dr Collins. 'I'd like that. I'm getting a little stir crazy in that hotel room.'

Katie thought that her father was looking even more frail than the last time she had seen him. He came to the door with a loose-woven grey shawl around his shoulders and the circles under his eyes looked inkier than ever.

She told him that Siobhán was conscious, although she didn't tell him that she wasn't yet able to speak, and that there was no predicting if

399

she would ever fully recover her mental faculties. She didn't tell him about Nola either. There would be plenty of time for that when Nola had been charged and convicted.

'Well – what a relief that Siobhán's awake,' said her father. 'You hear of people staying in a coma for years, don't you, and when they do wake up, all their friends have grown old and the world has changed beyond their recognition.'

'Have you eaten?' Katie asked him.

'Ailish left me a potato pie. I'll heat it up when I get hungry.'

'Well, make sure you do.'

He stared at her for a long time, saying nothing, his eyes searching her face as if he were trying to see her mother in her.

'You're all right, though?' she asked him.

He nodded. 'I'm all right, my love. But you know what they say. The way to avoid the tragedies of the past is not to let them happen to begin with.'

He paused a little longer, and then he said, 'So how's your murder case coming along? I saw something about it on the TV news this morning. You've found another dead priest, then? Father O'Gara? I'm sure I knew him once, Father O'Gara.'

Dr Collins was sitting close to the fire but she still gave a shudder, as if she had felt a sudden draught. 'Oh, God,' she said, and that was all she had to say, because Katie knew exactly what she was seeing in her mind's eye.

As concisely as she could, Katie brought her father up to date on her investigation. 'We're still looking for these characters, these Fidelios.

There's no way of telling for sure if they've got hold of Monsignor Kelly and Father ó Súllibháin, but we can't think of anyone else who would have wanted to abduct them.'

Katie's Father said, 'It's the church behind this, you mark my words. The church will do anything to protect its own, in my experience. The church will even sacrifice the innocent, if needs be. I had to deal with the murders of two children in Blackpool once, two girls, nine and eleven, both strangled, and I'm convinced to this day that they were going to tell their parents what their priest had been doing to them, but they were silenced. You know, *silenced.*'

He pulled his shawl tighter around his shoulders. 'My forensic evidence mysteriously went missing, and I couldn't find a single credible witness. But I know who did it. He's dead now, so there's no point in pursuing it, but he should have been punished at the time.'

Katie said, 'What I need to find out is the real identity of this Reverend Bis. If I can find *that* out, then hopefully I can find out who he was acting for when he approached those four priests to form the St Joseph's Choir.'

'Go back to your evidence,' said her father. 'Haven't I always told you that? The devil hides in the detail.'

'I don't really *have* much evidence, do I, except for Father Heaney's notebooks, which could mostly be fantasy for all I know, and a whole collection of harp wire and piano wire and bassoon string. And a rat. And a detonator.'

'Fair play, that's all you have, like. But go over

401

it again, and when you've done that, go over it again. And if you have any witnesses, nag them and nag them until they're sick of the sight of you. These days, it's all rush, rush, rush to get a case wrapped up, so that it looks good in the media and, most of all, it doesn't put too much of a strain on the budget.'

Katie lifted both of her hands in surrender. 'Whatever you say, detective sergeant. I have the translation of Father Heaney's notebooks in my briefcase, and all of the notes that my team have been compiling on my laptop. When I've had a large drink and something to eat and a couple of hours' sleep, I'll take another look at them. And then I'll take another look. Are you satisfied?'

Katie's father gave her a faraway smile. She had a disconcerting premonition that he wasn't going to live for very much longer. She looked across at Dr Collins and she thought that Dr Collins had sensed that feeling of mortality, too, as if Death had passed by the half-open living-room door, and glanced inside, and seen her Father sitting by the fire. *Don't you worry about missing your wife, boy. You'll be seeing her soon enough.*

Before they left, Dr Collins excused herself and went to the lavatory. While she was away, Katie's father inched himself forward in his armchair and took hold of Katie's hands in his.

'Now, tell me, have you made up your mind yet?'

'About what? About John, you mean?'

'He's a good man, Katie, and I can tell how much he loves you. Let me tell you something, a love like that doesn't come into your life very

402

often, if at all, and you don't want to let it slip through your fingers.'

Katie said nothing, but her father squeezed her hand even tighter, and said, 'I know what you're thinking. You're thinking that you have Siobhán to take care of, and me, and the entire well-being of the city of Cork and everybody in it. But you have your own life, Katie. Michael will take care of Siobhán and Ailish will take care of me, and the city of Cork can take care of itself.'

'You really think I ought to go?'

He gave her that faraway smile again. 'It's your decision, girl. But I'm just reminding you that you have only the one life. I will never be able to hold your mother in my arms again, and I weep for the loss of her every single day. It's bad enough weeping for the loss of a love you once had. Don't be after weeping for the loss of a love you never had at all.'

When they arrived at Katie's house, Katie switched on the table lamps and drew the curtains and turned on the central heating. Barney was wildly pleased to see her, and kept jumping up and down and thumping his tail against the furniture. Katie let him out of the kitchen door into the back yard and then came back into the living room.

'Drink?'

'Oh, please. Brandy, if you have any.'

'There – kick off your shoes and relax,' Katie told her. She poured a brandy for Dr Collins and a vodka for herself and then they both sat back on the sofa side by side and let out simultaneous sighs of relief.

'*Slàinte,*' said Dr Collins, lifting her glass.

'*Fad saol agat,*' Katie replied. 'Long life to you.'

'What a hell of a day it's been,' said Dr Collins. 'And, my God, it's been so much worse for you, what with your sergeant being killed and these priest murders and everything.'

'I've had better days, if that doesn't sound too cynical.'

Dr Collins looked across at her. 'Do you know something, you're not like any female Garda officer I've ever dealt with before. Not a senior officer, anyway. All of the female Garda officers I've dealt with, in the upper ranks, it's like they're constantly trying to assert themselves because they're women. They behave more like the men than the men do.

'But you – I don't know. Like I said before, you're very strong, but you're so much *yourself*. It's your very femininity that makes you strong.'

Katie gave her a quick, noncommittal smile. 'How about something to eat?' she suggested. 'Pizza, or I have some cold chicken, if you fancy that. I could throw a salad together.'

'I hope you don't think that I'm coming on to you,' said Dr Collins.

'As a matter of fact, I think you are, but I'm not upset about it. I'm flattered.'

Dr Collins blinked at her furiously. 'Oh. Oh, I see. I'm sorry.'

'Honestly, don't worry about it. I'm flattered, that's all. I have to admit that I thought you were a bit of a gorgon when I first picked you up at the airport, but I admire what you do and I've grown to like you as a person. So, when you pay me a compliment, I'm flattered.'

Dr Collins looked at her, biting at her lip, and there were so many stories in that look, so many disappointments.

'All right,' she said, at last. Then, 'How about a chicken sandwich?'

Once she had eaten, Katie no longer felt so tired, so while Dr Collins went to have a shower, she took Stephen Keenan's translation of Father Heaney's notebooks out of her briefcase, sat on the sofa with a large vodka and started to read it page by page.

Barney lay uncomfortably close to her, his jaw resting on her foot, one eye open and one eye closed. He was always suspicious when there was a stranger in the house.

Katie's father had made her feel careless, because the truth was that she hadn't yet read any of these notebooks, not line by line. She had only listened to Stephen Keenan's summary, and skimmed through a few pages to get the general tone of what Father Heaney had written. She knew that Patrick O'Donovan had read them more closely, but he might not have been looking at them with the same eye as hers.

According to the notes that Stephen Keenan had scribbled in the margin, Father Heaney had written *'Vita Brevis'*, 'Life Is Short', at the top of the very first page and underlined it 'three times, heavily, as if he was really trying to emphasize it'.

Next, he had gone on to describe his career as a teacher at St Anthony's, in Douglas, and how successful he had been as a choirmaster – especially on that glorious day in 1979 when his choir had sung for Pope John Paul II. It was not until page forty-three that he came to describe the secret meeting in the house in Montenotte when the Reverend Bis had asked him to put together a new boys' choir for St Joseph's Orphanage.

'The Rev. Bis declared that without question this would be the sweetest children's choir in all of church history; and so I asked him how he would be able to compare *this* choir with the choirs of the sixteenth century, the beauty of whose singing is (of course) known only by reputation.

'The Rev. Bis assured me that there would be empirical proof of this choir's supremacy. It would be a choir to delight the ears of God; and God would reciprocate by appearing before them in all His splendour, His robes shining like the sun.'

Katie skipped a few pages. Stephen Keenan had mentioned that Father Heaney had used obscure nicknames and puns and anagrams in order to conceal the identity of most of the people mentioned in his diary. Some of these names had taken him hours to decode, and many of them he hadn't been able to decode at all. In the Latin version, Father O'Gara had been called *Procul Rana,* which could be roughly translated as 'a far frog'. Stephen Keenan had eventually realized that this was an anagram of 'Fr. O'Gara'.

When he had talked to Katie about his translation, he had repeatedly referred to 'the Reverend Bis'. On the page, however, Katie saw that

406

Father Heaney had always written it as 'Rev. Bis'.

Maybe I'm fooling myself, thought Katie, but that looks to me like an anagram of *brevis,* meaning 'short'. And Father Heaney had prefaced his notebooks with *Vita Brevis,* and underlined it.

Why hadn't Stephen Keenan seen it? Maybe it had been far too obvious for a complicated analytical mind like his. But 'short' or 'shortie' could well have been Father Heaney's nickname for the cursor – the go-between who came to recruit him to organize the choir – especially if that go-between had been a noticeably short man, high up in the diocesan hierarchy.

And who fitted that description more than the Right Reverend Monsignor Kevin Kelly, VG?

Katie opened her laptop and switched it on. It took her only a few minutes to locate the history of the diocese of Cork and Ross and the clergy who had worked for the bishop's office and the diocesan secretary's office over the past thirty years. One of the younger recruits to the bishop's office in October 1980 had been the Reverend Kevin Kelly, who had distinguished himself in his ecclesiastical studies at St Patrick's College, the national seminary for Ireland, in Maynooth. His exact position in the bishop's office was unclear, but for a young priest he appeared to have been unusually close to the bishop himself, who at that time was Bishop Conor Kerrigan.

Katie found several newspaper photographs of Bishop Kerrigan at important diocesan functions and celebratory masses, and the young Reverend Kelly was almost always at his side. In some pictures their heads were close together and they

407

were clearly sharing some confidence or other.

In his prime, Katie recalled that Bishop Kerrigan had been an uncompromising fundamentalist – anti-abortion, anti-birth control, anti-euthanasia, an unshakeable believer in transubstantiation and the reality of angels. His favourite saying was, 'Remember – man is called by grace to a covenant with his creator.'

Towards the end of his life, however, he had rarely appeared in public and had given no interviews. The official explanation had been that he was suffering from pancreatic cancer.

Dr Collins came back into the room, wearing Katie's white towelling bathrobe, her hair wound up in a turban. Barney immediately sniffed and lifted up his head and made a *whuffing* noise.

'Enjoy your shower?' Katie asked her.

'Heaven,' she said, wiping her steamed-up glasses. She looked at Katie short-sightedly, with an expression that seemed to suggest that it would have been even more heavenly if Katie had shared it with her.

'Well, I'll take one myself now,' said Katie. 'Come on, Barney, out in the yard for your evening business. How about another drink? Or something else to eat?'

Dr Collins shook her head. 'I'm fine for now. How's it going with the notebooks?'

'I still have a lot to read. But I think we have a clear indication that all of those four priests were recruited by Monsignor Kelly, and that Monsignor Kelly was acting on behalf of Bishop Kerrigan.'

'And what does that tell us?'

'So far, not very much that we didn't know already.'

Dr Collins sat down next to her, her bathrobe opening to reveal her pale bare thigh. Katie put down the notebooks and closed her laptop and stood up.

'Anything you want, just help yourself,' she said.

Dr Collins nodded, as if to say *I wish*.

Forty-five

Katie let Barney out of the kitchen door, and then she went through to her bedroom and undressed. Wrapped in a towel, she walked back along the hall to the bathroom.

She stood in the shower for over three minutes before she started to wash herself, her head tilted up, her eyes closed, letting the warm water gush over her. Her late husband, Paul, had installed the power unit for the shower himself, because he had always considered himself a bit of a handyman, but it had always vibrated loudly whenever the shower was turned on.

Because of that, she didn't hear the front doorbell chiming, and she didn't hear Dr Collins call out, 'Somebody at the door, Katie! Do you want me to answer it?' If she *had* heard her, she would have said absolutely not, especially since she wasn't expecting any visitors.

She was thinking about the advice her father had given her about John. She knew that her father was right, and that real love is a precious rarity. At the same time, however, she had worked so hard to reach the rank of detective superintendent, and she was so dedicated to her job and her team of detectives, that she knew that she would feel genuinely bereaved if she walked out on them. It would hurt, and hurt badly, and it would hurt her team, too. And then there was Siobhán, of course, and her father himself.

She was soaping her shoulders when she heard a loud bang from the hallway – so loud that it made her jump. She recognized at once what it was, and she immediately turned off the shower.

She stood in the shower stall, not moving a muscle, listening hard, while the last of the water gurgled down the drain and the shower head dripped. She didn't call out. Somebody had fired a shotgun in the hallway and it wouldn't have been Dr Collins, which meant that there was an armed intruder in the house.

Very carefully, she slid open the shower door. She listened again. At first there was nothing, but then she heard a dry cough and the sound of somebody going into the living room. She was surprised that Barney hadn't barked, but then he was probably too busy snuffling around the dead leaves at end of the yard, trying to pick up the scent of shrews.

She stepped out of the shower and reached for her towel, but as she did so it slipped off the towel rail and down behind the brown wicker laundry basket. She was about to reach over and pick it up when she heard another dry cough, and a knocking noise, like the barrel of a shotgun

410

knocking against the side of the coffee table, or the arm of a chair.

She went to the bathroom door and eased down the handle. She opened it only an inch, but when she peered into the hallway she could Dr Collins's right arm lying on the floor, and the white sleeve of her towelling bathrobe was spattered with blood.

Oh, Jesus, she thought. *Oh, Holy Mary, Mother of God, she's been shot, and she isn't moving.*

She opened the door wider so that she could see into the living room. Because of the acute angle between the two doors, she could see only one of the armchairs, a lamp, and part of the window, but a hunched-up shadow was moving across the curtains, as if somebody was swaying from side to side.

She eased herself out of the bathroom. The front door was still ajar and a strong breeze was blowing in from the street outside. She could see the street lights flickering behind the trees, and the glistening of the water in the harbour. Dr Collins was lying on her back, both arms raised, with a bloody hole in her chest the size of Barney's red dog bowl. She was staring up at the ceiling and her mouth was wide open as if she were just about to shout something. Katie's white towelling robe was bundled up around her waist.

Katie crept towards her bedroom, keeping her back to the wall. Her discarded clothes were still strewn across the bed, but it wasn't her clothes she was after. It was the flat TJS hip holster that was lying on top of her chest of drawers on the

411

left-hand side of the door, with her nickel-plated Smith & Wesson .38 revolver.

She picked up the holster and gently tugged the gun out of it. As she did so, there was another knocking sound from the living room, and yet another cough, and then a man in a dark green sweater and black jeans suddenly stepped out into the hallway, carrying a double-barrelled shotgun in his left hand and all of Father Heaney's notebooks in his right.

Katie cocked her revolver and pointed it at him, holding it in both hands.

'Drop it!' she shouted at him, almost screaming.

The man flinched, jerking up his right elbow so that all of the notebooks fell on to the floor. He tried to swing the shotgun around, but very awkwardly, and the barrel caught on the radiator on the opposite wall. Katie shot him, twice, in the chest.

The man toppled backwards, dropping his shotgun. He tried to keep his balance, but he stumbled over Dr Collins's body and fell heavily on to the floor, both legs swinging up into the air together, like a rocking horse. His left hand scrabbled for his shotgun but Katie bent down, picked it up, and tossed it back along the hall, out of his reach.

'Look – you've only fecking shot me,' the man croaked at her. He looked down at his chest and there were two dark stains on his sweater. Blood was bubbling out of one of them, so Katie must have hit him in the lung.

Katie stared down at him unblinking, keeping her revolver pointed at his face. He had jet-black hair that had been cut lopsidedly, as if he had done it himself. He was of medium height, pudgy, with a roundish face and a nose like a pink broad bean.

Katie said, 'I *know* you. Your hair's a different colour, isn't it? But it's you all right. What the hell are you doing in my house?'

'You've only fecking shot me,' the man repeated.

'You've just shot this woman,' Katie snapped back at him. 'You've killed her.'

'I need a white van,' the man begged her. His voice had become a thin, reedy rasp. 'I'm bleeding to death here.'

'You're Brendan Doody, aren't you?' said Katie.

'You've only fecking shot me. I'm dying.'

'You're Brendan Doody, aren't you? I've seen your photo, Brendan. You've dyed your hair black but you can't tell me it's not you. What in the name of Jesus are you doing coming to my house with a shotgun?'

She went to the front door and closed it.

'I was told to,' said Brendan Doody.

'Who told you to?'

'I can't tell you. He'll kill me.'

'You're going to die anyway. What difference does it make?'

Blood slid out of the side of Brendan Doody's mouth, and he coughed. 'I need a white van. I'm drowning here. I'm drowning in my own blood.'

'Who sent you here, Brendan?'

Brendan Doody took three bubbly breaths, and then he wheezed, 'The monsignor sent me. He said I had to shoot you as soon as you opened the door. But it wasn't you, was it?'

413

'Did you shoot Father Lowery, too, and Detective Sergeant O'Rourke?'

Long, concentrated pause. Then, 'O'Rourke? Was that his name? I'm sorry. Please. I didn't know what his name was. He shouldn't have followed us. Please, I'm dying here.'

'Why did you do it, Brendan?'

'The monsignor said I had to.'

'Did he tell you why?'

'He said that if I didn't he would call for the guards and tell them it was me who killed Father Heaney and then I'd have to go to the Mountjoy for the rest of my life.'

'But it *wasn't* you who killed Father Heaney, was it?'

Brendan Doody shook his head, and coughed up more blood. 'I said that it was but it wasn't.'

'But why would you do that?'

'The monsignor said that I had to help the bishop because the bishop was in terrible trouble and it was the bishop who made sure that I was taken in and taken care of when I was a small kid, like. He dictated me a letter to say that it was me who killed Father Heaney and then I had to say that I was going to kill myself, too, but I didn't. One of the priests found me a room in Grawn and I had to dye my hair and tell everybody that my name was Tommy Murphy.'

All of this came out in a bubbling slur that Katie could barely understand. But there was a panicky look in Brendan Doody's eyes and she could tell that he was prepared to tell her everything if she would only call for an ambulance and save his life.

'The *bishop?*' she said. 'What kind of trouble are we talking about?'

'Please,' he pleaded with her. 'I don't know what kind of trouble. I truly, truly don't.'

'But wait a minute. Which bishop do you mean? They took you in at St Patrick's long before Bishop Mahoney was appointed. You don't mean Bishop *Kerrigan?*'

Brendan Doody nodded. His eyes kept rolling up into his head and each breath was shorter and shorter.

'But Bishop Kerrigan died years ago,' Katie persisted. 'How could he be in trouble?'

'Not dead,' said Brendan Doody.

'He's not dead? Then where is he?'

'Dripsey. Big house. Near the monument. I did some decorating there.'

'And that's where he is now?'

Brendan Doody nodded again. 'I'm supposed to go there now. Meet the monsignor. He said it's the time.'

'It's the time? The time for what?'

'Please.'

Brendan Doody's head dropped back on to the carpet and his eyelids half closed. He was still breathing, however, and when Katie knelt beside him she could feel a pulse in his neck. She stepped carefully around Dr Collins's body and went into the living room to call for an ambulance. After that she called headquarters and asked to be patched through to Inspector Fennessy.

'Liam?' She told him what had happened and Inspector Fennessy simply said, 'Jesus.'

'Brendan Doody said Bishop Kerrigan is still

alive and kicking and that he lives in a house near Godfrey's Cross in Dripsey.'

'Come here to me? I don't believe it!'

'That's what he said. He also said that he was supposed to go there after shooting me and meet up with Monsignor Kelly. *"It's the time,"* he said, although he didn't tell me what time. But if Monsignor Kelly has gone there, there's a fair chance that our Fidelio characters have gone there, too. In fact, they probably took him there.'

'This is pure amazing. How do you want to play it?'

'Get your team up to Dripsey and see if you can identify the property. I expect that any one of the locals will tell you. There's only a post office and a couple of pubs and one of those is closed.'

'So what do we do once we've located it?'

'Nothing at all. Just keep an eye on any comings and goings until I can get there. I have to stay here and wait for the paramedics and the technical boys and some back-up, but as soon as they've arrived I'll be with you.'

She went back into the hallway. Brendan Doody was still alive, although she didn't know for how much longer. She stood looking down at him and for the first time in her life she didn't feel any remorse at having had to shoot a man, or guilt that she had questioned him before calling for the paramedics. He had shot and killed Jimmy O'Rourke in cold blood; and Dr Collins, too; and Father Lowery. It was no excuse that he was mentally slow and emotionally vulnerable, or that Monsignor Kelly had exploited him for his own distorted purposes.

416

She saw flashing blue lights outside and it was only when she stepped over Dr Collins and saw herself in the hall mirror that she realized that she was still completely naked.

Forty-six

By the time Katie arrived in Dripsey it was almost twenty past eleven. Dripsey was a small village in the hilly countryside twenty kilometres to the west of Cork City, on a tributary of the River Lee – *Druipseach* – 'the muddy river'. The tributary had once provided the power for a paper mill and a woollen mill, but both factories had long gone to ruin.

A very fine rain was falling, more like a veil of wet chiffon than rain. The windows of the Weigh Inn pub were still brightly lit, but the Lee Valley Inn was in darkness. Katie drove around the left-hand curve in the road, which was the social centre of the village, and headed further west to Godfrey's Cross.

It was here in 1921 that an IRA ambush had been foiled by the British army after a tip-off from a local woman, and a monument had later been erected to the IRA men who had been captured or wounded, and those who had later been tried and sentenced to death.

Katie turned into the car park beside the monument. Four squad cars were parked at the far end, under the overhanging trees, as well as

417

two Garda vans.

She climbed out of her car and Inspector Fennessy came across to meet her, accompanied by a uniformed sergeant. Inspector Fennessy was wearing a black raincoat with the collar turned up and he looked tired and strained, like a worn-out schoolmaster.

'We've found the house so. It wasn't difficult. Everybody in the Weigh Inn knew it, but all of them think that some retired writer lives there. None of them seem to have a clue that it's Bishop Kerrigan.'

Katie buttoned up her coat. 'Considering that Bishop Kerrigan is supposed to have gone to meet his maker years ago, I'm not surprised. I Googled him and he should be eighty-seven by now, if it really *is* him.'

'We carried out a quick reconnoitre,' Inspector Fennessy told her. 'There are three vehicles parked in the driveway – a grey Ford Transit van and two saloon cars, a Toyota and an Opel. I have two men keeping an eye on the house, and about five minutes ago they reported that the downstairs lights are still on, as well as the staircase and two of the upstairs rooms, but they have not yet seen anybody inside.'

Katie nodded and said, 'All right. Normally I'd want to wait this out, at least until daylight, but if they have Father ó Súllibháin in there, and they're torturing him, we need to go in without any messing. Monsignor Kelly could be in there, too, but we don't have any idea whether he went with them willingly or unwillingly.'

'So what's the plan?' asked Inspector Fennessy.

'The plan is we drive straight in there, block off their vehicles and surround the house front, back and sides. We give them one chance to open the front door, and batter it open if they don't.'

'Nothing too complicated, then?' said Inspector Fennessy, with the faintest hint of sarcasm. He had always been one of the subtlest of Katie's team, preferring to set up elaborate stings to catch the criminals he was after, with listening devices and phone taps and misleading text messages. Battering down doors was not really his style.

They assembled all of the gardaí together beside the monument, twenty-four of them in all, and Katie explained what she wanted them to do.

'These people are violent and sadistic and very unpredictable and we have no clear idea of what their agenda is. Because of that, we need to get in there fast and restrain everybody immediately, no matter who they are. We can separate the perpetrators from the victims once we have them all locked down.

'We believe that Bishop Conor Kerrigan may be inside, as well as Monsignor Kevin Kelly, one of the vicars general. I want them restrained, too, just as quickly and securely as the others. Whatever they say to you – even if they threaten you with excommunication – don't hesitate.'

The men all looked so grim that she had to add, 'Excommunication, that was a joke.'

'Oh, right,' they said, but none of them laughed.

The Garda sergeant divided his men into groups – seven of them to cover the back of the house, four on either side, and the remaining eleven to enter by the front door, either by invitation or by force.

They were walking back to their cars when Inspector Fennessy's mobile phone rang. He answered it and said, 'Yes. Yes. Well, how about that?'

'What is it?' Katie asked him.

He closed his phone. 'They found the van with the crozier on it, in a country pub car park not far from Macroom. Empty, and partly burned out. It seems like your instinct was correct, ma'am. Sorry if I doubted it.'

Katie laid a hand on his sleeve and gave him a smile. 'Don't worry,' she said, 'I'm too flah'd out to feel smug.'

They left the monument car park in a convoy, with Katie following Inspector Fennessy. He took a left at the cross and drove down the winding, unlit road – which, if they had followed it for another eight kilometres, would have taken them all the way back down to the River Lee. After less than a kilometre, however, he turned right, in between two tall stone pillars and a pair of rusted iron gates that looked as if nobody had closed them in decades.

They jolted along a narrow, gravelled driveway between overgrown bushes, which lashed at the sides of their vehicles. The rain was so fine that Katie's windscreen wipers kept up a monotonous rubbery squeaking. She was beginning to feel more than physically tired: she felt emotionally exhausted too, almost as if she could cry.

After half a kilometre, a large grey stone house appeared among the trees. It was one of the grand nineteenth-century houses that had been built for the owners of the Dripsey paper mill, with a mansard roof and clusters of barley-sugar chimneys and a wide porch with twisted pillars. As they slewed to a halt right in front of the porch, two gardaí came out of the shadows on the left-hand side of the house and jogged over to join them.

'Still no movement,' said one of them. 'The curtains in the lounge are wide open but if there's anybody in there they must be lying on the floor.'

'Let's just get inside,' said Katie. She and Inspector Fennessy hurried up the steps to the front door, closely followed by the uniformed sergeant and three gardaí, one of them carrying a battering ram. The rest of the gardaí split up and disappeared around the sides of the house to cover any other exits.

The front door was solid oak, weathered to a pale grey colour. The cast-iron knocker had the face of a leprechaun, with a disconcertingly mischievous smile, as if he knew exactly what Katie's business was here, even before she had knocked.

Katie took hold of it and banged it three times, as hard as she could.

'*Armed gardaí!*' she shouted. '*Open the door!*'

They waited for a few seconds, but there was no response, so she banged the knocker again.

Still no answer. Katie stepped away and pulled out her gun. 'That's it. Let's have it open.'

The garda with the battering ram stepped forward without hesitation and slammed it into the door panels. This was a heavy duty Stinger, weighing thirty-five pounds, and the door burst open immediately. Katie ducked into the hall, followed closely by Inspector Fennessy and the rest of the gardaí.

'*Armed gardaí!*' she repeated. '*Come on out and show yourselves!*'

She crossed the hall to the living-room door, which was half ajar. Inspector Fennessy joined her and gave the door a kick to open it wider. Katie nodded at him and he quickly glanced inside.

'Anybody there?' she asked him.

'Doesn't look like it.'

Both of them pushed their way into the living room with their guns held up stiffly in front of them, but there was nobody here, not even lying on the floor.

'Search the rest of the house, quick!' Katie ordered. Three gardaí clambered upstairs, while two more went through to the kitchen and the dining room and the downstairs cloakroom. For a few minutes, the house echoed to the sound of slamming doors and hurrying boots.

Eventually the sergeant came back into the living room and held up both hands. 'Nobody home,' he announced.

'Then where in the name of Jesus have they got to?' said Katie. 'Their van and their cars are all here. Don't tell me they're *walking.* Where would they walk to?'

They went back outside. The rain was growing more persistent and Katie could hear thunder. *Just the weather for a disastrous night like this.*

She walked around the right-hand side of the house, where there was a wet stone patio with a rose pergola, although the roses were badly neglected and most of them were shrivelled. Inspector Fennessy came up to her and said, 'What now?'

422

'I don't honestly know, Liam. We search the house to see if they left any indication of where they were going, and how. Maybe they have accomplices who came to pick them up and take them away before we even got here. In which case, they could be absolutely anywhere at all. They could be halfway to Mayo by now.'

She walked through the pergola to the back of the house. Apart from a light in one of the kitchen windows, the gardens were shrouded in darkness. She stood quite still and listened to the rain falling through the trees, and the occasional rumbling of thunder.

'Right,' she said, after a while, more to herself than anybody else. 'I think I'm going to call it a night. Let's put a guard on the house for now, and we can come back in the morning and make a really thorough search.'

She turned around, but as she did so she heard a high piercing wail, almost unearthly. It faded away almost immediately and then there was nothing but the sound of the rain, and the gardaí talking to each other, and squad car doors slamming.

'Did you hear that?' she asked Liam.

'Did I hear what?'

'That sound. I don't know. It was like somebody crying.'

Inspector Fennessy listened for a few seconds. 'No,' he said, impatiently. 'I can't hear a sausage. And I'm beginning to get very wet here, ma'am.'

More thunder, but then Katie heard that same falsetto wail. *There!* she said, triumphantly. 'You must have heard it that time!'

'It's a vixen, most likely,' Inspector Fennessy told her. 'They make all kinds of weird noises, vixens, especially when they fornicate. Like Montenotte girls.'

He started to walk back through the rose pergola, but as he did so the high-pitched sound started yet again, and this time it didn't fade away. It grew louder, and sweeter, and more harmonious.

Katie and Inspector Fennessy stood staring at each other.

'I never heard a vixen singing *"Gloria"* before,' said Katie.

'Me neither, I'm afraid to admit. It's *them,* isn't it? It's those fecking Fidelios. They're only out here *singing,* for Christ's sake.'

'Ssh,' said Katie, raising one hand to her ear. 'Can you work out where it's coming from?'

They both stayed silent for almost half a minute. The *'Gloria'* continued, although it swelled and diminished in the wind, and now and then it was blotted out by thunder. Eventually, Inspector Fennessy pointed into the darkness and said, 'Just about there, I'd say. From behind those trees.'

'I think you're right. Call Sergeant O'Brien back, would you? Let's get down there and take a look.'

While Inspector Fennessy went to tell the Garda sergeant what they could hear, Katie made her way down a flight of stone steps that led from the patio to the lawns. The lawns sloped at quite a steep diagonal to the south-west, and they were bordered by a copse of tall, mature oaks. As she made her way down the slope, Katie could hear the singing more and more clearly. There was no doubt that it was coming from somewhere beyond the trees. *A cappella,* unaccompanied, in the style of the chapel, but sweeter than any singing that she could imagine. Somehow the rustling of the rain and the distant rumbling of thunder made it all the more enchanting.

Inside the copse, it was very dark at first, and she had to tread very carefully to avoid making too much noise. As she went further, however, she saw a single bright light shining between the trees, and it became easier to see where she was going. She looked back. The criss-cross beams of at least fifteen flashlights were coming down the slope behind her.

The singing continued, heartbreakingly beautiful. Katie made her way to the very edge of the copse. She kept herself close to an oak that was thickly covered in ivy, by way of camouflage, and peered between the leaves.

Beyond the copse there was a grassy field, in which a pressure lantern had been hung on a tent pole. Around the lantern stood three figures dressed in extraordinary costumes. All of them were robed in white, but one of them was wearing a tall pointed *capirote,* while another one had a hat like a bishop's mitre, and the face of the third figure was covered by a white, expressionless mask, like a clown. In the strongly contrasting light and shadows they looked like characters out of some religious nightmare.

It was these three who were singing, their hands pressed together as if in prayer. Katie recognized the chorus from her *Elements* CD, but if these were the same boys who had sung on that record, their voices had filled out and matured and developed an otherworldly dimension that made Katie feel that she was standing in a cathedral, rather than a rainy field in west Cork in the middle of the night.

But it wasn't only the ethereal singing that made Katie feel as if she had entered another reality. Close behind the Fidelios, three tall scaffolding poles had been erected, each of them at least four metres high, and each with a shorter length of scaffolding clamped across the top to form a T shape. They were arranged in the same way that the crosses on Calvary had been arranged, when Christ was crucified.

On each scaffold a naked man had been bound with his arms spread wide. Each man was bruised and scratched and streaked in blood, and each man was wearing a crown of razor wire. Their heads were slumped down on their chests so that Katie found it hard to recognize them at first, but when the man on the left-hand scaffold lifted up his face to the sky and soundlessly opened his mouth, she realized with a shock that it was Monsignor Kelly. He appeared to look in her direction, but she very much doubted that he could see her, concealed amongst the ivy, especially since he had so much blood in his eyes.

The man hanging in the middle was emaciated and white-haired, with yellowish skin and a ribcage like the back of a kitchen chair, and Katie could only guess that this was Bishop Conor Kerrigan. On the right, a sallow man with a round

426

head and a pot belly hung motionless. His left cheek was swollen with one huge inky-coloured bruise. This must be Father ó Súllibháin, whom Tómas the gardener had described as 'Father Football'.

Inspector Fennessy caught up with her, and the rest of the gardaí now came crashing through the copse.

'I don't believe what I'm seeing here,' said Inspector Fennessy. 'This is like the Stations of the Cross gone mad.'

'Come on,' said Katie. She had never felt so determined in all of her career, although her voice was shaking. 'Let's put an end to all of this. Can somebody call for the paramedics and the fire brigade? Like *now,* please.'

She took out her revolver and stepped out from behind the tree, followed by Inspector Fennessy. The three Fidelios immediately stopped singing, and stepped back towards the scaffolds.

'Stay where you are!' Katie called out.

The three Fidelios backed away even further, until they were standing right next to the scaffolding poles, one by each of them. They moved almost as if they had been directed by a choreographer.

'I said stay where you are! If you move one inch more, I'll shoot you!'

The three Fidelios stayed where they were, but slowly raised their hands. Katie stalked up to them, keeping them covered, and said, 'Let's have those masks off, shall we?'

The man with the pointed *capirote* lifted it off and tossed it sideways on to the ground. He was a bulky man, round-shouldered, but he looked just like the cherub that Mrs Rooney had described, up in Ballyhooly. His hair was curly and his cheeks were round and ruddy and, most unnervingly, he was smiling at her, as if he had done something especially sweet to please her.

'Denis Sweeney, is it?' Katie demanded.

The man shrugged. When he spoke, his voice was a throaty treble, like a young boy's, or a woman's. 'I have all kinds of names for myself.'

'Such as?'

'The Grey Mullet Man, I call myself sometimes, or, when I'm feeling bombastic, the Exactor of Divine Recompense. But Denis Sweeney will do.'

Inspector Fennessy said to the other two Fidelios, 'You two – get those masks off before I fecking blow them off.'

They did what they were told, and dropped their masks on to the grass. They looked exactly like their pictures on the Fidelio website, with bulging brown eyes like hamsters and receding chins.

'The Phelan twins, I presume?' said Katie.

'That's them,' said Denis Sweeney. 'They sing like angels but they don't converse much, except with each other.'

'All right,' Katie told him. 'I want all three of you to lie flat on your faces on the grass and put your hands behind your backs.'

'No,' said Denis Sweeney. In the distance, there was another deep mumble of thunder.

'*No?*' said Katie.

'That's right, no. I refuse.'

'Well, all I can tell you, Denis, is that if you

don't do it willingly these officers will be forced to make you do it *un*willingly. With batons, if necessary.'

Denis Sweeney looked up at Bishop Kerrigan and smiled. 'It was all his fault, you know. A man of God shouldn't make promises and then go back on them.'

'Denis, this is your last chance. Lie flat on your face on the grass and put your hands behind your back.'

'There's a problem there,' said Denis Sweeney. 'The problem is that I'm holding in my right hand here a wire, and this wire is connected to the double coupler at the top of this scaffolding tube. Do you know very much about scaffolding, do you?'

'What are you trying to tell me?'

'I'm trying to explain to you that if I drop flat on my face on to the grass, I will inevitably pull on this wire and the crosspiece will topple off and Bishop Kerrigan will topple to the ground along with it. Now a fall like that would be life-threatening enough for a man of his age but there's another problem, which you may not yet have noticed.'

'What are you talking about?'

'I'm talking about the second wire, which is fastened around his testicles and which will castrate him when he falls.'

He nodded towards Monsignor Kelly, hanging from his scaffold, and then to Father ó Súllibháin. 'The same for these two. If the Phelan twins pull on their wires, that'll be two more instant castrations.'

Katie stepped up close to him, still pointing her gun at his chest. He had tiny clear beads of perspiration on his upper lip. She looked up quickly at Bishop Kerrigan and saw that he wasn't lying. A thin wire, like the wire they used to cut cheese in supermarkets, was wound tightly around his scrotum. It made his tiny penis stick up like the penis of a newborn baby boy, or a cherub in a Renaissance painting.

Denis Sweeney said, 'I was going to castrate them all anyway, if nothing happened.'

'What do you mean, "if nothing happened"?'

'What do you think we're doing here tonight? They made a promise to us, did they not – this bishop, and this gligeen of a reverend, and those four priests, but then they never kept it. We gave up our manhood for what they promised us. It was the only thing in the whole world that a boy would give up his manhood for.'

Katie stared at him. 'You *believed* them?'

'Of course we believed them. They told us that Bishop Kerrigan himself was going to make us the most astounding choir that the world had ever known. With our singing, Bishop Kerrigan was going to bring the glory to the diocese of Cork and Ross, and when I say the glory I mean The Glory with a capital T and a capital G. He was going to do what Pope Sixtus V had never been able to do.

'We were orphans. Nobody had ever loved us, not even our own parents. We had never known anything but material poverty and emotional rejection. Suddenly these priests were offering us the earth. No – much more than the earth. They

430

were offering us heaven, too.'

Inspector Fennessy said, 'Let go of the fecking wire, Sweeney.'

'No.'

'I said let go of the fecking wire.'

'Wait a second, Liam,' said Katie, 'I want to hear this.' She turned back to Denis Sweeney and said, 'Bishop Kerrigan promised you that if you agreed to become *castrati*, you would get to meet God? Like, for real?'

'Yes. But we never did, and then we were told that Bishop Kerrigan had died and the choir was disbanded. All of us were left emasculated, with nothing at all to show for it – not even The Glory. None of us ever told anybody what had been done to us. Would you, if that had happened to you? But we never stopped believing that we could meet God one day.'

'So what made you kill Father Heaney and Father Quinlan and Father O'Gara? And why have you strung up Bishop Kerrigan and Monsignor Kelly and Father ó Súllibháin like this?'

'Because we heard that CD, of course. We heard our own voices again, and we realized how much we uplifted people, and we remembered why we had given away our manhood. We wanted to try it again, that's all. We *knew* we could do it. Don't you try to tell me that God would allow sixteen innocent boys to be castrated for nothing. That is not the God that I believe in.

'I went to see Monsignor Kelly and told him that I was thinking of re-forming the choir with as many of the boys as I could find. He said he would help me as much as he could, but I wasn't

431

to mention to anybody what had been done to us at St Joseph's. He gave me some money and he gave me the van and he wished me luck, but that was all.'

'But why did you have to commit murder?'

'Why do you think? I got together with the Phelan brothers and we formed Fidelio and we sang our hearts out, but God *still* didn't show Himself. Monsignor Kelly stopped answering my calls, so I went to meet Father Heaney, but Father Heaney said he couldn't and he wouldn't help us, so I gave him nothing more than what he justly deserved.'

'Did Monsignor Kelly know that it was you who killed him?'

Denis Sweeney glanced up at Monsignor Kelly with an expression of total disgust. Monsignor Kelly was still conscious, but he was beginning to tremble as if he were having a fit.

'I called Monsignor Kelly, yes, and this time he took my call and I told him that it was me who did away with Father Heaney. But he said that if anybody found out that Bishop Kerrigan had tried to create a choir of *castrati*, and why, it would be a disaster for the church. An absolute catastrophe. He said so long as I promised to keep quiet and not to harm the other three priests, he could arrange for somebody else to take the blame.'

'Oh, yes. Brendan Doody.'

'I don't know what his name was. Some handyman.'

'But you didn't keep your part of the bargain, did you? You didn't stop killing? You went after

432

Father Quinlan, and then Father O'Gara?'

Denis Sweeney suddenly lost his temper, and his voice became even more shrill. 'Because Monsignor Kelly let it slip that Bishop Kerrigan was still alive. He said that I shouldn't keep on trying to see God because Bishop Kerrigan hadn't been right in the head and that was why they retired him and told everybody that he was dead. But I think that he was lying to me. I think that all of the clergy in the diocese were terrified that Bishop Kerrigan would actually make God appear – scared shitless, because God would then see for Himself how greedy and corrupt they were – how they lined their own pockets, and abused innocent children, and lived off the fat of the land.'

He looked up at the night sky, blinking against the raindrops that fell in his eyes. He was breathing deeply with emotion. 'You ask me what we're doing here tonight? We have punished the wicked and we have cleansed the unbelievers and tonight we are going to sing for God and if God appears tonight then these three sacrifices will be allowed to live.

'If not...' He looked down again, and suddenly gave Katie that sweet, disarming smile. 'If not, we will bring them down to earth, which will complete our retribution. Water, air, fire and earth. The four elements, about which we sang so sweet.'

The Garda sergeant came up behind Katie and touched her shoulder. 'Paramedics on the way. Fire brigade too. Five minutes tops.'

'Thanks,' said Katie. 'Be sure to tell them no sirens.' Then, to Denis Sweeney, 'I'm going to give you one last chance, Denis. I want you to let go of

433

the wire and lie on the ground. Otherwise we will have to shoot you. Do you understand that?'

Denis Sweeney kept on smiling, and as he did so he wound the end of the wire around his wrist, and twisted it tight. 'If you shoot me, and I go down, Bishop Kerrigan is coming down with me.'

'I thought you believed in Bishop Kerrigan.'

'I do. I did. But God is more likely to appear, isn't He, if He sees that somebody who really believes in Him is going to be sacrificed if He doesn't?'

'Do you know something, Denis?' put in Inspector Fennessy. 'You're a fecking header, and no mistake.'

Denis Sweeney still didn't stop smiling. 'I want you to do something for me now, please. I want all of you to go back at least as far as the trees. My dear brothers and I are going to start singing, and if the Lord appears to us, it will be like the sun itself coming out, and I wouldn't wish any of you to be hurt or blinded.'

'Header,' Inspector Fennessy repeated.

But Katie said, 'Do as he says, Liam. We have to keep this very, very calm. We've lost enough priests already, don't you think?'

'Whatever you say, ma'am,' said Inspector Fennessy. He turned around to the Garda sergeant and flapped his hand to indicate that all of his men should step back a few paces.

Denis Sweeney looked at Katie and she saw something in his expression that she had never seen in anybody, ever. It was a longing so intense that it was painful. Perhaps he was longing for the man he never was.

434

Forty-seven

The Fidelios began to sing. They started with *'Gloria'*, by Guillaume de Machaut, and then they sang *'Ave Maria'*.

Although there were only three of them, their harmony was hair-raising, even more moving than the *Elements* CD. The scenario was surreal, with those three naked priests hanging suspended from their scaffolds, but Katie couldn't help herself being transfixed by the sound of their voices, soaring higher and higher, and when she looked around she saw that the gardaí were standing in the rain as if they had all been turned to stone.

Ye watchers and ye holy ones,
bright seraphs, cherubim, and thrones,
raise the glad strain, Alleluia!
Cry out, dominions, princedoms, powers,
virtues, archangels, angels' choirs: Alleluia!
'Alleluia! Alleluia! Alleluia! Alleluia!

At the final *'Alleluia!'* Bishop Kerrigan unexpectedly lifted up his head. His face looked like a bloody skull, with empty sockets for eyes. He opened and closed his mouth three or four times without uttering a sound, but then he screamed, *'It cannot be!'*

His voice was reedy and thin, but he screamed

loud enough for Katie to be able to hear him over the singing.

'*It cannot be!*' he repeated. '*The Lord will never show His face! It is not for us to call on Him! How can we presume?*'

Exhausted, his head dropped back on to his chest, so that all Katie could see was his crown of razor wire. But in a few desperate words he had probably explained everything.

He may have believed once that God would show Himself, but perhaps he had gradually come to realize that it was never going to happen, no matter how sweetly we sing to Him. Perhaps he had seen at last how arrogant it was, for humans to expect that their maker should prove His existence, how lacking in faith and how futile. That was what could have driven him over the edge, mentally, and led to his resignation, or his removal.

Now the Fidelios were singing the '*Kyrie*'. Even though each of them was still grasping one of the wires that would have brought down the cross-bars, they were able to hold out their arms and join hands. Their singing rose to a pitch that was almost beyond human hearing, so that it was not so much a sensory experience to listen to it but a spiritual one. Katie felt as if the air around them was crackling with static, and she could literally feel her hair standing on end. Even the rain was sparkling.

Kyrie eleison!
Christe eleison!
Kyrie eleison!

And then – without any other warning at all, no rumble of thunder, no sudden downdraught – a dazzling fork of lightning struck all three scaffolds. The *krakkkk!* of electrical energy was deafening, and Katie was knocked over backwards into the grass.

Each of the three scaffolds crawled and crackled with blinding sparks, which jumped between the three Fidelios, too. Their faces became blazing masks, and smoke poured out of their wide-open mouths. On the scaffolds themselves, Monsignor Kelly and Bishop Kerrigan and Father ó Súllibháin were all shrivelling up, faster and faster, until they resembled nothing more than figures made out of brown autumn leaves.

There was a final *snapp!* like a short-circuited fuse and then there was silence. Smoke drifted away through the rain, and the flaking ashes of the three incinerated priests softly tumbled after it.

Inspector Fennessy helped Katie back on to her feet. 'Jesus,' he said. 'Maybe they did it. Maybe God *did* pay them a visit, after all.'

Cautiously, still seeing after-images of lightning floating in front of their eyes, they approached the three scaffolds. Inspector Fennessy kept on looking upwards, as if he was half expecting a second bolt to hit them from the sky, but Katie said, 'You know what they say. Lightning never strikes twice. And even if it did, you wouldn't see it coming.'

'Well, these poor gowls certainly didn't.'

The three Fidelios were lying between the scaffolds, their faces blackened, their white robes covered with elaborate brown curlicues like Hebrew lettering, as if they had been sent a written message from God. *Mene, mene, tekel, upharsin.*

Inspector Fennessy bent over them, one after the other. Then he said, 'Serious, do you think it *was* God?'

Forty-eight

The following afternoon Katie drove up to Knocknadeenly to see John. It had been raining for most of the morning, but now the sun was shining and the road ahead of her was blinding.

When she reached Meagher's farm, Aoife, his collie, came running across the farmyard to greet her, and in the back of Katie's car, Barney barked and jumped around and threw himself against the windows in excitement.

John came out wiping his hands with a cloth. He hadn't shaved, but she always liked it when he didn't shave. He was wearing a pale blue checked shirt and jeans, and a tan leather belt with a silver buckle in the shape of a longhorn steer.

'You're looking very western,' she said. She came up to him and he took her in his arms and kissed her.

'I've just been cleaning up,' he told her. 'I'm all packed and I'll be leaving tomorrow afternoon.'

They went inside the farmhouse, and through to the kitchen, which was very clean and bare

438

and empty. No spice jars, no saucepans hanging on the wall, no geranium pots on the windowsill. A strong smell of Dettol.

'I saw the news,' said John. 'That was truly freaky, wasn't it? RITUAL PRIEST KILLERS STRUCK BY LIGHTNING. Jesus. But they didn't mention you.'

'There's a lot they didn't mention, and there's a lot they never will. Like Bishop Kerrigan still being alive, for instance. And what was *really* going on there.'

'At least you weren't hurt, sweetheart. And at least this goddamned priest killing thing is all wrapped up. You couldn't have timed it better.'

Katie put her arms around his neck and kissed him, and kissed him again.

'Let's go to bed,' she whispered.

He kissed her back, first on the forehead and then on the lips.

'Why?' he smiled. 'Are you tired, girl?'

They made love with the sun shining through the bedroom window. All of the pictures had been taken down, so there was a pattern of faded rectangles on the wallpaper. *No room so empty as a room that no longer has pictures in it,* thought Katie. *When the pictures are gone, that means that you will never be coming back.*

Halfway through lovemaking, she reached down with one hand and took him out of her. Then she immediately turned over so that she was lying on her stomach, with her face turned away from him.

'Katie?'

At first she didn't answer, so he leaned over her and said, 'Katie? What's wrong, sweetheart?'

'Hurt me,' she said.

'What?'

'You heard. Hurt me.'

She opened her legs, reached behind her and grasped his penis. She positioned it between the cheeks of her bottom and said, 'Go on. You know you want to.'

'Katie – what's this all about?'

'I want you to hurt me, that's what.'

'What the hell for? I wouldn't hurt you for the world.'

'Not even if I said I wasn't coming with you?'

There was a very long pause. Then John said, 'You're not coming with me? You mean like you're not coming with me now, or ever?'

'I can't. Not ever.'

'You don't love me, is that it?'

She twisted around and her eyes were crowded with tears. 'Of course I love you. I love you like I've never loved anybody else. But I can't come with you, it's impossible. All of my life is here and all of my family is here and how can I just abandon them?'

'Katie. Oh, Katie. Oh, Katie.' John put his arms around her and they held each other tight as if the tighter they held on to each other the slower the time would pass by, or even stop altogether, so that they could hold on to each other forever.

Forty-nine

The next morning at 11 a.m. they held a media conference at Anglesea Street, and Katie gave the press the full story of what had happened at Dripsey. Or at least the story that she and Chief Superintendent O'Driscoll had devised in collaboration with Bishop Mahoney's office. They had agreed that there was no good to be done to anybody by releasing all of the details of St Joseph's Orphanage Choir, and Bishop Kerrigan's deluded dream of heavenly glory.

Katie was leaving the building with Detective O'Donovan when she heard somebody call out, 'Katie!'

She looked around. As she did so, all of the crows rose up from the roof of the car park opposite, silently, and flapped away. It was Paul McKeown, rather more smartly dressed than when she had first met him, in a grey blazer and black trousers and shiny black shoes.

'I was hoping to see you,' he said. 'I wanted to talk to you about Denis Sweeney and the Phelan twins. My God – I can hardly believe they got struck by lightning.'

Katie looked at her watch. 'Listen,' she said, 'I've got half an hour. Why don't we go for a coffee and I can tell you all about it. Patrick – I'll see you this afternoon, about two if that's okay. We need to go over the evidence in that Ringa-

441

skiddy drugs fiasco.'

'Fine by me, ma'am,' said Detective O'Donovan, and walked away.

Katie took Paul McKeown back into the station and upstairs to the canteen. It was deserted, except for a single garda in his shirtsleeves, eating a late breakfast of bacon and eggs and reading the *Sun*. Katie went to the counter for two cups of coffee and then she and Paul McKeown sat by the window.

'Now,' said Katie. 'You want all the grisly details, I suppose.'

But Paul McKeown was looking at her with a frown on his face like a sympathetic doctor. He said, 'Before that, tell me what's wrong.'

'I'm sorry? It's all over, apart from collating all of the evidence, of course, and writing my report.'

'No, I meant what's wrong with you.'

'Come here to me? I don't know what you mean. There's nothing wrong.'

Paul McKeown reached across the Formica-topped table and took hold of her hands, and for some reason she couldn't really understand, she allowed him to.

'Katie,' he said, 'I've been running the Cork Survivors' Society for long enough to know when somebody's hurting.'

'Oh, I see. And you can tell that how, exactly?'

'What – apart from the fact that you've been crying?'

Katie was about to tell him not to be so ridiculous. Not only ridiculous but incredibly personal, especially since he hardly knew her. But she suddenly found that her throat was so tight that

442

she was unable to speak, and that her eyes were brimming with tears.

'You don't have to tell me about it,' said Paul McKeown. 'Whatever it is, Katie, it's your business. But if it'll help.'

She still couldn't speak. All she could do was sit there holding Paul McKeown's hands, with tears running down her cheeks, because she had lost little Seamus after his first and only birthday, and she had lost Paul, no matter how much of a chancer he had been, and she had lost Jimmy O'Rourke, and she had seen Dr Collins killed, and now she had lost John, too.

Paul McKeown handed her a paper napkin and she dabbed at her eyes. After a while, in short, choked-up bursts, she was able to tell him why she was so upset. He listened to her with a serious expression, not interrupting once.

When she had finished, however, he said, 'Let me tell you this, Katie. If you lose too many people, you're in real danger of losing yourself, too. I've seen it happen far too often. Don't let it happen to you.'

Fifty

At 3.30 p.m. they announced that it was time for passengers to board Aer Lingus flight 722 to San Francisco, via London and New York.

John finished his beer, picked up his hand baggage and his laptop, and walked out of the airport bar. He went down the escalator to the main concourse and stood in line, waiting for customs and security. The woman in front of him was talking loudly on her mobile phone. 'Don't you worry, I'll be back by Thursday and then I'll give him a reefing, I can tell you, the gowl.'

Rather bitter-sweetly, it occurred to him that he would never have to speak Corkinese ever again. No more 'how's it hangin', boy?' or 'goin' for the messages' or 'he was readin' the hole off your wan'.

He had almost reached the customs desk when somebody laid a hand on his shoulder, very gently, almost as if they had touched him by accident.

The publishers hope that this book has given you enjoyable reading. Large Print Books are especially designed to be as easy to read and hold as possible. If you wish a complete list of our books please ask at your local library or write directly to:

Magna Large Print Books
Magna House, Long Preston,
Skipton, North Yorkshire.
BD23 4ND

This Large Print Book for the partially sighted, who cannot read normal print, is published under the auspices of

THE ULVERSCROFT FOUNDATION